ELIZABETH BOWEN

TO THE NORTH

PENGUIN BOOKS

To D.C.

Penguin Books Ltd, Harmondsworth, Middlesex, England
Viking Penguin Inc., 40 West 23rd Street, New York, New York 10010, U.S.A.
Penguin Books Australia Ltd, Ringwood, Victoria, Australia
Penguin Books Canada Ltd, 2801 John Street, Markham, Ontario, Canada L3R 1B4
Penguin Books (N.Z.) Ltd, 182–190 Wairau Road, Auckland 10, New Zealand

First published 1932
Published in Penguin Books 1945
Reprinted 1984

Made and printed in Great Britain by
Richard Clay (The Chaucer Press) Ltd,
Bungay, Suffolk
Set in Monophoto Baskerville

Elizabeth Bowen was born in Dublin in 1899, the only child of an Irish lawyer and landowner. She was educated at Downe House School in Kent. Her book *Bowen's Court* (1942) is the history of her family and their house in County Cork, and *Seven Winters* (1943) contains reminiscences of her Dublin childhood. In 1923 she married Alan Cameron who held an appointment with the BBC and who died in 1952. She travelled a good deal, dividing most of her time between London and Bowen's Court, which she inherited.

She is considered by many to be one of the most distinguished novelists of the present age. She saw the object of a novel as 'the non-poetic statement of a poetic truth', and said that 'no statement of it can be final'. Her first book, a collection of short stories, *Encounters*, appeared in 1923, followed by another, *Ann Lee's*, in 1926. *The Hotel* (1927) was her first novel, and was followed by *The Last September* (1929), *Joining Charles* (1929), another book of short stories, *Friends and Relations* (1931), *To the North* (1932), *The Cat Jumps* (short stories, 1934), *The House in Paris* (1935), *The Death of the Heart* (1938), *Look at All Those Roses* (short stories, 1941), *The Demon Lover* (short stories, 1945), *The Heat of the Day* (1949), *Collected Impressions* (essays, 1950), *The Shelbourne* (1951), *A World of Love* (1955), *A Time in Rome* (1960), *After-Thought* (essays, 1962), *The Little Girls* (1964), *A Day in the Dark* (1965) and her last book *Eva Trout* (1969).

She was awarded the CBE in 1948, and received the honorary degree of Doctor of Letters from Trinity College, Dublin, in 1949 and from Oxford University in 1956. In the same year she was appointed Lacy Martin Donnelly Fellow at Bryn Mawr College in the United States. In 1965 she was made Companion of Literature by the Royal Society of Literature. Elizabeth Bowen died in 1973.

I

Towards the end of April a breath from the north blew cold down
Milan platforms to meet the returning traveller. Uncertain thoughts
of home filled the station restaurant where the English sat lunching
uneasily, facing the clock. The Anglo-Italian express – Chiasso,
Lucerne, Basle and Boulogne – leaves at 2.15: it is not a *train de luxe*.
To the north there were still the plains, the lakes, the gorges of the
Ticino, but, as the glass brass-barred doors of the restaurant flashed
and swung, that bright circular park outside with its rushing girdle
of trams was the last of Italy.

Cecilia Summers, a young widow returning to London, was
among the first to board the express. She had neglected to book a
place and must be certain of comfort. She dropped her fur coat into
a corner seat, watched the porter heave her dressing-case into the
rack, sighed, got out again and for a few minutes more paced the
platform. By the time she was seated finally, apathy had set in;
when two more women entered she shut her eyes. Getting up steam,
the express clanked out through the bleached and echoing Milan
suburbs that with washing strung over the streets sustained like an
affliction the sunless afternoon glare . . . As they approached Como,
Cecilia and her companions spread wraps and papers over the
empty places; but an English general got in with his wife, creating
a stir of annoyance. The general took one long look at Cecilia, then
put up *The Times* between them.

At Chiasso they stopped dead, it appeared for ever. Rain fell
darkly against the walls of the sheds; Cecilia began to feel she was
in a cattle truck shunted into a siding. English voices rang down the
corridor; Swiss officials stumped up and down the train. She thought
how in Umbria the world had visibly hung in light, and a bird sang
in the window of a deserted palace: tears of quick sensibility pricked
her eyelids. As the wait prolonged itself and a kind of dull tension
became apparent, she sent one wild comprehensive glance round
her fellow travellers, as though less happy than cattle, conscious,
they were all going to execution.

The St Gothard, like other catastrophes, becomes unbearable

slowly and seems to be never over. For some time they blinked in and out of minor tunnels; suffocation and boredom came to their climax and lessened; one was in Switzerland, where dusk fell in sheets of rain. Unwilling, Cecilia could not avert her eyes from all that magnificence in wet cardboard: ravines, profuse torrents, crag, pine and snow-smeared precipice, chalets upon their brackets of hanging meadow. Feeling a gassy vacancy of the spirit and stomach she booked a place eagerly for the first service of dinner. She had lunched in Milan too early and eaten little. She pulled a novel out of her dressing-case, picked up her fur coat and ran down-train behind the attendant. The general sighed; he was romantic, it pained him to see a beautiful woman bolt for the dining-car.

In the dining-car it was hot; the earliest vapours of soup dimmed the windows; Cecilia unwound her scarf. She watched fellow passengers shoot through the door and stagger unhappily her way between the tables, not knowing where to settle. The train at this point rocks with particular fury. It seemed possible she might remain alone; this first service, with its suggestion of the immoderate, does not commend itself to the English; also, Cecilia by spreading out gloves, furs and novel, occupied her own table completely, and had the expression, at once alert and forbidding, of a woman expecting a friend.

She was not, however, unwilling to dine in company. Looking up once more, she met the eyes of a young man who, balancing stockily, paused to survey the car. A gleam of interest and half-recognition, mutually flattering, passed between them. They retracted the glance, glanced again: the train lurched, the young man shot into the place opposite Cecilia.

Unnerved by the accident, or his precipitancy, she rather severely withdrew her gloves, handbag and novel from his side of the table. The young man touched his tie, glanced at his nails and looked out of the window. Cecilia picked up the menu and studied it; the young man with careful politeness just did not study Cecilia. When the waiter planked down two blue cups her companion looked at the soup; she just heard him sigh. He was in no way pathetic and not remarkably young: about thirty-three. She was to say later she had looked first – and regretted now she had done so – at his Old Harrovian tie: the only tie, for some reason, she ever recognized. He picked up his spoon and she noted his hands: well-kept, not distinguished-looking. By the end of five minutes he had composed himself for Cecilia, from a succession of these half-glances, as being square and stocky, clean shaven, thickish about the neck and jaw, with a capable, slightly receding forehead, mobile, greedy, intelligent mouth and the impassive bright quick-lidded eyes of an agreeable reptile. Presentable, he might even be found attractive – but not by Cecilia.

The wine-waiter took their two orders, came back and put down the bottles. The train flung itself sideways; the bottles, clashing together, reeled; Cecilia's and his hands flew out to catch them. Their fingers collided; they had to smile.

'Terrible,' said the young man.

She agreed.

With his napkin he polished a hole on the steamy window and looked through. 'Where are we?' he said.

Cecilia, doing the same, said: 'It looks like a lake.'

'Yes, doesn't it: terribly.'

'Don't you like lakes?' said Cecilia, with irrepressible curiosity.

'No,' he said briefly, and lakes disappeared.

'This must be Lucerne.'

'Do you think so?' the young man said, impressed, and looked through again. Woolly white mists covered the lake: through rifts in the mist the dark inky water appeared, forbidding: they ran along an embankment. Malevolence sharpened his features; he seemed pleased to catch Switzerland *en déshabillé* – some old grudge, perhaps, from a childish holiday. 'Why,' thought Cecilia, 'can I never travel without picking someone up?' His manner and smile were, however, engaging. She looked sideways; torn darkening mists streamed past her eyes; above, on the toppling rocks where the hotels were still empty showed a few faint lights. It all looked distraught but perpetual, like an after-world. And in an after-world, she might deserve just such a companion: too close, glancing at her – if any shreds of the form still clung to the spirit – without sympathy, with just such a cold material knowingness.

For his part, he considered her broad pretty hands with their pointed fingers and narrow platinum wedding-ring, her smooth throat with the faint *collier de Venus* and gleam of dark pearls inside the unknotted scarf, her shoulders, the not quite unconscious turn-away of her head. She had charming dark eyes, at once sparkling and shadowy, fine nostrils, a pretty impetuous over-expressive mouth. A touch of naïvety in her manner contrasted amusingly

7

with the assurance and finish of her appearance; she was charmingly dressed. One glance at her book – in the austere white covers of the *Nouvelle Revue Française* – made him fear she might turn out pretentious, even a bore. The very thought of an intellectual talk as they writhed through Switzerland over a muggy dinner made him sweat with discomfort and put a finger inside his collar. Looking again, however, he saw that the pages were uncut. He supposed she had borrowed the book from someone she wished to impress. In this he wronged Cecilia, who had chosen the book this morning, to please herself only, in the arcades at Milan.

'I hope,' he said, with engaging deference, 'you weren't keeping this table for anyone?'

'I'm sorry?' Cecilia inquired, returning her eyes from the lake.

'I said, I hoped you weren't keeping this table?'

'Oh no . . . One could hardly expect to.'

'No,' he said. 'No, I suppose not.'

She found his way of not smiling a shade equivocal.

'With the train so full,' she said coldly.

'Here comes the fish: sole, they say – Do you know I thought for a moment . . .'

'What?' said Cecilia, who could not help smiling.

'I thought for a moment we'd met.'

'I don't think so.'

'No, I suppose not.'

She saw no reason why he should be amused. It amused him that a woman with such command of a look – for never (he thought) had he been more clearly invited to dine in company – should keep such an odd little flutter behind her manner. She remarked rather nervously: 'Last time I came back from Italy someone thought I was a Russian . . . A Russian,' she said, and looked sideways into the window – for they now ran through a cutting – where a reflected faint shadow under the cheek bones, with a sparkling petulant vagueness, accounted for the mistake.

'It would depend,' he said gravely, 'what Russians one knew.'

Cecilia complained that she did not care for the fish. The indifferent wine set a pretty flush under her eyes; though she told herself she did not like him her manner animated and warmed. If she did not like *him*, she loved strangers, strangeness: for the moment he had the whole bloom of that irreplaceable quality. Dim with her ignorance, lit by her fancy, any stranger went straight to her head – she

8

had little heart. She could enjoy in a first glance all the deceptions of intimacy. With one dear exception, she never cared much for anyone she knew well.

His name was Mark Linkwater. From the casualness with which he had let this appear in their talk, she took him to be a young man of importance, in his own eyes if not in the world's. It would seem likely the world shared his view of himself; he would be far too shrewd to admit what he could not impose. If, therefore, she had not heard of him, the ommission must be concealed. She felt round and discovered that he was a barrister. The ground cleared, they went nicely ahead.

As a companion for dinner, she suited him admirably. It is pleasant to be attracted just up to a point; he had asked, so far, no more of women than that they should be, on varying planes, affable. Touchy and difficult in his relations with men, the idea of personal intimacy with a woman was shocking to him. The train fled away from the lakes, up the valley from Brunnen, with a shriek on past Zug to Lucerne through the muffling rain, dashing light on wet rocks and walls, lashing about its passengers as though they were bound to a dragon's tail. With a hand put out now and then to steady glass or bottle, Mr Linkwater gave Cecilia his view of Rome.

He had come from Rome. 'Oh, Rome?' she exclaimed. 'How lovely!'

He shrugged: 'Too many nice people.'

She was surprised. He reflected on Roman society, but had enjoyed himself. Though not, evidently, a son of the Church, he was on the warmest of terms with it; prelates and colleges flashed through his talk, he spoke with affection of two or three cardinals; she was left with a clear impression that he had lunched at the Vatican. As he talked, antiquity became brittle, Imperial columns and arches like so much canvas. Mark's Rome was late Renaissance, with a touch of the slick mondanity of *Vogue*. The sky above Rome, like the arch of an ornate altar-piece, became dark and flapping with draperies and august conversational figures. Cecilia – whose personal Rome was confined to one mildish Bostonian princess and her circle, who spent innocent days in the Forum displacing always a little hopefully a little more dust with the point of her parasol, who sighed her way into churches and bought pink ink-tinted freesias at the foot of the Spanish steps – could not but be impressed.

Mr Linkwater, eyebrows alone expressive in the fleshy mask of

9

his face, talked very fast with a rattling fire of comment. It was dry talk of a certain quality; Cecilia found it amusing. Though no doubt all London would hear this later, she had to be flattered.

He liked talking and was amused by himself, but did not put up this barrage for no other reason. The fact was, he had caught once or twice while he talked a rather strange look from her, gloomy, dreamy, exalted, and feared that given an opening she might begin talking about herself. She might tell him life was difficult, or how terribly things upset her. Married and so communicative: he dreaded to be involved with her – His fears were groundless, she was only wanting to tell him about Umbria – More probably she was a widow, for the unhappy decisiveness with which she had ordered her wine bespoke the woman obliged for years to do things for herself and who did not enjoy doing them.

Neither Cecilia nor Mark had nice characters; all the same, this encounter presents them in an unfair light. On a long journey, the heart hangs dull in the shaken body, nerves ache, senses quicken, the brain like a horrified cat leaps clawing from object to object, the earth whisked by at such speed looks ephemeral, trashy: if one is not sad one is bored. Recollect that this was a journey begun after lunch, through a blighted fag-end of Italy, through Switzerland in the rain. At the moment, also, both their personal backgrounds were inauspicious. A quarrel had precipitated Mark's departure from Rome: anger shot red through his present mist of depression. Cecilia, a widow of twenty-nine, was wondering why she had let frail cords of sentiment and predilection draw her back from Italy to the cold island where, in St John's Wood, the daffodils might not be out. She had spent too much money and got too few letters while she was abroad; she wondered if she were ruined, if friends had forgotten her. Mistrustful, tentative, uncertain whether to marry again, she was quite happy only in one relationship: with her young sister-in-law, Emmeline.

Mistrust, in fact, underlay the whole of the interlude, which finished with brandy for Mark and a green Chartreuse for Cecilia. Still, they got on well enough, each determined to please while closing the heart against pleasure. They were both left with curiosity, some little piqued self-regard, and promised to meet in London, if not again on the journey: he made certain she was in the telephone-book. Back in her carriage, Cecilia blew out her air-cushion, wrapped her fur coat round her knees and, with a murmured apology, put up her feet by the hip of the general's wife. She could not afford a sleeper. She read for a little, took two aspirins, then nodding, decided that Markie's manner (for Markie was what his friends called him) had been impertinent: she would avoid him tomorrow.

Returning next morning from breakfast Cecilia saw from the corridor Mr Linkwater humped at the far end of a carriage, on a flying background of battle-fields under new culture, unsuccessfully shaved and looking distinctly cross. Avoiding his eye she passed hurriedly on down the train. At Boulogne the day was windless, the boat slipped from shore to shore like a pat of butter over a hot plate. Markie discovered Cecilia; for some time they paced the deck. Folkestone appeared, the flags on the Leas lifeless, hotels staring out at nothing: England showed a blank face. Nodding inland Markie said: 'Are you staying here long?'

'I have no idea,' said Cecilia.

II

'What is the matter, Emmeline?' said Lady Waters.

Nothing was the matter, but Emmeline found this too difficult to explain, so she looked mildly at Lady Waters out of the corners of her shell-rimmed spectacles, and said nothing.

Lady Waters was quick to detect situations that did not exist. Living comfortably in Rutland Gate with her second husband, Sir Robert, she enlarged her own life into ripples of apprehension on everybody's behalf. Upon meeting, her very remarkable eyes sought one's own for those first intimations of crisis she was all tuned up to receive; she entered one's house on a current that set the furniture bobbing; at Rutland Gate destiny shadowed her tea-table. Her smallest clock struck portentously, her telephone trilled from the heart, her dinner-gong boomed a warning. When she performed introductions, drama's whole precedent made the encounter momentous . . . Only Sir Robert, who spent much of his time at his club, remained unaware of this atmosphere.

Lady Waters had had no children by either marriage. Her first had made her Cecilia's aunt-in-law, her second, Emmeline's first cousin once removed. Cecilia had met Henry Summers (Emmeline's brother) for the first time dining at Rutland Gate. One was not a connection of Lady Waters's for nothing; Cecilia had heard a good deal of Henry and Emmeline Summers, while they had had frequent occasion to smile at the name of their Cousin Robert's new wife's hypothetical niece, who was always abroad or had just left London. Then Cecilia and Henry, both bidden to dinner, had met; unconscious, chattering amiably while their relative's large premonition darkened and spread above them, they became friends, intimates, lovers and quite soon afterwards married. That dangerous marriage was after Georgina Waters's own heart: when, within less than a year, Henry died of pneumonia, she had to conceal her relief that, given Henry's nervous make-up and Cecilia's temperament, there had been no time for worse to come of it.

That marriage so brief as hardly to lose its character of an event had transformed Cecilia from a young girl at once vehement and mysterious into a bewildered widow. She did not know where to turn. Incredulity, with which she had entered upon her happiness, remained the note of her grief. Emmeline Summers's suggestion that they should set up a house together had worked out well. At that time both young women had found themselves solitary: Cecilia's mother, never very affectionate, her whole heart given to her two sons killed in the war, had re-married soon after Cecilia met Henry and gone to live in America; Henry and Emmeline Summers had been orphans from childhood, with no relatives nearer, few friends more trusted, than Sir Robert Waters, their father's cousin. They brought themselves up side by side, Henry some years ahead; very much alike, as though the same tree had divided. During the year of her brother's marriage Emmeline, perhaps a little forlorn, had been much abroad; one might say that she and Cecilia had had hardly time to take stock of each other before their eyes met across a grave.

Their views of life and their incomes combined comfortably; they did not ask too much of each other and from one happy point of departure both went their own ways. Emmeline had put some of her capital into a business, in connection with which she left home for most of the day; while many acquaintances and a quick succession of interests soon kept Cecilia once more amused and alert: she went out a good deal. Lady Waters, however, still viewed the arrangement with an unshaken mistrust. Women could not live together, sisters-in-law especially. How much did they speak of Henry, how lively a bond was their loss? While Lady Waters considered that unreserve, in other company than her own, must be debilitating, reticence could only be morbid. Painful expectancy brought her frequently to their house; as they did not come to her with their troubles she came to them, and was their constant visitor. This they could think of no way to prevent.

They had gone to live in St John's Wood, that airy uphill neighbourhood where the white and buff-coloured houses, pilastered or gothic, seem to have been built in a grove. A fragrant, faint impropriety, orris-dust of a century, still hangs over part of this neighbourhood; glass passages lead in from high green gates, garden walls are mysterious, laburnums falling between the windows and walls have their own secrets. Acacias whisper at nights round airy, ornate little houses in which pretty women lived singly but were not always alone. In the unreal late moonlight you might hear a ghostly hansom click up the empty road, or see on a pale wall the shadow of an opera cloak . . . Nowadays things are much tamer: Lady Waters could put up no reasoned objection to St John's Wood.

Cecilia's and Emmeline's house was in Oudenarde Road, which runs quietly down into Abbey Road, funnel of traffic and buses. It had big windows, arched stairs and wrought-iron steps at the back leading down to a small green garden. Cecilia, hesitant over the agent's order, looking about at the temptingly sunny spaces of floor, had remarked: 'It's a long way from everybody we know . . .' But Emmeline said: 'We never know whom we are going to meet.' From the first glance the house had smiled at them and was their own. So here they had settled.

This afternoon of Cecilia's return, when, unannounced at her own request, Lady Waters swept her furs and draperies through the narrow hall into the drawing-room, Emmeline had been doing the flowers. She did not often do flowers and was uncertain of the effect. Tulips spun and flopped at her in the wide-mouthed vases: how did Cecilia ever make tulips stand up? Lady Waters begged Emmeline to go on with what she was doing, saying she also loved tulips, but presently asked Emmeline why she was so restless. The simple arrangement of tulips could not account for this pausing and stepping about – Lady Waters had never done flowers. Emmeline wished she had told the maid she was not at home: as she was generally out at this hour it had not occurred to her. It would, however, have taken more than a formula to turn Lady Waters away: if one were out she came in and waited. Unfamiliar afternoon light in the drawing-room and Emmeline's thoughtful solitude had been precious . . . Emmeline's manners were perfect, but when she was very much bored she seemed to contract physically and took on an air of mild distress.

When Emmeline had nothing to say, or could not trouble to think, she would turn her head sideways, appearing thoughtful. She paused gently before she spoke, as though fearing she must disappoint you. She was tall, with slight narrow figure and hands; her movements were leisurely and inconsequent. At twenty-five she looked very young, or perhaps rather ageless. Her red-bronze hair, not cut very short, sprang from a centre parting to fall in loose waves each side of her narrow oval face. The spring of her hair, the arch of her eyebrows, her air between serenity and preoccupation made her look rather like an angel. She was not quite angelic; though she was seldom exactly difficult Cecilia sometimes found her a shade perverse: she mistook theory for principle. Her spectacles, which from an independence that would rather blunder than be directed she seldom wore, had frail tortoiseshell rims the same tone as her hair, and made her look very much more serious and intelligent. She had put on her spectacles now to look at the tulips, for she was very short-sighted: they discomfited Lady Waters.

Vaguely trailing a tulip, Emmeline stood by the tallboy smiling in silence at Lady Waters. It was hard to believe that her manner could mean nothing. Lady Waters, who had apparently come to stay, loosened her furs impressively and settled among the cushions. She had a fine, massive figure and dressed with expensive disregard of the fashions.

'It is disturbing for you,' she said, 'Cecilia's perpetual rushing abroad and then home. It is a pity she cannot settle.'

'It makes variety,' said Emmeline, looking into the tulips.

'One can have too much variety.'

'Can one? . . . I rather like sometimes having the house to myself, though I shouldn't like it always.'

Lady Waters, naturally pouncing on this, remarked that Cecilia could not be a restful companion. Emmeline, deferring in silence to this opinion, abandoned the tulip, sat down in a low chair and pulled at a strand of green wool in the knee of her skirt: this appeared to absorb her. Her faculty for idleness was remarkable; Lady Waters thought she must be anaemic.

'Cecilia,' their relation continued, 'never seems to be happy when she is not in a train – unless, of course, she is motoring.'

'It depends rather where she is going.'

'She goes where she likes: it's neurosis. I'm really anxious about her.'

'I often wish she would fly.'

'She would arrive too quickly,' said Lady Waters. 'Also, I understand that one cannot talk in an aeroplane. I really dread these journeys; she picks up the oddest acquaintances.'

'Yes,' agreed Emmeline.

Though Lady Waters spoke of her niece with severity and deplored her behaviour to everyone, her real feeling for Cecilia was of the warmest: she liked her a good deal better than she liked

Emmeline. Heart-to-hearts with Emmeline often proved un-rewarding; Cecilia was better value, more generous, less recessive; Lady Waters had known her from childhood, had successfully married her once and hoped to do so again. So that she was accustomed to speak of Emmeline far more guardedly, merely saying that that glacial manner was unfortunate in a girl, and that Emmeline kept her intelligence for the office. Henry Summers, however, had had his weaknesses; it was always possible Emmeline might run deep.

Drawing up her black moiré skirt and approaching one foot to the fire, Lady Waters glanced thoughtfully round the room. 'You have made it all look very bright,' she said, 'I hope Cecilia will notice. Do you *really* expect her? Has she wired to say she is coming?'

'She hasn't wired to say she is not.'

'So you stayed at home to welcome her. That is really good of you, Emmeline; I know how you value your working time. I do hope she will not disappoint you. When did you hear from her last?'

Emmeline, wondering how to get Lady Waters out of the house before Cecilia – at any moment – arrived, looked up anxiously at the clock. Her movement was not unobserved; Lady Waters warned her at once against tension. The only way with Cecilia was absolute calmness: Henry had always found that: it was Georgina's own way; Cecilia and she got on perfectly.

'And – I know, Emmeline, you won't mind my suggesting – you must not let Cecilia dominate you. In an unconscious and very sweet way, she *is* very pervasive. You and I who love her can say so between ourselves: she *has* a strong personality. For you who are younger and much more unformed that must often be difficult. In a way, I am like that myself: I have a strong personality; I need the strongest self-discipline. Marriage makes one look into oneself . . .' She paused.

'I expect it does,' agreed Emmeline.

'Now Cecilia, tragically, never had time for the discipline stage in marriage; her marriage was all like a dream. I feel sometimes it simply enlarged her egotism. While with you – as, of course, in a sense, with poor Henry also –'

'– Will you stay to tea?' put in Emmeline.

'No, I must be going on to the nursing-home. I am glad to have had this talk alone with you, Emmeline, we so seldom meet. You do understand what I mean? It has been so much in my mind.'

'Absolutely,' said Emmeline.

'You are clear-sighted,' said Lady Waters, patting Emmeline's knee.

'You really can't stay to tea?'

'No, thank you; I simply looked in to see if you *were* expecting Cecilia, and cheer you up just a little in case she had changed her plans. I rang you up twice this morning but there was no answer: perhaps you had better speak to the maids? Cecilia so hates to have messages overlooked. But I am glad to have had a word with you: one cannot say much on the telephone. You will think over our little talk?'

'Oh, yes, Georgina . . . Yes.'

'And I brought a few tulips, to give Cecilia a welcome.'

'How very kind,' said Emmeline, looking round for the tulips.

'However (thinking she might have put off) I left them outside in the car, and as you have made the room so pretty already and your vases seem to be full, I think perhaps I will take them on to the nursing-home.'

'I expect that would be best.'

Lady Waters wrapped her silver fox round her chin and pulled on her black suede gloves. 'And how *are* you?' she said looking closely at Emmeline. 'There has hardly been time to hear. You are looking a little tired; the spring, I expect. Such a beautiful day, so still. You must come round next week and tell me all your news. Robert was asking for you only yesterday. And how is your little kitten Beelzebub?'

'Benito? He's quite well, thank you.'

'A tom kitten?'

'More or less.'

'I expect that is best – And mind, tell Cecilia I shall expect her tomorrow; in fact she might ring up tonight: I shall be at home. I must hear all about Italy.'

'I'll remind her.'

'Now I must really go; they don't send up tea at this nursing-home after five o'clock. *They* met at my house, you know, Felicia and Ronald, and now there's this tiny boy. It does seem extraordinary.'

'Doesn't it.'

Emmeline went out with her cousin as far as the steps. '*There's* a taxi, now,' Lady Waters said, looking down the road. 'But it seems to be standing still.' She kissed Emmeline, the chauffeur shut the door; with a last significant look and a wave she was gone. As the Daimler turned off into Abbey Road someone tapped the glass of the taxi, which creaked into motion and drew up again at the gate where Emmeline stood. 'Thank heavens,' Cecilia said, getting out, 'the Daimler is unmistakable.'

'How long have you been sitting there?'

'It cost one and three extra: I thought she would never go. I watched that new chauffeur of hers smoke three cigarettes; I suppose he thinks in St John's Wood it doesn't matter – Oh, how *are* you, how are you, angel . . .'

At the first sight of Emmeline a delicious sense of homecoming had rushed to Cecilia's heart. They went up the steps arm-in-arm; the parlourmaid came out smiling; a thrush sang; the taxi-man carried the suitcases up the steps. Cecilia kissed Emmeline.

'What did Georgina want?'

'I don't know – Tell me about the journey.'

'It was not bad. Though as I found that I was overdrawn at the bank I didn't take a sleeper.'

'Cecilia, you are tiresome with your bank!'

'I have six hundred lire; I'll change that back into English and not cash a cheque till May. Don't be cross with me – Darling, how funny those tulips look!'

'They fell out again,' explained Emmeline.

'And I met a man in the train.'

'Someone you know?'

'Well, I know him now. We weren't really meaning to talk, but I looked at his tie – No, he wasn't nice really, though he made me laugh; he was self-satisfied and looked rather sensual.'

'How?' said Emmeline.

'Oh you know how people look – or you ought, but you never notice. Still, I dare say he was unhappy. You are so *ignorant*, darling. Still, it is nice to be home with you . . .'

Cecilia, strung-up, excited, not knowing where to begin, like a child at Christmas, pulled off her scarf and turned to look out of the window. On the iron steps to the garden sparrows were chittering, the unmoving boughs of the plane were in pale bud; next door a cherry-tree was in bloom. There was a brightness over the air but no sun.

'It's always the same kind of day when I come home! Oh, those thrushes, Emmeline: I shall weep!'

'Why?'

'The birds in Italy –'

'You haven't asked after Benito,' Emmeline said reproachfully.

Benito was brought in, but looked rather stodgily at Cecilia, sat down almost at once and began to wash: he was really Emmeline's kitten. 'He's too sweet, but take him away,' said Cecilia, bored. 'He'll frighten the thrushes – I do hope Georgina didn't annoy you? I can't help feeling I brought her back into the family.'

'She brought you some tulips.'

'Oh, where?'

'But she took them on to the nursing-home.'

'Which nursing-home? Why?'

'I don't know.'

'Poor darling: you wished she'd been dead for a hundred years?'

'Yes,' said Emmeline gently.

Cecilia picked up their own tulips and put them in place with a touch. She said: 'Half way through the St Gothard, when I thought I was going to die, I thought what a nice house we lived in. I felt much worse, though, at Chiasso – Oh, that man's name in the train was Markie.'

'Did he say so?'

'No, he said his name was Linkwater. But I saw "Markie" in handwriting across the corner of his cigarette case – he was that kind of young man.'

'Shall you see him again?'

'I might or might not. He's a barrister. *You* wouldn't like him.'

'Poor Markie . . .' said Emmeline, balancing with an elbow against the mantelpiece. Cecilia thought what a lovely thing Emmeline was; how she brightened the drawing-room with her satirical gentleness, her uneffusive glow. 'I meant,' cried Cecilia, penitent, 'to bring home so much from Italy, to be nicer myself, I mean – and here I go, simply gossiping about men.'

'Still,' said Emmeline, 'it *is* nice, having you back.'

Cecilia, her senses still running ahead from the speed of the journey, looked round. The drawing-room, still clearly seen as though strange, but already misting across with her sense of her life here, was exceedingly dear to her: two or three things, she noticed, were in the wrong place. In these first few glances she seemed to visit herself. Life here, still not quite her own, kept for these few more moments unknown tranquillity. She had forgotten the heavy smoothness with which armchairs ran over the parquet, the sudden muting of steps as one crossed a rug. The mirrors were bright with reflections of grey-green gardens; in one was a cherry-bough. Firelight fingered the cups on the tray between the armchairs; arched deep recesses were dark with books, the walls all daylight: the long pale-green curtains hung from their pelmets like pillars, placidly fluted.

The white marble mantelpiece, graced and a little hidden by Emmeline's leaning figure, was of its period, rather ornate and high. But here Cecilia's eyes paraded a whole array of dear objects, sentimental and brittle. If elsewhere the room in its studied restraint might seem cold or formal – high windows down to the parquet, white cushions, cabinets spaced out round the glossy walls – the mantelpiece broke out into a gala of femininity. Clear as a still-life in the limpid afternoon light, the ornaments smiled at each other and might be supposed after midnight to dance and tinkle: candlesticks dropping with lustres, tapering coloured candles, fans tilted aslant, shell tea-caddies, painted patch-boxes, couples of china cats spotted with flowers, ramping dark ivory Chinese dogs, one widowed shepherdess with only the clock to smile at, a tall rosy clock from Dresden (a heart on its pendulum, silent under a shade), a small gold clock, ticking. There were curling-up photographs of Benito the kitten and drawings of a steel cathedral cut out by Emmeline but not framed. And, drooping out of a claret-glass, three white roses; roses a girl had worn at a party, a little brown at the tips.

Cecilia's eye lit on these. 'A party?' she said. 'Last night? Oh, you never told me!'

III

At the party where Emmeline wore the white roses she met for the first time a friend of Cecilia's, Julian Tower: thirty-nine, very tall and immaculate, with hair brushed back from a high forehead, grey eyes in deep sockets and a pleasant, formal smile. She had heard Cecilia complain of his manner as almost excessively moderate; worse, that he looked like one of those nice English actors who look so much more like gentlemen than like actors that beside them an ordinary gentleman would appear theatrical. All the same, she had heard of him as agreeable; he struck her as sympathetic. Though he came a good deal to Oudenarde Road, she had always been out at that hour or having a bath before dinner. It seemed to surprise him that *she* was Cecilia's sister-in-law; he looked at her doubtfully.

'But why not?' said Emmeline. 'You would not expect us to be alike.'

'Oh, no,' he said, still unconvinced, and remarked how funny it was that they had never met. 'Though I've known you by sight for some time without knowing you were you – Or do you and she make a point of not knowing each other's friends?'

'No, why?' she said surprised. 'Surely that would be foolish?'

They danced and sat down again. Emmeline, who had drunk throughout the evening nothing but iced tea, remained cool-looking and – as uproar heightened around her and couples yelled into each other's crimsoning faces – so singular in her correctness of manner as to seem solitary, though she was never alone. Once or twice she gazed round, turning her head on her slender long neck, as though wondering why she had come to this party at all. Having left her glasses at home she recognized nobody till they came into close range, when consternation would mingle with her surprise.

Julian, already at some disadvantage through not feeling quite himself, wished they need not have met so far on in the evening. Very modern lighting heightened an unreality; the high walls were blanched with light at the corners and cornices, rooms seen through doors had a flat, hard brilliance, like lit-up mirrors. Julian with a brandy and soda, Emmeline with another glass of iced tea withdrew to a settee half way up the staircase, in an alcove alarmingly flooded with white light. In her bright silver dress her figure appeared shadowless: she blinked, watching people go up and down.

'I'm afraid,' Julian said, 'you don't think this is much of a party.'

'Don't you?'

'I hate most parties: I hardly ever go.'

'I am rather enjoying myself,' she said, 'I go to a good many.'

She sipped her tea, gazing past him neutrally, while he more and more wished they had met elsewhere. A diffident man, he relied too blindly on formula: it was his idea of a party that having drunk more than you wanted you asked questions you still rather dimly considered impertinent: nothing mattered next day. His wits, from which he had early parted for this false confidence and woolly sense of expansion, were now badly needed for Emmeline. Evidently his party manner did not go down well with her; she made him feel foolish, as though he were wearing a paper cap.

'Cecilia's quite well,' she said, after an interval.

'She's in Sicily, isn't she?'

'Not exactly, no; tonight she is in the train, before that she was in Umbria. She will be back tomorrow.'

Emmeline delivered this information a shade sadly; it must have a cold ring for him now. For she had fancied she saw in Cecilia, towards the end of the winter, the earliest symptoms of boredom with Julian Tower. She did not speak of him nearly so often, and certainly saw him less. Or else, conceivably, he had been getting tired of her, which she must have resented. Mutability seemed to Emmeline natural; if her own friends, like her evening dresses, outlasted Cecilia's, it was simply because she did not wear them so hard or – to pursue the sartorial image – cut so close to the figure . . . In this case Emmeline was mistaken: it was simply that Julian – who had inherited a rather too flourishing family business of more than two hundred years' standing – had had less time recently than the most indulgent of women could understand. His thoughts still turned to St John's Wood; he was still more than half in love with Cecilia and half hoped to marry her. He knew quite well she had been in Umbria, not in Sicily. But perversity moves one at times to affect an ignorance that must pass for indifference as to the movements of some dear friend, or to put a faintly malicious construction on their behaviour, for the sake of some stranger too bored to tell truth from error. Emmeline took little interest in his mistake.

'Cecilia tells me you're always busy,' he said. 'You do something special, don't you?'

'I am a shipping agent: I run a travel agency.'

'I see. Like Cook's.'

'No.'

'Just a travel agency . . . How very nice.'

'Yes, it is nice.' Evidently this was an affair of passion: glancing once or twice at his white tie, no higher, always returning her eyes to her frosted glass – in which she kept tipping about an icy circle of lemon, a long spray of mint – she began to talk rapidly, fully alive. 'Our organization is really far-reaching,' she said. 'We can tell anyone almost everything: what to avoid, what to do in the afternoons anywhere – Turkestan, Cracow – what to do about mules, where it's not safe to walk after dark, how little to tip. We have made out a chart of comparative dinner times all over Europe, so's people need not waste their evenings; we are just bringing out a starred list of places good out of season and manufacturing towns that sound awful where there is really something to see. We keep very much up to date. My partner is doing a rather interesting graph of civic intelligence. We've got a slogan: "Move dangerously" – a variant of "Live dangerously", you see. It took us some time to think out, but I think it's effective. We're having it stamped on our circulars.'

'But do your railway companies like that?'

'I don't know,' said Emmeline, 'we haven't asked them. The great thing is to reach a particular public.'

'I see. But with so much forethought surely your clients are always only too safe?'

'Oh yes, physically,' she said with some contempt. 'But what everyone feels is that life, even travel, is losing its element of uncertainty; we try to supply that. We give clients their data; they have to use their own wits. "Of course" – we always say to them – "you may not enjoy yourselves." '

'I see . . . Will you send me one of your circulars?'

'I wonder,' said Emmeline, raising her eyebrows anxiously, 'if that *is* such a very good slogan? It seems to need some explaining – Forgive my asking, but after all you are one of the public: do you think you have taken the point *now*?'

'Yes,' Julian said gravely. 'It has made me want to begin to travel all over again.'

'That was what we hoped,' said Emmeline, brightening. 'Of course,' she said naïvely, 'we charge quite a high commission. But we take personal care of clients: we are beginning to get well known.'

'Where are your offices?'

'Woburn Place. They are a little expensive, so far.'

'Still, I believe in façade. May I come round one day and talk to you about Central Europe?'

'Yes, do come, and I'll show you that graph of civic intelligence. Where do you want to go to in Central Europe?'

'I – I hadn't quite thought.'

'Then,' she said – and for a moment lifted from his white tie the eyes of an ecstatic – 'you could really go anywhere?'

'More or less,' agreed Julian, elated in spite of himself.

'Come round soon,' said Emmeline, 'and we'll talk this over. If you're busy all day, come round after hours, we sometimes stay open till half-past six and have sherry for clients. They come in when they're back and give us their impressions: we get them tabulated. It keeps us in wider touch. My partner can't move, he gets sea-sick and air-sick and quite often train-sick, and I haven't got time to go everywhere. So we are glad to work in with clients.'

'You don't deal only with Bloomsbury?'

'No,' said Emmeline. A shade of distinct displeasure passed over her face; evidently that kind of thing had been said before. 'All round Woburn Place,' she said fluently, 'there are temperance hotels full of people from Wales and the North, so intoxicated at having left home at all that they are ready to go on anywhere. When they walk round the squares after breakfast they see our posters.'

'Do they walk round the squares after breakfast?' said Julian doubtfully.

'Yes,' said Emmeline, finishing up her tea.

A couple, having passed up and down several times looking fiercely into the alcove at Julian and Emmeline, sat down at last on the stairs just below the settee. The girl had a backless dress and a mole on one shoulder-blade. She leant up close to her partner in speechless affection, dropped her glass downstairs, giggled re-signedly and had a drink out of his. The atmosphere grew less temperate.

'Like one currant in icing,' said Julian.

'What, what?'

'That spot on her back.'

'Oh dear, I can't see it!' said Emmeline in despair. He glanced at the white roses pinned to her shoulder, the soft curtain of hair falling over her cheek as she leant forward beside him, trying to focus the other girl's back. He remembered what a cool note her name struck in Cecilia's talk. Her thin arms, blue-veined inside the elbow, were crossed on her knee; the fingers curled idly up. He tried to say something to bring back her eyes to his own, to command her mild interest and lovely attentive face.

'I'm so glad,' said Julian, 'we met at this party.'

'So am I,' Emmeline said, giving up the mole in despair. 'I always like parties; for one thing I often meet clients or people who may be. But I really like dancing.'

'Shall we dance?' said Julian, discouraged.

'No, I think the floor is too full.'

A young man, coming downstairs, said: 'Emmeline, you have cut me five times.' He showed some disposition to linger.

'I'm so sorry,' said Emmeline.

'Perhaps,' Julian said quickly, 'you ought to be talking to somebody else?'

'No; do you want to? Anyhow, I must be going. I never stay late.'

'I think I must have heard your voice on the telephone –'

Emmeline looked so thoughtfully through the young man that he moved away. 'You may have,' she said, 'I say: "Hullo? . . . all right: hold on!" ' Her voice trailed off: too considerate to inquire, she wondered how late it might be. She gazed at Julian, wishing he were a clock.

Had she wished, she could not have seen into him very far; she was short-sighted in every sense. Watching slip past her a blurred, repetitive pattern she took to be life, she adored fact – the exact departure of trains – and had taught herself to respect feeling. At a dance on a battleship she had been kissed by a sailor while searching the stars for Orion through a pair of opera glasses he lent her. He had breathed hard, knocking the opera glasses out of her hand – but now she remembered more clearly how the launch with her laughing companions ran under the bulk of the ship, and the stars at one startling moment . . . Since the sailor, she seemed to have been surrounded by shadowy people, acting without impetus, with no spring of passion to their behaviour, not throwing cracked opera glasses, as he did, into the sea.

She was glad to have met Julian, though he promised to be still one more of those shadowy friends, and was aware of his interest and moderate kindness as of the touch on her shoulder of the white roses at which he glanced so often, or of the silvery folds of her dress falling down in the bright light. Drifts of hearsay came through her memory: that he was either rich or extravagant, solitary or difficult, that he had once been married or would not marry, that he had an aunt or sister living above the Wye valley or near the Severn. She wondered if he loved Cecilia, if she would love him, whether *she*, Emmeline, on the outside of this mystery, would ever love. Nothing could be as dear as the circle of reading-light round her solitary pillow.

'I think perhaps I'll be going home.'

'Will you tell Cecilia I'm hoping so much to see her?'

'Yes . . . You could ring her up.'

He picked up her glass and his and stood up in the staring alcove; she smoothed her dress out and looked down into the hall. There she saw men as trees walking, her mind already at home in the dusk of her white room outside the lamplight. Already spring air began to blow through their house at night: driving up through St John's Wood you saw the pear-trees, while bare branches across moonlit walls seemed also to be in blossom. They went downstairs into the noise; as she turned to say Goodnight someone clutched Julian's arm and said 'Julian –' When he got free and turned round again, Emmeline was quite gone.

Back from the party where she had met Julian Tower, Emmeline, shivering slightly before the extinct fire, had unpinned the roses and dropped them into a glass. The Dresden clock stood still at some ghostly hour: this was her last night alone in the house . . . The map of Europe was never far from her mind, crowds rushing from platform to platform under the great lit arches, Cecilia's face sleeping against the cushions as the Anglo-Italian express tore into France from Switzerland on the return journey.

IV

Cecilia was interested to hear that Emmeline had met Julian, at that party last night, while one was asleep in the train.

'He's nice,' she said, 'isn't he? What did he say about me?'

'He asked if you were in Sicily.'

'Nonsense,' exclaimed Cecilia. She said later, 'Julian hasn't got much vitality.'

Cecilia resumed home life at high pressure: before she was into her bath two people had rung up to know whether she had arrived. Then – as she could not bear to miss anyone – she was called twice from her bath to the telephone, and stood steaming and talking, while patches of damp from her skin came through her wrapper. It would have been sad to return unnoticed. All the same, as she lay turning on with her toe more and more hot water, melancholy invaded her. She thought how at sunset the little hills lapped like waves round Urbino, and having brought her whole pile of letters into the bath with her read them, all blotchy with steam, with tears in her eyes, dropping sodden envelopes on to the bathroom floor.

Some quite new friends of Cecilia's dropped in by car at about ten o'clock: conversation continued till past midnight. Once or twice a shadow passed over Cecilia's face; she wished she were not overdrawn, she wished she had not picked Markie up in the train and given him her address; she feared she would soon know her visitors far too well; she wished Emmeline would not sit looking through them so gently, with such distaste. 'I wish,' she thought once or twice, 'I were still in Italy.'

A garage was amongst the advantages of Oudenarde Road. Emmeline's car, however, was not much use to Cecilia, as Emmeline drove off early to Woburn Place and seldom returned before dinner. Sometimes they drove to the same late party together, Emmeline's silver slipper pressed delicately on the accelerator, sometimes the time and place of their dinner engagements permitted Emmeline to drop Cecilia. On other occasions Cecilia had to take taxis, and very expensive they were. She could not help feeling that Oudenarde Road was rather far out: Emmeline, however, had been so anxious to settle here. The morning after Cecilia's return Emmeline, having started the car, looked in to remind Cecilia she must ring up Lady Waters and tell her all about Italy.

'She must ring me up,' said Cecilia. 'I'm half dead.'

'That's as you feel,' said Emmeline, dispassionate.

'Do I *look* terribly tired?' inquired Cecilia, rolling anxiously round to face the light on her pillows. Her breakfast tray was beside her; she had no intention of getting up.

'Oh, no.'

'You can't see from there,' said Cecilia crossly. 'You never can see how frightful anyone looks – I do wish, darling, you needn't take a dispatch-case about; it makes you look so fussy.'

'I am very busy: I brought work home.'

'How *is* Woburn Place?'

'Very well indeed,' said Emmeline, shining. 'We really are beginning to get known.'

'Yes, I'm sure you are. Do you find people pay up, or is it like running a hat shop? We really shall need some money – How much is six hundred lire in pounds?'

Emmeline told her.

'I shall really have to give up going out for a bit; I cannot afford ten shillings a night for taxis. It's extraordinary about money; I *don't* think I indulge myself, do you? I suppose I shall have to ask people up here instead; ten shillings isn't much if they're fond of one. But then, of course, the house bills go up. Perhaps I had better give up my 'cello lessons; I don't seem to be getting on. Do you think I had better give up the 'cello? Don't *hover*, darling; you can't be in such a hurry as all that. One really must be serious about money.'

'I'm sorry,' said Emmeline, 'but we're sending a Congregational Choir to Paris next week and we can't think what they're to do at nights. They are very broadminded, but ladies are in the party –'

'– Send them to waxworks – Or shall I give up the club?'

'Let's talk about money tonight.'

'No, that gives me a headache. Besides, I am going out.'

'By the way,' said Emmeline, 'Georgina says I am not to let you pervade me: she says you have a dominant personality.'

'I'm getting fat,' said Cecilia gloomily, 'which is far worse. Emmeline –'

But Emmeline had faded out of the door and gone. With a sigh,

Cecilia picked two more grapes from the bunch on her tray. She was a little greedy, but, though the attractive lines of her face and figure showed no bones anywhere, did not put on weight. Peeling the grapes, she wondered how best to avoid Markie if he rang up, and exactly how piqued she should feel if he never did. She regretted, also, having sent Julian from Gubbio, in reply to his rather long letter, a picture post-card, though chosen with some care. She wondered what to put on . . . Before she was half dressed she had vacillated to the telephone by her bed and rung up Georgina – Lady Waters insisted that they should call her Georgina, saying she did not feel like an aunt or an elder cousin at all, but an intimate – They had a long and, for Cecilia, unwisely intimate talk. While Emmeline simply said, gently and not very often, that she wished Georgina'd been dead for a hundred years, Cecilia daily declared her to be a scourge and a menace. Yet it was Cecilia who telephoned, who was magnetized to Rutland Gate. She could seldom bring herself to disclaim those masterpieces of temperament or caprice attributed to her by aunt-in-law. And again at moments like this – twenty past ten on a restlessly sunny morning when she was half dressed, had nothing special to do before lunch and was tempted to feel she did not exist – there was no doubt Georgina was reassuring. Cecilia felt herself crystallize over the wire, and reck-lessly made an appointment for tea.

Hanging up the receiver, Cecilia caught Henry's eye. There were few photographs in her room and Henry dominated the mantel-piece, his narrow and rather faintly and charmingly equine face expressive of apprehension and some amusement. The photograph fixed a look that in life she had hardly known; the perpetuation of the half-look that in life was so rare and fleeting disconcerted Cecilia. If there had been irony in his affection for her she had not observed it. To the tune of their passion and curiosity, exasperation and tenderness there had been, so far as she was aware, no under-tone. Left alone with this photograph, she had entered – not without chagrin or sometimes a faintly cold touch of something about the heart – on quite a new phase in her relations with Henry. Eye to eye through the picture-frame, they built up a whole past they had not shared, became in childhood cheerful, ruthless antagonists, sceptical of one another in adolescence. As man and woman, it seemed, they had still to meet. Sometimes – by those queer inter-changes when she sat most alone, in the cold widowed solitude of her room – their whole married year seemed annulled; sometimes it seemed they had not been lovers ... In the photograph Henry looked at you like Emmeline, but more guardedly, more satirically. You read the same skating quickness of thought, less resolution, more feeling, the same reluctance or inability to engage oneself closely with life on any terms. In spite of an almost fantastic detachment of manner and delicate frame, Henry had shown more vigour and less detachment than Emmeline – had he not married Cecilia? The face of her husband, remote in anger or invisibly close in passion, was gone: had she known or touched him? All she had touched was dust. But Henry, raising his eyebrows, drawing down a little his upper lip, was still with amusement deprecating something or someone – or perhaps simply deprecating his own amusement.

Hanging up the receiver, Cecilia felt this was unfair. Henry had had his weaknesses: had *he* never gossiped to Lady Waters? ... She dressed, touched her mouth up, took out a pair of fresh gloves and, with the morning before her, walked down to Baker Street Station to save twopence. At the florist's she pinned a carnation into her coat.

Cecilia lunched in St Leonard's Terrace with three young friends – not a party, they just dropped in – three young married women. The conversation was esoteric: they spoke of happiness; knee-to-knee round the painted table, nibbling salt almonds and twisting the long-stemmed Venetian glasses they confessed they could not understand themselves; each, as she talked, took on an air of childish rarity and importance. They were young women delicately compact as hyacinths; one wore frills down her front, she was going to have a baby; one showed a glowing reticence, she had a lover; one, a bride, was called from the *soufflé* to telephone to her husband. Going upstairs to coffee they all advised Cecilia to marry again.

Emmeline lunched not far from Woburn Place at a shop called 'The Coffee Pot', with Peter Lewis, her partner. She read a book about Poland, he blue-pencilled a manuscript; they ate poached eggs on spinach, each paid for their own lunches and did not speak to each other. The place was full of pleasant young men and women, secretaries of the surrounding learned societies, lunching elbow-to-elbow. Young women in more of a hurry ate salad up at a counter, perched on high scarlet stools: young men are seldom in such a hurry as all that. Emmeline, who knew most of them, nodded and smiled going out, looking less unapproachable than she had looked at the party. When she got back to the office, Cecilia rang up from St Leonard's Terrace to say she now found she had six hundred and fifty-eight lire: how much would *that* be? A client with passport trouble came in and asked Emmeline to ring up a consulate. Peter was worried when someone came in to ask silly questions about Brazil just as he was getting on with the graph; he threw the graph at Emmeline and rang up some shipping companies. Their secretary, recently down from Lady Margaret Hall, who worked for ten shillings a week and the experience, made more mistakes than usual in her typing and looked gloomily over the wire blind at the sky. There had been several personal calls for her lately: Emmeline said perhaps she had better go home. Peter complained she made more noise than was possible with her typewriter; her touch must be unsympathetic. She had hands like mattresses; also, he did not approve of pin-money girls.

'But we can't afford one who isn't,' said Emmeline, sketching a new poster on the back of an envelope.

'I'd pay nearly ten shillings *not* to have her.'

'She may marry,' said Emmeline hopefully.

'I don't see how she can, poor thing.' Hunching his shoulders as though in a high cold wind he added: 'She doesn't like us.'

'I think she likes the experience.'

'Then she ought to pay *us* ten shillings a week.'

'We might sack her,' said Emmeline, 'that would all be an experience.'

'I don't see how we can.'

It always came back to this. Neither liked to suggest that the other should learn to type. Emmeline finished the poster, he amended the lettering; meanwhile she upset some green ink over his graph. She was surprised, and a little annoyed with him; she had had no idea the green ink was about ... All the same, a colourless harmony presided over the office, in which they both took up personally a very small space. Capacity for the direct side of business apart, they were an ideal partnership. Their office, a room with fine cornices overlooking a courtyard, had once been someone's back dining-room and was divided by folding doors from the premises of an archaeological society where almost complete silence reigned. Peter and Emmeline each had roll-top desks of their own, hers by the window, his under the green glare of a lamp he hardly ever turned off. Their secretary occupied a deal table half into the fireplace; she had wedged the legs with blotting-paper but when her violence became excessive they would both look up and wince. There were maps stuck over with flags (to denote the position of clients), their own posters, three shelves of files, a small safe of which only the secretary could remember the combination, a hat-rack, a cupboard for tea-cups and sherry. Two swivel chairs were provided for clients, who could thus face either Peter or Emmeline ... As Cecilia said, it all looked very workmanlike. Cecilia did not, however, care much for Peter, who looked, she said, rather too Peter-ish.

After another stiff hour of concentration, not interrupted by clients, Emmeline put on the kettle and soon poured out pale tea into thick bright pottery cups. The parlourmaid rang up from Oudenarde Road, on Cecilia's behalf, to say they were right out of sherry: would Emmeline bring back a bottle with her and be home early?

During Emmeline's talk with the parlourmaid Peter remained by the fireplace, blowing his tea with an air of slightly disdainful discretion, as though he were thankful he had no ties. Emmeline knew nothing and wished to know nothing of Peter's life; their partnership having been based on a strong common interest – or strictly, fervour – and a little spare capital on both sides: up to that, they had only met at those rather dispersed and apparently hostless parties they both attended. Though he knew almost everyone she knew, and apparently thought them frightful, she never discussed him elsewhere. He spoke sometimes of catching a train; she had seen him once in a restaurant quarrelling with a haggard young friend ... Nothing urgent came by the four o'clock post; having filed a picture post-card from a client in Prague under 'testimonials' they decided to close the office and take their projected new poster round to a friend at the Southampton Row school of art. On the way, Emmeline wondered if they were prepared for the Whitsun rush; this led Peter to re-open the question of their publicity; he also felt they were not doing enough with airways. Turning left, they paced Theobald's Road for some time in an agitated discussion: when they got to the art school their friend had gone. Peter, who had this form of incipient mania, could not remember if he had remembered to lock up the office, or whether he had only thought he *must* lock up the office; Emmeline found she had left a cheque on her desk, so they went back quickly to find the office unlocked and a client there.

An elderly gentleman in an overcoat, only too clearly another friend of Sir Robert's, stood eyeing between alarm and respect the posters, the blotted graph and the sugarbowl. Only an excellent lunch and the strongest regard for Sir Robert could have brought him to this end of London at all. As they came in, he had been in the act of picking up his bowler; apprehension had gained on him; meeting Peter's stern eye in the doorway he looked decidedly trapped.

'I'm afraid,' said the client, still with some faint idea of escape, 'I am after hours?'

'Not at all,' said Peter, shutting the door firmly.

'We are so sorry,' Emmeline said, putting on her spectacles and sitting down at her desk, 'to have kept you waiting. We've had a terribly busy day.' Mopping up the last of the green ink she said something about publicity.

'We are directing our own publicity,' Peter took up fluently. 'And the exceptional rush on airways has kept us so busy we do not know where to turn.'

Reassured by Emmeline's mildness, Sir Robert's friend put down his hat again, spinning his chair in her way. He spoke of Sir Robert; they chatted; he went on to inquire after Cecilia. Peter, after a glassy half-look that said 'Yours' to Emmeline, unwound his scarf from the hat-rack, flicked down his hat and went off to wash, leaving them to it. Gently, with a series of feathery touches to right and left, Emmeline rounded the rambling old gentleman down the straight path to business. Though he had no wish to leave England so soon his wife, it appeared, was determined to do so; he did not care where they went so long as it was not again to Biarritz. Guessing that he spoke no languages and would want bridge, Emmeline reached down the appropriate files, marked: 'Lakes'. Peter, running cold water over his wrists at the end of the corridor, heard them talking about mosquitoes. Listening critically, he thought Emmeline's manner insufficiently feminine; he could have done it better himself.

Emmeline got back late with the sherry; whoever it was had gone. The drawing-room, however, was still rich with strange cigarette-smoke; Cecilia, in black, wandered among the furniture with the air of not having yet readjusted herself to solitude. As Emmeline came in she said: 'I suppose I do lack background . . .'

'Who has been telling you that?'

'Julian.'

'Oh?' Emmeline said, surprised. 'Did he come to tea?'

'Yes,' said Cecilia, gloomily. 'I was to have seen Georgina, but I wired and told her life was too difficult: she will be furious.'

'I'm sorry about the sherry.'

'Oh, *that* didn't matter.'

'Why, did he annoy you?'

'He depressed me,' said Cecilia, lighting a cigarette. She blew three rings of smoke and watched them dissolve critically: 'It is all very well to talk to me about backgrounds,' she went on . . .

V

Julian had depressed Cecilia by talking about his niece, a girl of fourteen. Though his manner took light from her animation he had arrived preoccupied: she had assumed that this must be something to do with herself, but soon wished she had not asked him what was the matter.

Pauline, an orphan, had been controlled for the last five years by a committee of relatives, of which Julian, as her guardian, was unwilling chairman. His brothers and sisters all felt he got through life too easily, forming too few ties and buying too many pictures; it was not without some sense of justice that they had inflicted this minor worry. He paid the child's fees at boarding-school (no one had left any money for Pauline), visited her once a term and took her to plays in the holidays. Her confirmation, which seemed to him premature, the fixing-in of a plate to correct prominent teeth and treatments for flat feet and curvature had all been reported to him. Her complexion, his sisters told him, time would correct; he heard with relief that though highly nervous she was not astigmatic and had no digestive trouble. His eldest sister ordered her clothes, for which he paid, a sister-in-law took her in for the holidays or arranged for her circulation among relations.

But for the last week of these Easter holidays there had been a break-down; no one could have Pauline. The family intimated to Julian that they would be satisfied with any arrangement he chose to make, and suggested a week in his flat in London, visiting the museums and getting to know her uncle. Pauline, said his sister-in-law, is full of interests and wonderfully responsive. She put Pauline into the London train and retired into a nursing-home, where she had a baby.

So Pauline was, at present, in Julian's Westminster flat, where she played the gramophone and talked a good deal to the house-keeper. She stitched name-tapes on to her new summer-term outfit, sang to herself and was terribly little trouble. But his housekeeper did not like children; his flat was not arranged for a little girl. His community with all bachelor uncles in the great tradition of English

35

humorous fiction did not console Julian. He saw that this must be funny, but suffered acutely. For his niece, who read Ian Hay, the situation was full of charm. She was diligently little-girlish; whimsicality distorted their conversation. She alternated between the romp and the dream-child, occasionally attempting the mouse, when she effaced herself noticeably. With a sense of guilt that was profound, he did not know which of these aspects was most distasteful. It was at him that she day-dreamed, at him that she thundered about the flat; her assaults on his attention were like the firings-off of a small gun.

It was not, Julian said to Cecilia, the gramophone that he minded, though she scratched his records and walked a whole box of needles into a rug: he was out so much, it was not fair to complain. It was not that, having been recommended to drink much milk, she was always white round the mouth and left clouded glasses about on the mantelpiece. It was not that she rubbed her chilblains with small pieces of camphor. He did not know what it was . . . When he went down to the school the headmistress took him aside to tell him Pauline was psychologically interesting; she seemed to be proud of Pauline. The headmistress had made Julian think of a man who once came into his flat with a new fire extinguisher. 'I should like to interest you,' he had said, 'in this new line we are showing . . .' The headmistress, failing to interest Julian, had liked him less.

'It is not . . .' he said, looking heavily round Cecilia's drawing-room. 'Oh, she's doing her best, poor child; I can feel her doing it.'

Cecilia said, surely one could put up with anything for a week?

In fact, it was less the niece than the uncle that worried Julian: something in him that would not bring off the simplest relationship, that could be aware of any relationship only as something to be brought off; something hyperconscious of strain or falsity. This descent of an orphan child on his life might have been superficially comic, or even touching. But the disheartening density of Proust was superimposed for him on a clear page of Wodehouse. The poor child's approximation to what she took to be naturalness parodied his own part in an intimacy. She mortified him on his own account, and on account of the woman so drearily nascent in her immaturity: he confronted again and again her look, as she chattered and romped, the unavowable anxiety of the comedian. He was estranged from her, as though she were transparent, as he was estranged from almost all women, by a rather morbid consciousness of fraternity.

After three days of her company, he felt like a pane of mean glass scrubbed horribly clean, like a pool dredged of its charming shadowy waterweeds. Those inexactitudes of desire that sent him towards Cecilia, those bright smoky movements of fancy became remote and impossible. Society, peopled with nudes, became unseemly as a Turkish bath; he could look nowhere without confusion, least of all at himself.

To be with Cecilia made a slowing-down and a break in this anxious consciousness; it was like falling asleep. Aware of her pretty figure in black on the sofa beside him, her head turned his way, her expressive hands – that, unlike other hands, seemed to exist to touch, to communicate their vitality – he relaxed under the enchantment of a delectable strangeness, this foreignness to himself that passed for her mystery. To be with her, so nearly to love her was to lend oneself wholly to an illusion, to hang in a drop of light in the lustres along her mantelpiece, to be reflected for less than a moment, like a bird's shadow flashing across a mirror, in her dazzling ignorance of oneself.

Julian knew too well that in grumbling about his niece to her he was presenting himself in a most unattractive light: one should discuss one's difficulties only when they are over. Intoxicated by his utter failure to please, he went on to complain that Pauline's age was difficult, that he did not care for responsive women, that she annoyed the servants and blew in her glass when she drank; all this, he said, need never have mattered if it were not so clear she would never be one of those people whom, in spite of all their failings, it is impossible not to like.

'But, my dear,' said Cecilia briskly, after what seemed some hours of this, 'she's only a girl, after all: she can't eat you.'

'I know.'

'What do you mean by responsive?'

'Like a bear you have to keep on throwing buns at.'

'Oh dear: I wonder if I am responsive? She doesn't read yellow novels or smoke in her room?'

'Oh, no, she is most respectable; she chaperones herself the whole time.'

'Isn't she pretty at all?'

'I'm afraid not.'

'Spotty?'

'I'm afraid she is, rather.'

'Oh dear, poor little thing.'

'It's horrible,' said Julian, lighting her cigarette for her, 'to be talking like this about a child. But she rattles me terribly. I can never just look at her; I always feel as though I were catching her eye.'

Cecilia, realizing that what he really wanted was to talk to her about himself, not Pauline, was a little mollified. 'Don't be neurotic, Julian,' she said more kindly.

'I don't feel she can be enjoying herself. I've got a woman to take her to museums and things, and she's been to a film with a friend, but I think that shocked her.'

'Poor little thing. Would you like me to ask her to tea, or something like that?'

'Oh, well,' said Julian. This, as a matter of fact, had been in his mind, but the way Cecilia put it it did not sound possible.

'I would, only what should we talk about all the time? She'd be so bored . . . Why didn't you bring her this afternoon?'

'Don't be silly, Cecilia,' said Julian sharply.

Cecilia, startled, knocked ash very carefully off her cigarette. 'Well, you know,' she said, 'you do get things on your mind.'

'What a bore I must be.'

'Oh, no.'

Cecilia was, as a matter of fact, rather fond of children; she felt sorry for poor little Pauline shut up in that cold flat and would have liked to do something for her, though not to please Julian. Naturally she was irritated with Julian, who should have known better than to sit beside her, after three weeks of absence, looking at once haggard and dumpy like a widower with five children. She had amused herself for a short time by her impersonation of a dissipated and heartless woman. Her Aunt Georgina's example gave her a horror of searching talk; all the same she liked to receive confidences if these were conferred prettily, with some suggestion of her own specialness, not dropped on her toes all anyhow, like a bulky valise someone is anxious to put down. Looking thoughtfully past Julian while he maundered on about Pauline, she remembered the one occasion when he had kissed her passionately, and looked again at his rather beautiful mouth. She was aware of her power to overbear in him something speculative and recessive, to be not for one instant his sister. After that dreary letter to her in Italy, after pretending to Emmeline he did not know where she was when she went abroad –

here he was, consulting the married woman about his niece. The brittleness of the pretext – for such, in a flash that brightened the afternoon, it did now appear – at once piqued and soothed her: though their interview was remaining so frank and serious, he had come for a touch of the subtle excitement she could command. But their inequality seemed immense: she could never marry him.

She told herself, she would have married Henry again and again. Turning half round, her elbow among the cushions, fixing on Julian a melancholic dark look, she missed Henry with impatience, as though he had gone to come back and was already too long away. From her marriage a kind of vulgarity Julian's tentativeness aroused in her had been absent, and that year when, however little she knew of Henry, she had best known herself, had a shadowy continuity among her impressions. Henry was with her casually, as though he came strolling into the room; there were cues he could never resist, incidents that provoked him to actuality. Without being aware, before or after his death, of his influence as an influence, she still took impressions on his account and often suspected her judgements were not her own. The mantelpiece was too high, he would always have thought so; with double discomfort she felt draughts to which he would have objected steal through the shut French window between the curtains. Now she could hear him agree, with that easiness that was so slighting, how very nice Julian was . . . These moments when he and she met – he going up, she down on a moving staircase, when their fingers brushed for a moment across the handrail – still left Cecilia perplexed and smiling.

Julian did *not* volunteer that Cecilia lacked background; it was Cecilia who suddenly saw this and asked him if it was so.

'Perhaps,' said Julian, wondering why she was not more tiresome. But charm – or what passed for her charm – apart, her satirical honesty, with her habit of rounding briskly upon herself, kept her at all times from being quite a bore. He was not, however, disposed to discuss her character . . . There were quite long intervals when he did not think at all of her, when her personality was like an engaging book on a shelf by one's chair that one has only to put out a hand for, but does not put out a hand for. Perhaps half the pleasure in some of these visits remained in returning to somewhere where she was not. Some effervescence she set up in him, subsiding, left a sediment, bitter-sweet, of a doubtful quality that he did not analyse. He wished sometimes he could forget her, and, since last night, thought sometimes of Emmeline, whom it might become impossible to forget.

Pauline was all alone in the flat, waiting for her Uncle Julian to come home. Life was not gay here: the late afternoon, ticked away by small clocks all over the flat, had been more than long. She had, it is true, been out before tea; she had asked Mrs Patrick, the housekeeper, if it would be suitable for a young girl of her age to go out all alone for a ride in a bus. (Pauline had been told what happens in London and warned, especially, to avoid hospital nurses.) Mrs Patrick, with hospital nurses also in mind, said it depended entirely upon the character of the bus. Taking thought, she had recommended the No. 11. The No. 11 is an entirely moral bus. Springing from Shepherd's Bush, against which one has seldom heard anything, it enjoys some innocent bohemianism in Chelsea, picks up the shoppers at Peter Jones, swerves down the Pimlico Road – too busy to be lascivious – passes not too far from the royal stables, nods to Victoria Station, Westminster Abbey, the Houses of Parliament, whirrs reverently up Whitehall, and from its only brush with vice, in the Strand, plunges to Liverpool Street through the noble and serious architecture of the City. Except for the Strand, the No. 11 route, Mrs Patrick considered, had the quality of Sunday afternoon literature; from it Pauline could derive nothing but edification. So, anxious to get Pauline out of the flat, she recommended a ride with confidence.

Fully subscribing to Pauline's idea that a young girl cannot be too careful, she would not, she said, have countenanced a No. 24, which goes down Charing Cross Road. Pauline blushed, she had heard about Charing Cross Road. So she boarded a No. 11 at the corner of Smith Street, rode to Liverpool Street, admired the grimy glass arch of the station and rode home. Tomorrow, she promised herself, she would take the No. 11 in the other direction, to Chelsea, to look at the artists. There had been no hospital nurses, no one had looked at Pauline. Back in the flat, she had seed cake and toast for tea before Mrs Patrick went out. Pauline thought to herself what a good thing it was that she was a dreamy child, full of interests, who liked playing the gramophone.

Shadows drew out in St James's Park, twilight swung a clear veil over the sky. Kneeling up to the window Pauline sought the company of the wild-violet evening and some few lights. She went to the other window: across the E-shaped court gay low lamps sprang into flower in other drawing-rooms, tea was taken away: Pauline sighed; this was the hour for intimate talk. Here she hung alone, at a toppling height in the London sky.

Pauline fingered the switches, but light poured into the pictures only, leaving the heart of the room cold. Olives writhing in the mistral, campanili flat in the sun, shadows gashing white water, a hare's blood dripping into a glass all blazed alive at her with unfriendly vigour, as though she had opened windows into the wrong world. The room with its bunch of shadowy furniture became full of vacancy, in which Pauline hardly seemed to exist. A nice room, she thought, and suitable for an uncle – it had a too intelligent, muted luxury, a gloom of rugs and deep chairs, rather *triste* repose: in the shelves gilt lettering just did not catch the light – but needing a woman's touch ... When Big Ben struck, there was no one to whom to say, as she always did, that this made her think of the wireless.

Pauline had been given to understand that girls were a softening influence. She felt that her Uncle Julian might well confide in her; with this in view her searching eyes seldom left his face. 'Little Pauline,' he might begin. She had hoped much of this lamplit hour. He had been disappointed in love ... Or a lady in violets and furs might come to the flat: Pauline doubted, however, if that would be respectable ... At her confirmation classes they had worked their way through the Commandments: at the seventh, an evening had been devoted to impure curiosity. She had been offered, and had accepted, a very delicate book and still could not think of anything without blushing. She felt she had erred in accepting the delicate book when she lacked impure curiosity, but the other candidates, all averting their eyes, had held up their hands for it and she did not like to be out of anything. So that now flowers made her blush, rabbits made her blush excessively; she could no longer eat an egg. Only minerals seemed to bear contemplation ... Trying the switches again and moving one lamp to a mirror, Pauline curled her lip back to study the gold band over her teeth. Was this why no one had spoken to her on the bus, or had she that look of indefinable purity?

She could not help feeling that she was a lonely child. She stretched out on the divan, one hand under her cheek, and, as

41

Julian still did not come and the windows darkened, reflected that she was an orphan, had had a French great-aunt and a troubled family history, had been confirmed when she was thirteen, was alone in her rich uncle's flat five storeys up, and that her favourite poet was Matthew Arnold. These dramatic facts of her life fully coloured an hour's blankness.

Then she heard Julian's key in the flat door. He perceived for a moment her pensive figure among the cushions, and, as she sprang up to embrace him and kiss him just short of the ear, could not be thankful enough this was not his wife.

'All alone?' he said heartily.

'Ever so happy,' said Pauline.

The remark was unanswerable. 'Still, it's too bad,' said Julian. He felt really guilty and wished he had brought her chocolates or something to eat.

Pauline said she had been for a nice 'explore' on a bus.

'Good,' said Julian, and glanced at a letter he longed to open.

'I love buses,' said Pauline brightly. 'I sat inside but saw everything. It was just like *Punch*. Such a sweet nun got in: we smiled at each other.'

'Do you like nuns?' said Julian.

'They have such sweet faces,' said Pauline firmly. 'It was a No. 11; coming back, the City looked quite enchanted.'

'It doesn't enchant me.'

Approaching, she stood at his elbow and watched with large eyes while he mixed himself a whisky and soda. 'Do you really like that?' she inquired, 'or do you only drink it because you are tired?'

'Yes . . . I mean, no.'

'Horrid old office, keeping you so late.'

'As a matter of fact I went out to tea.'

'I thought you never went out to tea.'

'Well, I do.'

'I expect it was fun,' said Pauline. From one glance at his face she turned quickly away, blushing: there was a pause full of delicacy. He suggested that they should go to a film at the Polytechnic, a film with no nonsense in it, about lions.

VI

'Who *is* Mark Linkwater?' said Lady Waters, about three weeks later.

'A friend of Cecilia's.'

'My dear Emmeline, if I did not know that I should not be asking: that is just why I ask.'

'He's a barrister,' replied Emmeline, after a moment's considera-tion.

'I dare say . . . I understand from Cecilia you don't like him?'

'Yes, I do,' said Emmeline unexpectedly. 'He's unlike most people.'

Lady Waters's manner intensified. 'How?' she said.

'Rather bumptious,' said Emmeline, smiling.

'I did not care for his manner.'

'Who is that that is bumptious?' inquired Sir Robert suddenly, putting down *The Times*. He loved and esteemed Emmeline – did he not send her clients? – and was delighted to have her with them at Farraways for the week-end. Farraways, a small country house in Gloucestershire, had been left to Georgina for life by her first husband, Cecilia's uncle: it had been offered to Cecilia and Henry for the honeymoon, but they had preferred Spain. It was a dull-faced, pleasant Victorian house with big bow windows, low window-sills and a long view down a slope of the Cotswolds. The other guests for this week-end were a young married couple, the Blighs, who might, Lady Waters was certain, still save their mar-riage if they could get right away from people and talk things out, and a young man called Farquharson who had just broken off his engagement on Lady Waters's advice. At present, this Saturday at about half-past five, the Blighs, who would have been passably happy if Lady Waters had left them alone, were quarrelling at the far end of the garden, while Mr Farquharson, who would have got along nicely married to almost anyone, was writing long letters of explanation to everyone up in his room. Sir Robert, his wife and Emmeline still sat round the tea-table in the drawing-room bow window. Emmeline could think of no reason to get up and go away.

Sir Robert in the country was like a dog; he liked to be taken for long walks (which was chiefly why Emmeline was invited); indoors he sought human propinquity, but while seldom sitting apart from his wife or her friends took no part in the conversation. Anything could be discussed, Sir Robert remained unconscious. His interruption today was without precedent, and must be the effect of Emmeline. Lady Waters was rather annoyed.

'A friend of Cecilia's, Robert,' she said repressively.

'Which friend of Cecilia's?'

'A Mr Linkwater.'

'Never heard of him – do *you* think he's bumptious, Emmeline?'

'My dear, it was Emmeline who just said so.'

'Then I dare say Emmeline is quite right.'

'But I like him,' said Emmeline.

'If we are disturbing you, Robert,' said Lady Waters, 'we had better go into the garden.'

'No, don't do that,' said Sir Robert, and put up *The Times* again quickly.

Emmeline, who had been eating a lump of sugar, said thoughtfully: 'I don't think bumptious is really the word.'

'Oh, I've no doubt he is clever. But I did not like his expression; there was something about his eye that I did not like; it reminded me of a basilisk.'

It was beneath Emmeline to ask Lady Waters where she had seen a basilisk. She said: 'He's not at all sorry for himself,' selecting the very quality that had not commended him to Georgina.

'Why should he be sorry? I've no doubt he has a very nice time. Cecilia seems very much taken up with him.'

Emmeline, who had a transparent skin, turned faintly pink as she said: 'I don't think they meet much.'

'Nonsense,' said Lady Waters. Her look drank in the blush; she was accustomed to find Emmeline quite impassible. 'Evidently,' she said, 'you agree with me.'

'I don't quite know what we are talking about,' said Emmeline with extreme gentleness. She looked out wistfully at the garden. She had not come down all this way into Gloucestershire, in the middle of what she and Peter considered the Whitsun rush, to sit indoors discussing attractions as though they were at Rutland Gate. She had no doubt that Cecilia had already told her aunt all about Markie, far more than she knew. Emmeline, longing to play tennis before dinner, rather sadly selected one more lump of sugar and crunched it up.

'All that sugar cannot be good for you, Emmeline – All I can say is, I hope this will not come to much.'

'I don't see why it should.'

'You are very young, Emmeline.'

'You don't think the others might like to play tennis?'

'I don't think they are much in the mood,' said their hostess darkly.

'You don't think it might cheer them up?'

'I'll take you on, Emmeline,' said Sir Robert joyfully.

'Don't get hot,' said his wife, as the pair stepped out through the window. Sir Robert did get very hot; in his braces he was soon rushing about the court. He played, however, a stonewall game and beat Emmeline, who was erratic. Gerda Bligh soon appeared in an arch of the beech hedge, mournfully, like Cassandra, while Tim Farquharson, attracted by the sound of the balls, put down his pen and came to hang round the court. He was a little afraid of Emmeline, who had been his ex-fiancée's friend; for her part she found him a harmless young man, though inferior.

'I've written eight letters,' he could not help saying to Gerda Bligh when the set was over.

'They won't go till Monday now,' said Sir Robert cheerfully. 'You should have given them to the postman.'

'But nobody told me.'

'Yes, that's too bad; you should have given them to the postman.'

'*Does* an afternoon post come in?' said Emmeline suddenly. Her white sweater slung round her shoulders, absently knotting the sleeves round her neck, she turned to look at Sir Robert as though he had said something she did not quite know how to take. Her hair blown back, she had for a moment a curious distant look, not like a woman's.

'Naturally,' said Sir Robert, who from the moment he had not too willingly hung up at Farraways his own quite honourable hat, had accepted everything here in its fixed order.

Emmeline getting up, left them; she walked rather slowly away from the white seat in front of the beech hedge, as though she might never return. Did she expect a letter? Perhaps even she hardly knew what drew her indoors, or set her feeling her way through the dark hall to the table where posts lay. By the gong, she 'found Markie's letter: square, blue and compact – and at once wished he had not written.

'A letter has come for you, Emmeline,' said Lady Waters, appearing.

'Yes, Georgina.'

'I see you have found it.'

Not replying to this observation, Emmeline went on upstairs. Though Lady Waters naturally had not examined the letter, she had seen from across the hall that the vigorous handwriting was unfamiliar, and wondered what stranger could be in close enough touch with Emmeline to know where she was for two days. It was quite simple: Markie, knowing that Emmeline was to be with the Waters somewhere in Gloucestershire, had looked up Sir Robert in *Who's Who*.

He wrote:

Dear Emmeline – As Wednesday does not suit you, what about Friday? I can put something else off: we must not let this fall through. So please do wear yellow and do not be late again. I'm sorry you found me tiresome the other night, though you cannot expect me to agree with you. Had that never happened before? It is quite usual. And really there did not seem to be much to say; you do rather dispose of any little thing one brings up. However, no doubt we shall find more to say later on.

If it would restore confidence, we will go and dance somewhere on Friday, instead. Or you can tell me more about trains – you did not seem to think much of my books. Anything you like. I do miss you: it is that funny look in your eyes, like a foal coming up wind to inspect you. I would do anything to amuse you, but the fact is you are so dazzlingly beautiful I really don't care if you're amused or not.

Don't be late on Friday; there's never enough time. And don't put off, like last week, or I shall come round and fetch you. Cecilia would be amazed. How nice she is; I'm so glad I talked to her in the train. Remember me to your aunt – or cousin? – who said I must be an extrovert.

Yours,

P.S. – Friday: 8.15.   Markie.

Emmeline pushed this bumptious letter into a drawer, but still did not feel quite alone. It was not in her nature to shut a drawer violently; an edge of the blue envelope still stuck out. Her room was full of late light that, reflected through the big windows up from the lawn filled the mirrors, struck on the polished bed-end's mahogany whorls and blinded a print of calm ruins hanging over the mantelpiece. Emmeline, as though someone had touched her, was confused by a curious pleasure and trepidation. She heard Markie's voice and confronted his sceptical eyes, the eyebrows above them twitching up in a question: her faculties stood quite still. Seeing herself in the mirror she turned away, dreading the touch of a thought, even her own. She received from the glowing walls of her room an impression of space, of a vast moment.

This impact of Markie upon her was disproportionate with her life. No one had troubled her, something in her had forbidden anything but indirectness and delicacy. A splinter of ice in the heart is bombed out rather than thawed out. At her desk in the window she wrote back quickly, before reflection could intervene:

Dear Markie – Yes, I can come on Friday, thank you, though it seems a pity you should have to put something off. I will try to be punctual, though we are kept very late at the office just now. I do not mind if we dance or not. I am sorry you thought me unreasonable; I suppose other people are often surprising.

I can leave my car at the garage just round your corner so you need not call for me. But why should Cecilia be 'amazed'?

Yours,
Emmeline.

Remembering that this letter could not leave here till Monday, and that it would be quicker to take it with her to London, she slipped it into the drawer beside Markie's and, at dinner, thought of their odd companionship among her gloves and handkerchiefs.

Cecilia, though she had trouble enough with her friends, never expected anyone to act out of character. She felt so certain Emmeline would think Markie awful that she had mentioned the prejudice to her aunt as a *fait accompli* and had prepared the way for his dining at Oudenarde Road with a good deal of apprehension. True to her resolution to take fewer taxis, she had been seeing her friends at home; hence her orbit and Emmeline's touched more often. Cecilia had long fixed Emmeline in an idea of her own as fastidious and mildly difficult and, though hurt if she deprecated

47

the close friend of the moment, found Emmeline's distaste for most of her circle – or a distaste she liked to attribute to Emmeline – rather tonic and bracing: Cecilia did not think much of most people herself. Emmeline's standpoint was one of Cecilia's few landmarks.

When, some days after their journey, Markie had rung up and invited himself to see her, Cecilia, not wishing to meet him on these terms, had countered at once by an invitation to dinner, which she as soon regretted. 'He is clever, of course,' she had said to Emmeline, 'and hard-headed . . .' but she felt discouraged and thought of going to bed with a temperature. All the same, she had begged Emmeline to be there. She did not feel Markie would mix at all well with most of her friends, and would rather face, afterwards, Emmeline's coolness than their polite reserve. She invited, to make a fourth, a young friend just down from Cambridge who should be too much flattered at being present at all to be critical of his company.

Markie came and – at least in the general view – conquered. Turning rapidly to and fro between Cecilia and Emmeline – having almost no neck he veered bodily from the waist, which gave one an alarming sense of his full attention – or traversing round the table his rapid fire of talk, he dominated the party. His wit was incisive, spectacular, mordant: the young man from Cambridge, *ébloui*, hardly glanced at Cecilia . . . It was one of those one-man evenings which, though successful, leave one rather depressed. Cecilia, yawning when they had gone, kicked off her gold shoes before the fire.

'Markie,' she said, 'is fatter than I remembered. And poor little Evan was quite dumb.'

'He's more thick than fat,' said Emmeline, accurate. 'And Evan was listening.'

'He must learn not to listen like that – like a fish. I'd forgotten he was so young. Markie talks like all young men of Evan's age long to talk, but that's no reason why he should be encouraged.'

'Still, I think they enjoyed themselves.'

'I've no doubt they did,' said Cecilia. 'But did we? That is the question.'

'I like Markie,' said Emmeline, leaning her cheek on the side of the mantelpiece. 'I think he's so funny.'

'You wouldn't care for him really; he isn't at all your sort of person.' Having disposed of this, Cecilia shook out the sofa cushions that Markie had sat on and lay down among them herself. 'But then,' she continued, crossing her ankles, 'whom does one really like? That's what I keep asking myself. Here we go ruining ourselves asking people to dinner. I shall begin going out again, Emmeline; I don't think taxis are really much more expensive and it's easier to get away from people. Here I am, worn out listening to Markie; it's like watching something catch too many flies on its tongue. And I shall have more of it, I'm lunching with him on Thursday.'

'Are you?' said Emmeline, who was lunching with him on Saturday.

Cecilia's lunch with Markie had not been a success; he was so rude she felt he could only have asked her out of politeness: she felt pale and gloomy. When they parted: 'Well,' he said briskly, 'this has been delightful.' She could not agree with him. To make matters worse, they had run into Lady Waters . . . However, Cecilia's dividends were coming in, her new clothes had arrived; she was having a very gay time and all possible interest in Markie soon dwindled away. She only regretted having spoken of him to Lady Waters, who never forgot, with whom the subjects of former confidences remained mournful and monumental, a whole hall of petrified kings . . . Markie, too well advised to encounter Cecilia over the wire, soon traced Emmeline to her number at Woburn Place.

Emmeline, during these weeks, had seen Markie a good many times. He impressed her with his good sense, his extensive and intimate knowledge of Europe, his quickness of mind and the information on almost all topics he could command. While he talked, she would look at him thoughtfully: she had had no idea till he wrote that he found her difficult. For some time she had found his physical personality vaguely unpleasing, though she took little stock of these things: she jumped as though she had been struck the first time he put out her way an eager but nerveless hand. He had the effect of suspending her faculties not unpleasantly, like some very loud noise to which one becomes accustomed. She was surprised by the kind of woman he admired in restaurants and had had no idea till he wrote that he thought her beautiful. For some time – until, in fact, their own friendship was well established – she took him for granted as some sort of family friend: such had come and gone. He sailed in her waters under Cecilia's ensign.

When Emmeline realized Cecilia no longer saw him she was alarmed; it was as though a door shut upon her and Markie, leaving them quite alone for the first time: the nature of their relationship changed for her. When she understood that Cecilia had not realized *she* still saw Markie, taking fully for granted that he was out of the family, Emmeline was dumbfounded. Reserve had kept her at all times from discussing her friends with Cecilia, whose incuriosity was immense: at this point, a profound shyness inhibited Emmeline. This was her first break with innocence. Something weakened in her defences that were not till now defences, so unconscious had they been and so impassable. The soft, inquiring foal's eyes she still fixed on Markie had a new shadow behind them. The evening of that enlightening talk with Cecilia she had promised to dine with Markie: she almost did not go: she went, and she came away shaken. He had not been slow to interpret that new wary shadow behind her eyes.

'Wednesday,' he had repeated, leaning into the car as he saw her off, just after midnight. But Emmeline, every nerve quivering from that collision, had leaned away from him in her white fur coat. 'I can't,' she had said, despairing. She shot into gear, accelerated, and the small car went spinning, terrified, up the empty streets to St John's Wood. Emmeline, trembling, went to her room and wept. She recollected his goodness of heart, his engaging friendliness, how his face lit up when they met. There had been some mistake. Stepping out of the yellow dress she had put on so cheerfully she had racked herself with contrition. All next day she worked desperately, to the exclusion of thought, and today, two days later, came down to Farraways, where she would walk with Sir Robert.

In the drawing-room at Farraways, where they were waiting for dinner, a distinct gloom was lightened by the appearance of Emmeline. Gilbert Bligh had forgotten his black tie and been obliged to borrow one from Tim Farquharson, whom he disliked; he did not dare reproach Gerda who would have replied that she was not a valet; that they had not enough servants was one of her tragedies. Tim Farquharson, unable to post his letters, had re-opened several and come to the conclusion that he had not done himself justice. Sir Robert, leaning on the piano, was showing a book of drawings to Gerda Bligh, who would have preferred to stay in her room for a good weep. Lady Waters, arranging a fur on her spangled shoulders, looked magnetically at her visitors. Emmeline had, in fact, entered a web where the prey still fluttered . . . But the drawing-room with wide-open windows, bowls of white lilac and young fire seemed to be full of friendly people. She smiled, and said she hoped she was not late.

'Emmeline's looking well this evening,' Sir Robert could not help saying proudly to Gerda Bligh.

'As though,' Gerda said, sighing – for her time for all this was over – 'she'd been reading a love-letter.'

Sir Robert, who knew his Emmeline, smiled politely and put the drawings away.

VII

Gerda Bligh was not really a fool, she was an honest girl of about Emmeline's age, with a tendency to hysteria. Having read a good many novels about marriage, not to speak of some scientific books, she now knew not only why she was unhappy but exactly how unhappy she could still be. She was in spirit one with those many young wives whose mortifications are aired in the evening Press. Gilbert bought evening papers to read the murders, but Gerda went straight to the Woman's Page. It is true, she was more fortunate than Mrs A. (Mill Hill), Mrs B. (Sydenham) and 'Discouraged'. Her husband did not, for instance, bring home friends from the office who smoked their pipes round the gas fire, ignoring her while she got the tea. Gilbert's friends, when they came to dinner, made quite a fuss about Gerda and bored him. Advice to run upstairs between the cooking and serving of supper to put on a smile and a fetching crêpe-de-chine frock did not concern her; if she suffered from lack of sympathy it was not at the end of a day's ironing. Her difficulties, however, were in the main the same; husbands can be as unresponsive over a sole from Harrods as over the sardine tin. She rearranged the drawing-room: Gilbert took no notice or said he liked it as it had been before. He complained that she lost things when she had simply put them away. When they mislaid the corkscrew at sherry-time she could only say, tremulous: 'Well, I am not a butler.' He would reply: 'But we buy new corkscrews every week.'

Gerda was lonely: she was the daughter of a retired admiral, marriage had isolated her from her relations in Hampshire, from whom she had been divided before marriage by intellectual discontent. Gilbert's friends said he had picked her up at a dance near Portsmouth from which he had better have stayed away. She lacked sympathy: only Lady Waters was needed to unsettle Gerda completely, and Lady Waters she met at some lectures on Adler they both attended. It turned out, Lady Waters had known and had deeply distrusted Gilbert's mother, so that she took a particular interest in the young pair. After some talks, Gerda could not imagine how she had ever stayed married so long. The Blighs as a couple dined fairly often at Rutland Gate, but it had been a shock to Gerda to find, when they came to Farraways, that her friend had a lien on Gilbert also, and must have asked them to lunch alone in alternate weeks. Gilbert remarked with complacency, taking off Tim Farquharson's black tie late that Saturday night, that Lady Waters thoroughly understood him: it had shocked Gerda to feel that their marriage had been discussed. That with Gerda herself Lady Waters had now superseded the evening papers did not make it more pleasant when she saw Gilbert pacing the borders behind the beech hedge with Lady Waters, thoroughly talking things out.

Emmeline quite liked Gerda but wished she were not here. After breakfast on Sunday morning Gerda waylaid her in the garden.

'Where are you going?' said Gerda, pathetic.

'Nowhere particular.'

'What an awfully pretty dress,' said Gerda, herself looking re-markable in lime-green. She had ash-blonde hair brushed sideways over her forehead and rolled at the nape of her neck, and large over-expressive eyes in a pretty expressionless face that lengthened at least an inch when she felt doleful. She knitted her brows when she spoke but had a threateningly calm manner. 'Did I hear you say,' she went on, 'you were going to church?'

'Later,' said Emmeline, who had arranged this with Sir Robert.

'I wish I were; I love dear old village churches.'

'Do come.'

'I couldn't,' said Gerda, 'you see, my ideas are upset.' Sitting down on a step of the sundial she looked up at Emmeline so appeal-ingly that Emmeline had to sit down also. Tufts of aubretia hung over the stones; the frank tawny faces of pansies surrounded them; a dewy fresh exhalation came up from the matted roots of the plants. The sun streamed over the rock-garden. Gerda glanced at her small feet in high-heeled green sandals, at Emmeline's, longer and narrower in snake-skin shoes. 'I used to love church,' she said, sighing.

'Still, you could join in the hymns.'

'They upset me frightfully. Fine weather makes me feel awful, too.'

'Perhaps we shall have a wet summer,' said Emmeline.

'You look so happy,' said Gerda, fixing on Emmeline her dark, morbid eyes.

'I ate such a large breakfast,' said Emmeline.

'Still, you are happy, aren't you?'

'Oh, yes,' said Emmeline. She was so happy that she could have kissed the sundial; everything seemed to be painted on glass with a light behind. She smiled at the glint of sun on poor Gerda's hair: grief was a language she did not know. 'Something smells nice,' she said, 'is it thyme or rosemary?'

'Catmint,' said Gerda, whose mother was a keen gardener. 'Do you think one's relations with men are always impossible? I sometimes think women were born solitary.'

'My sister-in-law thinks that.'

'How I should like to meet your sister-in-law! You know, Emmeline, I should really never have married. One cannot abide by an emotional decision one's whole life.'

'Does Georgina say so?'

'It's what I've always felt.'

'Still, it might be dull not to marry.'

'Oh, Emmeline, if you only knew!'

'I don't,' said Emmeline, placidly shredding a leaf. Flowers grew, and on this fine morning chorused with scent and colour: she thought idly, free will was a mistake, but did not know what this meant. Gerda went on to say it would have been sad to have missed motherhood. Emmeline could not remember how many children she had, and asked her: Gerda said she had two.

'How nice. Do you want any more?'

'Not now,' Gerda said gloomily.

'One of each?' said Emmeline, the excellence of the arrangement making her smile.

'Not one of each: two daughters. Emmeline, what shall I *tell* them? Am I to watch them grow up and make the same frightful mistakes? Suppose they come to me and say they wish they had never been born?'

'I don't expect they would mean it: people so often say that.'

'But one never knows.'

'How old are they?'

'Four and two. But they won't be that always.'

'No – But what is the matter, Gerda? Are you wanting to run away with somebody else?'

'I don't think I could,' said Gerda – this was her great subject. 'I seem to be quite used up: I seem to have no energy. Besides, it may sound extraordinary, Emmeline, but I'm not *interested* in men any more. You and I are the same age, and you have so much before you; it seems extraordinary. Perhaps I don't meet anyone who appeals to my mind. Besides, I really am fond of Gilbert, and there would be such a fuss. Besides, no one has asked me to.'

At this point Tim Farquharson appeared in the rock-garden, picking his way down the curly paths. He was in better spirits this morning and would have liked a chat. He stood still and stroked the top of his head nervously, as though the sun were too hot, for he had put himself wrong with Gerda the night before. Too much preoccupied to be aware how things went with the Blighs, he had remarked to Gerda that unhappy couples were boring ... Gerda and Emmeline with their two pretty bare heads, sitting shoulder to shoulder under the sundial were just what Tim wanted, but he did not know how to approach.

'So that's where you are,' he said.

'Yes,' replied Emmeline – but Gerda, still smouldering, lowered her eyelashes.

'Did I hear you say you were going to church?'

'I am,' said Emmeline, 'later.'

'Shall I come? I can't make up my mind.'

The church bells had begun in the valley beyond the house, so Emmeline left Tim Farquharson, unhappy and undecided, stork-like among the aubretia. A woman could have done much for him in these ways; he began to regret his engagement, especially as Lady Waters, beyond remarking that he had now to rebuild his life, had not taken much interest in him this week-end, and Sir Robert, forgetful and never quite up to date, kept asking the date of his wedding and sending his love to Jane.

'What is that?' he asked, sniffing.

'Catmint,' said Gerda. 'I don't like it.' She turned away from him moodily.

Emmeline walked away through the tulips brimming with light. 'So long,' she thought, 'as Georgina is pleased with them all and they do not depress Cousin Robert ...' She was bewildered by confidences; she may have lacked some faculty, key to the maze, or been on some plane or another a kind of idiot. Till now, a face not approaching or some fixed object had delayed her drifting fancy an instant, till it trailed on like a vapoury shadowless thin cloud over a tree. She laid hold on nothing. Now, like a cumulus mounting in dazzling soft rocky whiteness, one pleasure in an identity, Markie's, reigned in her perfectly clear sky.

She did not immediately turn to the house, but went down the garden. Looking out through an arch in the beech hedge, down the shining country at the low stone walls' broken shadows and trees in the blue bloom of morning powdered with light, while the church bells struck on the air their invisible pattern, she thought less of Markie than had an intimate sense of his presence, quickening with confidence and delight: last week's shock fell away.

Sky crowded the arch with light, the hedge with its ardent young leaves was the burning green of May. She bent from the hedge one leaf, serrated, with delicate sappy veins, and looked through it at the sun. Her finger-tips went transparent: here and in the veins of the leaf ran the whole of spring . . . The bells changed, Sir Robert was waiting: the leaf sprang back to the hedge.

Markie had told her a story about beech trees.

Last November, he said, he spent a week-end in the country, impure country where London's genteelest finger-tip touches the beechwoods. He had not enjoyed himself; his friend's wife, like most wives, was specious, doors opened with arty latches, the house stank of cold steam from imperfect heating: he had a touch of liver.

'Was he a great friend?' asked Emmeline.

'No, just a man I knew.'

Markie, for the good of his liver, went for a walk by himself after Sunday lunch, uphill into the woods. No birds sang: it had been worse than that day in Keats. Leaves, rotting and rusty, deadened his steps; the afternoon had been sodden and quite toneless; it began to be dark early. Down there, between the dreary trunks of the beeches, houses lay like a sediment in the cup of the misty valley: great gabled carcases, villas aping the manor, belfried garages where you could feel the cars get cold. There were no lights, not a thread of smoke from a chimney. Afternoon stupor reigned; there was nothing more that they wanted; down there they all sat in the dark. Gardens extensive and cultured, with paved paths and pergolas, ran up the sides of the valley, some had lakes where a punt could measure its length, not turn, some bird-baths for sparrows to drown in. To Markie the foreshortened villas appeared enormous, bloated as though by corruption . . . Then someone's wife opened a cold piano: she tinkled, she tippetted, she struck false chords and tried them again. God knew what she thought she was doing. The notes fell on his nerves like the drops of condensed mist all round on the clammy beech-branches. Markie's left shoulder-blade had begun to itch violently: he ground it against a tree. Penetrated by all these kinds of discomfort he had raged in the bare meek woods ... The piano stopped, he went downhill again to tea.

The fire, as he had foreseen, was dead out; the room was, however, stale enough to be warm. Flustered by his return, his hostess had dabbed at her face with an impotent powder-puff. He had said: 'How nicely you play!' She said, 'But I wasn't playing. I don't know what I was doing: what was I doing?' Her husband did not know either: he knocked ashes about in the fire and said it was out. 'Did you have a nice walk?' they had asked him.

'Where did you go?' Markie could not remember. 'Oh well,' they said, 'all the walks are the same round here. But it's pretty country, isn't it?' No one else came in: they said they lived very quietly. 'Still,' Markie's friend had said, 'it does grow on one.'

Emmeline, considering this when he angrily came to an end, had inquired: 'Is it a ghost story?'

Markie had simply looked at her.

'But why did it make you so angry?'

Though the story seemed to have no point, it had saddened her in the hearing. Retrospective anguish had made quite a poet of Markie. She was not clear, however, whether he meant people should not marry, or should not live in Buckinghamshire. His contempt for such placid pools in the life-stream surprised Emmeline.

Hurrying downhill beside Sir Robert, they took a short cut over slippery grass. Emmeline wondered what Markie would do at Farraways.

'Your aunt talks of taking tea out this afternoon,' said Sir Robert, who could never be clear that though his wife was Cecilia's aunt she was Emmeline's cousin. 'She thinks you might all like to look at the Roman villa.'

'Do *you* want to?'

'It always looks to me more like a rockery; they have discovered some pavement but that is locked up on Sundays. However –'

'I should much rather play tennis or go for a walk. Do you think we could?'

'Perhaps,' said Sir Robert, brightening. 'Perhaps. It would

certainly leave more room in the cars. In fact in that case they need only take one car. We will see how the land lies . . .'

'We'll be late: there's the last bell!'

'The Vicar is always some time in the vestry: he mislays his things. He lost the banns last Sunday, poor fellow. Do you remember him, Emmeline?'

'I don't think I've met him.'

'I could have asked him to drop in to tea if it hadn't been for that villa.' Sir Robert held open the white gate, they hurried across the churchyard; the last good-humoured bell saying: 'Come – come – come!' The straight sunny tombstones looked sociable, fresh wreaths were laid on the breasts of the graves. You could almost see the dead sitting up holding their flowers, like invalids on a visiting-day, waiting to hear the music. Only the very new dead, under raw earth with no tombstones, lay flat in despair: on one grave a whole mass of flowers had wilted; no one had had the heart yet to put any more . . . As Sir Robert approached, two little boys touched their caps and slid off a tombstone.

On the altar red candles-flames trembled, opaque in long shafts of sun. The bell stopped, the organ had not begun: in the light perpendicular church there was almost complete silence. But in the vestry you heard the choir holding its breath and the Vicar bustling about, still looking for something.

VIII

Pressing back with a creak the lid of the picnic-basket, Lady Waters took out two thermos flasks and a box of cucumber sandwiches: a Genoa cake followed. 'It's a pity,' she said, 'we are still too early for strawberries.'

Her guests smiled but did not say anything. Having motored twenty-five miles they sat on a stump of the Roman villa, their feet in a pit. The car was drawn up at some distance under an oak; the chauffeur paced gloomily round it. Behind them, above the villa, Sunday seemed to inhabit the steep twinkling leafy silence of woods this side of the valley. On a green notice board nailed to a post was neatly set out in white the possible date of the villa, with the conditions under which it was to be seen any day except Sundays. No paling forbade them to prod the masonry, but the mosaics, as Sir Robert expected, were all locked up, and though they had lain on their stomachs on the lid of a kind of cucumber frame they could see through ground glass and wire-netting nothing but their own shadows on what looked like cement.

As Lady Waters said, tea would be very refreshing. The custodian, who lived near by in a gothic cottage picked out in green to match the notice board, was himself at tea with his family; he looked at them cynically out of a latticed window. Gilbert Bligh, as though magnetized, could not help glancing back and back again at the cottage.

He said: 'That would be a nice job.'

'Especially on a Sunday,' said Tim bitterly.

'I wonder who gets it. Somebody's gardener . . .'

'Gardeners may be cross,' said his wife, 'but they are not generally rude.'

'He's not being rude,' said Gilbert, 'he's just having a look at us. After all, Gerda, a cat –'

'– *Gilbert!*' cried Gerda, biting her lip and writhing. The enforced introduction by Gilbert of proverbs into his talk was a constant annoyance. Gilbert's reasoning followed the main stream of racial good sense: he frequently rounded up at a point where to avoid a

59

quotation or skirt an aphorism would in itself have been precious. With the oblique and recondite nowadays at a premium, Gilbert could see no reason why he should not affirm the obvious: Shakespeare had done so. 'What is the matter, Gerda?' he said mildly.

'Children, children . . .' said Lady Waters. The Blighs as a turn, she felt, were taking up more than their share of the week-end programme: like a pair of indifferent acrobatic dancers they came bounding again and again from the wings without an encore. This was rather hard on Tim Farquharson. She was seriously annoyed with Sir Robert and Emmeline for staying behind, though circumstances had forced her to conceal her annoyance. She had relied on Sir Robert to stroll with Gerda among the ruins, on Emmeline to engage Gilbert while she had her long-postponed understanding talk with poor Tim. One or two kind words before lunch, and a glance charged with comprehension between the courses had, however, brought Tim up once more to the footlights, in his own view at least. So much cheered was he that, observing the Blighs' disorder, he concluded that Lady Waters had asked them to show him what he had escaped.

In the Blighs' present state of exasperated susceptibility, their attention to one another was almost lover-like. They broke off conversations at dinner to glare compellingly at one another across the table; they dogged one another about the house and garden to see what the other was doing and interfere. Having been assured by their hostess that their melancholy condition was interesting, they saw no reason to efface themselves. Lady Waters, to relax, as she said, the strain of propinquity, had put them in two different bedrooms, each side of a passage. But backwards and forwards between their two rooms, to the alternate discomfort of Emmeline and Tim Farquharson, the tide of battle had rolled far into last night. No sooner did one Bligh appear to compose itself than the other bounced in to renew the conflict; when the aggressor retreated the first Bligh, thinking of something really conclusive to say, would dart in pursuit with a furious patter of slippered feet. Gilbert, in spite of his placid exterior, showed as much zest as Gerda.

Lady Waters asked Gilbert to take tea to the chauffeur, who was, she feared, a little annoyed at being taken out on a Sunday. She overruled her servants as she overruled her *protégés*, but having gained a point could be full of consideration. Gilbert went off with a cup and the best of the sandwiches; Gerda, thinking of something crushing to say, sprang up and went wobbling after him in her high-heeled sandals.

'They seem rather upset,' said Tim Farquharson, looking after them.

'They're unhappy,' said Lady Waters.

'Well, I don't feel *too* happy, but somehow one couldn't go on like *that*.'

'You're not unhappy,' said Lady Waters: she looked at him keenly. 'Not now: you are simply making some readjustments.'

'I don't think it can suit me.'

'My dear Tim, life is a succession of readjustments.'

Tim, looking depressed, said he had no doubt she was right. Lady Waters observed the droop in his nice profile. A sort of dependence in Gerda's tottering movements had made him nostalgic: there was something in having a woman come after one, even to quarrel.

'*I* should hate,' he said, 'to inflict my moods on anyone.'

'But you have unusual reticence.'

'Still, it feels queer now to realize one's moods are no one's affair.'

'Emmeline noticed you were unhappy.'

'I'm afraid I rather bore her,' Tim said, stretching his feet out and looking gloomily at his socks.

'No, I don't think so. But she has a very reserved manner.'

'I suppose reserved people do take things harder. I often wish I weren't reserved.'

Lady Waters looked thoughtfully down the valley. 'Feeling,' she said, 'is ingrowing.'

At this point, unfortunately, the Blighs came back. Gerda said the custodian was still staring.

'My *dear* Gerda,' exclaimed her hostess, 'if it upsets you so much we had better move up the valley. But I like the idea of bringing back life to this old place. Perhaps we are in the atrium.'

'What is an atrium?'

'A kind of lounge.'

Gerda thought of ashtrays and wicker chairs. 'It must have been very cold,' she said.

'It was, very cold. You see, at home they were accustomed to build on the shady side of a hill, and the Romans were not adaptable.'

'Then they cannot have been good colonists.'

'Well, they were,' said Gilbert annoyingly, cutting the Genoa cake.

'Were they like Anglo-Indians?' asked Gerda, ignoring him.

'One cannot be certain,' said Lady Waters. Gilbert had opened his mouth to say Romans had central heating, but the discussion seemed to be closed. Lady Waters looked monumental, her scarf draped about her.

A brief silence hung over the party; Gerda sat sucking her green beads and brooding. Gilbert wondered why something at once consequential and dreamy about his hostess's manner had reminded him of the Dormouse. ' "So they were," ' he said aloud suddenly, ' "Very ill." ' No one took any notice. Tim Farquharson, slowly digesting that brief little talk, began to think kindly of Emmeline. He thought she looked all the time like a girl at a party to whom one has not yet been introduced: from that point almost all girls had declined for him. He had noticed in time that Jane (who had been his fiancée) was likely to be self-centred; Jane's very charming appearance had ceased to atone for her habit of interrupting or looking elsewhere when he began to tell her about himself. Emmeline was so far from interrupting that quite a long second ensued before she would reply. He wished she had come to the villa. He feared, however, that she might think this a rather too quick readjustment, what might even be called a rebound.

Conversations with Lady Waters left Tim always rather unsettled, with the feeling of having not quite come up to scratch, of having said either less than she had expected or more than it pleased her to hear. He felt like some homely piano, that after some chords idly struck by a practised executant has been shut again with a bang and a sad inward jangle of wires. He doubted if she were entirely good for him but dared not pursue this too far, as if it were not for her encouragement, he would have still been engaged to Jane. Her hold on his vanity was, however, inexorable; while her country house and her tea-table were accessible he must not consider himself his own . . . As the opposite hill went bright gold and a chill stole up the valley Tim wished he had been married some years, without being engaged. Through a haze of regret for Jane he beheld Emmeline.

As that chill stole up the valley, and the woods with their gold outline, in which evening announced itself by a whisper, receded in darkness and mystery, Gerda slid closer to Gilbert to lean on his shoulder for natural warmth. The smoke of their cigarettes, wavering up, melted. The dead house, less than a plan in masonry, tightened its hold on the fancy, the living eye with its colours, the heart with its quickness to clothe an unknown hill. Here, where exiles had lived, today's little party of exiles cast round in spirit, to find nothing . . . Lady Waters said it had been a beautiful day, but they ought now to be going home.

Sir Robert and Emmeline, guilty and happy, played tennis a little, walked a short way and had tea out under the lime tree. The Vicar did drop in to tea, between children's service and evensong: he said there had been three christenings.

Sir Robert congratulated the Vicar. 'The village is getting on.'

'Yes,' said the Vicar with ascetic enthusiasm, 'our weddings and christenings balance; the young couples do very well. And then there are always the growing families.'

Emmeline, leaning back in her long chair, looked up through the lime. She loved to be with Sir Robert and liked the Vicar. Looking back at the house she saw through the open windows rooms undiscovered in shadow, empty and kind. The departure of Lady Waters with her plaintive interesting party had reassured house and garden, in which a native conventional spirit crept out to inhabit the rooms and alleys, shaking away the decades with their mounting petulance like creases out of a full silk skirt. Lilac embowered the arbours where love had once sought seclusion or grief privacy. The whole garden, tilting down to the west, gave to the afternoon sunshine its smooth mown lawns and May borders.

Here Emmeline, step-child of her uneasy century, thought she would like to live. Here – as though waking in a house over an estuary to a presence, a dazzling reflection: the tide full in – she had woken happy. But already a vague expectation of Monday and Tuesday filled her; looking out from the shade of the lime already she saw the house with its white window-frames like some image of childhood, unaccountably dear but remote.

'– Emmeline agrees with me, don't you, Emmeline?' Sir Robert was saying.

'Oh, yes.'

'Now do you indeed?' said the Vicar with interest, turning round in his chair.

'I . . .'

'*Emmeline!*' said Sir Robert, shaking his head.

'Limes have a soporific effect,' said the Vicar smiling. Words could not express how pleased he had been to find Lady Waters from home and, instead, this thin girl with the social passivity of an angel, pouring out tea with her left hand unsteadily, gracefully under the lime tree. Indeed, had he not heard what was unmistakably Lady Waters's car hoot, as it never failed to hoot, at the lych gate while he was conducting service, the Vicar might not have looked in at all. He owed Lady Waters no duty: if she ever did go to church, she said, it would not be to high church: these play on emotion.

'Do you like lime tea?' Emmeline asked the Vicar. But Sir Robert, whose conscience was sensitive, said on the same breath: 'You know, they will find that villa shut up. I said so three times, but they would not believe me: do you think I ought to have said so again?'

'You did what you could,' said the Vicar, who understood that Sir Robert blamed himself less for letting the others go than for being so happy without them. 'No doubt they enjoyed the drive.'

'No,' said Sir Robert, still worried, 'they don't care for motoring, they all said so. However, I dare say they'll be as well there as anywhere else.'

The Vicar said: 'Modern life becomes increasingly complex. It seems a short time since motoring was in itself a pleasure. As in fact, it is still to me; I never fall far short of that anticipation with which I first mounted my brother's high red Minerva – of a type, Miss Summers, that you would not remember: it had a door at the back. I wore a dust coat and goggles; the ladies were heavily veiled. I am still surprised by the speed at which things fly past. But nowadays the whole incentive to motoring seems an anxiety to be elsewhere.'

'I know,' agreed Emmeline.

'Do you share this indifference?' inquired the Vicar anxious.

'No, I like driving my car.'

'It is hardly fair to say that,' said Sir Robert, pursuing his own train of thought. 'I feel it is nice of all these young people to have driven so far to visit an elderly couple. As you know, we've got little to offer at Farraways in the way of amusement – no wireless, no swimming pool, nothing, I feel sure, that they are accustomed to – What else are your friends accustomed to, Emmeline? However, they seem to be finding their own amusements: happy among themselves no doubt. That young Farquharson seems a little below par; I understand from something my wife said he's been badly treated: girl threw him over the evening before the wedding. Still, no doubt he'll do better. But those young Blighs seem devoted, never apart: it's quite pretty to see them. They are about the garden all day together, like boy and girl. That young Mrs Bligh's very unaffected and nice: intelligent, too; she's interested in the Minoans. I'm lending her Evans's book when we get back to town. For such a pretty young woman she knows a remarkable lot – isn't that so, Emmeline?'

'More or less,' said Emmeline, smiling at him.

Next morning, Tim Farquharson motored Emmeline back to London. She had come by train (her car was having new pistons fitted) and would have been as glad to return that way. She so much impressed on Tim the urgency of her business, and made early rising such a condition of her company, that they left Farraways soon after sunrise, stealing out past the doors of sleepers. Mists still filled the valley; the tulips stood up asleep. Something caught at her heart as they started, though she told herself she was leaving nothing behind.

The roads were empty: Oxford, where they had hoped to breakfast, was still asleep, so they rushed the Chilterns and breakfasted at High Wycombe. Tim Farquharson, watching her pour out his coffee, said he did hope they might meet again. They swerved north a little at Uxbridge and spun into London by the great empty by-pass of Western Avenue. Small new shops stood distracted among the buttercups; in the distance aerial glassy white factories were beginning to go up among forlorn may trees, branch lines and rusty girders: here and there one was starting to build Jerusalem. Emmeline smiled at London, where her friends still slept under that haze of shining smoke.

Skirting the rotten ribs of the White City, Tim asked her *when* they might meet: she was uncertain.

IX

On Friday, a cold cloudy evening, Emmeline rang the bell of one of those very high, dark-red houses in Lower Sloane Street. A light sprang up over the door and a manservant admitted Emmeline to a darkish hall.

Markie lived in a flat, completely cut off, at the top of his sister's house: she was a Mrs Dolman. They made a point of not meeting, cut each other's friends at the door, had separate telephone numbers and asked no questions. One, in fact, might have lain gassed for days before the other became suspicious. It was all, Markie said to Emmeline, more than simple: to her it had sounded elaborate. Markie's meals, separately cooked, went up to the top in a service lift; he gave orders and scolded his sister's cook down a speaking-tube. When a cook, outraged, left, Mrs Dolman, setting out grimly to look for another, dialled through to Markie warning him to eat out until further notice. Delicacy did not exist in Markie's family, in which only a brutal good sense put the brake on egotism. He and she, exacting hard terms from each other without compunction, wrangled cheerfully on the stairs or insulted each other by telephone. The agreement worked well for both parties; he secured more than moderate comfort with no anxieties; the Dolmans, whose minor economies were remarkable, could keep on their large rather disagreeably imposing house whose lease had been purchased almost for nothing during the War.

Emmeline wished Markie lived in the Temple. She did not like the look of the servant who let her in; she felt she was forcing her way through a strange woman's house. None of Markie's other friends can have shared this prejudice, of which Emmeline was ashamed.

'Straight on up,' said the servant, when Emmeline asked for Markie. He was perfunctory, knowing she must have been here before. Before she was up the first flight he switched the hall light off: evidently they economized. There was no staircase window; light filtered down through the banisters from a much higher floor. As Emmeline felt her way up in her long yellow dress, like a ghost astray, a door shut above and with firm, quick steps, well knowing her way, a woman began to come down. She came humming, snapping a bracelet on to her wrist; stiff taffeta brushed the stairs. Emmeline, apprehensively raising her eyes, saw a stocky, vigorous figure trailing a cloak, a line of faint light from above on some fuzzy hair. Seldom conscious enough to be shy, Emmeline, pressing back to the wall, found herself wishing to dematerialize. They came practically face to face.

'Mustn't pass on the stairs: bad luck,' said the strange woman, halting against the banisters. Emmeline felt herself cynically regarded by unseen eyes. She had the sense of a powerful presence, of a familiarity that was startling, close to her in the dark. She heard slow, heavy breathing, and taffeta creaking against the banisters.

'Going up to Markie's?'

'Yes,' said Emmeline.

'Know your way all right?'

'Yes, thank you.'

'Right you are.' A bare muscular arm, with the bracelet, came up to pat the hair and adjust a shoulder-strap. 'Well, good night: have a nice time – Oh, and turn out that light as you go up: I never waste anything.'

She went on down with a rush; Emmeline in her chiffon went on up silently. Markie's door was open; he stood at the head of the stairs.

'Hullo,' he said. 'Meet my sister?'

'I think so: yes.'

'What a bore for you – Come in, Emmeline.'

It would have occurred to Cecilia to ask why Markie, hearing his sister engaging his friend on the stairs, had not come down to introduce them instead of listening cynically above. Emmeline did not know what was wrong: she gave Markie her hand, which was chilly from driving, and they went into the flat. Here Markie's curtains were drawn on the last cold daylight, the lamps were all lit, pictures and glasses shone. One stepped back from summer, late light in squares and gardens, into the seasonless glare of festivity. Emmeline's world, that had hung shining throughout the week like a bubble on some divine breath, contracted suddenly to this room – staring, positive, full of shelves and tables – the scene of some terror from which she had lately fled. Today, at last, was Friday. 'Here I am,' she thought, smiling to reassure herself.

Markie helped her off with her coat; they smiled at each other and said nothing. Markie folded the white fur coat and put it down, liking the silent intimacy of her arrival. Misty with short-sight, her eyes dwelt anxiously on his face, as though there were someone here that she did not recognize. Something slipped from her, on the instant, like a bright cloak, leaving her colder.

'Sherry,' Markie said.

'Is your sister married?'

'Oh yes, she has a husband.'

'What is he like?' pursued Emmeline gravely.

'Oh, just a man,' said Markie, bored, bending above the wine-cooler. 'I've got some new sherry I want you to try; I ought to have opened it – something to do with gas: he directs companies.'

'She's rather like you.'

Suddenly straightening himself to stare at her, holding the bottle and corkscrew, he said: 'You do look lovely, Emmeline!'

Emmeline, like a tall crystal lamp in which the flame springs up, at these words shone taller and brighter. Having turned his way at once absently and intently, she remained still listening, as though he had not yet spoken, her eyes fixed on his with docility as though his pleasure commanded her and she could not turn away.

'You don't wish we were going out?' he asked with a certain amount of confidence.

'No, I like being here.'

'*I'd* much rather.' Drawing the cork, he filled their two glasses. Emmeline took up hers and drank.

'How do you like it?'

'Yes,' she said, vaguely sipping.

'Or don't you know?'

'I'm afraid I like almost anything dry.'

Markie gave Emmeline up, but was pleased with the sherry. 'I suppose you do dislike *something*,' he said, refilling his glass accurately. 'But I wonder so much what goes on with you, all the time.'

Markie's rather imposing, finished bad manners – which nervousness and a pressing sense of the unusual had accentuated, for he was not himself – were lost on Emmeline: he might have been quite ordinary. With a surprise so mild as to be either innocent or satirical she said: 'Do you want to know?'

68

Markie, after a moment's reflection, said perhaps he did not. His eyes were on Emmeline's cool bare arms held out to the fire. With her clear reticence she was as calm as a stupid woman, without that drag on the nerves.

'All the same' – he was beginning – when from the neighbourhood of the bookshelves a reedy, ghostly whistle made Emmeline jump. She started violently, spilling her sherry. 'What's that?' she exclaimed.

'Only the cook whistling.'

'But why?' This seemed to Emmeline funny, she laughed immoderately. 'Why does she do that? What an extraordinary cook! Our cook doesn't whistle.'

Markie, whose sense of humour was not agile, saw nothing funny about his domestic arrangements. He was accustomed to lead laughter rather than be surprised by it. He explained rather coldly that the cook, having no other means of communication, whistled up the speaking-tube when dinner was starting up in the lift.

'But supposing your cook couldn't whistle?'

'I suppose we should have a bell.'

'But why don't you have a bell anyhow?'

'I suppose because our cooks can whistle.' He returned the cook's signal and went to open the hatch: Emmeline, seeing she had annoyed him, waited anxiously. A small table behind the sofa was set with silver and glass on a green damask cloth: Emmeline, self-reproachful and nervous, feared that the lift might stick. She had never dined here before, only come back after a restaurant.

'I'm so sorry, Markie,' she said. 'But it sounded as though your cook had got in behind your books – like a cat, you know.'

The lift appearing, Markie took out a tureen with plates and some silver dishes which Emmeline helped him put down beside the fire. 'I had no idea,' he said, rather slightingly, 'you were domestic.'

'Everything seems like magic in this flat.'

'Why do you get so rattled?'

'I'm sorry: I don't feel rattled. Am I?'

'My dear, you've been like a cat on hot bricks ever since you came.'

Emmeline, putting hot plates on the table, confessed 'I was startled, meeting your sister.'

'But I told you she lived here.'

'Oh, yes.'

'*Well?*' said Markie, twitching his eyebrows up in exasperation. 'I don't see why that should upset you. I know she's a bore.'

'Is she? I'd like to meet her properly.'

'What, at tea? Of course, if you like. But I can't see why you should want to. She'll be rude for one thing; she's always rude to my friends.'

'She made me feel like a tramp,' said Emmeline, bringing this out with a rush.

'No, she didn't,' said Markie sharply. 'And you wouldn't mind if she had. I know quite well what she made you feel. Don't be childish, Emmeline: the thing's too absurd!'

While this discussion took place they sat down to table; Markie looked angrily at her across the glasses. Emmeline, bowing her head in despair, pleated an edge of the table-cloth. 'Nonsense,' Markie went on: his manner was at its coldest and most aggressive.

'You asked me,' said poor Emmeline. She looked bewildered – like a gentle foreigner at Victoria, not knowing where to offer her ticket, to whom, if at all, her passport, uncertain even whether she has arrived – Her friends had never been angry: she dared not meet Markie's eyes.

Then: 'I'm so sorry,' he said, with an abrupt alteration of manner. 'You make me feel frightful: do look up and smile . . . *Emmeline*, you don't know how I've been looking forward to this!'

'So have I,' she said, looking up and smiling.

'Is that why we're both so cross?'

'I expect so,' said Emmeline quickly.

'But we are enjoying ourselves,' Markie said with authority, and once more she sprang to agree with him. The dinner at once took on the air of a celebration: here was Emmeline beaming, exalted, floating all ways in light. She was too happy.

'Don't burn yourself –' exclaimed Markie, having just done so. Emmeline had, however, forgotten her soup; she took up her spoon quickly. 'What a good lift,' she said, 'bringing up soup so hot!' Her tone was heartfelt; she looked round for more to praise.

'Angel . . .' said Markie, forgiving her, in the moment, for having put him out and disarmed him, for having made him feel, perhaps for the first time, not quite all he could wish. 'Angel . . .' Markie repeated, leaning across the table. 'Emmeline – I've been thinking of nothing else!'

Emmeline straightened one fork, then another, looking down at her hand.

'It's really been frightful,' he said, with unfeigned surprise.

'But you have so much to think of,' she tried to suggest, with an anxious lift of the eyebrows.

Her concern was not for his work – his energy was terrific; ambition was written all over him; his ability, when allowed to appear, was beyond question. She knew of his reputation: Markie was 'rising' with the inevitability of a lighted balloon. But she was literal, and believed in a fearless exactitude between friends and lovers: over-statement troubled her with its mystification and false accents; in love she would speak the bare truth, or allow it to be inferred. Respecting so much and regarding so steadily the unconscious Markie, she could but be appalled when Markie spoke of himself. She sought the hearth, he led her into a theatre: reluctant, she was made free of a mock-heroic landscape with no distances, baroque thunder-clouds behind canvas crags. It seemed impossible for him to speak of himself naturally, and in those emphatic pauses preceding self-revelation she did not know what she dreaded to hear him say. Though she might love him, she must dread at all times to hear him speak of their love: it was not in words he was writing himself across her. She might be said to be drawn, with a force of which she was hardly aware, by what existed in Markie in spite of himself. 'We should be dumb,' she thought, 'there should be other means of communication.'

When the fish was finished, he pushed the dishes into the lift; soon the cook whistled again and Markie took out a duckling, the sweet and a coffee-machine with a glass dome. The arrangement, rapidly growing on Emmeline, was delicious; she longed to get up and whistle back to the cook. Markie, feeling he had said too much far too early, calmed down, anticipated the spacious evening ahead and, refilling their glasses, asked what she had been doing. She spoke of Woburn Place, parties with and without Cecilia, her week-end at Farraways. 'A nice house?' he said, 'how old?' She considered: 'Seventy.' She said it had been very fine and she liked the country.

'I must say I *don't*,' said Markie. 'What do you do all day?'

'Nothing particular. I played tennis.' Looking at him with compunction – for she had now no more to tell – she recalled that extraordinary happiness of which he had been the author. How

71

could she speak of the hedge, the Vicar, the print of ruins, Sir Robert, the bells? Suddenly very shy, perplexed by this paradox of intimacy and isolation, she sat looking at Markie a moment as though he were not there.

In that moment, he felt her go distant: he got up and restlessly stood by the fire, darkening inwardly with dissatisfaction and ennui. Wondering why he had wanted her, why she had come, he looked at her lovely long neck, her hair pale with lamplight, her face that obediently turned at his movement, but turned unseeing.

'Did you read my letter?' he asked.

'Of course, or I shouldn't be here.'

'Then is all that all right?'

Consciousness of him and tenderness flooded her look: nodding, she put out her hand to show she could say nothing. Taking the hand but impatiently letting it go he objected: 'But then shall you always –'

'– I don't know,' she said, her voice trembling. Standing up to see him more clearly – for his face had appeared from the table an angry blur – she once more looked at him fixedly, in rather a wild kind of inquiry, as though this were for him to answer. In her ignorance, her open-mindedness, her docility, she appeared to Markie adorably funny and young. Collecting himself, a hand on each of her shoulders, he kissed Emmeline: firmly, lightly and cheerfully. 'There . . .' he said, letting her go.

At the kiss so sagely administered Emmeline's eyelids fluttered, as though someone were tickling her under the chin with a buttercup: she thought of the sailor. When she looked at Markie who, standing there solid, said nothing more, she could not help laughing: that had been only that . . . That distorting horrible fear of the other night and the other kiss was undone: she felt as happy as though it were last Sunday morning, beside the hedge. While she stood laughing at him in her yellow dress the coffee-machine bubbled and Markie pushed up two armchairs. Something became entirely satisfactory: Markie made coffee and Emmeline watched him; smoothing out the long folds of her dress she relaxed in the armchair. Nursing one foot, tipping brandy about in his glass, Markie began to talk very quickly, as though she had been a whole roomful. As he had told her, she was so dazzlingly beautiful he did not care, really, if she were amused or not. This equable evening over, there would be others ahead.

X

Cecilia had not asked Pauline to tea in April: the more she was with Julian the more the child stuck in her conscience. The idea of that sad young creature moping in Julian's flat while he and she had pursued their own selfish pleasures became increasingly painful: by June her susceptibilities festered about it, as round a thorn. While asking herself if this enraged sense of obligation on Julian's behalf denoted increasing affection, Cecilia became quite unable to let the matter alone. Whenever things for a moment hung heavy between them, Cecilia would ask reproachfully: 'How is poor little Pauline?'

When Cecilia asked after Pauline – signalizing, as he had learnt too soon, a distinct drop in the atmosphere – Julian became depressed and could only say she seemed to be happy at school. It was unwise of Cecilia to dig at his conscience: each time, he retreated into an introspection from which her vivacity could not retrieve him. Watching her charm and prettiness through a dark glass, he would ask himself if she were worth the constant effort she seemed to expect. This was unfair, for he found in her something flowering, effortless, innocently exotic, apart from his anxious ineffectual conscience as from his life.

So that when Cecilia, on their way home in his car from a play they had not enjoyed, pursued for the third time since April: 'But how do you *know* she is happy at school?' Julian lost his temper, flushed like a woman and asked, with a good deal less point than violence, how she supposed one knew anything? Cecilia, impressed, said she supposed she had now ruined their evening. She turned his way eyes misty, enormous, dark as they crawled through bright blocked Piccadilly.

'What have I *done*, Julian?'

'You organize me,' said Julian, already, however, ashamed. He stooped to pick up her little gold bag that had slipped to the floor of the car.

'I have enough to do,' flashed Cecilia, 'organizing myself. I wish you had never told me about that child!'

'Oh *really*, Cecilia . . .' After all (as she said herself) it was quite usual to have nieces: Cecilia sometimes went on as though Pauline were his illegitimate daughter. This was no doubt his fault.

He added: 'I'm going down there next week: you had better see for yourself.'

'Going where?'

'To the school.'

'Do you mean, come too? . . . I should love to: I've never seen a girls' school.'

'You didn't go to one?'

'Good heavens, no! I think that will be very nice. Let's take down something for the poor little creature to eat: they say girls are always hungry. *Do* you mind being organized?'

When she turned like this, impulsively, lights catching her dark eyes and spangling her pale face and furs, Julian did not mind anything. Cecilia glanced down with some complacency at her spray of orchids: peace was once more restored. Julian suggested that they should take the whole day out and lunch in the country. But Cecilia said no: Buckinghamshire was too small, not many times the length of his car; they would soon overshoot the school and run out of the county; they must not overshoot the school. The fact was, to lunch at a country inn one must be in love (she thought). The musty red entrance, hat-racks, long solid menu, short wine-list were bare of charm for her nowadays. She could not attempt this with Julian . . . So they agreed to go down on Saturday, lunching first at her house.

On Saturday (the day after Emmeline dined with Markie) Cecilia and Julian set out in good spirits. It had been impossible, from Pauline's polite letter, to tell if their visit would be acceptable, but they both felt they must be doing the right thing. The sun shone: Cecilia – leaning back in the big open Bentley as they slid out through the traffic passing car after car – reflected that, while with discretion she had always enough money, it must be nice sometimes to have a little too much. She looked amiably into other cars, watched Saturday couples pushing perambulators along the pavements and wondered if she should like children, and kept pointing out to Julian houses in which she was glad she did not live, always a little too late.

She said suddenly: '*Shall* I go to America?'

Julian, forced to change gear by a block in the traffic, said: 'No – why?'

'Mother's always asking me to, but she may not mean it. But I know I should like New England. My mother's adorable nowadays, just like an elegant old American: she and I always do take colour quickly. Every room she comes into seems to have been just given her as an expensive present, and she looks as if she'd been unwrapped from tissue paper. I don't know why she and I don't have more to say. Her husband's so nice. However, I dare say they will be coming to Europe again.'

'Do you think seriously of going?'

'It is just an idea,' said Cecilia frankly. She had not meant to send up her own value at quite this rate. 'It seems foolish to have an American mother and not see her.'

'It's foolish not to do so much that one doesn't,' said Julian, glancing sombrely at the speedometer. 'But what about Emmeline? Could you leave her alone?'

'Oh, I shouldn't stay there for ever. I expect I miss Emmeline more than she misses me.'

'I suppose she'll marry,' said Julian, somehow saddened by the idea.

'I don't see how she couldn't, and yet I don't see how she could. No one is nice enough for her: any marriage of hers would be a mistake. Besides, she is so detached – What a heavenly day, Julian: how well you arrange things!'

They cleared London and ran out into the country. Cecilia blinked; they were doing seventy on a straight stretch of road. Julian drove in silence; she raised her face happily to the sun.

Chilly cloudy yesterday (when she had a little dreaded this expedition) was quite forgotten. The chestnuts were all in flower, sunshine enamelled the buttercups, beeches glittered over their emerald shadows, cows stood knee-deep under the hawthorns. The Chilterns ran up over the snug red-brick farms: it was all as pretty and gay as a calendar. The countryside flashed as they drove, as though someone were waving a bright-coloured handkerchief at Cecilia. 'Oh dear, are we here?' she exclaimed, as Julian drew up at a white gate in a wall.

Here they really were, at the school gates, and here had a slight argument. It looked pleasant enough, with limes drooping over the wall, but though Julian reminded Cecilia how much she had wanted to see a girls' school, Cecilia would not go in; she said he had better fetch Pauline out. She was sleepy, and had to do up her face; she could not meet a headmistress or talk, she said, just at present to young girls. She made Julian run the car up a lane, where he left Cecilia, eyes shut beatifically, under an elder-tree. Considerably exasperated, he walked up alone to the house.

The school was a pleasant brick country house, with wings added. Pauline, speechless with apprehension, awaited him in the hall. Her hair was plaited so tight that her eyes popped out of her head; she wore the butcher-blue school tunic and gave him a muted kiss.

'Where is your car?' she said anxiously.

'I left it backed up a lane.'

'Oh, but it's such a nice car. You could have driven it up . . . Where is your friend?' she added, blushing, avoiding his eye.

'She's in the car.'

'Oh,' said Pauline, obviously relieved. It became clear to Julian he should not have brought Cecilia; in fact Pauline seemed to feel he was on the brink, every moment, of an enormity. Pauline said the headmistress was sorry to be in London: Julian bore up. She added that she, Pauline, had a friend, Dorothea, who had been excused cricket to come and talk to them. At these words Dorothea, punctual as a conjuror's rabbit, appeared through an archway. Very affable, Dorothea had the situation at once in hand, covering Pauline's blushes with a smooth stream of talk.

'I feel so sorry for men,' she said, 'coming down to a girls' school – Where did you say your friend was?'

'Up a lane, in a car.'

'Dear me,' exclaimed Dorothea, 'she *will* think us inhospitable!' She hurried away to look for Cecilia. Pauline, looking after her friend with affection, explained: 'She is in the orchestra.'

Cecilia, opening her eyes, was surprised to find Dorothea looking kindly into the car. Dorothea, explaining that she was not Pauline, told Cecilia to get out and come with her: she collected the dazed Cecilia's gloves, fur and handbag and hurried her up through the garden into the hall. 'Here we are,' she said, beaming. Forming her little party up into twos, Dorothea marched them out through a side door, across a lawn, round some trees in the direction of the playing-fields: they were to watch cricket.

Cecilia found herself with Pauline: quite dazed by the violence with which the real succeeds the imagined she found Pauline less childish than she expected, taller and – she could only express it as more unmarried. Dorothea, who had thick legs, bustled ahead with

76

Julian; she was very much in demand when her friends' families came down, and with her jolly, direct manner had a great line in fathers and uncles.

'I've heard so much about you,' Cecilia said charmingly to Pauline, but the child appeared suffocated. Hearing a bat strike a ball Cecilia added: 'Do you play cricket?'

'Yes,' said Pauline, 'but I hate it . . . We had an overhand bowler once, but she ricked her arm . . . There's a girl here called Summers, but she says she is no relation of yours and does not know you.'

They approached the cricket ground and a small pavilion backed by a wood. 'That's our games captain,' said Dorothea, pointing out a solid girl fielding point, in a panama hat. 'That girl eating grass at longstop is called Summers: she says she must be a cousin of yours and thinks she has met you.'

Pauline preserved a horrified silence. One girl, run out by another, carried her bat back to the pavilion with an obvious air of relief. 'It is not a match,' explained Dorothea, 'or feeling would run higher.' The field, rigidly self-conscious, appeared to ignore the visitors, though one or two girls glanced sympathetically at Pauline, and Cecilia's clothes came in for some sidelong attention. Julian remained unnoticed. The party watched two overs, then they were moved on by Dorothea to look at the school gardens.

The gardens were planted like rows of neat little graves, someone had a cement rabbit, someone had built a sea. Pauline, looking drearily at some sprouting annuals, said that Dorothea and she had a garden but never won the prize. They turned in by a side door to the gymnasium, where Dorothea, with a flash of blue knickers, turned a dignified but *dégagé* somersault on the bar, let down and swung the ropes, displayed the vaulting-horse and said they must see the studio.

'The work here,' said Dorothea as they stood wilting under the skylights, 'doesn't amount to much: there are one or two little things of mine . . .' 'She draws divinely,' breathed Pauline. Cecilia paused to admire a spray of painted azaleas, but Dorothea hurried her on. 'These are some things of mine,' she said modestly, opening a portfolio.

'My legs ache,' Cecilia exclaimed irrepressibly, as they left the studio. 'Do you think we could possibly sit down?'

The girls, in some consternation, considered the matter: there did not seem to be anywhere, unless one went into a class-room and sat at desks. Pauline suggested that they should sit, very very quietly, in the chapel. Here, under the organ-loft, they seated themselves in silence. Meditation seemed to be indicated: Cecilia glanced at her fingernails, Julian read the inscriptions on tablets let into the walls. 'Three of our old girls have died, twenty-six are married.' Pauline explained in a whisper . . . The strain was beginning to tell on Pauline, but Dorothea remained a rock.

'I think, tea,' said Cecilia, as they filed out of the chapel.

'But you haven't seen the laboratory . . .'

'I'm afraid I *must* have some tea. We passed such a nice hotel. You can come out with us, can't you? We brought some strawberries.'

The early strawberries had been expensive, but Cecilia had said the girls would appreciate that. The girls glanced at each other; even Dorothea blushed. 'It's *very* kind of you,' they both said, lowering their voices. One could not doubt the poor things were hungry. They said they were not allowed in hotels, but there were some very nice tea-rooms approved by the school . . . They walked back past the playing-fields; the girls were still playing cricket.

In the tea-rooms, some other girls were being entertained by their families: they smiled distantly at Pauline and Dorothea, their mothers glanced suspiciously at Cecilia and Julian, who did not look like parents. Pauline was in an agony; she felt that Cecilia's appearance, not to speak of her manner to Julian, really did require some explanation.

When Pauline had got Julian's letter, saying he hoped to bring down a friend, Mrs Summers, who wished to meet her, she had gone hot all over and prayed for guidance. Such a thing had never been done before. It was too much to hope that Cecilia would look motherly: her Uncle Julian would not go motoring for the afternoon with a motherly soul. Pauline had turned, desperate, to Dorothea: she was most fortunate in her friend.

'Oh, I think they will be all right,' Dorothea had said. 'They must be getting engaged: they may tell us at tea. She *is* a widow, of course, not a *divorcée*? An uncle of mine got married the other day: such a jolly, sensible person; we all like her. Not young, naturally.'

'I don't think he would marry a sensible person,' said poor Pauline.

'Why, is he aesthetic?'

'I think he is lonely. I noticed that when I stayed there. I expect a man misses having a woman about.'

'Oh yes, they must be engaged,' Dorothea concluded. 'Or else he would never compromise her by bringing her down here. Did you see any signs of it coming on?'

'No – The thing is, will *she* compromise *us*?'

'We must hope for the best.'

'You *are* a support, Dorothea,' Pauline had sighed.

When all four sat down to tea in the hot little room with its printed table-cloths, Dorothea and Pauline, released from the ardour of hospitality, were able to give the couple their full attention. Not a blink of Cecilia's, not a flicker from Julian escaped their scrutiny. Solidly, heartily eating, the girls missed nothing: their eyes were watchful over the rims of their cups. Chaste jollity, with a hint of congratulation began to pervade Dorothea's manner; Pauline's look, sidelong, marked every interchange with intensity.

Perplexed, Cecilia lighted a cigarette: indicating a notice the waitress asked her firmly to put it out again. Julian said Indian tea disagreed with him: the waitress said there was no China. 'Ridiculous!' cried Cecilia, and all the mothers turned round. Cecilia, smouldering like a Siamese cat at a show, was glad to find that their strawberry punnets left stains on the table-cloth.

'More cakes?' said Julian, seeing a plate empty.

'Thank you,' said Dorothea. 'The school-girl's appetite is notorious.' She and Pauline had done quite well: their hosts had not looked after them but they had passed things to one another and, with apologetic glances towards Cecilia, refilled their cups . . . In the rather heavy succeeding silence Cecilia glanced at her wrist-watch and thought of the cool road.

The girls thanked them repeatedly for the strawberries.

'They were my idea,' said Cecilia with some complacency. For the first time she met Pauline's eyes, full upon her – anxious, expansive, pleading. This square child and the little lonely half-ghost in the flat upon whom she had lavished a vagrant sympathy were not, after all, so different . . . Dorothea, however, thundered across the possible intimacy of the moment.

Dorothea – upon whom some inner fermentation of tannin and strawberries must have acted as an intoxicant – precipitated to speech by Julian's quite open glance at the clock, leaned forward impressively, raising her tea-cup. 'Well, I am sure,' she said meaningly, 'we wish everyone luck!'

Magnified by her spectacles, the archness of the look that she cast at Cecilia and Julian was unmistakable. There was a slight pause in the tea-room, an acceleration of interest. The mothers paused, tea-pots suspended over their daughters' cups. Pauline, eyes downcast, face crimson, thanked her Uncle Julian (turning to settle the bill with a good deal of attention) for their delicious tea.

Later: 'I think *that* went off well,' said Dorothea to Pauline, as having waved good-bye to the car they walked back to the school.

'But they didn't *tell* us,' objected Pauline, not yet recovered from a profound sinking.

'If they are not engaged,' Dorothea said huffily, 'they ought to be. If they are not, I think *her* manner was most peculiar. Of course, Pauline, I shouldn't dream of criticizing your *uncle* – However, of course if you feel –'

'No, you were splendid,' said Pauline, rallying.

'I must say,' said Dorothea, 'I thought it went off well myself.'

Under the beech trees pierced and sparkling with sunset, Julian and Cecilia drove for some miles in silence. The country looked pretty, but she had seen it before. She remarked: 'That seems a very good school.'

'*Do* you think Pauline's happy?' said Julian shyly.

'It's bad enough being a woman,' exclaimed Cecilia with passion, 'but I can't think why girls of that age were ever born!'

Julian appeared to agree; they were once more silent. 'What,' he said at last, 'was that other girl's name?'

'Dorothea – we heard it often enough.'

'She was very kind,' said Julian, looking ahead stonily through the windscreen.

'She's not shy: I suppose that's a dispensation of Providence.'

'Why?'

'She's so plain, poor girl: she's like a curate.'

Julian, not turning and with an effect of great suddenness, said: 'Did you hear what she said?'

Cecilia, looking serenely at her cigarette case, said: 'Yes. Did you?'

His look crept round to her profile. 'I wish we were,' he suggested.

'But how could we be?'

'I mean, engaged.'

'Yes, I know you do,' said Cecilia, exasperated. 'And I mean, how could we be when you haven't proposed to me?'

'But that's what I'm doing.'

'Yes, I know, it's frightful: it's like a fly walking over one! It's really too crass of you, Julian – simply because of that over-fed child! I may sometimes wonder whether I'd like to marry you, but you might see I didn't want to be asked. If I can't marry anyone who wants to marry me more than you do, I won't marry: I'm perfectly happy the way I am!' Tears of vexation brightened her eyes in the sunset: she repeated: 'I'm perfectly happy with Emmeline.' Flying beeches sent shadows over her face. 'I don't love you, you don't love me!'

'For heaven's sake, Cecilia –' said Julian, appalled.

'For heaven's sake what?'

'Don't get so excited. I'm more than sorry I spoke.'

'So am I . . . You don't know what you want.'

'I've no doubt you are right,' he said bitterly.

As they approached London, Cecilia took out her lipstick. She said: 'Shall we let this drop?'

XI

Cecilia, finding herself in Knightsbridge with no engagements, rang up Lady Waters at Rutland Gate, at about one o'clock. She was tired and would be glad of a little sherry and lunch in the dark quiet dining-room, even at the price of a Real Talk. Lady Waters, who seldom lunched out and was truly hospitable, said this would be delightful. 'I shall be alone,' she said, 'but for little Gerda Bligh.'

'Little Gerda who?'

'Gilbert's wife.'

'Oh yes,' said Cecilia, blankly. 'Well, thank you ever so much, Georgina, I'll come round.'

Lady Waters liked to have someone about the house; the pre-occupations of Emmeline and Cecilia's uncertainty gave Gerda an opening. Lady Waters and she had been shopping together; after lunch they were going on to a lecture. Cecilia, arriving, was very much bored to find Gerda with her little air of muted vivacity, flitting about the drawing-room. Contriving to look as appealingly rustic in London as she had looked exotic at Farraways, Gerda wore a large chip straw hat and frilly frock with a fichu. With a cold eye, Cecilia watched her tucking her gloves away behind a sofa cushion with all the coy propriety of a favoured squirrel.

This tall crimson drawing-room, even its cushions, still felt to a great extent Cecilia's own. Here she and Henry had met, and the room kept a smile for her in its formal shadows ... From Sir Robert's mother came down the brocaded paper, the gilt-slung pelmets, chandeliers, mirrors, Sèvres vases and ormolu clock. From indifference to decoration or a passive respect for the Waters family feeling Georgina had left the drawing-room much as it was – she had installed more sympathetic lighting and approached the arm-chairs suggestively into têtes-à-têtes. She had been right: the room remained an imposing second to her personality, and guests were as much alarmed as magnetized into indiscretion.

Here Henry, feet on the white hearth-rug, back to a roaring fire, had first smiled at the young Cecilia sitting under a lamp. Here, both not unaware of their Georgina's rather marked inattention, they had withdrawn to a distant sofa after dinner. Disregard, frivolity, voluntary coldness of heart had for years overlaid this memory for Cecilia – the slate is too small, not much can remain written – but even now something stirred when she came in, as though a spring were less dry or frozen than choked, obliterated by dusty leaves.

Cecilia, her feet in the white hearth-rug, facing the cold summer hearth, looked into the mirror between the Sèvres vases and retilted slightly her charming hat. It was not of Henry she thought, if she thought at all.

Lady Waters, in black and eécru, sat looking earnestly at her niece. 'It seems a long time since we met. What have you been doing?'

Cecilia just glanced at Gerda. She said to herself, she *had* been feeling expansive, but how could one talk now? 'Time does fly,' she said, 'once it begins to be summer . . . I've been trying on a new evening dress.'

'I hear you've been going out a great deal,' said Lady Waters, with that air with which lesser women prefix: 'A little bird told me' – but her confidante would have been an eagle. 'I hope you are not doing too much?'

'Too much for what?' said Cecilia. 'I never do anything else. Don't tell me I'm looking tired,' she added, 'I'm discouraged enough already, from trying on. Dressmakers' glasses make one's figure look nice but one's face awful. I can't think why – they can't hope to sell one a new face.'

'You're not looking *tired*, exactly . . .' said Lady Waters, annoyed by Cecilia's nonchalant way of standing – fur slung from one shoulder, rose stuck into her buttonhole, lighting a cigarette as though she would well manage life on her own account. Darkly, she saw her niece going about with too many men, talking too freely, being too affable . . . Meanwhile there sat Gerda, hands folded like Cherry Ripe; a model of sweet dependence. In spite, however, of her young friend's pretty deference, Lady Waters felt her to be a clear-sighted girl, no doubt a far finer character than Cecilia.

'Gerda and I,' she said affectionately, 'have been buying eiderdowns.'

'*Eiderdowns?*' said Cecilia, her whole figure a query. She could no more imagine her aunt in a domestic bargain department than she could imagine a yogi there.

'Lovely eiderdowns,' agreed Gerda, nodding.

'Wasn't it rather hot?'

'Eiderdowns are reduced at this time of year,' said Lady Waters with an air of remarkable pleasure in this discovery. 'Like fur coats you know: Gerda saw them advertised in the *Observer*. It is worth while to remember, Cecilia.'

'I know,' said Cecilia, indignant. In fact there was little that one could teach her about running or stocking a house: though economy may not have been her forte she was exceedingly competent. If she preferred, at this season, evening dresses to eiderdowns, the need was practical and immediate. 'Emmeline's and my eiderdowns don't wear out,' she said. 'I suppose we are quiet sleepers.' Particles of white fluff seemed to float through the air; she felt prickly all over and could have sneezed.

Gerda sighed: 'Gilbert smokes in bed; he burns holes in our eiderdown.'

'Who's Gilbert?' Cecilia inquired, wondering what there would be for lunch.

It appeared later that the question had been indelicate. Lady Waters, drawing Gerda's arm through her own, swept behind Cecilia into the dining-room in some displeasure. Cecilia felt quite sorry: she had hardly glanced at the little creature and had forgotten she might be married. Watching across the table how Gerda hung breathless upon Georgina's lips, she very soon placed poor Gerda as a child-wife. Gerda, who had dropped her hat in the hall as they passed through, frequently tossed back her short fair hair: her manner towards Cecilia remained propitiatory. Cecilia, however, did not like women to whom the diminutive could be applied . . . It did not occur to Cecilia that, having invited herself to luncheon and being preserved by the excellence of the Rutland Gate cooking from the material rigours of pot-luck, she might take her company as she found it. She remained forbidding. 'Really,' she thought, 'if this is Georgina's latest, she is coming down in the world.'

The lunch was excellent. Even with all its leaves out, the table, designed for parties, was very large. Light caught the damask's involved pattern of roses and pheasants, and six sprays of early sweet peas, arranged by the butler, sprouted out of a small silver vase.

'Emmeline will have told you about our few days at Farraways,' Lady Waters said to her niece.

84

Emmeline, coming back placid and shining, had said almost nothing, and Cecilia, knowing Emmeline could not be amusing about people, had not asked. She had understood there had been more of Georgina's 'cases' and that no one talked about her . . . 'Of course,' said Cecilia blandly.

'It was a quiet week-end,' said her aunt, 'but sunny and peaceful. I hope, however, that Emmeline was not bored?'

'No, I think she loved it.'

'I think Emmeline's wonderful,' Gerda said with a sigh. 'We had some lovely talks.'

'Oh, yes?' said Cecilia, who did not believe this possible.

'She's so understanding.'

'She is when she listens.'

'Cecilia,' said Lady Waters, 'underrates Emmeline.'

'Yes,' said Cecilia placidly.

'But,' their hostess said, affectionately reproachful, 'Gerda did not care for my poor Tim.'

'Oh, I never said *that*, Lady Waters! I just said he hadn't much self-control.'

'He was not at his best, naturally.'

'Why?' said Cecilia, helping herself to a cutlet.

'He has broken off his engagement – surely Emmeline told you?'

'But, Georgina, what an extraordinary thing to do!'

This was just what Sir Robert had said, when at last he had got the facts right. He had begun to say, with some vigour, hard things about having had poor Tim under his roof at all, till he recollected the roof was Georgina's. 'You take a conventional view of life, Cecilia,' said Lady Waters. There was a silence heavy with disagreement. 'Tim,' she added, 'is sensitive, and he behaved with real courage.'

'Young men may *do* these things,' said Cecilia, 'but need they discuss them?'

'Anything,' Gerda said with a sigh, 'must be better than the wrong marriage . . . All the same,' she went on with her little privileged air, 'I really do think he made rather a fuss. His feelings were not out of sight for one single moment. I suppose unhappiness takes people different ways. However unhappy I may be, I hate to attract attention . . . But I thought you were wonderful with him, Lady Waters.'

'Tim *who*?' said Cecilia suddenly.

Fond as she was of Gerda, Lady Waters could not help regretting, while on the subject of feeling, this opportunity to bring herself up to date with Cecilia's affairs. Cecilia, with fleeting half-looks in her aunt's direction, and small interrupted movements as though to speak, flirted heartlessly with this curiosity. Gerda's candid eyes never leaving them, Lady Waters again and again felt herself checked. When Cecilia, making a rapid gesture, upset her wineglass, Lady Waters observed, while the butler was still mopping: 'You certainly are not yourself today.'

'I so seldom am,' said Cecilia.

Looking large-eyed round the sweet peas, Gerda appeared to ask what Cecilia might be like when she was herself. Aware, as lunch proceeded, of losing ground a little with Lady Waters, Gerda found herself wishing Cecilia had not come. Eiderdowns having made talk impossible during the morning, Gerda had still a good deal more about Gilbert to tell her friend.

'You are doing too much,' Lady Waters went on.

'Nerves,' said Cecilia modestly.

'You smoke far too much.'

'Perhaps it is simply that.'

They both knew it was not. This Monday morning Cecilia was, as a matter of fact, decidedly overwrought. Besides the agonies of decision – green, white or flame-colour? – she could never order a new evening dress without a sense of fatality: how much would have happened before it was worn out? . . . On Saturday there had been that disturbing passage with Julian: when she came in, desiring only a hot bath and introspection, she had had to dress at once and go out to a dinner party. Social activity right on top of a crisis had the same effect on Cecilia nervously as, on her inside, exercise taken too soon after a meal: undigested experience hung heavily on her spirit. She had stayed in bed, restless, all Sunday morning – was this a touch of heart or a touch of liver? – and saw provokingly little of Emmeline, out all day: later some friends had come in to talk in the garden and stayed too long.

'I think,' she said, after a longish pause and some salad, 'I shall really go to America.'

'Nonsense, my dear,' said her aunt, having heard this before. She did not think that Cecilia would care for a country where no one had heard of her, and also knew well that Cecilia's mother (her own sister-in-law by her first marriage) had intended the invitation rhetorically and might be considerably put out by Cecilia's arrival. On the first point she was wrong: Cecilia, a social Columbus, could have asked nothing better than a continent full of strangers, and knew well how to build up a rumour in a day.

'– Oh, dear child,' Lady Waters continued, turning to Gerda, 'remind me that I want you to do a little telephoning for me after lunch: it would be such a help.'

Poor Gerda realized that this was her congé. 'I will indeed,' she replied. 'And, if you don't mind, at the same time I'll just ring up Nannie, to see that the babies are all right.'

'Surely,' said Lady Waters, surprised, 'you have no reason to think they are not?' She did not care much for babies once they were born; also this was quite a new development in her Gerda, who had spent long days at Rutland Gate without anxiety.

'Oh,' said Cecilia swiftly, 'have you got babies? Twins?' Her look expressed some surprise that Gerda had not got the children somewhere about her: Cecilia's ideas of maternal devotion were most exacting. 'I suppose,' she said, 'you have a very good nurse?'

'Nannie is wonderful. All the same, I do have to try so hard not to be fussy.'

'Gerda,' said Lady Waters, 'is quite right.'

'I know,' said Cecilia, 'if *I* had any children I should always imagine they were on fire or being choked. But I dare say I am hysterical.'

Gerda gazed unhappily into her cup of gooseberry fool. She was thankful when lunch was over. If only all Lady Waters's relations had been like Emmeline . . .

'You are very naughty, Cecilia,' said Lady Waters, when they were back in the drawing-room and Gerda with a long list of messages, hastily improvised, had been sent off to telephone in the study. 'You are not nice to my Gerda.' Time, however, was short. 'Now tell me,' she said, settling comfortably in her chair, hands crossed, 'whom you have been seeing?'

'Oh, everyone,' said Cecilia happily.

Lady Waters took a bold line. 'Emmeline,' she observed, 'does *not* seem to care much for that friend of yours, Mr Linkwater. Her manner rather impressed me: I think a good deal of Emmeline's judgement.'

'Markie? Oh no, Emmeline hates him. But that doesn't matter, Georgina; he and I never meet.'

'You would not call a man Tommie or Bert or Alf,' said her aunt distastefully, 'why should you call him "Markie"?'

'Everyone does: it's written all over his cigarette case. He's really a frightful young man,' said Cecilia blithely. 'However, I don't call him anything nowadays.'

Lady Waters, dissatisfied, looking broodingly at her niece, could best have summarized a cosmic and ravenous curiosity by asking: 'Then whom are you calling what?' For evidently there was someone. These bright eyes, the air of a spring bubbling, this capriciousness, of a woman who has been found charming, even today's nervosity were impossible to misread. If Cecilia did not love, she was loved. Besides, Lady Waters knew she had evening dresses enough for the social cycle: if she needed a new one she must be seeing someone too often. Regarding Cecilia more kindly, as one regards an oyster soon to be opened, or an engaging new novel certain to entertain, she hesitated between other lines of approach, while Cecilia, smiling and not unconscious, looked down at her pretty hands.

'You know,' said her aunt, 'I am sometimes anxious about you.'

'Oh dear, Georgina, why?'

'You are still quite young.'

'Well, I always hope so.'

'You are, and you have a very open generous nature and quick sympathies: I dread sometimes your being imposed upon.'

Cecilia, feeling, as always at the outset of these encounters, like someone exposing her palm for sixpence at a bazaar to the vicar's wife disguised as a gypsy queen, objected: 'I don't think I really should be, Georgina: I'm quite selfish.'

'You have an emotional nature.'

'I like being susceptible.'

'Emmeline,' said Georgina, closing in swiftly, 'seemed to be anxious about you. I could see she had something on her mind.'

'If she thinks it's Markie she's frightfully out of date,' said Cecilia rashly. 'But I don't think she'd be so stupid.'

'Indeed,' remarked Lady Waters, without expression.

'Not that poor Markie wasn't respectable: he wouldn't pick one's pocket. But all my friends now are so very respectable: they take me to see girls' schools.'

'Dear me,' said her aunt, 'are they widowers?'

'No, they have nieces.'

'*I* see,' said Georgina, with ominous calm.

Cecilia began to wish she had lunched at Woollands. Dreading her own discursiveness she found she had come to a point where she must either talk about Julian or go. With Henry, Emmeline, with Georgina even, it had been always the same: it all had to come out. Emmeline's detachment, Georgina's cavernous receptivity alike provoked her to volubility. With delight pursuing the butterfly-shadow of feeling, Cecilia liked far too well to discuss her fancies. Sir Robert's white wine, then this dark-red drawing-room had slain their thousands: this magnetic gaze of Georgina's went straight to Cecilia's head. Here even Henry had wavered, inventing when he had no more to confide . . . Scenes flashed, words danced through Cecilia's brain; her relations with Julian appeared more and more remarkable.

Only one fact deterred her – Julian's appalling eligibility; she could discuss her heart but not her prospects. For all her sibylline grandeur, Georgina remained an aunt: one could but dread her approval. She would track Julian down, sum him up, invite him to dinner – or worse, to tea.

Lady Waters, with whom nothing sifted through to oblivion, had every common noun filed for reference and cross-indexed. The obscurest connections were not over-looked by her, mention of objects as innocent as grouse or a bicycle started a bell ringing: small talk offered little retreat from her perspicacity. 'Nieces,' she said. 'It's curious how I am always hearing of nieces . . .' She paused: uneasy, Cecilia heard the filing-cabinet click open. 'That friend and client of Emmeline's, that Mr Tower, a tall man I met in her office, *he* had a niece, I remember. He and Emmeline were talking of schools in Switzerland: I thought she seemed quite animated. "Why, Emmeline," I said, "I had no idea you were an education bureau!" '

'Animated? – Oh no, not possibly. Julian bores Emmeline: they never meet.'

'Then no doubt it was as a friend of *yours*,' her aunt said smoothly, 'that she had sent him circulars –'

Gerda edged, breathlessly, round the door. 'Only me,' she said, and sank with a puff of billowing skirts into the white fur rug at her patron's feet. 'I've had *such* a time; you must have thought I was lost! It made that buzzing, gone-away noise at me every number I dialled: you know how a telephone makes one feel, Lady Waters, quite in disgrace! But I got all your messages right, I think.'

'Thank you, Gerda.'

'Lady Zweibacher didn't seem to like my little squeaky voice: she kept asking for you. "Lady Waters is engaged," I said, "she can't come to the telephone." I was right, wasn't I?'

'You were quite right, Gerda,' said Lady Waters.

'There goes *that* cat,' thought Cecilia gloomily, 'well away.' The topic, now open to discussion, would not be easily dropped. Though alarmed she was not, however, entirely sorry.

XII

'Our accounts balance,' said Emmeline, after nearly two hours of silence at Woburn Place. They had sent their secretary out for the afternoon; she had said she feared accounts were not in her line, as she read English at Oxford, and her presence made Emmeline nervous while adding up. Peter Lewis preferred to call their secretary 'the stenographer', the word brisked him up with its ring of efficiency and things went more slickly, as in a film of American office life. The stenographer got fewer personal calls nowadays and had begun to look gloomy: though it was a relief not having her sprawling to telephone over Emmeline's roll-top they now feared they might have her with them for always.

Peter, who had been tiptoeing round the room cracking his finger joints, opening and shutting things in an agony of suspense – he had no head for figures either – cleared his throat and said: 'Then you mean we are all right?'

'Yes. In fact we are six pounds seven and nine to the good that I cannot account for.'

'You don't think we should have an auditor?'

'Not while things are going so well.'

'What a good thing people have to pay cash down for this sort of thing,' Peter remarked happily. 'One of my friends has just gone bankrupt over a bookshop: all his friends came and he couldn't bear dunning them.'

'Oh dear,' said Emmeline. 'What's become of him?'

'He's living with me till we can think of something for him to do. Of course I've got no pistols or anything in my rooms, and there's nothing that one could hang from, but I see him look at the gas fire every night when I put it out.'

'He can't type, can he?'

'Not at all well. Anyhow, I don't think I should like to have him about here; he rather rattles me.'

Emmeline, wondering what one could do, sat looking unhappy till Peter suggested they might make tea. 'Of course,' she said thoughtfully, watching the kettle boil, 'if we did run this place on credit we could make anybody go anywhere. But I don't think it would do.'

'It would be madness,' said Peter firmly; she had to agree.

Business recently had been brisk, Emmeline's fervour and Peter's determination to talk shop everywhere having attracted a good many clients, a number of whom remained. Their propaganda was simple: on her return from Farraways Emmeline had sent off circulars to the Blighs, Tim Farquharson and the Vicar she met at tea. She received newcomers with sympathy, even with tenderness, while Peter's air of according unwilling respect to a client's intelligence was highly flattering. If they were not always efficient (in the most exacting sense) they were solicitous; their two charming grave young faces turned his way gave any client a sense of his own uniqueness; their rather high rate of commission was justified by a personal touch freshly and delicately applied. Arriving at one's destination one found a post-card, stamped with the office slogan, wishing one every pleasure. Markie swore he had met a client who having bribed and fought her way to Belgrade on the wrong ticket found her hotel room full of roses ordered by Emmeline. They were persuasive: one with bookings to Stockholm to see the architecture. Tourists went in wishing to paddle from Heyst sands and came out viewing without passion the abstract purities of distant provincial towns to which she had sent them could feel sure that in Bloomsbury Emmeline would passionately be estimating their reactions. A gentleman from the north who, after a frightful fortnight in Silesia (which he had expected to find at the toe of Italy, full of orchestras), went in to wreck the office, was found with a large handkerchief, beseeching Emmeline not to cry. 'There, there,' he said, 'a girl like you's not fit for this sort of life.' She had not wept: he had mistaken the blink behind her spectacles.

Their integrity was an asset; Peter seldom and Emmeline never lied. They said: 'You may not enjoy it the whole time, but you'll be glad to have been there . . . You may be uncomfortable but the people have nice manners and you will never be bored . . . Yes, the cooking *is* oily, but you know that is good for one's inside . . . No, if that is your wife you cannot take her to their theatres . . . Quite right, if you don't keep wrapped up at sunset you may die of pneumonia, but you can buy beautiful native shawls . . . Well, yes, it *is* cold there, but you soon don't notice . . . It is hot there, even at nights, but they have such clean ice in the cafés . . . Yes, it is unhealthy, but it's the most beautiful place in Europe: I'd rather die of that than anything else . . .' No one could have been more distressed than Emmeline at the misunderstanding about Silesia and Sicily. 'I *told* him it was very abstract, but he kept on saying, "Yes, yes, that's just exactly what I should fancy." '

The day on which Lady Waters and Julian had met in the office had been what Peter called a visiting-day: everyone seemed to look in. They had not done much that morning except dictate a few letters to the stenographer, who looked sceptical. Then a young man who had once tried to marry Emmeline and still hung about (he does not come into the picture) had looked in to say he had persuaded his aunt to go south that summer by means of Emmeline, and would they be sympathetic as she had never travelled without her husband, who was just dead. 'Yes, yes,' said Emmeline. 'Does she want to be quiet or noisy? Does she know she may be too hot?' . . . Then Julian – happening, he said, to be in this part of the world – had looked in for another word with Emmeline about Central Europe. Sitting down by her desk he had had a good look at Peter who, seeing that this occasion was to be social, leaned away from them on the mantelpiece admiring his long fingers, cleaning up his nails with a nib. They discussed co-education in Switzerland: Julian said at once that this would not do for Pauline . . . Then Lady Waters looked in on her way to a lecture on ethics at University College. Emmeline introduced Julian and explained that they had been talking about his niece. Lady Waters, glancing from one to the other, had discounted the niece at once. She said that she did not believe in co-education and soon went away with a rustle.

'Is that your aunt?' asked Julian.

'No, she's my cousin by marriage.'

'But Cecilia speaks of her as an aunt.'

'She is Cecilia's aunt, then she married my father's first cousin. She married,' said Emmeline, explaining carefully, 'twice, you see.'

Julian was left with a pleasant impression that if he married Cecilia Emmeline would be his relation twice over. He did not, however, desire to duplicate any connection with Lady Waters.

'I feel sometimes as though she were *my* aunt,' said Peter, who had been asked to tea to discuss Havelock Ellis . . . Julian could not stay long: he admired a new poster and regretfully went away. Fortunately for business – though Julian's Bentley and Lady Waters's Daimler, lining the curb, must have given the premises quite an air – visiting-days were infrequent. Peter and Emmeline could regard the six pounds seven and ninepence as a bonus for unremitting effort and the entire sacrifice of their social life up to six o'clock.

This afternoon, Emmeline having done the accounts with such good results, they felt light-hearted: the office was so very pleasant without the stenographer that they were not anxious to go home yet. They cleared off the last letters and pinned up the finished graph; Peter politely rejected a sketch of Emmeline's for a poster: a Handley Page looping the loop full of passengers. He ripped open another packet of Gold Flake while they discussed getting more closely in touch with Intourist with a view to doing more about Russia. An electric kettle arrived, a present from Markie who had complained that the place smelt of gas. Peter, depressed for a moment, said, would this mean getting re-wired for power? 'Oh well,' said Emmeline cheerfully, 'We can afford *that*. But perhaps it will boil on the light plug.' She tried and it did . . . She got out her car and dropped Peter at Imhof's, where he was going to buy some records to cheer up his poor friend.

Emmeline – who liking life better than ever, took no chances – crawled sedately west for a little, in second gear, down the Easton Road, in the lee of a lorry clattering with steel girders. Leaving the hoarse dingy clamour, the cinema-posters of giant love, she turned into Regent's Park, swept round under lines of imposing houses and, out of the park again, steadily mounted to St John's Wood. First the stucco villas, smoky, sunk in their gardens, had the air of pavilions mouldering after an exhibition, retreats forgotten and disenchanted, unkindly eyed from the rasping buses. She bore left from the bus-route; the houses brightened along roads silent and polished, the air freshened: this was a garden. The glades of St John's Wood were still at their brief summer: walls gleamed through thickets, red may was clotted and crimson, laburnums showered the pavements, smoke had not yet tarnished a leaf. The heights this evening had an airy superurbanity: one heard a ping of tennis-balls, a man wheeled a barrow of pink geraniums, someone was practising the violin, sounds and late sunshine sifted through the fresh trees. Someone was giving a grand party: more gold chairs arrived; when they flicked lights up a moment in the conservatory you saw tall frondy shadows against the glass. Emmeline wished them joy – but it depressed Cecilia to hear the music of parties to which she was not invited.

At Oudenarde Road the drawing-room windows were open. Cecilia, surrounded by cushions, sat out on the iron steps overlooking the lawn. She was not going out tonight and had had, since lunch, her hair shampooed and re-set: soft waves round her face made her look very young and she wore a pink cotton frock. 'Darling?' she said, as Emmeline, having put the car away, came round the house and, sitting down on a lower step, pulled her hat off and gazed down the garden. In the foreground Benito sat washing himself thoroughly, one leg up like a mast. 'Don't . . .' Emmeline said and pulled at the leg gently: he had all day to wash in.

'Tired at all?' said Cecilia.

'No, it's been a good day. I did the accounts and they came out.'

'Why not make Peter do them?'

'He can't add.'

'I see no point in that young man – Emmeline, I haven't seen you for ages: where did you go all yesterday with that horrible Connie Pleach? I don't like her, she thinks I'm a parasite: if I am, that's not her affair. Anyone can see her affection for you is unholy – where did you go?'

'Into Sussex, to see her father.'

'Oh, has she a father? If her affection is *not* unholy, she likes you because you have got a car. I've had an awful day: I went to lunch with Georgina.'

'Oh, she asked you?'

'No, I asked myself: it was madness, as it turned out. We had a rather nice egg thing for lunch – remind me to get the recipe from her. There was a sort of girl there, like a bad illustration to Hans Andersen.'

'Gerda Bligh. She's not bad really: she's unhappily married.'

'Gilbert smokes in bed. Did I tell you I'm getting a new evening dress? Orchid-green: ravishing with the skin, though you might not think so – Oh, *listen*: Georgina's convinced you think I'm in love with Markie!'

Emmeline, who was stroking Benito, paused with her hands on the kitten and said nothing. A sort of vigilance in her attitude caught Cecilia's attention.

'Guilty,' she said: 'the back of your neck's blushing. I thought you said no one had talked about me. It's so lovely and like you, darling, to be fifty years out of date when you do gossip!'

'I didn't say anything . . .'

'Angel, why should I mind?' laughed Cecilia, leaning down, in a haze of fragrance from the shampoo, from the upper step. 'You left poor Georgina so perfectly happy for more than a week. Unwisely – as it turned out – I did disillusion her, saying, of course, that I never saw Markie nowadays, that he was too fat, a bore, a bounder, an egotist, altogether a frightful young man –'

'– Stop!' said Emmeline passionately.

'Why?' asked Cecilia, caught up in mid-air.

'Don't say that. You should take the trouble to see that it's not true!'

'What's not true?'

'He's my friend: I like him so much, I see him so often.'

'Whatever on earth do you mean?'

'I like him,' repeated Emmeline, quivering.

Up to a point Cecilia made quick adjustments. 'Well,' she said equably, 'if you do, you do. It seems to me a peculiar taste, but I can't help you.' Countering what she took to be hysteria, she put on a motherly air, very concrete and sensible. 'Don't for heaven's sake,' she commanded, 'get into a state of *mind*.' Her tone, her manner patted the quivering Emmeline: she had seldom to cope with Emmeline, but had coped, so far, admirably. This was nice of Cecilia, whose best Georgina-story for years had just fallen remarkably flat.

'I'm sorry,' said Emmeline, much more calmly. 'But I did think you were unjust.'

'No doubt I am,' said Cecilia. 'After all, your precious Markie practically cuts me dead – Do you really see him? How odd: how often? What a dark horse you are!'

She could not have said anything more unfortunate. 'I haven't been meaning to be,' said Emmeline, miserable. 'It's worried me very much.'

'Don't take things so *hard*,' cried Cecilia, exasperated. 'Markie's your friend, not mine: you see him, I don't, we're both pleased: what more do you want? Naturally I don't think you've been making mysteries: why ever should I? If I hadn't been so insanely self-centred I might have noticed. I am sorry I was unpleasant: consider it all unsaid. They say he'll go far, and he certainly is amusing – Though I don't mind telling you, Emmeline, I wouldn't trust Markie an inch: I don't like his mouth. However, no doubt you're good for him – Now are you calm again?'

'Yes,' said Emmeline humbly.

'Because if you are, I should like to go on talking about myself – I said it was madness to lunch with Georgina: I'll tell you why exactly. Deprived of Markie she was after me like a lioness: I went to pieces completely. So she took the bloom off something I wanted to tell you – I don't know that it has much bloom really, in fact it has no bloom: I'm worried. Julian's proposed to me.'

Emmeline, startled, said: 'You didn't tell *her* that?'

'Oh no. But I don't know how much she may have gathered.'

'Oh, *Cecilia* . . .'

'It was a most wretched affair. What *is* the matter with Julian?'

'So you said –?'

'I was furious – naturally I said no. He sounded as though he just thought he might as well. Something a child said at tea put it into his head.'

'At tea where?'

'At that school, darling: don't ask silly questions!'

'I hope,' queried Emmeline, raising a gentle face of concern, 'you weren't unkind?'

'Well, I hope not. I seem to remember saying something rather nasty about a fly. He seemed rather low afterwards – not disappointed but mortified. Perhaps I was unkind . . . But Julian's little perfunctory way of saying things as though he felt they might be expected always has made me see scarlet. The idiot!' exclaimed Cecilia. 'Why have men got no background? Nothing they say ever seems to have any context. What do they think about all day long? One hears all this about the City, but I cannot believe Julian really does very much. He is naturally rich and attracts money, but I know he spends half his time in that office simply fussing about.'

'One can't help fussing about in an office, I've noticed that.'

'But you're not important about it.'

'There's so much time one cannot account for.'

'Not at all,' said Cecilia. 'If I don't know what I'm doing at every moment I do at least know what I'm trying to do. But half the time one is asked to believe men are working, I think they must simply exist in a kind of stupor.'

So much that Cecilia thought had never occurred to Emmeline that their talks kept, after all these years, freshness, and topics were inexhaustible. Disturbed, and sorry for Julian, Emmeline sat silent.

Cecilia, wound up and angrily beating together the tips of her fingers, continued: 'A man can't tell you sanely about himself; he either knows nothing at all or goes all morbid – Oh yes, I know you think I am horrid about Julian, but really he has annoyed me. It was like someone blowing his nose before he kisses you . . . There's so much to be said for Julian, he *is* in a kind of way lovable, when he doesn't propose, and he's been charming to me. Wealth does make me feel rather *éblouie* – do you think I'm wrong, Emmeline? There's a feeling of being tucked in all the time, which I like, when one's going about with Julian, as though he were carrying round a rug. I don't think I hurt his heart but I'm sorry I hurt his vanity. In a way, the less he wanted to, the nicer it was of him to propose if he felt he ought: I suppose one should look at it that way. Can I really have been unkind? – Do *say* something, Emmeline!'

Emmeline started. She had sat staring so fixedly at Cecilia that Cecilia had disappeared; instead, she had seen spinning sentences, little cogs interlocked, each clicking each other round. She sat blinking at this machinery of agitation that a word spoken two days ago had only now set going. She was an earnest but not an intelligent listener . . . 'So you said no?' she said finally.

'That's what I keep telling you. – Don't say you only hope I may not regret it.'

'That's what I was thinking,' said Emmeline candidly. 'Shall you see Julian again?'

'Of course: I should miss him fearfully.'

'Mayn't it be difficult?'

'Why? From the fuss you make, darling, one would think no one had ever done this before. It won't be so nice, naturally; once a man has begun to propose it is always unsettling.'

'But if you think he didn't mean to, why should he do it again?'

'It sets up a train of thought,' said Cecilia wisely. 'You really are very young, Emmeline: I suppose I ought to take better care of you than I do. Do be sensible about Markie. I suppose I should ask him to dinner, it gives the thing countenance.'

'My dear Cecilia!' cried Emmeline, with a surprise that abashed Cecilia.

'Then you'd rather I didn't?'

'It seems rather pointless,' said Emmeline mildly.

'You see,' said Cecilia, worried, 'I don't *love* Julian. It doesn't come off, somehow. It does seem a pity – I could be so much in love.'

This Emmeline doubted. She was aware, with concern and affection, of the diligence with which Cecilia courted the passion, exposing her heart hopefully like a child who has hung out a box where birds will not nest. Romantic, ingenious, melancholic, Cecilia lent the whole force of her temperament to this expectation. Her ear always pressed to the whorls of the shell, she heard something always, but not the sea.

What could be wrong? Not a sense or a faculty failed with her. It could not always be Henry: having come and gone he was generally present, but not like this. He may, indeed, have thought worse of her for this impotence. Her heart – for she tapped at it constantly – seemed in order. She had loved: she was honest and did not exalt the idea of fidelity – what has once happened, happens again. Here she was at a standstill, her plot only half spun out. Sometimes she asked herself if she had loved even Henry at all. Then, brushed past by the younger Cecilia – a girl's glowing face for a moment seen in a crowd near her lover's shoulder – Cecilia felt slighted and jealous. She *had* loved, but could not recapture the tune of her bridal days ... It could not always be Henry.

Emmeline knew it was not, still, Henry, but was his death. More shocked by this than she knew, a little dwarfed by the accident, Cecilia could not estimate now what she suffered then: the sombre memory went beyond her compass. Death gone, one rejects the ordeal instantly: grief, great in momentous passing, leaves one a little smaller. Obstinate in its refusal to suffer, the spirit puts up defences; the frightened heart repairs itself in small ways. Very few remain ennobled; one has to live how one can – it is meaner living, gaudy, necessitous, full of immediate pleasures like the lives of the poor.

When a great house has been destroyed by fire – left with walls bleached and ghastly and windows gaping with the cold sky – the master has not, perhaps, the heart or the money to rebuild. Trees that were its companions are cut down and the estate sold up to the speculator. Villas spring up in red rows, each a home for someone, enticing brave little shops, radiant picture palaces: perhaps a park is left round the lake, where couples go boating. Lovers' lanes in asphalt replace the lonely green rides; the obelisk having no approaches is taken away. After dark – where once there was silence, a tree's shadow drawn slowly across the grass by the moon, or no moon, an exhalation of darkness – rows of windows come out like lanterns in pink and orange; boxed in bright light hundreds of lives repeat their pattern; wireless picks up a tune from street to street. Shops stream light on the pavements, upon the commotion of late shopping: big buses swarm to the curb, small cars dart home to the garage, bicycling children flit through the birdless dark. Bright façades of cinemas reflect on to ingoing faces the expectation of pleasure: lovers laugh, gates click, doors swing, lights go on upstairs, couples lie down in honest beds. Life here is livable, kindly and sometimes gay; there is not a ghost of space or silence; the great house with its dominance and its radiation of avenues is forgotten. When spring is sweet in the air, snowdrops under the paling, when blue autumn blurs the trim streets' perspective or the low sun in winter dazzles the windows gold – something touches the heart, someone, disturbed, pauses, hand on a villa gate. But not to ask: What was here?

With the quick fancy, the nerves and senses Cecilia could almost love. She enjoyed the repose of small intimacies, susceptibility she could command, reflections of passion momentarily commanded her. With her, the gay little streets flourished, but, brave when her house fell, she could not regain some entirety of the spirit. Disability seems a hard reward for courage.

XIII

It was nearly midsummer: behind a film of thin opal the sun rose early – not long, however, before Emmeline was awake. She woke with a start, as though someone had spoken, not a shred of night mist clung to her brain: the day began from the moment as though she had opened a book at the right page. Getting up, she looked into the garden where she and Cecilia had talked so late last night. Something moved in the plane tree: fearing this might be Benito – so small, so high up – Emmeline, for whom the tree was a blur, put on her spectacles. But it was the one-eared cat from next door, a noted *flaneur* in other gardens. Every leaf of the plane now appeared in delicate outline: last night while they talked it had darkened and towered, edgeless, into a burnished sky. The next-door cat leered at Emmeline, scrabbled further into the leaves, then calmly walked head first down the mottled tree-trunk. At the foot it swayed off like a leopard, one rippling curve of malignity. Silence: the peaceful twitter of some alighting sparrows. This clear film over the silence of gardens was lovely; the day like a magnolia seemed still to be sleeping in pale bud. Down in the Abbey Road, traffic was just beginning.

Pausing now and then to glance out of the window, Emmeline wrote to Markie:

Dear Markie – Thank you for the letter I found at the office, and for the copper electric kettle which came yesterday afternoon. It boils very well. It will be nice to have tea without smelling of gas.

Yes, I thought about you on Sunday. I wondered what you were doing. I was in Sussex. I'm sorry you didn't like the people you went to lunch with; why did you go? What you said in your letter makes me feel very happy. But you mustn't think all that. I am quite ordinary. If I seem stupid sometimes when I am with you, or as though I were somewhere else, it is because nothing else has been like this.

This morning looks beautifully early, I wish you were awake. It looks like a day slipped in between Monday and Tuesday, that has nothing to do with the week. I wish you were here. There is so much I should like to say that I seem to have nothing to say. Perhaps some day words will be different or there will be others. When you get this it will be Tuesday evening and what I see now will be gone.

Cecilia asked how you were last night and was interested hearing about your flat. She said she wished she lived in Lower Sloane Street. Just now when I looked out there was a one-eared cat in our plane tree: it walked down. I did the office accounts yesterday and they came out. I think that is all my news.

Emmeline.

As Emmeline finished the letter she sighed, sorry to say good-bye to the moment and Markie: a little door shut between them as she stuck down the envelope. Pulling on her red leather slippers she crept downstairs, where she slipped a light overcoat over her pyjamas, unhasped the drawing-room window and went out. The foot of the garden was screened by summery poplars: next door they were still asleep behind drawn curtains. Here there were few flowers; their white irises over for the summer, that would be all till next year's daffodils. The garden bloomed in monochrome, silvery variations of green; some sheeny flag-leaves, a bush of rosemary somebody had forgotten: here a leaf of ground ivy caught the light like a petal. Daisies pirated everywhere and the next-door clematis showered over their wall. Emmeline saw justice everywhere: they suffered their neighbour's cat and enjoyed his clematis. Unashamed of their flowerless garden she stood, looking round, in the dew in her red slippers.

She heard the side gate click and thinking: 'The milkman,' did not turn round. But it was Markie who crossed the grass and appeared beside her, pale and puffy in a dishevelled white tie.

She exclaimed: 'But I thought I had locked the side gate!'

'You forgot,' said Markie, and looked at her oddly.

'But it can't be seven o'clock!'

'As far as I'm concerned,' said Markie, 'it's still yesterday: I haven't been to bed.'

She looked in surprise from his tie to his face. Sure enough in his eyes dull as ashes, his glance restless, aggressive and quick as though still in company, she found the stale lights of yesterday unextinguished. Behind his strained eyes she saw the passionless pressure of dissipation, the whole fumy void of a night which, like hell, had no clocks, in which no remission was to be hoped of the hours. He added: 'I've been to a party.'

'Nice?'

'Just a party,' said Markie, shutting his eyes.

'Anyone there?' pursued Emmeline, interested.

'No one you'd know – at least I hope not.'

This aspiration of Markie's touched Emmeline, but depressed her: she would have liked to have known his friends. On the subject of parties she had less prejudice than he thought. It was true, she had not cared for those parties, when she was very young; they had been silly with syphons, spoiling one's dress, and young girls did not know how much to drink. She did not care much for parties where everyone disappeared and everyone else looked mysterious, where people wept or were sick, or for those affectionate parties from which it was hard to come singly away. She had, however, spent many quietly pleasant evenings under adverse conditions... Markie had a good head; if he had been very drunk he was not drunk now. Only, like spirits upon his breath, a rather dreary portentousness still hung about his manner. From his clothes, it appeared that the party must have begun grandly, though possibly it had transferred itself from place to place.

'But how did you get here?' she said.

'We got into a car to drive a man home to Hertfordshire; coming back we went round in loops, I don't know who was driving: possibly no one. I saw the name of your road – though it seemed unlikely – I stopped the car and got out. Curiosity.'

The oddest preoccupation and curiosities pucker the weary mind that carries itself like a burden not to be put down. It was true, he had been to Oudenarde Road only once, and that not in daylight; its pilasters, steps and incline of gardens were strange to him. He said: 'I didn't expect to find *you*.' They had certainly surprised each other. Emmeline, just a shade anxiously, smiled.

'It's a nice house, isn't it?'

'Very,' said Markie.

'But shouldn't you go back and get some sleep?'

'Good God, no; that would do me in!' Sleep, in fact, would be fatal: he was due at his chambers by ten, before that he wanted simply a bath and some coffee. He declared he was all right so long as he did not sleep. Besides, he was still feeling sociable – 'Though I can't be pretty,' he added.

He was not: it was certainly not vain of Markie, calling this morning. He laughed, but kept irritably turning his head as though the skin of his neck were too tight, and tweaking his crumpled tie. To get his tie like this, someone must have been holding him tight round the neck, perhaps in the car. It was not yesterday with his chin and jaw. Markie's appearance, however, while rather absently noted, meant little to Emmeline, for whom it was as though some ragged and bulky cloud interposed a moment between herself and her fixed idea of him – and in that moment, even, the cloud's edge brightened. She was touched, it was dear of him to have come: for, liking repose so much, he could not have hoped very much of their sleeping windows. If he were pleased to see her she could not determine. Their garden was lively with callers this morning – who had been first? The tom cat.

Markie took in her overcoat, her hair in soft uncombed strands, bare ankles and red slippers dark with dew. He said: 'Why do you wear your spectacles when you're not dressed?' Knowing he liked her better without her spectacles, Emmeline took them off quickly and, blinking at him, explained that she had been looking for a cat. She suggested, 'You could have coffee here.'

'Oh, can I? Very well – thanks.'

They went in through the drawing-room. Whatever Markie had come here hoping to see, he seemed now to observe nothing. The servants were just down: Emmeline went to the head of the kitchen stairs. 'Coffee,' she said, 'at once, please, and toast and things.'

Then she shut off the kitchen, with its buzz of discreet surprise. Markie, having implored Emmeline not to ask him about the party, now went on to tell her a good deal. His recollections were mostly vindictive; she gathered he thought all women better away from parties.

'But they're supposed to look nice.'

'They don't.' Still producing a stream of cold volubility he leant up against a table and knocked off some books which clattered about the parquet. This, with the sound of the tray being carried tinkling into the dining-room to the tune of an explanation from Emmeline, effectively woke Cecilia.

'What's the matter?' she called. 'Is it lunch time?'

'There's Cecilia,' said Emmeline.

'Oh yes, how *is* Cecilia?'

Emmeline, slipper-heels going clop, clop, clop, ran up breathlessly to Cecilia's door. 'Give Cecilia my love,' called Markie. Cecilia, indignant, still webbed-up in dreams, rolled round to stare at Emmeline in the yellow dusk of drawn curtains. She 'slept high' on a whole pile of frilly pillows, the telephone sentinel by her bed. 'Emmeline, what *is* the matter?'

'It's Markie,' said Emmeline, outlined against the daylight. 'He's just having breakfast.'

'Why? Is he staying here?'

Cecilia, confused, had a vague recollection of having said last night she might ask Markie to dinner; of this good disposition on her part he seemed to have taken rapid advantage.

'He's been to a party.'

'That awful party next door?' Cecilia, who had been mortified by the sounds of the gold chair party (in fact some roads distant) far into the night, told herself this was exactly the sort of party Markie *would* go to. 'There's no bacon,' she added, reviewing the larder dreamily.

'I don't think he feels like bacon; he just wants coffee. You don't mind? He sends you his love,' said Emmeline anxiously.

'Thank him,' replied Cecilia. 'But I must say I think we should all be better in bed.' Diving round on her pillows she resumed the repose of a goddess. Emmeline went downstairs again.

Markie's coffee had come; he sat looking heavily at the tray with its pretty Chinese cups. The dining-room with its airy white curtains, roses and slender furniture made the plain fact of eating seem quite irrelevant: here Emmeline pondered over a grapefruit among the cool reflections of morning, or Cecilia dissected the pretty emotions by candlelight. Markie looked out of place here. Emmeline brought out a comb from her pocket and did herself up vaguely, sitting down opposite Markie. 'This feels like after a ball,' she said.

'Why?' But he mellowed: Cecilia's coffee was excellent.

'Well, perhaps not . . . Cecilia is sorry there's no bacon.'

'You look lovely,' he said, 'though your nose is a little shiny.'

'Oh dear . . .'

'Still, it's a nice colour – why don't you write to me?'

Emmeline was surprised, she had understood men avoided re-criminations at breakfast and that it was women who erred in this way. Perhaps, however, this was not breakfast for Markie: she felt she was living his day and her own at once. 'But I did,' she said.

'No, you didn't,' said Markie, taking more black coffee.

'I just have. I've just been writing to thank you for that electric kettle.'

'Oh yes,' scoffed Markie, 'that's what *I* always say.'

'Why should I tell you I wrote if I hadn't written?' said Emmeline, colouring.

'All right, *all* right,' he said, pacific. 'Then give me the letter now.'

'*No*,' exclaimed Emmeline, startled by her own vehemence.

'Why?'

She could think of nothing but: 'It was meant to be posted.'

'Well this will save you the stamp.'

'Anyhow,' said Emmeline, 'it's a foolish letter.' She looked at him thoughtfully, pushing back her hair from her face: that Markie should read her letter became impossible. His presence, his black-and-white bulk above the breakfast tray, made what she had written meaningless. Till now, she had offered to no friend her hours outside time: now the budding magnolia, plucked and discarded, breathed its unmeaning fragrance among the fumes of coffee. Not a question, less than a smile – her hour, her letter faded, unanswerable. Not to speak was her instinct: she should not, in most secret ink, ever have spoken. But she had not yet spoken: the letter was still unread. Yet, embracing once more her integrity, Emmeline's heart smote her. For here Markie was: in his presence – within reach, if he cared to kiss, of his kiss, within reach, if she dared to put out a hand, of his hand – this idea of pleasure as isolated, arctic, regarding its own heart only, became desolating to Emmeline as a garden whose flowers were ice. Those north lights colouring the cold flowers became her enemies; her heart warming or weakening she felt at war with herself inside this cold zone of solitude. She desired lowness and fallibility, longing to break the mirror and touch the earth.

'All the same,' she said, 'I'll give it you if you like . . .'

'That's very sweet of you, angel,' said Markie, touched. But his thoughts had wandered, he was regarding himself in the flank of the silver kettle, in which he appeared like the Frog Footman, shockingly globular. 'I don't look much,' he said, 'to write letters *to*.'

Some idea he had had of wresting her letter from her had vanished before she answered, leaving him moderately ashamed. Her odd shyness and her reluctance of fancy had, before now, provoked him; he did not know how much or whether pleasantly.

His feeling for her, held up, found its way out in a kind of boister-ousness and toughness on a plane where these were likely to be supportable; he had wit enough to be inflamed by his own bad taste. On the whole he was nastier to his other friends than he was to Emmeline: the perpetual adolescent in sensitive natures remained his victim, but in her the adolescent was still unborn. An idea of tussling with her for a letter she would not give him, uncertainly taken up, had quite soon bored him ... Besides, he valued her sweet, lame letters.

'Quite a picture ...' said Markie, and looked round the room where between the window and mirror he and she hung like fishes in bright water, equally opposite each other in daylight. Not quite eye to eye, pairs of gold-fish in those little crystal aquariums poise for hours together over the shells and glass ornaments, hardly more animate than the unrippling water, making a pattern. In Markie, prickly and strident nervousness evaporating from his manner, this piscine acquiescence to the bright stillness became apparent, while to Emmeline these lucid minutes were native and kind as an ele-ment. It was their first breakfast together.

A rose dropped petals; almost as silently past the window a bicycle spun downhill. The postman began to come uphill, knocking from door to door. Big with fate for the sleeping Cecilia, were it only an invitation to dinner, the letter bag bumped up their steps.

'Post ...' said Emmeline, snapping the silence idly.

'Expecting anything?'

'No.'

'I should like there to be a letter from me, but there's not.' Groaning into his coffee cup, Markie soliloquized:

'*How* on earth am I going to get home?'

'You telephone for a taxi – but there won't be any taxis up here yet. When one's catching an early boat train one orders one over-night ...' Her voice trailed off, it hardly mattered; Markie was not listening.

Upstairs, Cecilia woke up again. '*Emmeline!*' she called urgently.

Emmeline looked at Markie as though their days together were over, as though she had only the moment in which to speak. 'I'm glad you came,' she said hurriedly, and brushing the back of his chair with her hand ran upstairs. He sat staring at her empty place, at a heap of petals that, while she sat saying nothing, her long fingers had gathered, turned over and sifted one by one.

Cecilia, now very wide awake, sat up pulling her pink dressing-gown round her shoulders with an air of immense resolution: a splash of daylight fell into the room. 'Was I dreaming,' she said, 'or did you come just now and tell me that Markie was in the house?'

'He's just having breakfast.'

'Well, I must say I think this is very bohemian of Markie. I'd have said so before if you'd given me time to wake up. I suppose he's not shaved or anything.'

'He didn't mean to come in.'

'I still don't know what he's doing in St John's Wood.'

'I'm going to drive him home.'

'You can't drive round London with Markie looking the way he probably does. Besides, you're not dressed yet. If there aren't any taxis he'd better ring up a garage. Really, darling, I don't see how you can run a travel-bureau if you can't get a man back to Sloane Square without all this fuss.'

Emmeline strolled off into the bathroom and turned her bath on. If Cecilia and Markie did not meanwhile arrange otherwise, she still proposed to drive Markie home. Her two friends' communication seemed to be brief and angular; through the bathroom door she had a glimpse of Cecilia in pink ruffles, still rather angry, leaning over the banisters ... Going back to her bedroom, Emmeline found her letter to Markie behind the blotter. She put a match to the corner and watched it burn. A very little of Emmeline quivered off in hot smoke; she blew down the flame and brown ash fluttered on to air spinning already with sound and sunlight: the day was in full bloom.

XIV

It sometimes startled Cecilia to think she and Julian might now be engaged, kissing each other officially, much on the telephone, trying to find a house. To Julian, who was very busy, this realization occurred in sharp gusts, disarranging his habit of mind, like some wind through a room full of papers; he endeavoured to keep himself closed against the disturbance. At the same time, his one halting impulse – linked with the speed of the car through the glowing country – began to take on a roughness, the whole prestige of savagery: something seen, as it were, by the tail of his rational eye but never looked at quite squarely. He was on the nervous edge of feeling and almost suffered: he moved cautiously, always preparing to wince, as though stiff from a first day's riding. Chagrin played some part in his mood: he felt a born minor character. In the course of that week after Saturday – in which, besides the unusual pressure of business he had a good many engagements – he received, with some books of his she sent back, a pleasant note from Cecilia, saying how much she had enjoyed the school and their day in Buckinghamshire.

Julian's sister returned from abroad: on Thursday, as she requested, he met her train at Victoria. Her greeting expressed that deprecating affection to which, from his family, he was accustomed: they all felt he should do more. Too much exhausted to speak, as they drove to her club, she suggested that they should lunch together tomorrow: she had three days in London on her way through to Shropshire ... Julian, having extracted himself from another engagement with a good deal of embarrassment, wondered where he should give her lunch. Wherever he took her she never seemed to enjoy herself; on the other hand, she liked to feel everything possible had been done. When once they had lunched at his flat she appeared more depressed than ever, saying: 'Of course you are right to live very simply.' He decided to give himself, at least, a good lunch.

Julian's sister, a pale tall woman dressed with neutral English good taste, appeared to be handsome, though her features were indistinct as though seen through wrappings of gauze. Her head drawn in like a duck's on her long neck when she smiled gave the smile a disconcerting quality of indulgence. A discouraging woman to meet for the first time, she seemed at all times to be smothering mild resentment at what one had done or said: she appeared to endure life with laudably little fuss. She was some years older than Julian, lived in Shropshire and seldom said or did anything actively unkind.

Slipping off her suède gloves before lunch on Friday she looked about her, appraising the restaurant without comment. Julian said he hoped this place would amuse her, and she said it seemed to be very bright.

Julian asked after Cadenabbia: she said it had been much as always and she did not think she would go again. She told Julian he did not look well, and inquired after Pauline: her manner at this point took on a slight air of reproach, resembling Cecilia's.

'Oh, she's very well,' Julian said, with the briskness his sister always provoked. 'I was down there on Saturday.'

'Oh yes, at the school? She wrote that you were expected.'

'She seemed quite pleased to see me,' said Julian doubtfully.

'With girls of that age,' said his sister, 'it is impossible to be certain. Pauline is painfully shy; it is impossible for her to express her feelings in any way.'

Julian looked round the tables at couples lunching, so gay and intimate. Among all this mirrored pleasure, these lights and faces, he missed Cecilia acutely: blurred by the inhibitions of Pauline, upon which his sister dwelt with such gusto, their last bright Saturday seemed to recede . . . *Hors d'oeuvre* appeared; his sister took up her fork doubtfully: though he assured her these were a speciality it soon appeared she would eat nothing but radishes and an olive. 'You took Mary down with you?' she resumed (Mary was their sister-in-law). 'Pauline said, "*They* will be coming." '

'No, a friend came with me, a Mrs Summers: she was anxious to see the school.'

'She thinks of sending her daughters?'

'No.'

'She did not care for the school?'

'She has no daughters.'

The strain of this interlocution – in which every question by taking the form of a statement made it clear that only one answer would be acceptable – was beginning to tell on Julian. He felt he had never said 'No' so often; each time he received from his sister a faint vibration of outrage, as though she suspected in him some quite gratuitous impulse to contradict. She paused when he told her Cecilia had no daughters, her long dim face like an uninspired Madonna's becoming strained with the effort to put something difficult delicately. 'Julian,' she began –

'Yes, Bertha?' said Julian boldly.

'Julian, you must not be hurt . . . I am sure this white wine is excellent, but do you think I might just have some Vichy water?' Nothing was easier (Bertha had 'an inside'), but Julian, who had been bracing himself agreeably, went flat, as though Cecilia had disappeared. Spinning one glass on its base till it clinked wildly on another, he said: 'Look here, do you still think I ought to marry?'

'Oh yes, a man's life is so empty . . . I'm afraid,' she said, looking round, disconsolate, 'my Vichy water is giving a good deal of trouble.' Julian turned irritably to the waiter. 'But, of course,' she said, 'as you did not marry, you can always take Pauline abroad when she leaves school. It would be nice for her to travel a little, and I think she is fond of you.'

'I'm afraid I couldn't do that, possibly.'

'I should take her myself to Florence, but the climate is so uncertain. All the same, Julian, you must not become too set in your way of life; one does become set in one's way of life about middle age, I have noticed that in myself, I quite see it in you. There is a great deal, I am sure, in taking an interest in younger people: I am sure you will find Pauline an interest as she grows older . . . Of course we all felt it a pity you did not marry, though I quite see you may not feel you could do so now. A young wife would be unsettling, and a woman of your age might not fall in with your life as you might expect.'

'Exactly . . . Here comes your Vichy.'

'There is no one at present that you . . .'

'Nobody,' snapped her brother.

'Then I do not see how you can marry,' she said placidly.

Devastated by the correctness of this opinion Julian turned moodily sideways, just not to catch at the moment, Markie's eye. Markie, pulling in his chair opposite Emmeline's at a corner table, had been explaining to Emmeline why her appearance, the first night of all at Oudenarde Road, at dinner, had been such a surprise:

he had heard of her as a sister-in-law. But what, asked Emmeline, did a sister-in-law look like? Markie's eyes, travelling round the restaurant, settled on Julian's sister, who illustrated his point perfectly. '*That*,' he had said, directing Emmeline's happy unfixed gaze.

Emmeline put on her spectacles. 'Why,' she exclaimed, 'there's dear Julian!' She radiantly smiled and nodded, Markie knew Julian slightly but did not connect him with Oudenarde Road. 'Oh,' he said, 'do you know him? Who's that he's lunching with?'

'I've no idea.'

'Obviously,' said Markie looking again, 'it is not his idea of pleasure.'

Heads together over the table, they both laughed. She still felt sorry for Julian, but he was far off, at the small end of a telescope. In a sort of ecstatic distraction she took off her spectacles, glanced once more round the room that swam with reflections of her own happiness, then back at Markie, who did not again let her look away. Fans whirring silently made icy discs on the air: she dropped her gloves and sat listening.

For his part, Julian had been surprised to see Emmeline – particularly straight, slight and beautiful in a green dress – sitting down opposite Markie. He had had no idea of all this. With a very solid respect for the young man's ability, impressed – though he never knew quite how agreeably – by the amount of noise Markie made and his personal vigour, Julian discounted a good deal else that one heard: he was always amused to meet Markie. All the same, he did seem an odd companion for Emmeline. Emmeline had, moreover, told Julian she never lunched out on week-days as this kept her too long away from the office: he could not believe her to be disingenuous. Today must be an exception – from her look and air, her absorption, the exception was radiant.

'Whom,' said his sister plaintively, 'do you keep looking at?'

Julian explained that Markie was one of our coming young men: raising her lorgnettes his sister looked carefully. 'He looks to me more dissipated than anything.'

'He lives hard and works hard: I couldn't do it.'

'I shouldn't advise you to try; it would not agree with you. Who is the girl?'

'A Miss Summers.'

'Oh, your friend's daughter?'

'No, Bertha. I told you, she has no daughters of any kind.'

Returning the lorgnette a moment to Markie's table his sister said with distaste: 'They seem very much in love.'

With a shock, Julian realized that this was true.

The shock was startling, an utter exclusion from something, a door slammed in his face. He did not know what he had lost, not Cecilia: there was no question of losing Emmeline. This tête-à-tête with his sister, this mournful association with her in gloom and impotence, as though before birth, by some unkind twist in heredity, they had both been shanghaied together, drove home like a stake through his heart the idea of solitude. Catching a tone of Bertha's, marking her slow movements, he had a sense of unseemly familiarity with himself, as though chained opposite a mirror . . . Had Cecilia appeared in the place opposite, he would have besought her clemency with a kind of fury, sent out for roses, touched her fingers across the table. No living contact seemed ever to have been his own. Those tears of chagrin she shed, last week in the bright sunset, glittered terribly in his memory: her vexation transmuted itself to a kind of terror: from what advance of the cold and dark in him had she stepped back? Less in desire than desperation he clung in thought to her warm and sensuous hand.

'That is not a young man,' Bertha said, '*I* should like to send any girl about with. She looks quite young.'

'Oh really, Bertha, I think you're a little arbitrary.'

'No doubt times change . . .' There descended once more upon her, like more gauze veils, an absolute lack of interest. 'What is this?' she said, 'turbot?'

'Turbot.'

Bertha liked the turbot, which was not at all rich. Radishes had not impaired her appetite: a brief pause suspended the pricking discomfort of dialogue. Avoiding the corner table, Julian's eye roved round the room, to find with relief a couple who smoked in silence eyeing each other glumly, a pale girl, downcast, pulling at her lace handkerchief, two short-haired women nonplussed by each other, a flushed man rolling his brandy round in a glass, with eyes for no one, a blonde in a red hat being insistent angrily – then with despair met Markie and Emmeline in a mirror.

The set of Markie's shoulders, his pose of quiescent vitality, leaning forward on his crossed arms, proclaimed the conqueror. Julian looked no farther: he found he had thought of Emmeline as beyond desire.

At the end of luncheon, Bertha sipped white coffee politely, an eye on her watch. She wondered if it would appear unkind or ungrateful – after the radishes, that nice turbot, a chicken *en chasseur* she had after all refused and the *crème brulée* that was her choice – to leave Julian before he had finished his cigarette. Her time in London was limited; at half-past two exactly she wished to go shopping. She wanted a massage after her journey, a fitting at her corsetière's, a new silver saucepan to boil milk in her bedroom, a chat with her specialist and one of those mackintosh coats she had just seen advertised for her dog. She desired to visit her hat shop, which concealed itself upstairs in Mayfair with a discretion so sinister one might expect to rap three times on a panel or be regarded narrowly through a grille. The ostensible reason for her departure was that she had arranged to buy Pauline a new party frock. The child, who had outgrown her confirmation dress, wrote that she was to be prominent among the sopranos when, on the speech day, the school choir inaugurated the proceedings with song. So Bertha had promised to seek out a modest and innocent dress and send in the bill to Julian.

'I do not think,' she said finally and with the kindest intentions, 'that there is really much more to say.'

Upon this note they parted.

Julian paid the bill and saw Bertha out. He bowed, in passing to Emmeline, but she did not see him. Outside, watching Bertha's taxi go off, he remained for a moment hypnotized by the glare and vibration of traffic – long cars nosing like sharks, vans whirring in gear, the high tottering buses. Then, stopping another taxi, he slid off into the stream. He was returned to his quiet room at the office and to the telephone.

'Hullo?' said Cecilia. 'Oh, Julian, how nice to hear your voice!'

'I just thought I'd ring up.'

'I'm so glad.' There was a pause.

'I hope I haven't rung up at a bad time?'

'Oh no: I've got people to lunch but they'll get along nicely. She eats nothing, she's making her husband diet and they inhibit the other man. There was such a nice lunch, so I'm eating it all. Oh, Julian?'

'Yes?'

She thought he was really bad on the telephone. 'I only wondered, what have you been doing?'

'I've been giving my sister lunch.'

'Did she enjoy herself?'

'I don't know.'

'How terrible. I do wish –'

'What did you say?'

'The line's bad, isn't it?' said Cecilia, nervous. 'Something keeps on buzzing.'

'Does it? I don't think –'

'I'm so sorry if I said anything – I mean I did mean what I said but I needn't have said it like that – Are you there?'

'Yes.'

'I do wish you'd come and see me.'

'Do you think it would be a success?'

'Oh yes; that sort of thing always is.'

'Then I'll –'

'*Oh my God*,' said Cecilia. 'I've left the door open!'

Silence sent a sharp vibration across the wire. Julian, hanging up, stared a moment more at the dumb black instrument, then touched a bell for his secretary. He resumed the kind of day that was Peter's ideal: people coming in quietly over carpets, trays of papers put down or taken away, a muted efficiency, telephoning in a tone of governed irritability, interviews of a varying smoothness, and, at one blink from Julian, a dark green blind twitched down by the secretary to forbid the bold afternoon sun that approached his desk.

Cecilia's lunch party, having heard through the open door the first phrase of the interlude, had exchanged less than a glance and, all raising their voices, maintained a strenuous conversation till she came back. They were not English for nothing.

XV

After lunch Emmeline said good-bye to Markie at the corner of Woburn Place and hurried back to the office. Here the stenographer sat alone; Peter, having in vain awaited his partner's return, had gone out to keep an appointment. It was, indeed, half-past three: Emmeline's unpunctuality was without precedent; the clock's incredulous face confronted her from the mantelpiece. No detail of Emmeline's entrance, agitated and bright-eyed, escaped the stenographer who, twitching a new sheet of paper into her machine, typed on with emphatic diligence. 'Life,' she implied, 'is a serious business for *some* of us, still.'

'Mr Lewis left you a note,' she said.

'Thank you,' said Emmeline, who had already found it.

'He was sorry to miss you: I think there was something he felt he had to decide.'

The stenographer's estimation of Peter was at times depressingly obvious; towards Emmeline her attitude had remained, so far, cryptic. Watching Emmeline take her hat off and fold back her long green sleeves, she observed: 'It does seem a pity to work in that dress.'

Emmeline never came to work in anything but a coat and skirt, or a linen dress as severe: her employee saw no reason why this departure from precedent should be allowed to pass without comment. In fact, the slightly hectoring intimacy of her manner showed that on such an occasion she felt they might well be girls together.

'It won't hurt it,' said Emmeline frigidly.

'Green suits you rather,' remarked the stenographer.

'I hope I haven't missed anyone?'

The stenographer, on a note of polite regret, said, well, yes, someone *had* been in just now, asking about Andorra. What had she done? She gave them the folder about mule-tracks and Mr Lewis's pamphlet 'Espadrilles'.

'I'm afraid that was quite wrong. They should have had "Unknown Republics".'

'I'm sorry,' said the stenographer with dignity. 'I'm afraid it did not occur to me that Andorra was unknown.'

'Well, it is,' said Emmeline, searching among her papers.

'My people go there so much.'

'They are unusually fortunate.'

Emmeline seldom encouraged the stenographer; it was Peter who tried this, and Peter, consequently, whom the stenographer despised. Finding the paper she wanted, Emmeline stared at it but could read nothing, as in a dream. Something disturbed her with its insistence, some humming at the back of her mind that was not a mind. She thought: 'We mustn't lunch out again.' She thought of that eager client going away discouraged, reading Peter's cynical little horror 'Espadrilles', written for lady-artists. She had failed horribly in her charge.

At the same time, she could not help wondering if it would be nice in Paris. She had spoken today to Markie of Peter's project that she should fly to Paris to get into personal touch with two young Serbs who had started a sister agency. Much new ground might be opened up, on both sides, by an association: what Peter suggested was not (she must make this perfectly clear) partnership, but what he called 'interplay'. The terms of such interplay being so nebulous that they were hard to write down, a personal interview had become desirable: Emmeline's French was better than Peter's, also she liked flying. If all went well, if Emmeline liked the Serbs and they liked Emmeline, Peter and she would be free to speak of 'our Paris office', while the Serbs could refer in similar terms to Woburn Place. Both sides of the Channel, this ought to broaden the base of a client's confidence.

Markie, hearing of Emmeline's project with indulgence, had suddenly said he thought he should like to come too. He was very busy, but they could go at a week-end.

'But the Serbs mightn't be there on a Sunday.'

'They'll be there,' said Markie, 'if I know anything about Serbs.'

'But do you?'

'Naturally.'

She had said, wrinkling her forehead: 'But we don't know that they're keen: just dropping in on Sunday might seem a bad start, rather unbusinesslike. You see, we may have to woo them.'

'You'll be all right; tell them you're far too busy to come any other day and that they must take you when they can get you. Throw your weight about like anything, Emmeline.'

'Yes,' said Emmeline. 'I mean to.'

So Markie said they would fly to Paris together: that should be very nice. Emmeline had not thought of the enterprise quite that way. There was no doubt, however, that Markie's company would be pleasant: she could, anyhow, do nothing if he elected to book by the same plane. 'I hope,' she said gently, 'you won't distract me.'

'I swear not,' said Markie, blinking.

There was no doubt that her green sleeve rubbing against the desk distracted Emmeline at the moment. The silk was still warm from the sun; she still saw Markie's square-tipped fingers where the silk creased a little inside the elbow. She read and re-read that involved, complimentary letter in Spanish: one would think from its tone she had been proposing to the hotel-keeping in Malaga a visit from fifteen earls, though it was in fact fifteen art-students from Macclesfield who were wishing to make a walking tour in Andalusia. At the inclusive price she had quoted she must obtain for them everything: occasional chars-à-bancs, wine, the aesthetic amenities, accommodation in accordance with the proprieties – for, as they had intimated with an indescribable archness, their party was to be mixed. At the thought of these fifteen enthusiasts Emmeline's heart, on a better day, had gone up: just now she could only think of the ten toads, terribly tired, trying to trot to Tetbury – she was appalled. Her roll-top in its solemn surround of silence was a monument to the pretence of industry: in vain her stenographer's pointed tapping, in vain the clock: place and time, shivered to radiant atoms, were in disorder. There was no afternoon; the sun, forgetting decline, irresponsibly spun like a coin at the height of noonday. Emmeline, as though threatened with levitation, gripped the edge of her roll-top. 'Miss Tripp,' she said, 'I think I will dictate.'

The stenographer – unaware, naturally, that the call was to Emmeline's faculties – looked up willingly. Bored, she had been patching up her mistakes with a purple pencil. The mistakes were many, but machine-like efficiency is not, she had been given to understand, compatible with high intelligence. Though discouraged by Peter and Emmeline, she took their dictation in shorthand, which involved heavy breathing, took rather longer than long-hand, and was at times impossible to re-read correctly. She looked up smiling, as though at an invitation to dance: Emmeline should have been warned.

'Those Macclesfield students . . .'

'I've got them all filed.'

'Well, you haven't at present: they're here. I want you to take a translation down as I go along; I've got a letter from Malaga here and I can't think in Spanish.'

'One feels like that, sometimes,' said Miss Tripp.

'Ready?' said Emmeline, slightly raising her voice. Omitting the compliments, she dictated slowly a translation of the long letter. It was finished; they paused and looked at each other. 'Just read it through,' said Emmeline. Miss Tripp, with the air of walking a tight-rope, read the translation aloud. Emmeline heard it out with misgivings: this was not what she had dictated, it did not even make sense.

'It sounds odd to me,' said Miss Tripp.

'I'm afraid,' Emmeline suggested, 'it may be the shorthand. Do you think perhaps we had better go through it again?'

'I suppose,' said Miss Tripp tartly, 'they have secretaries in Malaga.'

'I suppose so: why?'

'I suppose a secretary in *Malaga* couldn't make mistakes?'

'I'm afraid no hotel would send off such a silly letter – No, never mind, Miss Tripp; go on with what you were doing; I'll just write down the translation myself.'

Miss Tripp, going scarlet, turned from Emmeline to the fireplace with a convulsive movement, as though she were about to dive up the chimney. 'It seems,' she said, 'I am not a success in this office: nothing I do is right.'

Emmeline felt for a moment they must be engaged in unholy theatricals: such things did not happen this side of the footlights. No one had struck this note in the office before. There sat Miss Tripp, trembling, in a vivid and not pleasing pink spotted frock that had no doubt last summer at Oxford seen happier days. No doubt she had punted in it, making meanwhile clear-headed remarks to re-cumbent friends in a voice that, penetrating the hawthorns, rang down the curves of the Cher and across the meadows. No doubt she had then been esteemed and admired: *this* seemed too cruel. What had Emmeline done – delaying with Markie, leaving the office unsmiling to clients, Miss Tripp unattended and prey, as it now appeared, to these morbid reflections? Where had she been? – she dared not account for herself. Over her bright day Nemesis fell like an axe. She said faintly: 'Do tell me what is the matter.'

Miss Tripp was quite ready for this. 'The matter is,' she said in a calm, analytical voice, 'simply, that I am human.'

Emmeline, utterly taken aback, stared at her secretary with a surprise that was most unfortunate. 'Yes?' she said.

But Miss Tripp had paused to let this remarkable statement sink in. She was in perfect command of herself: the clock ticked on, evidently some more from Emmeline was expected. 'But why not?' said Emmeline helpless.

'It does not affect you much.'

Emmeline wondered a moment if Miss Tripp had really no money besides their ten shillings, if she was starving.

'Though I dare say,' reflected Miss Tripp, 'that if one died in one's chair, or even just fainted, you *might* notice.'

'– I hope you are not ill?'

'Oh dear no,' said Miss Tripp, smiling bitterly. 'I find it hard to express my own point of view,' she went on fluently. 'Naturally I should never believe in allowing personal feeling to impinge on business relations: I think that's a fearful mistake. All the same, there are degrees in impersonality.'

'Oh yes . . . yes.'

Not for nothing had the unhappy stenographer said this all over again and again to herself in her bath; it came out with a patness, an impressive conviction that was confounding to Emmeline, for whom – she felt in a flash, with profound contrition – it was as though the very furniture, had complained. 'What you really mean,' she said, colouring, 'is, that you find us inhuman?'

Meeting Emmeline's clear and penitent gaze, Miss Tripp who was really quite young, lost her nerve, dropped her voice and began to mumble.

'What did you say?' said Emmeline anxiously.

'I said, that's for you to decide.'

'But I don't understand,' said Emmeline, in despair.

In rehearsing emotional dialogue, in or out of the bath, there remains always one point, unconsciously reached, at which one rings down the curtain. There is a shyness even in fancy; Miss Tripp had never heard herself going beyond this point. There was much she wished to have Emmeline understand but was not prepared to express. In Miss Tripp's bath there was always a later point when the curtain – having dropped, as they say on theatre programmes, for a few minutes to denote the passage of time – rose on an Emmeline fully enlightened, stricken, up to date with the whole arrears of Miss Tripp's feeling.

The arrears were stupendous. In the first place Miss Tripp had always greatly disliked being called Miss Tripp (which smacked to her of the ribbon counter) and would have wished to be called, as by friends, briefly, Tripp. More, she had hoped that, with Emmeline, the depressing gaiety of her surname might have given place to the softer 'Doris'. Then, she had dressed to attract, and for Emmeline's eye alone: as her dresses, striped, checked or polka-dotted, became more striking, her ties and jumpers more compell-ingly vivid, Peter might blink but Emmeline took no notice: with the same delicate, ignorant, abstract mildness might Tripp have been greeted had she appeared naked. At the period of the tele-phone calls Tripp had been going through a terrific emotional crisis; but though she had reeled from the telephone Emmeline asked no questions. When Tripp stared into blackness above the typewriter it had been: 'Headache, Miss Tripp! Then do go home.' Kindness became annihilating ... As for business experience – Tripp could see for herself her employers were inefficient. (Sitting by cynically while the pair blandished their clients, it did not occur to Tripp that one had something to learn in the way of charm, or might be instructed in sympathy.) If clients returned, Tripp saw plainly it was because Peter cajoled them, or Emmeline's air sug-gested that heaven was brooding over their enterprise: one did not think much of all this. As for salary, her ten shillings went in a half-week's bus fares and lunches: she was very much out of pocket. All this might have gone for nothing – but what had she, what remained? Tripp was not the richer by half a smile. She was (or saw herself) Emmeline's confidential secretary, countenancing for her sake the absurd Peter, that walking reproach to Cambridge, who squeaked and fluttered about her, more like a bat than a young man. But where was the confidence? Where were the smiles, the gleams of satirical understanding, the dear sense of impositions endured together, of jokes shared grimly enough, that should cement an association between females? Not by as much as a glance did Emmeline say: 'We are here to suffer.' When Peter, in concen-tration, rippled his finger joints, Emmeline shuddered – but not at Tripp. When Emmeline's head ached till she bit her lip and shaded her eyes from the window, she took aspirin silently. Flowers Tripp brought for Emmeline's desk were beautifully acknowledged, then, as papers began to mount up, removed to the mantelpiece. Emmeline had the air and eyebrows, the same fatal expression of being elsewhere, of the young man who had ignored Tripp at Oxford. Daily, this had all become more exacerbating: it was to work for a stone.

What Tripp could not hear herself saying (the momentary 'curtain' in her rehearsals), though night after night, turning on more and more hot water, she had savoured the rich cataclysmic effect of its having been said, was: 'I shouldn't stay here a moment if it were not for you.'

Were it not for Emmeline, Tripp's dash through life would have been electric. She would have been secretary to a member of parliament: having weathered with him the storms of political crisis she would, her material gathered, have withdrawn – leaving perhaps his affections not disengaged – to write a great, *the* really great, political novel . . . This career, mapped out daily in further detail, had all the mournful brightness of an alternative one does not adopt.

Here they both sat, Tripp and Emmeline, half-turned unhappily in each other's direction, in the drowsy glare of the Bloomsbury afternoon. It is extraordinarily difficult to make a strong scene sitting down. Emmeline kept repeating: 'I'm sorry you're not happy.'

'It's not that, so much,' said Tripp with the smile of one well accustomed to suffering. 'It's just that I never seem to be any *good*.'

'Oh, yes, you *are*: really.'

'What you want is an automaton.'

It was on the tip of Emmeline's tongue to say: 'We could not afford one.' Instead she said: 'Oh, but we like initiative.'

'My initiative seems to cast rather a blight. I don't mind Mr Lewis calling me "the stenographer" if that really seems to him funny, but I do mind him drooping about when I say things and cracking his fingers behind my back. What he would like, obviously, is a platinum blonde.'

'I don't think he would, at all. But Miss Tripp, if you really do feel we are wasting your time, if you don't feel you're getting the kind of experience that you wanted . . . You make me feel very bad: I do realize that you are working for us for almost nothing –'

'Of course,' said poor Tripp, awkwardness, misery and the idea of money making her more and more unpleasant, 'your and Mr

Lewis's business methods *are* very much your own, you know. Even if Mr Lewis did want a blonde kind of automaton, I don't think a girl of that kind would work here for a moment, if you don't mind my saying so. I do wonder sometimes if *any* other girl would. There's no routine, and when I move my elbow I knock my funny bone. When Mr Lewis yawns it goes right down my back. One's expected to take responsibility without being trusted –'

'– Oh, that's *not* true!'

'Well, without being acknowledged. If I hang up my hat on the rack, Mr Lewis moves it; he wants all the pegs for his muffler. If I hang it up in the washplace it falls down and the people from the archaeological society tread on it. Not that my hat matters; it's just an example.'

'Oh, but your hat does matter!'

'When your friends come in, I have to sit on the stairs.'

Emmeline, hearing all this with bent head, said, 'If that's how you feel, really . . .'

'I suppose,' said Tripp, chin up, 'you are sacking me?'

'Oh, no, *no*. But if you felt that there was something else that you might be doing . . .'

'Yes – I should be secretary to a member of parliament. That might lead to anything.'

'Of course,' agreed Emmeline, without a tremor of pity for the member of parliament. 'In that case, I feel we have really no right to be keeping you here . . . I'm just giving you a chance to sack *us*.'

She smiled, looking straight at Tripp kindly and anxiously, but with that myopic vagueness bound to remain for its object so disconcerting and sometimes cruel. Having left her spectacles in the restaurant she saw in Tripp's place simply an angry blur. 'You do see?' she added.

'*I* see,' said Tripp, stony.

'I'm so glad we've discussed things,' said Emmeline, gathering reassurance.

'I'm afraid I've hardly begun . . .'

'Oh . . . But you do feel it might be better – ?'

'No doubt I'm a fool,' said Tripp, 'but I'm staying – unless you sack me.'

'Staying?' Emmeline faltered.

'You may well be surprised, after all I've said. You may quite well ask why I've stayed so long.'

'I thought you enjoyed the work,' said Emmeline, hopeless. She looked round the dear, pale-green walls of her office, witnesses to such devotion, the stress of such happy excitement. The place was a studio to her, even a shrine.

'If I *enjoyed* booking students to Spain,' said Tripp crisply, 'I could do that at Cook's without having my hat walked on and spending half the afternoon on the stairs. You may find me invisible, Miss Summers, but it must be annoying sometimes that I can't be actually walked *through*.'

'What on earth do you mean?' said Emmeline. 'Really, we can't discuss this if it upsets you. I know this room's very small; I should like to extend our offices. If we have seemed unfriendly – I'd no idea – I can only say I'm more than sorry.'

Tripp produced a handkerchief, not to weep into but to examine from hem to hem with a hard ferocity. She had conducted the scene masterfully, so far, as she might have taken a punt up a crowded river: Emmeline could but respect her. Now, eyes red-rimmed, face congested as though by a spasm of indigestion: 'Sorry!' cried Tripp, '*Sorry?* I wouldn't work here at all if it weren't for you!'

'Oh . . .' said Emmeline. She stared at the fatal letter from Malaga, her mind recording a quite superficial astonishment: one had not expected Tripp to go off like this. What had one expected? Little – punctuality, bridling diligence, the impassable patronage of the educated young female towards employers who had respectively failed at the wrong university and attended none. She had been cheap, she wrote the King's English, absented herself at tea-time, and did not sniff . . . But all this time in Miss Tripp the juices of an unduly prolonged adolescence had violently been fermenting: now with a pop they shot out the cork from the bottle. The effect on Tripp, certainly, did not appear catastrophic: the bottle remained intact, Tripp's outline (at which Emmeline stole a look) was once more placid, as though some natural process had reached conclusion. Doubtless she felt much better. Certainly she felt justified: what Doris Tripp said, she stood by: it had to be right . . . For Emmeline, however, the air had become fumy.

Emmeline had enough with which to reproach herself. There was no doubt she had been as unscrupulous as only the pure can be. Her own passion for business, however disinterested, had led to the exploitation of Tripp – why ask why she was exploitable? – one had been affected by Peter's cynical: 'More fool she.' Of Tripp's interior, Emmeline had not for a moment attempted to take account. Emmeline's exaltation was dangerous and unsparing, she would have cut off her own hand to advance travel and had undoubtedly taken a finger or two of Tripp's. She had taken for granted that Tripp should stay late to work with her when there was high pressure: devotion to the business had been assumed. Had she been at all aware of something insistent, brooding, of the cloak spread for her to walk upon with an embarrassing flourish? The air did always clear, certainly, when Tripp left the office. It was too true, they *had* guyed her, her genteel self-sufficiency inviting the rather fairy-like malice of the two partners. Comparison with the seductive efficiency of a platinum blonde *had* been implicit in Peter's use of 'stenographer.' And this afternoon – oh fatal lunch, fatal Markie, fatal letter from Malaga – it had been Tripp who paid hard for Emmeline's straying faculties.

Her straying faculties – Alas, not only this afternoon was the office smaller and darker for an Emmeline ardently elsewhere, to a devotion in deed only, dulling, drained of the spirit. She was in love, and hung between earth and heaven: meanwhile the typed correspondence in black and violet, gathering dust a little, mounted up on her desk. Maps were maps, the world shrank in its net of red routes, of rails and airways: this was a small office regarding a courtyard, where Tripp bumped her elbow and Peter crackled his finger joints. Light, centring round one figure, withdrew from the distance, from continents into which she had shot her travellers like arrows, from rippled seas, ribbed hills, white-and-shady cities to which this office had been the arch.

Emmeline, who had been accustomed to walk so blindly, now found about lovers linked in the street her own transfiguration or malady. Now the emotional presence of Tripp, ham-faced Tripp with her wiry shingle and broad red knuckles, had a startling touch on herself. Here was feeling, clawed like a bear and winged like an angel. Some new weakness in Emmeline seemed to attract disclosures – had not, yesterday evening, the parlourmaid wept on her shoulder, saying she was betrayed? – Through some gap in the dyke the tide rose in points and ripples, at first slowly . . . Tripp blinked and put by her handkerchief. But not a note in her tone of courage, not one of those stealthy and avid glances had fallen short of its mark. As the tom cat's stealthy and battered entrance preceded Markie's so Tripp's convulsion repeated a hundred crises, masked between him and her in these spinning rings of excitement and pleasure, of which till now Emmeline hardly had been aware.

'If I hadn't come in in this wretched dress she would not have spoken.' But she had had to speak. Emmeline suffered an agony of the conscience: through herself the peace of the office had been destroyed.

She said to Tripp: 'Have we – have I really been stupid? *Have* I been inhuman?'

Tripp, pulling up again to the typewriter, said: 'That's for you to say.'

'There isn't . . . I can't do anything now?'

'I am *not* upset, thank you.'

'I didn't expect you were,' said Emmeline humbly.

Peter, coming in round the door some time later, said: 'Hullo, where's the stenog –'

'Gone,' said Emmeline. Her manner arrested Peter's attention: the afternoon and the office appeared unusual. 'What do you mean?' he said, 'bolted?'

'Oh, no. But she didn't seem very well, she was rather upset about something: I gave her a week or two's rest.'

'Did she ask for it?'

'I'm afraid I insisted rather. We'll get somebody else for a week or two. I'm sorry, I hope you don't mind.'

'As you feel. Let's get somebody who *can* type. To tell you the truth, I am heartily sick of the back of that girl's neck.'

'But she really is nice,' said Emmeline.

'I dare say. *Has* she got nerves?' Looking distractedly round him for Markie's kettle, he tipped some cold water out of it into a flower-vase, pushed the stenographer's table away from the fire-place and began to make tea. 'Cups?' he said, coming back with the refilled kettle. Emmeline went across to the cupboard, where she remained rather shakily, eating sugar. The stenographer's pink handkerchief lay crumpled under her chair.

XVI

The same day, Gerda was giving a little party. In her Ovington Square drawing-room the cushions were early displaced by a dozen or so girl friends; she had even invited Tim Farquharson, as she feared to be short of men. Some of the young men were thrown cushions and, pulling their trousers up at the knee, sat gingerly on the floor, some stood about in couples, some leaned on the mantelpiece while, from pouffes or the sofa, their partners in talk stretched up powdered white necks. There was a yelp of talk and some laughter: the party seemed to be going well. Gerda's line as a hostess was of adorable inefficiency; with the air of a lost child she tottered among her guests, in one hand a glass dripping sherry, in the other a semi-opaque yellow drink in which the skewered cherry appeared as a threatening shadow. Wherever a glass was put down a small sticky ring stamped itself: she pounced on these rings with her handkerchief with little reproachful cries (no one advised her to wipe the underneaths of the glasses). She bewailed the quality of the cigarettes, the heat of the room, the (so far) absence of Gilbert; she upset a saucer of olives. She was followed around by a young man she had known in the Navy, who each time she succeeded in placing a drink with a guest smiled proudly, as though she had sold a raffle ticket, and gave her another drink off a tray. He put the tray down and stooped to collect the olives; his name was Frank and he felt rather shy and masculine.

The girl friends and young men, however, were only the froth of the party; several interesting people were present – an unhappy-looking prophetic man, a psychologist, Sir Mark Blanes, Gerda's *accoucheur*, two young authors of novels about marriage with their placid, motherly wives, a rather bilious-looking South African magnate and a racing motorist Gerda had met out at dinner and invited five weeks ahead. There was an old admiral, not very distinguished, who sat in a corner with one of the girl friends, and a young, haughty producer who could not bear to be talked to about his work. The interesting people did not mix very well: the South African was a pacifist and disliked admirals, the authors avoided each other, the psychologist gloomed at the *accoucheur* and was rude to an actress whom he suspected of trying to pick his brains: it was his profession to find people interesting but he did not do so out of hours. The girl friends, however, provided a sort of padding: intense in their interest, unflagging in their responsiveness, punctual with their laughter, they passed on the great to each other from palm to palm like scarabs, enjoyed themselves hugely and gave Gerda's little party a very great air of success, though the racing motorist refused utterly to be detached from one of the authors' motherly wives, then went away early.

Lady Waters arrived rather late. Sweeping her draperies over some girls and some cushions, displacing some young men, she sat down and gazed round the room with impartial interest. The psychologist, who had met her, hastily looked away. Slopping sherry about, Gerda paused.

'Where,' said her friend, 'is Gilbert?'

Gerda shook her head helplessly. 'Kept, he *says*, at the office.'

'Dear me, that *is* very unfortunate. However . . .'

'I'm struggling along,' said Gerda. 'Frank's a tremendous support. I should love Frank to meet you –' She looked round, but the sailor had disappeared. The sherry having given out, there was now nothing for it but more cocktails; no doubt the guests could be taught to like them in time. So Frank was splitting up ice on the back landing.

Lady Waters, however, already had Frank docketed. 'Frank,' she said. 'Yes, I should like to meet him . . . Ah, I see you've forgiven my poor Tim! Who is that over there with Sir Mark?'

'I call him my Onkel Pieter; he's a South African.'

'I should like to meet him; he has a powerful face.'

'You shall, you shall! I'll find somebody else for Sir Mark.'

'Isn't Emmeline here?'

'She swore she would come; I expect she's been kept at the office.'

'And where is Cecilia?'

Gerda said, pouting: 'I didn't think Mrs Summers would care for my little party – Lady Waters, *sherry*? Oh dear, oh dear, there's none left!'

'I should prefer some orange juice.'

'Oh *dear*, we have no oranges!'

'Never mind, Gerda: find me your Onkel Pieter.'

128

Gerda, dashing across the drawing-room, tore the startled South African from Sir Mark; they had been discussing the Channel tunnel, would it or would it not promote good international feeling? Stumbling over the feet of the young men, Gerda explained that her imaginary uncle must meet her imaginary aunt. The South African seemed to expect little pleasure from this consanguinity. Though touched, as a solitary man, by Gerda's innocent fantasy – in return for which he sent her boxes of bonbons, took her to the Coliseum with supper afterwards underground at the Trocadero and, on the way back, sometimes kissed her on the brow – she offended him more than he could explain by mistaking him for a Boer. Steered to a chair by Gerda he sat down, knees together, not prepared to compromise.

'I have been talking,' he said sternly, 'about the Channel tunnel.'

'But God must have meant us to be an island,' said Lady Waters, who had been tuning herself to a Non-conformist simplicity she considered suitable for South Africans.

Emmeline, coming upstairs, heard a loud sound of hammering; a chip of ice rebounded against a picture quite near her face. The young man in shirt sleeves put down the hammer. 'I say, I *am* so sorry!'

'Hard work,' said Emmeline, smiling.

'Stop – haven't we met before?'

'The stairs are so dark,' said Emmeline, uncertain.

'At a dance . . . Antibes? Malta?'

'I've never been there.'

The young man, determined to get this right, came round from behind the bar and faced the window.

'*Oh* . . .' said Emmeline. 'Yes, we have.'

'I knew your face seemed familiar!'

'You lent me some opera-glasses . . .'

'Did I? I don't remember.'

'They got broken.'

'At a hotel?'

'On a battleship.'

'Queer,' said the sailor, shaking his head. 'It's quite gone. Still, I knew I remembered your face . . . I'm so glad we met.' He picked up the hammer.

'So am I,' agreed Emmeline.

'Well . . .' said the sailor; he glanced at the hammer, then at the lump of ice wrapped in flannel. 'It melts so fast,' he said gloomily. 'If I left it a few minutes longer the whole thing would slip into the shaker. But Gerda is in a hurry.'

'Then I mustn't keep you.'

'Meet later, I hope.'

'I hope so,' said Emmeline, going on up. Through the open door of the drawing-room streamed heat, smoke and voices, with late sunshine strained through the Ovington Square trees: this was one of those little drawing-rooms with large windows into which you step out as on to a platform among the tree-tops. There seemed no room for Emmeline even to stand: guests by this time were being pressed out through the windows. Pink floppy lilies dropped pollen into the sticky glasses; cigarettes fumed to death in little jade saucers. Flushed couples shouted unheard to each other, lost to the world. Nonentities gathered impetus as the party proceeded, celebrities mounted like hilltops into a haze of kind ambiguity. Gerda pounced on Emmeline as she came in; she would be just the thing for Sir Mark, who, deprived of the South African, rather heavily hung fire against the mantelpiece.

'My Sir Mark,' said Gerda excitedly, 'you *must* meet him – Sir Mark, this is Miss Summers; she's so clever.'

Sir Mark, who did not detach himself easily from a topic, spoke to Emmeline of the Channel tunnel.

'Oh,' she said, 'but I am a shipping agent.'

'Ha-ha,' said Sir Mark. 'Hum. Very good, yes, ha-ha!' Thumbs under his lapels he looked, however, rather anxiously round the room. Conversation with someone at whose joke you have heartily laughed without seeing the point is apt to become precarious. Since his student days, this kindliness of Sir Mark had been landing him in difficulties. Emmeline, for her part, tried hard to collect her ideas – the sailor was still so young, as though preserved in her memory. 'Besides,' she said, 'I'm claustrophobic.'

'Tut –'

'Are you?'

'Not at all – But in this connection some lines occur to me.' Sir Mark paused, cleared his throat and looked at Emmeline impressively. ' "*This fortress built for nature by herself, Against infection and the hand of war.*" '

'You mean what about quarantine? What about the Navy?'

'No,' said Sir Mark.

'Do you read Shakespeare much?'

'I carry him in my car –' But at this point, unfortunately, Sir Mark was called urgently to the telephone. 'I am afraid,' he said, 'this may mean I shall have to leave you.' Evidently it did: he did not come back. The life-stream is not arrested for one moment: a slight hush fell on the circle, aware of Sir Mark's profession.

'How *are* you?' Tim Farquharson said at Emmeline's elbow.

'Very well.'

'One can't hear oneself speak, can one?'

'No.'

'Tired?' said Tim, solicitous. 'Look, lean on my bit of wall. Can I get you something? I'm afraid there's no more sherry, but there's some sticky stuff left.'

At this point several more people arrived, including Gilbert, and Frank came in with some more drinks and the shaker. 'Oh, Frank!' cried Gerda: she led him across the room. 'Lady Waters,' she said, 'here's Frank!' Frank put down the tray and shook hands with Lady Waters: a very young, shy sailor. Gilbert, having apologized his way round the room, saying: 'Better late than never,' to the confusion of several people who had no idea who he was, obliterated himself among the girl friends, who were sorry for him. They were sorry for Gerda also and thought what a pity it all was.

'Who's Frank?' said Tim to Emmeline.

'He's a sailor.'

'Do you think perhaps he is Gerda's past?'

'Why?' said Emmeline.

'He seems so attached to her. And so much more the type one would have expected Gerda to marry – not that he's not very nice.'

'I've met him before,' said Emmeline. But Tim did not hear, the noise had become appalling. 'I wonder,' she said, looking anxiously round, 'if I could go home?'

'But you've only just come.'

'I know, that was why I was wondering.'

'*Tired?*' said Tim again: it seemed such a pity. She *was* very tired, the day with its curve of experience – Markie, Miss Tripp, the sailor, had been very long. Tim said: 'I wanted so much to talk to you.'

'I can't talk to anyone here –'

'Emmeline,' wailed Gerda, 'you're not going? My dear, you've only just come – oh, stop, Frank: just a minute – Don't go, Emmeline: Gilbert's just brought some sherry: he's trying to find the corkscrew.'

'Alas –' said Emmeline, slipping by inches away. Tim came after her. 'Look here, let me get you a taxi, perhaps we might both –'

'Thank you so much, I've got my car here.'

This seemed a pity, also. Tim, going crabwise downstairs beside Emmeline, went on: 'I'm afraid I must have been seeming like nothing on earth when we last met. I'm afraid I must have bored you fearfully. But ever since then, in a kind of way –'

'– Here is my car,' said Emmeline.

When Cecilia's lunch-party had gone, she stood with her hands to her head looking round the drawing-room. When they had quite gone she gave up enacting fatigue, shook out the curtains and tipped the ash-trays into the grate behind the firescreen. From now on, the afternoon was her own: no one else would be coming. Though she had held this out to herself as a pleasure, it was as though vaguely searching for something that had slipped away that she looked round at the books on the table, her own face in the glass ... The gold clock resumed its light little dialogue with the silence; she heard a movement like wind, the trees coming alive, in the shaded garden to which the steps running down from the window invited her cheerfully: there was a chair out under the plane. But she did not go out; the bright emptiness of this room with its smile fading became, brought up to the microscope of her nerves, a living tissue of shadows and little insistent sounds: the clock and the trees outside, a blind-cord tapping, her own dress rubbing against the sofa-back as she turned to listen.

The servants locked the door below and went out to a wedding. Then there was silence: in the long pause like a frozen gesture, in which not a petal fell, an arc of emptiness spanned Cecilia's horizon: she was so seldom alone. One of those small waves of country silence broke over London: she heard no traffic down in the Abbey Road. As though on a bare high hill from which for miles all round you can see no one approaching, she awaited herself with that constant question: what to do next?

The telephone's positive silence, the mirrors reflecting her pacing and pausing figure, began to oppress Cecilia, who left the drawing-room and went upstairs. She looked into Emmeline's room, which, with counterpane drawn up over the pillow, looked shrouded, as though no one slept here now. A friend's room with its air of guarding a final secret is like a death-chamber; here, still unknown, the sleeper seems many times to have died. Did Emmeline still see trains rushing across the ceiling, or was there a face now? Did colourless restless wishes touch the edge of her consciousness? Women are too like each other and far too different. Cecilia, not going in, leant against the doorway trying to read the name of a book by the bed, and thought: 'She is not my lover; she's not my child.'

Though the idea of parting from Emmeline could seem intolerable there was not much more, it occurred to Cecilia, than the idea of company in her company. Saying: 'I live with Emmeline,' she might paint for ignorant eyes, and even dazzle herself for a moment with a tempting picture of intimacy. But she lent herself to a fiction in which she did not believe; for she lived with nobody.

Nobody waited for her at the door of her own bedroom. Cecilia went in, changed a necklace and turned to face Henry's photograph. He had never seen Oudenarde Road; he and she from their end of London had not explored this neighbourhood slipping downhill: he had not known when he died that this house existed and that a shadowy part of his life would continue here. His ignorance made, for the moment, the room ghostly. Propped up in a frame on a mantelpiece against which he had never leaned, over a hearth before which he had not reflected – for like Emmeline Henry had been a great stander and leaner – he looked across at a bed in which he had never slept. Yet into these pillows Cecilia – her emotions becoming with solitude and the years ever more pointed and self-regarding – shed those tears of chagrin Henry had known so well. Before this looking-glass framed in its lights Cecilia, expectant, now hooked her own dress for parties with no one to touch a ruffle or smile at her in the glass. She nightly returned to this mirror, these pillows, her sense of being a far too general gift to the world: a rose in the public gardens, a novel for any subscriber to take out.

She wished it were midnight, but it was four o'clock. Nothing else paused; elsewhere London was humming. She thought: 'I will not telephone; I will not look to see if the post has come.' Her life became visible in the hour like water poured into a glass; momentarily no one cast a shadow, momentarily not a bell rang. Slipping off her rings one by one, she heard each clink on the table-top. The glass-topped table, flounced like a shepherdess, with tapering stoppered bottles, attendants to vanity, and Venetian powder bowl, was in itself pretty: she exclaimed in thought: Mine, but nothing replied: Cecilia. In the cupboards her dresses hung bosom to bosom coldly, as though they had never been worn. She ran down like a clock whose hands falter and point for too long at one hour and minute: the clock stops dead. She dissolved like breath on a mirror and trailed away like an echo when nobody speaks again . . . She thought of Henry, of Julian,

The telephone rang.

Cecilia plugged in her bedside telephone but did not immediately answer: she stood listening. The usual music became discordant – at once she felt how precious had been her solitude, that silence throughout her house with its archways and cool twisting stairs. She thought of her gay calm drawing-room with leisure written all over it, of those books to invite her leisure; how her bed and Emmeline's had only a wall between. She felt herself torn from something . . . Meanwhile, the stranger clamoured.

'Yes?' said Cecilia. 'Oh yes? . . . Do you? . . . am I? . . . how nice . . . Shall we really? Very well, Tuesday week, eight o'clock. No, I'm alone, so happy: you know I am always happy alone.'

XVII

Emmeline met Markie at Croydon: he was so very late she feared he would miss the plane. In her thin grey coat and skirt she sat waiting under the skylight on that sexagonal seat round the little pharos of clocks. A huge blue June day filled the aerodrome and reflected itself in the hall: she heard a great hum from the waiting plane hungry for flight. Such an exalting idea of speed possessed Emmeline that she could hardly sit still and longed to pace to and fro – but that would annoy Markie who did not like to be made to feel late. At about twenty to one he fell out of a taxi and hurried towards her with papers under his arm.

At the plane tilted up on its tail in a vast cement space like a dancing-floor, Markie, who had not yet flown, glanced a trifle suspiciously: blown sideways by the propellers Emmeline gaily swung herself in ahead. Walking uphill into the front car they became encased in a roaring hum, a vibration that shook the eardrums and, for some minutes while he arranged himself grimly, curdled his every thought: that summer, planes were not silent. Emmeline, intimating by gestures that for purposes of discomfort she had no stomach, took the place opposite him, facing back to the wings: they had a little table between. She was touched to discover that Markie had brought the *Tatler*, and wondered why.

The roar intensified, there was an acceleration of movement about the aerodrome as though they were about to be shot out of a gun; blocks were pulled clear and they taxied forward at high speed, apparently to the coast. For Markie the earth was good enough, he could have asked no better; he observed, however, from Emmeline's face of delight that something had happened: earth had slipped from their wheels that, spinning, rushed up the air. They were off. Dipping, balancing, with a complete lack of impetus and a modest assurance the plane returned to her element over the unconcerned earth: an immense sense of ordinariness established itself in the car and Markie, having compelled the waiter to understand they would want two brandies, opened a rather dull report.

Her eyes kept imploring him to look down and enjoy Surrey.

Surrey and Kent looked flatter and, like something with which one has ceased to have any relationship, noticeably less interesting – he had never liked either much. The grass, lawns and meadows, poorer in texture than he expected, looked like a rubbed billiard cloth. But to Emmeline some quite new plan of life, forgotten between flight and flight, seemed once more to reveal itself: she sat gazing down with intensity at the lay-out of gardens. No noise, no glass, no upholstery boxed her up from the extraordinary: as they smoothly mounted and throbbed through the shining element she watched trees and fields in the blue June haze take on that immaterial loveliness, that foreign and clear intensity one expects of the sky.

Markie looked up at her from the report a shade sternly; she pulled the *Tatler* towards her and looked at actresses. It was, however, impossible to stay stern with Emmeline, though she might sit among rows of indifferent business men looking wrapt and silly. Her hat off, her hair caught light from the sky all round; her face with its glow of childish delight softened to tenderness when she looked his way. His senses recovering from a numbness that had spread from the ear-drums began to take in pleasure; some idea of adventure asserted itself through his waking faculties: she was lovely and opposite him, they were flying to Paris. He began to discount hearing, to be aware of noise as sensible, visible, inimical only when one attempted speech, as vibration whenever the finger-tips touched an object, vibration of shadows and fringes of the silk curtains against the shining air. Inside, incredibly shadowy in a world of light, catching the full summer sun on its wings and fuselage and where the propellers made colourless discs of speed, the plane evenly passed to the coast, Kent drawn liquidly under it like a river.

Emmeline gave up the earth, but Markie, looking up two or three times from the report, found that though leaning back she was still smiling. Distracted, he pulled the *Tatler* towards him and wrote on the margin: '*What is the matter?*'

Taking the pencil, Emmeline wrote back: '*Happy,*' and twisted the *Tatler* round. Markie implied that, if *that* had been all it was, so, for the matter of that, was he. A few minutes later he was once more interrupted by Emmeline's pushing towards him, with a faintly anxious expression, another page of the *Tatler*, with: '*What is the French for "interplay"?*' He jotted down some alternatives: she considered them. Evidently the Serbs had begun, if not to oppress her, at least to take up the foreground; which was enough to make

Markie put the report down, pick up the pencil and wonder what to write next. Close in the strong light and distant in roaring silence her face appeared transparent; watching the thoughts come up like shadows behind it he thought of the Scottish queen's ill-fated delicate throat, down which, says a chronicler, red wine was seen to run as she drank.

She laughed and wrote suddenly: '*The Marseillaise makes Cecilia weep.*' He jotted with emphasis at the edge of a column: '*Extreme sensibility.*'

'*Nice.*'

'*In its place.*'

Emmeline seemed to think this lacked point; instead of replying she picked up the *Tatler* and began to look through, with an earnestness that was annoying, some Ascot groups which delighted her: she kept pointing willowy lacy ladies out with her thumb. Leaving her with the paper he tore a leaf from his pocket book, bit his pencil and for a moment paused.

'*Can't be true,*' he wrote. '*Can't believe we're together 2 whole days. You* ARE *nice to me.*'

Emmeline looked up from the paper, expression saying so much that there seemed little to add. She wrote back, however, '*There are those 2 Serbs.*'

Markie, smiling, crumpled one leaf and tore out another. The manner of this correspondence began to appeal to him: deliberation unknown in speaking, boldness quite unrebuked by its own vibrations and, free of that veil of uncertainty and oblivion that falls on the posted letter, the repercussions upon her of all he said. The indiscretions of letter-writing, the intimacies of speech were at once his.

While he pondered, while he sat writing idly and slowly, a bright white wave broke on their window: they cut through a cloud. Emmeline once more looked down; the serrated gold coast-line and creeping line of the sea were verifying the atlas. An intenser green blue, opaque with its own colour, showed far down in a sparkling glassiness their tiny cruciform shadow: they were over the sea. Very white cumulus clouds afloat like unperilous ice-bergs along a line of blue ether were their companions: over France more glittered, aerial dazzling cliffs. Like islands, each indented and charactered by their crumbling shadows, the clouds round the plane invited the mounting foot, and though the plane still held among all these distracting companions her forward course, one had the sensation less of direct and purposeful transit than of a pleasure-cruise through this archipelago of the cloud-line, over shadowless depths.

Enchanted, returning her eyes for a moment, Emmeline found his note.

'Or aren't you? These two days must be intolerable or perfect. You must know what I want: all I want. If I COULD *marry, it would be you. I don't know if you know what this means. I didn't think this could happen. For God's sake, be kind to me. Understand?'*

When at last, raising her eyes from the paper she looked his way, he was no longer waiting. Turned sideways, he looked at the air as though the note were forgotten. Perhaps he hoped little, perhaps he was certain of her. Understanding more sharply all she had understood weeks ago, uncertain less what than how to reply, she bent her head and began to draw patterns vaguely on the back of his note. Feeling of all kinds had stolen from her in this cold new reality of the cloudscape; conscious of the remoteness and uneagerness of his attitude she felt he, too, had written what he had written not on impulse, in urgency, but in a momentary coldness and clearness of feeling that was showing him where they stood. Stayed by this feeling of unimmediacy she reviewed one by one the incidents of their friendship, each distinct from the other as cloud from cloud but linked by her sense of something increasing and mounting and, like the clouds, bearing in on her by their succession and changing nature how fast and strongly, though never whither, they moved. She was embarked, they were embarked together, no stop was possible; she could now turn back only by some unforeseen and violent deflection – by which her exact idea of personal honour became imperilled – from their set course. She could not see at what point the issue became apparent, from what point she was committed: committed, however, she felt.

Markie started, took back the paper and added hurriedly, cross-wise: *'We could not marry.'* Returning the note he paused, so clearly waiting for her to answer that with an odd smile she wrote: *'Let us talk in Paris.'*

'No more to say.'

They looked at each other, and though their eyes never met without, on her part, a quick start of something more than emotion, the length and serious quality of this look – in which consideration, on her side gentle, on his searching, still played more part than feeling – pointed a pause in which both felt something gained or lost, though neither, perhaps, knew which. The aeroplane, mounting a little, crossed the pale French coast of dunes stained by shadows and forests; far off they saw the hazy mouth of an estuary, a river spanned further up by a bridge or shadow. Soon France was mapped out in pink fields, in pale and dark green fields; unlike England, more reasonable and distinct.

The roads – he and she looked down with a distant sense of arrival – the railways were empty; the buildings cut out and stuck up so precisely seemed glued to the scene. Earth had lost some of its magic; the light was perhaps harder – or was this France? The soil she loved, the civilization he honoured showed over-clear and metallic. Forests, however, with deep straight roads came back to reclaim the heart, and a cavalry school in a spreading pattern of chestnuts: below a horizon that seemed quite clear of illusion but where clouds in shadow still built embattled cities, Beauvais cathedral hung in a gauze of smoke. Recalling Markie's most recent journey she smiled and wrote on the *Tatler*: '*You always travel with Summerses.*'

Soon after the Oise, Le Bourget surprised them before they had thought of Paris. Markie's fingers tightened, blood roared in ears as the plane with engines shut off, with a frightening cessation of sound plunged downward in that arrival that always appears disastrous. Tipped on one wing, they appeared to spin over Le Bourget in indecision; a glaring plan of the suburb tilted and reeled; now roofless buildings gaped up at them; no one, however, looked up. Earth rejoined the wheels quietly and they raced round the bleached aerodrome in a whirr of arrival. Then, grasping their small baggage, tipped like grain from a shovel, they all stepped, incredulous, out of the quivering plane.

All round Le Bourget, France seemed to be flying her flags of colour. Emmeline waving good-bye to the pilot saw flowering mustard fields stretch to the sky; the hangars were scarlet with placards; the hotel flapped with striped awnings; from under the gaudy umbrellas of cafés old men, impassive, observed the arrival; little boys swung on the fence. It all looked very merry and amateur. Over all hung the bright sky, the subsiding wind of their speed. Only the grey-painted iron of French officialdom announced the *douane*. In there between two airy doorways they submitted their suitcases; Markie, stretching gratefully, lighted a cigarette. 'Well, here we are,' he said. There they were.

'What next?'

'I'm going to telephone to the Serbs.'

'Oh no, you're not,' said Markie. 'Not just yet.'

Paris, approached by its macabre north, wore its usual first air of being not quite Paris, or more like Paris than one foresaw. After hours of speed, its toppling grey immobility was impressive. Here were those façades brittle with balconies, awnings shedding hot dusk, chairs alert in the cafés and pavements running with life that crowd the eye in a moment and numb the spirit . . . Emmeline liked the Hôtel de Padoue in the Boulevard Raspail: Markie said this would suit him, too. As they shot through the more elegant quarters towards the river, some high white form of a fountain or fretted gloom of the chestnuts looked solider than the buildings, which creamy-grey in the sunshine were frail as plaster: odd echoes and silences ran along the arcades. The streets had been watered, the trees were already rusty and stale with summer . . . Oppressed by plunging once more in this shadowy network when she had been seeing lately so clear a plan, perplexed by some new view of life that, not quite her own, lent double strangeness to everything, Emmeline sat silently in the taxi beside Markie. They crossed the river and swerved up the left bank to their hotel.

Their rooms looked out at the back, on courtyards and unfinished buildings. The afternoon with its sense of suspended crisis – an afternoon of stretched moments, as might be one's last day on earth when fear and all sense of farewell had alike departed and only that very brief transit remained ahead – spaced itself out into pauses and hurried movement throughout the city again and again revisited but never fully known. From the hotel bureau Emmeline telephoned to the Serbs; they were affable, could not immediately see her but made an appointment for very distant tomorrow, when, to her surprise, they asked her, with her friend, to lunch . . . She and Markie found themselves in that most provincial and shady quarter of Paris, looking through gates at the Observatoire with its air of perpetual autumn: later they strolled down the gardens towards the Luxembourg. They talked of the Cirque d'Hiver, regretting it was not open, and wondered where they should dine.

'I suppose you might say,' he said, as they both sat down near the Luxembourg, 'that I shouldn't have come.'

'No,' she said. 'Why?'

'Then what do you think?'

'I don't know.'

Her attitude even said: 'Must I think at all?' as though, most alive in the heat and shade of the tree, she were reprieved from living. She spread out her fingers along the hot seat: he looked from her hand past her face up into the branches. An intense sense of being forced so close to the other as to be invisible, a fusion of both their senses in burning shadow obscured for the two, as they sat here, the staring quivering city, making remote for Markie a picture he must believe for always imprinted: Emmeline in her white dress watery with green shadow looking down at his hand approaching her hand – for Emmeline, Markie looking her way in an instant of angry extinction as though he would drown. A slackening of tension, the gentleness of the bemused afternoon – in which like someone who has lost his memory he was tentative and dependent and she, like someone remembering everything, overcome – carried them on to night with the smoothness of water, quickening to the fall's brink with a glassy face.

Past midnight, some few voices, or sounds with metallic echoes, dropped into the extraordinary silence behind the hotel.

XVIII

That Sunday evening Markie sat waiting for Emmeline on a gold wicker settee, facing the lift gates, in the vestibule of the Hôtel de Padoue. She had gone up for a pair of fresh gloves and a letter to post and would be only a moment, she said: she had not come down again. Mobility was not present in Markie's expression and attitude; impatience had burnt itself out to a dull smoulder. His eyes in a kind of extinction, blank of their evidence of an intelligence ravenous and satirical, fixed a shimmering point in the black-and-white vestibule tiles: passers-by stepped knee-deep into their cold light. Travelling at high velocity he had struck something – her absence – head on, and was not so much shattered as in a dull recoil. His mouth that Cecilia distrusted – too mobile, greedy, never unguarded even in its repose – sagged in lines of passivity. Something nonplussed in his attitude might have commended itself to the facile sympathy: a little checked Napoleon sunk into his flesh. He was tired from reading the unexpectedly difficult score of the day. In a stupor beyond impatience he sat waiting for Emmeline.

Sliding heavily in its grooves the lift came down twice, twice the gates clicked open: there was no Emmeline. She might have melted in some corridor of their hotel, her bodily vanishing would, to the nascent uneasiness underlying his reason, hardly have been incredible; for he had been oppressed since last night by sensations of having been overshot, of having, in some final soaring flight of her exaltation, been outdistanced: as though a bird whose heart one moment one could feel beating has escaped from between the hands. The passionless entirety of her surrender, the volition of her entire wish to be his had sent her a good way past him: involuntarily, the manner of her abandonment had avenged her innocence. As though she were conscious of her unwilling departure, of a disparity isolating for him in their two expressions of passion, he had read in her look today a kind of entreating gentleness. Following him with eyes that saw at once nothing and too much, she had seemed unwilling to be a moment apart from him: her finger-tips in the palm of his hand, in which every swerve and jar of the taxi became recorded, they had motored to Neuilly this morning to lunch with the Serbs.

They had lunched with the Serbs in a close little room with glass doors hot with sunshine. An urbane animation increased as their hosts refilled the pink wine glasses. Mme Scherbatskoff, French wife of one of the Serbs, laughed cautiously, glancing all ways and touching her steel necklace. Emmeline, pale but now very much the woman of business, swayed a little way like a reed in this current of sociability, but remained always rooted: Markie's respect increased. Over a dish of green figs their two notions of 'interplay' had been determined: the smoke of rich cigarettes scrawled the terms of the *entente* above the lunch-table. After lunch Markie, sitting with Mme Scherbatskoff in an arbour at the end of the villa garden, embarked rather wearily on a conversation at which they were both adept, while Emmeline indoors concluded her business with the two partners. She came out smiling – everything promised well – and walked down the red gravel path to the arbour with the two dark young men. There was a quiver of rockeries and hot gravel, burnt petrol hung over the privet and perfume from Mme Scherbatskoff's abundant corsage. They said good-bye, got a taxi and Markie and Emmeline drove out through the Bois to St Cloud.

The Bois with tall hemlock meeting the trees against a glitter of lake had been cool and glady: at St Cloud urbanity still had a ring round them. Versailles, St Germain would have been much the same. From the balustrades, from the stone rims of pools where there were no fountains heat quivered up; they looked over at tanks of opaque green water, an unpierceable wall of lime-trees (one had no sense of an eminence), back up the steps at the long perspective of statues and pollarded chestnuts slate-grey with summer. The terrace and hidden alleys were populous as a boulevard: this was a sultrily-bright Paris Sunday of Maupassant's, dramas behind the leaves. Voices made a sharp network throughout the forest, in which there was no silence. Round the chalets, parties sipped syrups; lovers sat somnolent in the shade: up the steep slope inlaid with flower-beds crowds stared out citywards from the high-up terrace. Distant, this fine hot Sunday, by less than three hours of airy transit, at Richmond, Kew, Hampton Court, love, family life, re-creation were being conducted, in a manner perhaps less steely and less accomplished but much the same. Round Paris and far to the south, empty France spread her plan of baked plains and highways, treed river-valleys and splintery limestone hills. West of London, slopes rushing with cars diluted in sunshine: the Farraways hedge arched its view of an older summer, the lime showered shadow on to a lawn with Cecilia sitting: from the air you would look at chimneys that reeled as you flew . . . Emmeline asked herself if this distended present, this oppressive contraction of space would be properties of air-mindedness. Emmeline, who had sent so many clients flying that her Bloomsbury offices seemed to radiate speed, now stood still with her hand on the bark of a tree in St Cloud – for they had gone a short way up an avenue – bark whose actual roughness blurred to the touch at the thought of so many forests, and longed to stand still always. She longed suddenly to be fixed, to enjoy an apparent stillness, to watch even an hour complete round one object its little changes of light, to see out the little and greater cycles of day and season in one place, beloved, familiar, to watch shadows move round one garden, to know the same trees in spring and autumn and in their winter forms.

'This is frightful,' said Markie, 'let's go on somewhere else.'

But Emmeline, very pale, leaning against the chestnut, said: 'I don't mind where we are so long as we *stay* where we are.'

Markie, seeing how tired she was, with a lover's tenderness and self-reproach, slipped a hand under her elbow. 'Come along,' he said gently.

'Where?'

'Well, let's sit down somewhere.'

Emmeline walked slowly beside him. There seemed to be nowhere to sit; other couples were everywhere – he could have no idea how little she cared. 'This is a wretched place,' he said angrily, 'to have brought you.'

'There wasn't anywhere else.'

Emmeline – hearing footsteps everywhere on the baked slippery grass, and leaves tearing as couples pushed through the undergrowth, seeing through the haze of myopia the shadowy hot-green forest – looked round her vaguely as though she did not know where she was, though a thought may have crossed her mind: had their triumphant cool flight been simply for this? Markie, reading into her look distress and embarrassment, felt that today of all days he should not have brought her here. The forest humming with pleasure translated itself for his anguished senses into a saturnalia; distraught with the agitations of a vicarious delicacy he hurried

Emmeline on, drawing her, with a hand still under her elbow, up avenue after avenue, wheeling her angrily round where perspectives met. They described, in their pursuit of a solitude always painted ahead, a deceptive mirage of space between further tree-trunks, a fairly wide circle, bringing them back to the terrace.

She said faintly, '*Where* are we going?'

'Back.'

'But we've only just come.'

'You know you're hating this place.'

'I'm not; I haven't had time. I just hate moving.'

'Then come somewhere quiet.'

'We're in Paris,' said Emmeline reasonably. Looking hard at her, he longed to suggest they should go back to their hotel, but did not know how she would take this. Two little girls, passing, looked curiously at the islanders with their hard bright eyes. Markie, characteristically forgetting the Serbs, felt their presence in Paris, the entire city and its environment to be his responsibility: overrating the afternoon's vulgarity and confusion he wondered she did not hate him for his imperfect control of circumstance. Sliding his fingers along her arm, he expressed penitence. Passion, with Markie, went in curves of caprice: under the fairly imposing surface of his masculinity there whirled currents of instability, of exactingness, of an incapacity to be satisfied, of whose ravages on serenity he was not aware: missing repose vaguely he made it impossible . . . Leaning on the balustrade, they looked over the tops of the limes at a hazy glare coming up from the Seine and Paris. All day the violent humility of his manner had been surprising Emmeline, who did not know what she expected, but not this. Her sense of the day was her sense of him: she felt bound to him closely but did not know where they were.

When they got back from St Cloud, about five o'clock, the sun was off their hotel, which was cool and dark again: shutters letting in slats of light were across the windows. They parted mutely; Emmeline had a bath, then wrote Peter a full account of the Serbs: she would not see him tomorrow, for now she and Markie were staying till Monday night. Markie rang for drinks to be brought up, drank, and recovered himself: he discovered he had been feeling guilty and nervous. Having sat for a time with no collar, looking through his glass filled and refilled at the stripy dusk of his room in which the ice slowly melted, he reflected that these things were, as he had once said to Emmeline, after all quite usual: he went down the passage and tapped on Emmeline's door. No answer; she must still be in her bath. Or possibly she was asleep; he tried the door-handle thoughtfully, thought better of it and returned to stretch out again on his hard green sofa . . . He woke up to find Emmeline in the doorway, in black and white, very fresh again: ready, she said, to go out. But as they stepped from the lift she had frowned at her gloves, which had dirty finger-tips: they were the wrong gloves, she said, and she had forgotten that very important letter to Peter Lewis. So she had disappeared again, like Eurydice: knowledgeable, the concierge put somebody else into their waiting taxi. Markie, unused to going about with a woman on these terms, had 'yet to learn that a woman who seems to be ready early is never ready.

They would be late going out: already beyond the glass doors a hot after-light filled the boulevard: shadowy trams crashed by . . . Markie shut his eyes, sick of the vestibule pavement which repeated itself on his eyelids in red and yellow. 'You've been *hours*,' he said, hearing her step at last.

Emmeline, smiling, gave in the key of her room to the concierge. Turning, she said: 'Darling . . .' her voice quite different and startled. In the glimpse she had had of him through the lift gates – to no other eyes very beautiful, eyes shut, slumping down in his chair without the least vestige of expectation – the fact of their being lovers had come close to her. Drawing her long fresh gloves up her wrists she smiled at him, dazzled and dazzling. Collecting himself, he stood up to face the innocence and entire confidence of her look. He was amazed, the uneasy moralist in him staggered to see her emerge in such radiant assurance from the distant and rather misty gentleness of the day. He could not account for her radiance, which nearly shocked him. The very fine conscience is, however, its own law; knowing no wrong, only what is repugnant.

The concierge, smiling, brought up another taxi. Emmeline, who had preserved throughout, with regard to their plans, her independence of attitude – for was she not here on business? – said: 'Where shall we dine?' Markie told her.

'Half the evening's gone,' he complained, as the taxi plunged down the boulevard.

'But you were asleep,' said Emmeline. 'I looked in.'

'It's been sheer waste.'

'I forgot to say anything to the lift boy, so he took me right up to the top. When I found where I was he had gone, so I walked down again: it took years.'

'Why not ring for the little beast?'

'One felt so silly. And then the chambermaid kept me: she was doing my room.'

'So you had quite a chat?'

'It was difficult not to talk. She hoped we're enjoying Paris: she thinks you're my husband – how pleased servants always are that one should be married. She asked if we'd been up the Eiffel Tower; I said no.'

Swerving violently at a corner, the taxi flung Emmeline against Markie, then out of his arms again. 'I like Paris taxis,' she said, holding on to the window-frame, 'they're like the Last Ride To-gether – Do you remember your cook that night? How annoyed you were.'

'One never knew where one was with you.'

'You made me feel rather a disappointment – Markie, *you* don't ever think I'm inhuman?'

He assured her she was not, with fervour: some tenebrous fear seemed to let her go. How much anxiety for this assurance had marked her surrender he had not the wit to inquire. Relaxing, Emmeline said: 'It feels funny, telling you everything that I do. Such little things get important.'

'You lead such a funny life, like a cat; always coming and going.'

'Don't all women?'

'*I* don't know: do they?'

'I don't know,' She looked out of the window at Paris, blurred tourist's Paris in which a few branches and figures were cut out distinctly on the pink-violet evening and brassy long lights began to blink in the cafés, catching the syphons and gilding the tired trees: everyone moved in a fever or feverishly stood still.

'Just how much,' he said, 'do you tell Cecilia?'

More than curiosity may have prompted the question. Emmeline turned in surprise. 'Oh . . .' she said, considering. 'She is so busy; we know each other so well. I don't think we say much – she knows, of course, that you're here in Paris.'

'Oh, she *does*?' said Markie.

His tremendous air of concern – for he took a rather low view of Cecilia, suspecting her of suspicion and worldly vigilance – im-pressed Emmeline in spite of herself. Rather anxiously, she went over that doorstep talk with Cecilia, who had certainly seemed annoyed but not really concerned. Cecilia had said with some force, she thought Markie's presence in Paris unnecessary and foolish. Would there not be the Serbs? And in the evenings two or three of Cecilia's friends, to whom she had written, would be expecting Emmeline – Emmeline had her own friends, but Cecilia did not think them as nice; they lived wretchedly and might not offer Emmeline dinner.

A slight chill passed over Emmeline, leaning closer to Markie who had stripped off her glove to turn over and kiss her hand. She felt untrue to Cecilia: an unspoken good faith, based on some understanding that life must not be allowed to pass out of a certain compass, existed between them and was not lightly to be abused. Upon the extravagances of Cecilia's behaviour something which seemed to be most of all her regard for Emmeline exerted a strong backward pull. Their alliance remained, on Cecilia's side certainly, largely defensive: Henry's death had been something ravaging, disproportionate; around Oudenarde Road a kind of pale was put up against one kind of emotion: nothing on that scale was to occur again. In their life together, as in a quiet marriage, Emmeline and Cecilia, inquiring less and less, each affectionately confronted the other's portrait of her own painting, finding it near enough to reality. It is this domestic confidence, this happy and willing ignorance of another heart that is most quick to suffer and least deserves betrayal. Emmeline, looking across the Channel, suddenly felt a stranger in her own home, a home she had perhaps never fully inhabited. Her new soaring confidence faltered, she dropped nearer the earth. Feeling how Cecilia's idea of her must persist, unchangeable as a ghost, that idea of an Emmeline like a cat, disengaged and placid, she knew she would not have the heart to say: 'That was never me'; and pain began to attend this birth in her of the woman. The new power, momentarily not bearing her up, became like wings dragging, a heaviness at the shoulders.

Looking down at her hand in Markie's she said: 'Don't let's talk about her.'

'*I* don't want to.'

'I love you so much,' she said, withdrawing her hand to steady herself, a little away from him, against the side of the taxi. Markie – either in protest at her withdrawal or because she deprived him of words – looked at her oddly, a shade satirically. These rare declarations of Emmeline's – preceded always by just such a little unconscious gesture of independence, as though she wished when she spoke to be most her own – had an effect on him that was silencing and disturbing: they had the frightening relevance of an indiscretion or something said unawares. He did not know how much he had come to rely in feeling on the enmity of the will, or how much he had counted in her on an alarmed reaction, on having her most his own in that precious sense of delinquency lovers enjoy. It was in the idea of outrage, of those tender agonies of the conscience, that he was most a voluptuary: the idea of guilt so enflamed him that the form surrendered in innocence seemed as cold as marble.

Their taxi steered between two lorries, bumped on an island and spun just clear of a bus. Emmeline laughed, seeing Paris spin round, and blinked at the crash of light. Markie stiffened and swore: his nerves were never too good.

'They're always like this,' she said, placid.

'Dagoes,' said Markie, no fatalist.

'Oh well, if one's killed one's killed.'

Markie was going to say he should mind very much, but at this point, fortunately, with a jerk that wrenched at its vitals the taxi drew up at Foyot's.

Parties of tourists strolled at the foot of the Sacré Coeur that was blanched with moonlight, or stood looking over the city. Markie and Emmeline mounted the last flight of steps: he was surprised to find himself right up here. Emmeline, who had been perhaps faintly tiresome, would not come round Paris with Markie, who knew indoor intimate Paris so well, and rejected firmly the evening he had designed for her: though she agreed that it might be amusing she feared that it might be stuffy. Though Markie could hardly regret a few naïve pleasures, he was amazed to find himself here in the moonlit dust. She liked the night air, she had said. 'Well, here you have it,' said Markie, puffing indignantly at the head of the steps.

Emmeline could not help glancing professionally at the tourists, wondering whose they were, if they were satisfied, whether in arranging to view the city of sins from this eminence they had contracted for a full moon. Their chars-à-bancs waited at the foot of the steps.

Moonlight fell glacial, sinister, Doréesque on the roofs of the city and caught a curve of the Seine. The breath of Paris came up chilled by the hour. It was nearly midnight: on this mean bare terrace one was served up cold to the moon. You could have seen a bird, but there were no birds, in the glassy sky.

'I'm so happy,' she said. 'I wish this were for ever.'

Markie, alarmed by the first approach of something he had been dreading, said quickly: 'It wouldn't last.'

'No. But we've got tonight and another day.'

'But you wouldn't have liked to marry me, would you?' he said, as though this were years from now and the whole thing over.

'I don't expect so,' said Emmeline, looking his way uncertainly in the moonlight.

'It would be a fiasco,' he went on, rather excitedly. 'I'm not the sort of person anybody could marry, much less you. You'd be disappointed: I couldn't bear that.'

'I wonder.'

'You delude yourself,' he said ungently. 'I couldn't live with you: point blank, Emmeline, I don't want to. I should feel myself dropping to pieces before your eyes.'

'That's as you feel,' she said, helpless.

'And also: what an impossible end for *you*!'

'But how am I to end?'

'I've no idea,' he said, with that nervous coldness she dreaded.

'But people do seem to marry.'

'Not people like you and me.'

'I should get in your way?' she suggested, trying to understand.

'Not much more, I dare say, than I should in yours. It would be impossible.'

'But if we love each other – this always parting, this always going away!'

Taking her arm rather roughly he steered Emmeline clear of a party of trippers: she spoke distinctly and might have been overheard. Frowning at her in the moonlight with some conviction – for he felt he was taking, if an ungentle, the honest way – he repeated: 'I couldn't live with you: it's impossible.'

Her clearness of mind deserted her; she could only feel he was angry. 'But what am I? What have I done?'

'Do you *want* to be married?'

'No –' she cried, terrified. Distracted by her short sight that could keep no count of his movements, the moonlight, the staring church and gaudy unreal scene, she made a bewildered gesture, like a deserted woman's. The church – for Markie an oppressive monument to futility – towered up high and frosty. An idea of the stored-up darkness of its interior – only apart from them by a door and curtain – stale gilt, cold incense and peering images in the perpetual scarlet of hanging lamps, created for Markie a kind of suction, setting up in him a nervous frenzy unlike the coldness of disbelief. The edge of his mind was restless with superstition: like natives before the solid advance of imperial forces, aspiration, feeling, all sense of the immaterial had retreated in him before reason to some craggy hinterland where, having made no terms with the conqueror, they were submitted to no control and remained a menace. Like savages coming to town on a fair day to skip and chaffer, travestying their character in strange antics, creating by their very presence a saturnalia in which the conqueror may unbend, feeling crept out in him from some unmapped region. His brain held his smallish, over-clear view of life in its rigid circle.

Emmeline could not bear him to be unhappy. She took his arm gently, glad to renew some contact. 'Never mind,' she said. 'Why are we talking? We're so happy. You make me so happy I don't know what to do.'

'Of course: we're in love, aren't we?'

Emmeline nodded. 'Now let's come away from here.'

'I'm horrible to you, angel!'

'No.'

'But you make me anxious: I don't think you know what you're doing.'

'I'll never be sorry.'

'We waste time,' he said passionately, as though for the first time seeing her, 'we waste time.'

The terrace was empty, but they did not wait to enjoy their solitude. As they went down the steps together – Emmeline recollecting how Cecilia had told her men always chose to explain things at the most curious times – Markie said much more cheerfully: 'If I shot anyone, I am the sort of man I should shoot.' One clock struck midnight, a little before the hour.

XIX

Lady Waters had not much difficulty in getting in touch with Julian, Sir Robert having unwittingly lent himself to the enterprise. She found Julian an unexpectedly difficult subject, but was at pains to maintain the connection through Pauline, for with Pauline's headmistress, Antonia Cherril, she rediscovered a friendship formed years ago on a Spanish journey. So she went down to visit the school, introducing herself to Pauline as a friend of her uncle's – Dorothea, even, admitted herself unnerved. She had Antonia to lunch to discuss adolescence and Antonia and Pauline to tea when the child was brought up to the dentist. Finally, hearing that Pauline had nowhere to go for the half term exeat, she invited the orphan to Farraways.

Pauline was alarmed but elated by the invitation. On the Saturday of the third week-end in June she set off across country by motor coach, in a dark-blue serge coat and skirt, in charge of the school matron who had relations near Cirencester. Unfortunately it was raining, bad weather was moving steadily south; the country looked steamy and roads ran like rivers. Though Lady Waters had promised Pauline her uncle, Pauline had heard nothing from him and did not know if he were really to be at Farraways. She was fascinated by Lady Waters, who made her blush . . . At High Wycombe they changed coaches: Pauline ate a bar of chocolate, Matron ate Marie biscuits out of an envelope. They passed through woods, over ridges, through villages dark with rain; when the *Daily Mirror* was finished Pauline and Matron looked out through the streaming windows, pointing out objects to one another: they became very friendly. Pauline's heart sank when at Cirencester Matron, looking suddenly common and kind in her large green hat, flopped from the coach to embrace her sister, while Pauline made her own lonely way to the car from Farraways.

The rain thinned and stopped; the car, clearing Cirencester, tore with a slick wet sound up the open road to Farraways: in the Daimler, massive as a conservatory awheel, Pauline, picking white fluff from her coat and skirt, felt more of an orphan than ever. At her feet reposed a moist parcel of turbot, a bottle of lime juice, a tin of cheese biscuits from the Cirencester grocer's. After some miles, the chauffeur stopped to inquire if she were comfortable, but looked with far greater solicitude at the turbot.

As the car took the turn of the drive Pauline, straightening her hat, saw the middle-aged stone house, porticoed, whose many polished dark windows had white frames. Before the front door a large lime dripped on to a lawn; just clear of the drops Lady Waters, in grey knitted wool, standing out on a duckboard, directed a gardener who was putting down numbers for clock golf. Stooping, Lady Waters herself stuck in the small red flag . . . Pauline, seeing these preparations for her visit, felt very much excited, as though the candles were being lit on a birthday cake. The car pulled up; she was let out to kiss Lady Waters, who said reproachfully: 'We have heard nothing definite from your uncle.'

'Oh *dear*,' said Pauline.

'However . . .' said Lady Waters. Smiling, she tipped Pauline under her anxious chin and led her towards the portico. Sir Robert, who had been looking out of the window, stepped back hastily in retreat. Light slipped through the clouds impalpably parting to touch the bronzed hay-fields and distant silvery trees for one of those moments, disturbing and gracious, with which wet June weather is interspersed . . . Pauline, feeling herself regarded with such kindness and so much disinclination to meet her yet, felt certain this must be Sir Robert. Lady Waters, however, said nothing; Sir Robert's companion, further back in the study, was an ornithologist, of no possible interest to her.

'I have heard nothing, either,' she said, making a confidante of Pauline as they went upstairs, 'of my niece, whom you know: Mrs Summers. This week-end has been rather difficult. But we have a composer with us, of whom I expect you have heard – This is your little room, Pauline: it is quite tiny.'

'Oh, how cosy; it is divine!' cried Pauline, clasping her hands. The room was in fact very small: they stood in a kind of canyon between the high polished furniture. The window looked over the porch; through looped muslin curtains the lime breathed in, sweet and damp.

'Mrs Summers will be next door, so you will not be lonely. You two are great friends already, I understand?'

'She *is* coming?'

'Her sister-in-law is in Paris, so it seems likely.' Lady Waters looked into the soap-dish, the ink-pot, the biscuit box: everything was in place. 'You must not feel shy here,' she said. 'This house has been home to so many young people; a great many little girls have slept in this very room. So you must feel quite natural with us. Are you fond of birds?'

Pauline wondered if they had an aviary. '*Very*,' she said.

'That will be very nice,' said Lady Waters, but did not give the context of the remark. Her eyes wandered, an expression of mild calculation came over her face: she was anxious to keep the ornithologist clear of Cecilia. 'My other niece,' she said, 'flew to Paris today – though she is not really my niece. Visibility looks to me poor today but it may have been different at Croydon; one never knows.'

'Never,' agreed Pauline. 'How I dream of flying!'

'That may have nothing to do with flying,' said Lady Waters, looking at her with interest. At this point, however, the telephone rang downstairs; having looked back once to remark: 'You remember your dreams, I hope?' Lady Waters left her young visitor. Pauline plunged the most vigorous of her blushes into soap and water and polished her cheeks to a high shine: discouraged by the allusion to shyness she wondered how to appear most natural. When the gong for lunch sounded she crept like a mouse to the stair-head, then pranced heavily down.

In the hall, however, her hostess was still at the telephone; she turned with an awful smile to enjoin silence. After some delays, Cecilia was through from London.

'I had thought,' Lady Waters was saying, 'that he could motor you down.'

'I have no idea where he is: he may be in Siberia.'

'Siberia? But he wrote from St James's Court.'

'Then he must be there.'

'The child has just come.' (Pauline fled to the dining-room.)

'Oh, the poor little thing: does she speak?'

'My dear Cecilia, your call must be very expensive – would you mind telling me if you *are* coming or not?'

Cecilia hesitated, sighing audibly on the wire. A voice said: '*Thrrree* minutes!'

'Oh yes: yes, Georgina, I'd love to – No, *don't* give me another three minutes! – The 3.55.' She rang off.

'There *is* no 3.55,' Lady Waters observed to the empty air.

It would end, of course, in a telegram and their sending the car to Cheltenham: Cecilia was a good deal of trouble to her relations: Georgina could see quite plainly, she never cared to commit herself in case something more amusing should turn up. This time, however, her hesitation and manner had been peculiar: one could be certain that something was in the air. Mentally all a-tiptoe, Lady Waters went in to lunch.

Her visitors, having assimilated each other imperfectly, still had the odd air of objects picked up at random. Pauline was still much agitated by what she had overheard: 'The child has just come' – what had Cecilia replied? Marcelle Veness, an unhappy woman composer who had lately quarrelled with her best friend and could speak to no one, gloomed at Sir Robert's right hand: she had spent the morning hatless out in the rain. An apologetic white dog coasted round the chair-backs; he belonged to the house and desolated by too many departures dared form no more attachments, looking at newcomers with a disenchanted eye: a nervy luckless little white dog that yearned for a sweet routine. The ornithologist, who never cared much where he was, talked on loudly and happily to Sir Robert. Sir Robert, however, could not give his mind to his friend; looking kindly at Pauline he asked her if she liked birds.

'It must be a joke here,' thought Pauline; she laughed heartily.

Lady Waters really had had no reason to count on Julian for this week-end; regretfully but distinctly he had declined her invitation. So regretfully that Lady Waters, who had naturally mentioned Cecilia, saw at once that there must be something behind this and wrote again. *Should* he unexpectedly find himself free, she said, he must let her know; Pauline was expecting to meet him and would be much disappointed. Julian, whose week-end engagements were quite substantial, was surprised and could see no reason to write again: he was alarmed by this hint, not the first, of Cecilia's relation's tenacity, which could do him no good.

Not at once dismissing the matter he had telephoned to Cecilia, who was appalled. 'On no account go,' she said, 'the place is a morgue. Besides, there is nothing to do there.'

'Oh, I wouldn't mind that . . . Do I take it you *won't* be there?'

'I may or may not.'

'I *could* go . . .'

'I see no reason why.'

Naturally, he was discouraged; Cecilia felt sorry later she had discouraged him. A week-end with Julian might have been pleasant – but not at Farraways. She was missing him these days; not that she saw him less but his absences seemed longer: the possibility of their ever falling in love remained, however, remote . . . Dreading, she could not say why, this next week-end without Emmeline, Cecilia decided that she would suggest to Julian, when he should ring up again, to cut his engagements for Sunday and take her into the country: she would be more than willing to cut her own. But he did not ring up again. Reflecting how many friends she had that were more amenable she thought: 'Really he is impossible: he is *too* touchy.' So before lunch on Saturday, in desperation, she telephoned to Georgina. She packed several books she never had time to read and a couple of old evening dresses she could not wear anywhere else: when she found the 3.55 did not exist she felt that life was against her and wept at Paddington. She telegraphed, begging Georgina to meet her at Cheltenham, knowing too well they all knew she had not cared to commit herself in case something more amusing should turn up.

When Pauline heard that Cecilia was really coming she recalled Dorothea's frightful remark and blushed into her lime juice. In spite of all this, she began to enjoy herself: a promising sparkle pervaded the flowerless lilacs and there were delicious new peas for lunch. She stared at the damp-haired woman composer, not having seen a woman drink whisky before; she ate gooseberry tart with short pastry and camembert with a delicious oozy inside; her skirt-belt began to tighten, a guarantee of repletion unknown at school . . . The unhappy celebrity, face like a drowned mask, meanwhile stared out of the window: she asked herself why she was here and could not have said. She was wretched everywhere; it did not greatly matter. Her empty studio, the stairs up which no one came any more had become impossible: one was bound to be somewhere. She had an untroubled contempt for her hosts and could hardly see them; stretching a hand out she began to eat biscuits quickly; finished one plate and looked round for more. It alarmed Sir Robert to see this poor lady, one moment unable to swallow, bolting so many dry biscuits.

Roaming the round table in search of biscuits, the composer's eyes of dark vacancy met Pauline's, and, without brightening, fixed her. She had not seen Pauline before: the child seemed incredible. 'Who are you?' she said languidly.

Everyone looked at Pauline, who choked and could not reply.

'Is she dumb?' Marcelle asked the table.

'Dear me, no,' said Sir Robert, while his wife, pleased at this evidence of returning vitality in her patient, looked compellingly at Pauline. 'Tell Marcelle who you are,' she said.

Marcelle did not cease to examine Pauline with distraught intensity. Wrapped thickly in a subjectivity through which the passions like taxi-lamps in a fog shed a murky glow, Marcelle could but be surprised when the mists thinned a moment, showing her something or somebody not herself. At such moments she had bought a dog because it was so like one, given someone a five-pound note because it was crackly or invited strangers to dine: it was her friends' privilege to patch up, later, any ensuing awkwardness, to remove the great Dane that encumbered her studio, reclaim the five pounds or dismiss the expectant party . . . Absorbed by Pauline she watched blush rise after blush, then looked down at the child's tie. She said: 'Do tell me why you are wearing that?'

'It's our school tie.'

'You don't think it's becoming?'

'No.'

'You're quite right,' said Marcelle. 'How terrible!'

'What is terrible, Marcelle?' said Lady Waters. She hoped Pauline was gratified: years afterwards the child might remember how Marcelle Veness had told her about her tie.

'Oh, come,' said Sir Robert, 'I think it is rather a pretty tie.'

'School was prison to me,' said Marcelle. 'Do you have to do what they tell you?'

'. . . I don't know.'

'But how can you not know?'

'Pauline cannot see herself,' interposed Lady Waters. 'It is difficult for her to say.'

The ornithologist, man of one single idea who had not been listening, said impatiently to Sir Robert, 'When do we start?' They were going out with field-glasses to the water-meadows, where they would stand for hours rooted and not speaking till they became to the objects of their observation as natural as willows. Or, drawing out foot after foot with a squelch they would advance step by step cautiously and as though by accident. For these meadows, strung in the rainy weather with pools and marshes, where in late spring fritillaries hang their delicate mottled bells, where young rivers barely emerge from the long fine grass, are pied with strange birds that flash over the water: the coot, the smew, the redshank, the common sandpiper; the yellow wagtail is numerous; there may be epoch-making appearances of the garganey, the ring ousel or the red-backed shrike ... Sir Robert wondered if he ought to ask Pauline to come with them. But there were no glasses for her, she would get her feet wet and it would seem unkind to keep asking her not to talk.

Marcelle, having given her hostess one glance of contempt, let Pauline go and subsided: once more the mists closed in. The butler provided more biscuits, but having lost interest in them she left the table ... Pauline knew she should never feel safe again.

'She has a good deal of temperament,' said Sir Robert: even his wife looked put out. So far, Marcelle had been one of her few reverses: Georgina could but regret having carried her off. Alone in her studio scrappy with torn-up letters Marcelle, poor soul, had for days been afloat in whisky: Georgina had bustled her out of it. Country air, some calm talks should do much for Marcelle. But she drank as much whisky here and was even more unresponsive: she played the piano at midnight and said next day it was out of tune. 'She'll get wet again,' said Sir Robert, as Marcelle strode past the window. For the clouds, which she seemed to attract, had closed in; once more it was raining steadily.

'Quarrels,' said Lady Waters, 'are terrible things.' Drawing Pauline's damp little hand through her arm she swept her into the morning-room. 'Never quarrel,' she said. 'Have you many friends?' She shook up a jar of bull's-eyes, gave Pauline one for each cheek and recorked the bottle: having made this concession to youth she went on to tell Pauline much of Marcelle's difficult life, and how it was said that she and her friend Diana had gone for each other with fire-irons. Though her version of this was modified, Pauline was greatly surprised: as her hostess's darkling accents bore in on her, more and more clearly did it appear that almost everything was improper.

Before dinner Cecilia arrived, a shade guilty, resolved within limits to be at her best. In the half hour before the dressing-gong she walked round the garden with Lady Waters.

Pauline, with a child called Loretta who had been asked to tea to amuse her, went cheerlessly round the garden the other way; whenever she heard Lady Waters she steered the surprised Loretta off down another path. Loretta, daughter of what Lady Waters called a retired actress, who lived in the village and was devoted to church work, had danced last winter in a sublimated kind of a pantomime, in which the fairies in purple chiffon had been more like some people's idea of a Greek chorus; she expected next winter to be one of the Lost Boys in *Peter Pan*. She had the finished naïvety of the stage child, appeared to be a born dancer and could not keep off her toes. Her behaviour surprised Pauline: springing backwards and forwards across the wet flower-beds, tossing back her hair like a little victory, Loretta talked about boys. Did Pauline know many boys, did she think them funny? Pauline said she knew no boys. Loretta said this seemed funny: kneeling down by the pool and smiling at her reflection between the lilies she brought a lip-stick out of her knickers and made up her mouth: her mother, she said, would be furious. No doubt she looked like a fairy, with bare legs and arms beside the pool in the rock-garden where the late spring flowers had fallen and the sundial, sad with no shadow, was streaked with rain ... Pauline, patient, wondered when she would go.

'There is no view this evening,' said Lady Waters, who stood with Cecilia looking out through the arch.

'No,' agreed Cecilia who had forgotten the view. Scents of pollen and lime-flowers trailed through the steamy garden; she yawned again, she had been up too late. Jarred by the late cry of a cuckoo, Cecilia found in the cloudy low arch of the sky, in the distant country like something reflected in water, the halt, the chill, the not quite oblivion of death. Pacing the garden, she never quite listened to what Georgina was saying, but looked at the roses battered apart by rain. Rainy petals littered the earth; more white roses, loose globes of colourless shadow, were still to fall; the La France were blanching. But glowing in early dusk the dark crimson roses, still close and perfect, drank in the sweetening rain: on their spined stems and dark leaves the crimson were like a painting – that drop so bright, so *real* on a petal's lip – but these were live roses, living through to the heart. Hoping that crimson roses might be her affinity, Cecilia resolved to go quite soon to America.

She resolved to go to America, where she saw confusedly many white porticoes in the sun. No more summer ghosts, no belated cuckoo deforming all the remembered sweetness of spring in his spoilt cry. In that continent bare of her youth she saw herself as a girl again. He won't come with me, she thought of Henry; we shall forget one another, she thought of Julian. Exhilaration possessed her; she saw a motor-boat cutting across a lake in the solid sunshine, horses hitched to a gate-post under the full moon. Strangers, the kindly touch of the unforeseen – it was high time she was abroad again. The heart is a little thing and one can coerce it; she would step up the cheerful gangway and go abroad. She saw the bright decks and gilt saloons, heard the bugles and silent throb of the liner steaming rapidly west: so one leaves behind one's little coffer of ashes.

'Surely,' she said, 'the cuckoos are late this year?'

'Cuckoos?' said Lady Waters, who had been thinking of Marcelle. 'No.'

'But it's June.'

' "In June, he is out of tune." But I understand that he stays till August.'

Outstaying by months his welcome. 'Terrible,' cried Cecilia.

'Yes, poor Marcelle!'

'Poor cuckoo! Does it all begin over again when it gets to Africa?'

'If you want to know about birds,' her aunt said with some displeasure, 'you had better ask Graham Watts. He allows us nothing but birds; he has no idea whatever of general talk. He has taken Robert out to look for a ring ousel; they will be both sneezing all night. But I do not think you will care for him.'

'Never mind: let's cheer up Marcelle.'

'You have rings round your eyes, Cecilia.'

'Oh dear yes: I look forty.'

'All the same, it's a pity that Julian could not come.'

'Oh yes, yes; he's so popular – What will you do with Pauline all day long?'

'She seems quite at home.'

'Oh yes, but she's like a rabbit. Shall I wear a rose at dinner?'

'Just as you like,' said Lady Waters disheartened. There would be no one at dinner for her Cecilia to shine at; she thought of her as a light, or at least a reflector; always in relation to someone else. Sir Graham might be discounted: in a few words she warned Cecilia against Marcelle. 'Though you might,' she said, 'persuade her to play the piano; it works off her feelings; otherwise she will wait till we've gone to bed.'

'But I should hate to hear her feelings. No, let's play jumbled birds with Sir Graham, or some round game with Pauline.'

'That would be very nice of you,' said her aunt, surprised.

'Not at all,' said Cecilia sweetly: wrist-deep in wet leaves she was picking a rose.

'Much as I like Marcelle, she would be no friend for you.'

'Oh, that's all right, Georgina: I shall be in America.'

Lady Waters received this with equanimity. Spattering on the rose-leaves, another shower began to fall.

Cecilia had been quite right, the place was a morgue, she had been here too much; old hopes and fancies lay with their faces upturned. Indoors, the red rose lost colour. The room where Cecilia slept was grander than Emmeline's; a high triple mirror reflected the rain falling, the four-poster's chilly chintz curtains were looped and tasselled: a widow keeps her prestige though she lie with a ghost. Cecilia's black evening dress was spread out on the sofa; viewing its shabbiness with compunction she felt how badly she had behaved. Hearing Pauline bumping about next door like a little moth in a lamp, Cecilia went into the passage. 'Hullo?' she said, tapping on Pauline's door.

'Hullo?' replied Pauline, appearing askance.

'It was just – I have hardly seen you.'

'No,' agreed Pauline, not raising her eyes.

'I'm so glad you're here this week-end.'

'So am I,' said Pauline politely.

Pauline, only anxious to please, did not know what to do next. What could have brought to her door this elegant, haggard young woman? Cecilia saw with dismay that the child *was* like Julian – that dolorous hesitation – though at the same time, poor little thing, so much more like a rabbit. She lacked his turn of the head, that charming, attentive smile and quick look that belied discretion . . . Something rose in Cecilia's throat as she thought of the wide Atlantic.

She said: 'Does your dress do up at the back? Perhaps I could hook it.'

'Thank you ever so much, it does up at the side.'

'In my day, they did up at the back. Would you like your hair brushed?'

'I brush my own hair, thank you ever so much.'

'Was that a nice girl you were talking to in the garden?'

'No,' said Pauline in a burst of confidence, 'she was a perfectly awful girl.'

'I thought so,' Cecilia said, nodding. Without further embarrassment they succeeded in parting.

XX

'I should let your uncle be quiet,' said Lady Waters, 'he will be tired after his drive.' Pauline, who had been hanging about the door of the drawing-room, disappeared hurriedly.

It did seem a long way for a man to drive for Sunday lunch on a showery morning. They had all been gratified when he rang up to propose this: only Cecilia was half-hearted. As Pauline and Lady Waters melted out of the doorway, Cecilia said satirically to Julian: 'Georgina seems to think you should lie down.'

Julian, who had hardly got clear of London before beginning to wish he had never started, hoped she would not be difficult. He was distressed to find her so nervous and melancholic. But he liked the house, the kind easy air of the rooms in which a quality Lady Waters admired in table-talk seemed no more than a jarring gramophone record, at any moment to be switched off. He liked Sir Robert, also the meal's conclusion with excellent brandy: he had, in fact, been feeling better since lunch.

Seeing no reason to sit in a draught, Julian got up and shut the door. In the morning-room Lady Waters, hearing the drawing-room door shut, smiled and got out the chess-board for Pauline.

'But I can't play chess.'

'Sir Robert would like to teach you.'

Sir Robert, however, had shut himself in the study with the *Observer*. His friend worked his way round the shelves, taking books out, sighing, and piling them on the floor; he digested easily and was anxious to be about again. Marcelle Veness, in a circle of cigarette stubs, stood chafing under the lime; good food and air having done, as her hostess predicted, their healing work with her, a raging boredom was beginning to set in. Magnificent in her pose of exasperation she was not unaware of Cecilia and Julian, whose eyes through the drawing-room window were fixed in awe on her. Oppressed by their segregation they clutched the idea of her presence.

Cecilia said vaguely: 'She *is* in a state of mind.'

'What is the matter?'

'Oh, love – Georgina will tell you.'

'So Emmeline is in Paris?'

'She says she saw you lunching somewhere the other day.'

'Yes.' After a pause, in which his impression of Emmeline came back sharply, he said: 'I was with my sister.'

'Were you?' she said with tremendous incuriosity. They both sat down on the window-seat, as near as possible to Marcelle. 'She looks rather bored,' said Julian.

'Poor thing. But she wouldn't think much of us.'

'I didn't know Emmeline knew Mark Linkwater?'

'Oh yes; she has lunch with him sometimes.'

'Apparently, yes.'

Cecilia said rather touchily: 'No one knows why.'

Julian looked at her oddly. 'She may think she likes him,' Cecilia went on, 'but Emmeline hasn't the vaguest idea what anyone's like. She may think he's amusing, but anything more – quite impossible. She's so fastidious and – well, if you knew Markie!'

'I wouldn't be sure,' said Julian.

'To begin with, he's got a Byron complex.'

'What's that?'

'If you don't *know*,' said Cecilia impatient, 'I can't tell you. All this *âme damnée* is such a bore.'

'All the same, in his own line he's exceedingly competent, not to say brilliant. Anywhere, he's hard-headed.'

'Oh yes. But they all say he leads such a nasty life.'

'I really don't know. He's amusing, for which one is grateful, and there's no doubt for some people he has got fascination.'

'If he has got brains, one has got to take them on trust: his manner with women is simply showy and tiresome. I wish I had never talked to him in the train – How fair you are,' she added, oppressed by his manner. These approximations of Julian's to what he took for a mean in judgement appeared by turns to Cecilia either desolating or funny: in fact she had little sympathy with his point of view.

With a smile at which her blood rose, for it was indulgent, he said: 'All the same, I don't think, you know, you can quite dismiss him.'

'How can one dismiss such a raging bore?'

'That, of course, is just as you feel.'

'Why should one be tolerant?' said Cecilia. 'Life is really too

164

short.' At the same time she had to laugh at herself, and at the pretty example of feminine prejudice she presented. Leaning back, still laughing, against the window-frame, she observed with her gentlest malice: 'Of course, he is positive; that is always something.'

Aware of the dart, Julian did not quiver: looking thoughtfully at Cecilia he said: 'He's very much attached to her.'

'Did he tell you? How do you know?'

'I just thought so,' said Julian, losing some ground. Encumbered by a sententiousness of which her irony made him aware, he expected Cecilia at any moment to round on him. He must plead guilty to an excessive and even officious concern with her sister-in-law's affairs, and felt, in fact, sadly like Lady Waters. But he could not forget Emmeline's face as she nodded to him across the restaurant.

Cecilia did not round on Julian: eyelashes casting their pointed shadow on her pale cheeks which a brush of unreal colour made more transparent, she sat looking down undecidedly at her cigarette. After a silence to which an uneasy desire to speak and fear of the truth contributed, she said with elaborate easiness: 'He's in Paris today, you know: they flew over together.'

'Really,' he said startled. 'Why?'

His manner confirmed her alarm; she said with marked concern: 'I suppose because he wanted to be in Paris.'

'Why didn't you go too? It would have been amusing.'

'My *dear* Julian – because I wasn't asked. She only told me what she was doing when she was half out of the door. I cannot run round after Emmeline, making us both ridiculous; I might as well take down my knitting and sit in her office. Emmeline's not a *jeune fille à marier*; ever since she was twelve she has done what she likes; she's completely clear-headed, her head is better than mine. Because I'm older than she is and have been married, do you expect me to sit up at nights for her with a cup of hot milk? I might just as well have tried to chaperone Henry. What an odd idea men always have of women's relations; you all seem to think we cry on each other's chests. Suppose I sometimes do wonder about what she's doing – questions one might ask another woman one couldn't ask Emmeline: she does make one feel common. Not that she'd think one was common, she'd merely think one was mad. How *can* you expect me to interfere with her?'

'I don't,' said Julian, retreating.

'Well then, Julian, don't fuss.'

'But she seems rather young.'

'So her clients all think, till they get her bills.'

'But this isn't business.'

'I didn't say so – really, Julian, you talk like an old maid!'

'I'm sorry: I thought you were worried,' said Julian tactlessly.

He caught from Cecilia the flash of a bright angry look; she threw her cigarette away, paused, then said weakly: 'You make me exaggerate. You suggest I'm suggesting the most preposterous things. I wish I had never said anything. But then whom am I to talk to? One must keep this from Georgina at any price ... I suppose I *am* worried; you see, it was I who picked Markie up in the train. If Emmeline likes him enough to be consistently charming, he would be mad if he didn't fall for her. He isn't a fool: he must know what's good when he sees it. But their marriage would be a catastrophe: I should do everything to prevent it. He's a bully; he'd make her wretched!'

'I don't think that need trouble you: he's quite unlikely to marry – at least, for years.'

'How do *you* know? So few men seem "likely to marry" – how awful they'd be if they did. But when it's a question of Emmeline –'

'He still wouldn't marry,' Julian repeated. 'It still wouldn't suit his book.'

'Why not?'

'For hundreds of reasons.'

'Money?'

'I dare say; for one thing.'

'But what do you know about Markie? You hedge and hesitate, Julian; it is enough to send one out of one's mind. You suggest he's not to be trusted.'

'My dear, you suggested that long ago!'

'I only said I thought so: you go on as though you knew. How well do you know him?'

'Hardly at all.'

'Then what do you know *about* him?'

'Nothing particular.'

Cecilia, getting up irritably, began walking about the room. She pressed one cigarette with a splutter into a rose-bowl, hesitated beside the piano and lit another. She stared down the garden at the concave, glassy distance from which an enemy army seemed to be marching. 'You make things impossible for me,' she said. 'If *I* suspected some woman of doing someone you valued harm I should tell you all that I knew of her. But these wretched little discretions – If Emmeline were your sister, *would* you have Markie about the place?'

'Not as things are,' said Julian, plainly disliking the question.

'You mean, not if they were in love?'

'If you like.'

'You saw them at lunch,' said Cecilia. 'But then – do forgive me, Julian – how can *you* tell?'

'You are overbearing, aren't you?' said Julian, so gently she saw at once that she must have hurt him. But a second and ice-cold perception succeeded the first. 'Perhaps,' she said, '*you'd* like Emmeline?'

'I don't know,' said Julian, startled. 'I hadn't thought.'

She said cheerlessly: 'So that you, of course, would imagine things.' The drawing-room in which she retreated from him to its furthest alcove, seemed large and over-cold for a tête-à-tête. His or her presence, she could not have said which, became superfluous and embarrassing in this solid and formal drawing-room which out of weeks of oblivion and shut-up silence had crystallized round its objects – brass bowls, the piano, a tall screen painted with lilies – a sardonic indifference to their company. Remembering he was supposed to have come to see Pauline, she made off towards the door.

'Where are you going?' said Julian.

'To find Pauline.'

'No, don't go; I want to talk to you.'

'We see each other so much.'

'Why won't you marry me?' Walking after her down the long room, he rather sharply dissuaded her hand from the door-knob. As his fingers touched the cold porcelain she drew hers away quickly, remarking: 'There seemed no reason.'

'You ask too much.'

'*You* expect too little.'

More amicably, however, she took his arm; they strolled back as though the window by which their talk had begun were entitled to its conclusion. 'Of course,' she said, 'if we were married you could interfere with Emmeline. But I don't really think it would do much good.'

The irony of her tone, with the ambiguity of the remark, kept him silent: still rather angry, he had to explore and reject every possible shade of her meaning while they stood, her arm through his, a picture of intimacy, like people married some years, looking out at the garden. Two or three lime-flowers, heavy with rain, fell; she heard again yesterday's cuckoo or its discordant brother. If this fresh understanding with Julian – or at least this return to a point where they had been more or less happy – could not lift the lowering sky or tune up the cuckoo, it at least set ticking again in Cecilia a clock that counted most hours of pleasure. Something unexpectedly sweet was dropped into her mouth opened wide for vacuous afternoon yawn. She felt grateful to Julian, quite contrite, and had he come rather better out of this question of Emmeline might have quite easily loved him.

Susceptible to that illusion of afternoon peace, so absolute in a strange house, and to the flowery drip of the lime with its wet leaves hanging, he remarked: 'I don't really think this is like a morgue.'

'I've been here too much.'

'Perhaps one could live in the country if one were married. Or could one?'

'Oh no, one could never do with the country for long – Then what *shall* I do about Markie?'

'I don't see what you can do, unless Emmeline asks you.'

Emmeline was, they both knew, never likely to ask. The question was begged, and begged, they both felt, ignobly. Already, however, Emmeline was remote; her face of sublime ignorance, that stirring and striking picture of love died out in Cecilia's nearness. Cecilia beside him, eyes downcast and aspect mildly dependent, quickened in him the strongly domestic impulse to batten down hatches and keep all worry away. Solicitude, tenderness are single-minded and narrow: from this the integrity of the home. In this moment before she was quite herself again – exacting and restless, gay with such a sharp edge of unfriendly melancholy – he would have sacrificed anything to this peace that was a mirage.

She thought: 'If I had gone on going out through the door, would he really have stopped me?' Sense leapt at the shade of a shadowy tussle about a door-knob.

'This poor little dog,' said Pauline, 'he has no friends.'

The white dog pattered after them round the garden; Pauline was taking her uncle to see the view. Lady Waters, forgetting the chess-lesson, had put down the bottle of bull's-eyes beside Pauline and gone out after Marcelle soon after lunch. No one else looked in, so Pauline had spent the afternoon happily, eating bull's-eyes and reading *The Woman Thou Gavest Me*. Time fled, she had discovered a masterpiece; when her uncle came in she had looked up all of a daze.

It was not bad out of doors. Pauline, breathing in the mild air upon depths of peppermint, felt she was swallowing ice. Having nothing to say she kept clicking her fingers and talked to the dog. 'His name is Roderick,' she went on, 'but he really answers to anything: I expect he is lonely. It is a sad life for a dog, if you come to think.'

'A dog's life,' said Julian, trying hard to collect himself. 'Why is he called Roderick?'

'I don't know. I didn't know what an ornithologist was till I looked it up in the dictionary. You see I never thought I should meet one, or a composer either. What a number of interesting people Lady Waters does know: she seems to know everyone.'

'I quite agree,' said Julian.

'But all her friends have very unhappy lives. Do you think that is usual?'

'I . . . what did you say, Pauline?'

'Are unhappy lives usual?'

'I really don't know.' This chance to get down to essentials with Pauline came at an unhappy moment. He asked hastily: 'How is your friend Dorothea?'

'Very well, thank you. She would have sent you her kindest regards, but I was not certain if I should be seeing you.'

'I wasn't coming.'

'But Lady Waters said she was sure you would come. When you telephoned this morning she said: "What did I say?" '

'And how are *you* getting on?'

'Very well, thank you; this half-term I am to be president of our form debating society. Dorothea and I are paving our garden; we may get an honourable mention, though naturally we do not hope for the prize.'

'I don't see why not; your garden seemed very nice.'

Julian heard Cecilia's voice in the distance. 'You enjoy being here, I expect?' he went on with immense concentration.

'Very much; it's a great thing to meet such interesting people. A girl of my age might easily feel *de trop*, but they are all determined to make me feel quite at home. Mrs Summers came in last night and offered to hook my dress, but it hooks at the side. Shall we sit down in the summer-house?'

They sat down in the summer-house; a curtain of honeysuckle hung over the door; Roderick followed them in and sat shivering. The church clock struck four; the sound rolled up from the valley through shredding, vapoury clouds. Pauline, petting Roderick, said nothing more; Julian wondered if it were raining in Paris, and if he should have another word with Cecilia before he left . . . He heard Lady Waters's unmistakable step on the path; the gravel creaked, the step passed; she looked, questing, this way, that way. Parting the honeysuckle, Lady Waters looked into the summer-house: against the watery garden, in trailing green light from the creepers, she looked very large and marine, like the motherly spouse of Neptune. Roderick shot out past her and hurried off.

'That's right, Pauline,' she said. 'Have you shown your uncle the view.'

'I couldn't find it,' said Pauline, flustered.

'No, the distance is cloudy today.' They made room for her in the summer-house. 'You are not,' she said to Julian, 'seeing us at our best; you must come again. And how do you think Cecilia is looking?'

'Quite well,' said Julian, surprised.

'I am not happy about her: she is pale, she is doing too much. Too many late nights. She needs someone to keep her in order: she will not listen to me.'

'That's too bad,' said Julian nodding at Lady Waters as though he could see it must be difficult, painful even, to be an aunt.

'She's talking again of America; she is anxious to see her mother. But I do not feel we must let her go. I think it is largely restlessness with her; I so wish she would settle down.'

'Very difficult, these days. I suppose the bishops, journalists and so on are right: this is a restless age.'

'All ages are restless,' said Lady Waters. Pauline, picking some honeysuckle to pieces, assented with eagerness. Looking with dissatisfaction about the arbour, their hostess said it was damp, so they all filed out and down the path to the rose-beds, Pauline trailing behind. 'But *this* age,' Lady Waters went on, 'is far more than restless: it is decentralized. From week to week, there is no knowing where anyone is. Myself, I move very little, but I am fortunate, I have my friends about me and human interests are inexhaustible. The human spirit is more than literature. What, I often say to myself, does one want with books:'

'I often wonder,' said Julian.

'Though the flow of ideas nowadays seem inexhaustible and all these new theories do certainly cast an interesting light on behaviour. I'm sure you agree? One may do so much, with a little judgement, by bringing theory to bear on life. Knowing that I am always willing to listen, friends bring me their difficulties; I am often surprised to find how a little talk, with a touch of some knowledge and penetration, may set things right.'

'I am sure that is so,' said Julian.

'Now Cecilia reads a good deal, when she is not running about, but I never think books mean much to her; she is emotional and needs some central interest. Emmeline has her work, but there is nothing of the professional woman about Cecilia; she is essentially feminine – don't you think?'

'There's not much of my idea of the professional woman about Emmeline.'

'Still, she has a turn for affairs and very good judgement: it seems possible she may not marry. So you are one of her clients?'

'I hope to be.'

'You think of going abroad? But not, I expect, for long?'

'No, that's impossible for me, unfortunately.'

'You are all,' said his hostess playfully, 'very much too anxious to leave England. Is that our naughty Emmeline's propaganda? Myself, I am a born islander, for better or worse – Pauline,' she added, 'run in like a dear child, and see if tea is ready: Sir Robert does not like to be kept waiting.' Pauline turned back up the path at a self-conscious trot; Lady Waters wheeled Julian off round a rose-bed. 'And how,' she said, 'do you find Pauline?'

'Quite in her element; it is really charming of you to have her.'

'We find her a very dear person; there is something appealing about her; so much sensibility under that shy look. She *is*, of course, shy, but so very responsive; she seems anxious to talk. She is devoted to you: quite a clear case of hero-worship. I shall not forget how her face fell when I told her you would not be coming, or how she lit up when you telephoned. And Cecilia, I really believe, had been more than half expecting you . . . Pauline is expecting, I think, to make her home with you when she leaves school?'

'I had hardly looked so far ahead.'

'It might not be easy, I can quite see, as things are at present: a young girl would hardly fit in with your present *ménage*; she would need a woman's sympathy and a woman's care ... However, so much may happen in four years.'

Julian felt bound to agree with her. He looked at a snail in the box border, at yesterday's roses, now spoilt and earthy, at tomorrow's buds coming out. She approved his manners, which were impeccable, his air of reviewing in courteous and mild abstraction all she had said.

'Pauline,' she continued warmly, 'has a spontaneous affectionate nature that is most winning. My husband has taken to her immensely: he is teaching her to play chess. And a charming sympathy has sprung up between her and Cecilia; all the week-end they have been inseparable; one sees Pauline follow Cecilia round with her eyes. Cecilia loves children; they bring out the sweetest side of her nature. Cecilia has missed so much; I should like to think that more was in store for her. It is hard to think of her youth as over, in any sense. It would need only a touch of happiness to bring her all out again, like a flower in sunshine. Since you came today, the pleasure of seeing a friend has given her quite a glow – Must you really go back tonight?'

'Alas, yes. In fact, if you won't think me rude I ought really to start before tea is over. I am due back for dinner at half-past eight.'

'We must not complain,' she said, with an air of distinct pathos. 'It has been most enterprising of you to come at all. Such a long drive, both ways. I can only hope,' she said, regarding him thoughtfully, 'you have felt it was worth while.'

Pauline came, panting, back.

'It is too bad,' said Lady Waters, crossing the hall that night with her little file of visitors on their way upstairs to bed, 'that Julian Tower had to go back so soon.'

'Indeed, yes,' said Pauline politely.

Cecilia said nothing: winding a wrap round her shoulders she stepped out into the porch. Above, the dark sky changed a little; something stirring behind the clouds shed a faint line of silver about the lime-tree. Cecilia looked up: while not a drop fell in the heavy darkness the clouds were in conflict, disturbed; light ran between like a messenger. Somewhere, the moon was rising. Somewhere, clear of earth's shadow, the radiant full moon received the whole smile of the sun. Clouds hid from the earth at this bridal moment her lovely neighbour, while to the clouds alone was communicated her ecstasy . . . Clouds closed in; the moon did not appear; darkness spread over the skies again; only the lime and a wet path silver for less than a moment had known of the moon's rising. The tree and path faded; cloudbound while that tide of light swept the heavens earth less than suspected the moon's perfection and ardour.

Cecilia sighed. 'It's horribly dark,' said Marcelle, throwing a match away into the darkness.

'That was nearly the moon,' cried Pauline.

'Yes, it's there,' said Cecilia, putting a hand out as though she expected the moon to fall into it.

Gathering up her furs, Lady Waters remarked: 'It's a pity: we should have had a full moon.'

Calling them all in, she shut the hall-door firmly.

'Perhaps,' said Cecilia, 'there is a moon in Paris.'

XXI

Coming down into clouds, Emmeline found with surprise cold showery weather in London. Evenings were shortened by rain, a chill like February's hung over squares and gardens. She had forgotten all this: her life, to which these last three days had given a new, perhaps its first conscious form, seemed bound up in a perpetuity of hot sunshine. She had had, however, little time for surprise: Woburn Place was humming, Tripp having been supplanted – for only some weeks they said and at great expense – by a Miss Armitage. Efficient as Nemesis and as unrelenting, Miss Armitage hustled the startled partners along; they worked at high pressure, as though they were organizing a coronation. A good deal of business had – or perhaps since their new employee's zealous research in the files merely seemed to have – mounted up. Groaning beneath this oppression, Peter was glad to have Emmeline home, and was plaintive with her for her absence of one more day.

Emmeline told Cecilia about the Serbs; Cecilia told Emmeline about Farraways and how Sir Robert had made her feel guilty by praising her shabby old evening frock. Monday evening at Oudenarde Road, when they dined together, was a cheerful vignette of intimacy; both talked more because they were conscious of some reserve. As though Emmeline had come back from a longer journey, Cecilia was full of little attentions. Drawing the curtains to shut out the rainy evening she asked at last, over her shoulder: 'And how was Markie?'

'Quite well; he sent you his love.'

'Summer's quite gone while you've been away,' said Cecilia, sighing.

Something made Emmeline smile; she said: 'Gerda'll be glad.'

'That little goose – why?'

'Fine weather makes her unhappy.'

While Cecilia remarked it was nice to think someone was pleased, Emmeline thought of the sundial at Farraways, of something about that bright Sunday morning that she had never recaptured, or even hoped to recapture. Cecilia, now looking at her less closely and anxiously, felt more at ease: Emmeline, though naturally tired, gave no sign of not being completely herself.

'So I have quite decided to go to America.'

'Indeed?' said Emmeline calmly. 'For how long?'

'That would depend. I thought you could have Connie Pleach here, or someone, to stay in the house with you. Of course I'll still keep up my half of it: I could well afford to, you see, as I'll be staying with mother.'

'You couldn't stay more than six months, though, because of the quota.'

Cecilia, who had not thought of this, was annoyed; the idea of America lost a good deal of its charm and vigour. 'It seems hard,' she said, 'that one should not be allowed to stay with one's own mother.'

'But, darling, you've never wanted to.'

'I do think it's annoying . . . I could pull strings, I dare say.'

'Or marry someone out there.'

'How heartless you are! Don't you want me back?'

'I can't imagine myself without you,' said Emmeline. So they shelved America. It did strike Cecilia a moment that the idea of Emmeline's imagining herself in any way, even to seeing her own shadow, was quite a new one. For she spoke of herself so little, as though she did not exist. Rather vague alarm returned; so that when the telephone rang Cecilia suddenly wondered: 'Can this be Markie?'

It was not, of course, Markie. Emmeline had made him promise not to ring up; they must go on as before, but more calmly, and meet whenever they could. She did not want life here disturbed by a voice that was too beloved, or ever alarmed by silences. The little white house pale with dusk, with rain streaming down its windows, was friendly tonight; here day-to-day life presented itself in mild outline and, after Paris, in delicate low-relief. She longed to inhabit with Markie the heart of the country, inaccessible, green and quiet, where telephones were not and lovers' meetings meant journeys. If they were to be little together they must be calmly apart.

Emmeline went to bed early; Cecilia read for a little and looked through her letters, staying to watch the fire die down. Restless, she crept up at midnight, tapped softly, and opened Emmeline's door an inch. She heard rain on the window, the clock ticking, an unstirring silence about the bed . . . Sitting up by her shaded lamp Cecilia wrote, later, to Julian:

'Emmeline's home tonight; she is tired and doesn't say much but seems quite happy: I regret, rather, anything that I said. Forget what I said: I don't think I was anxious really. She says it was hot in Paris – think of heat while we were at Farraways! – She had a nice week-end and quite liked her Serbs. So what a pair of old women we were!

'Which is not propitious for marriage. I don't think, really, Julian, that that would do. Of course there is always something, but we should wear that out. I wish you would not spoil me; it fearfully clouds the issue. What do we both want? Either nothing, or something quite different. But I thank you very much, all the same.

'Emmeline says they would only keep me in America six months because of the quota. I suppose you knew that: I didn't. How is one to be world-minded? Still, I may go, I dare say.

'What was Georgina saying to you in the garden: I could see it was heart-felt. Still, I agree, the place isn't a morgue, only like a quite nice Italian cemetery with photographs on the graves. And Georgina's unbalanced but kind. When old men like Sir Robert are dead, our civilization will go – don't you think?

'This morning, Pauline and I went out riding; she fell off but seemed to enjoy herself. She seems anxious to be affectionate, but can find no one she really likes. Though I always feel . . .' She wandered on, concluding: 'I may not post this,' and she did not. Her desk was full of such letters addressed to such friends, even stamped. Wondering if they would be posted if she were dead, she did not destroy them.

For weeks, wet weather trailed sadness over the newspapers. Wet lace was reported and sopping chiffons, debutantes were photographed shivering; ever so many functions were quashed by the rain. However assiduous the umbrella or kind the unrolled carpet, thousands of pairs of pale slippers must have been spoilt that summer. At Lord's the bats were silent; Wimbledon was suspended. Cecilia's social life registered this depression; Emmeline went to meet Markie with mackintosh buttoned up to the chin. No wonder Cecilia felt that life was escaping her, and Emmeline clung with intensity to one bright prevailing idea. Stripping off some distracting, sensuous, day-to-day pleasure the weather left nerves bare: one expected that even the gilded eighteen-year-old shivered, stepping into the ballroom. Across the mind's surface – on which a world's apprehension, strain at home and in Europe, were gravely written – the sense of a spoilt summer, so much prettiness wasted, darkly spread like spilt ink. Streets were to be navigated and parks desolate, pleasure-boats under tarpaulin and bands silent: the whole city became a mesh of unwilling hurry where nobody smiled or lingered. Unknown, the moon diminished; wasting itself upon vapours the sun smiled on.

The English went on putting up in so many unconscious prayers their request for happiness. As the holiday season approached glittering peaks and hot coasts, an idea of vineyards and lakes began to possess the imagination. Peter and Emmeline, still rather dazed by Miss Armitage, exploited the situation: bleached by rain on the palings their posters attracted more and more clients. Emmeline gave them the best she could of her now divided attention; when she went out to meet Markie she was quite often late.

The Summer Rush meant little to Markie, who rushed nowhere in summer: when she was late he was not patient. The more he possessed of Emmeline, the more he became exacting. The question of marriage, however, was not re-opened between them.

At the door of his flat, one evening about eight o'clock, he helped Emmeline out of her dripping mackintosh. She did not like driving her car in such heavy rain. 'But why not,' he said, 'take a taxi?'

'The nineteen 'bus was so near.'

'So you dripped in that 'bus for an hour – you're very late.'

'You mustn't be cross,' said Emmeline, who having gained in these weeks a new smiling power did not let Markie fuss her nearly so much. He said her hands were cold, chafed them; they went in to the fire. He said with authority that she was tired and had far better give all this up. Her look for a moment was serious and appalled; she thought he meant give up Markie. When he added 'That business of yours,' she laughed and said that was quite impossible: so much of her money was in it, apart from everything else.

'I meant, sell out, naturally. This would be your best time to, while things are going so well.'

'But I don't want to. What should I do all day?'

'I don't know: why do anything special?'

'I don't know: why do you?'

Ignoring this silly question he picked up to examine with some disapproval her right hand, whose forefinger showed a faint stain of ink. They had fallen into a habit of overruling, quite calmly, each other's opinions. Emmeline had to admit that this whole affair of careers for women did sound rather funny, the way Markie saw it, not unlike a ladies' race at regimental sports. Remarking: 'I'm not a houri,' she sat down on the floor by the fire, her shoulder against Markie's knee as he sat in the big chair, to comb out the wet strands of her hair that, separating in the warmth, resumed their own natural softness.

'I knew a girl once who had a shop, but she came to no good,' he said darkly.

'What did she sell?' said Emmeline, interested.

'Oh, paraphernalia – lampshades, book-ends that fell over, ash-trays that always caught fire, paper weights, those sticky Balkan toys – oh, yes, and flowers made out of oyster shells.'

'So what became of the shop?'

'As far as I know, it's still there.'

'Then what became of the girl?'

'Oh, Daisy – she quite went to bits.'

'Oh, dear: how?'

'She just went to pieces. She was a nice girl, too.'

'And gave up the shop?'

'Not as far as I know.'

'Then I don't see any moral,' said Emmeline, putting away her comb.

'There was one,' said Markie, one hand on the back of her neck to make her sit quiet. For she was inclined to get up and stroll round the room, as elusive in mind as in person. Emmeline did not ask what the moral might be: not from perversity, simply because she was hungry. 'There are too many shops,' she said. 'I can't think how they all pay. Especially gift shops.'

'What's that?'

'Daisy's kind, where you buy things to give other people you might not want for yourself – Do you think you could whistle for dinner? I feel quite hollow.'

Going across to whistle, he added: 'She doesn't think much of me.'

'Who, Daisy? Well, never mind, Markie, it can't be helped.'

Two or three of these disillusioned friends of his had cropped up now and again in their talk; Daisy's name, though not in this context, was now familiar. Emmeline, with whom fastidious in-curiosity reached a fine point, repeatedly shied away from them. She did not like to feel that they were unhappy; according to Markie they had been largely indignant; one way and another they seemed to have made a good deal of fuss. She could not account for their place in his own idea of his life, or reconcile the apparently rather pointless dalliance that had occurred with his derisive im-patience of sentiment and exclusively narrow ambition. She could only conclude that he felt time wasted at all had better be wasted thoroughly, and to this end put a pretty high value upon fatuity. If Daisy were all in bits – Emmeline had to perceive, as the lift came up and Markie took out the grilled chicken – Markie no doubt felt this was his fault; her fluttering shadow among her own lampshades remained important.

On small points, Markie quite liked being in the wrong and Daisy had certainly put him there. Her constant acute sense of having departed from virtue – for some time before Markie appeared, as a matter of fact, her behaviour had been open to criticism, but the more they saw of each other and the less he minced matters the more Daisy became the clergyman's daughter – lent charm to a frequentation that there was little else to support. Her bridling reproaches, her rather attractive blushes, her de-termination to keep things perfectly nice, her tears to be shut off at any time by his simply walking out of the shop, had been a source to Markie of endless satirical pleasure. In many ways, Daisy had suited him well, and he sometimes regretted her. She had brought up from some province an indestructible bloom of propriety. Bumping cheerfully round her back-shop, upsetting the book-ends, charring the ash-trays and tilting the lampshades crooked, he had spent evenings as natural and fresh and as nearly Arcadian as those tinkling sprays of shell blossom branching across the lamp-light. The salt of a little mild wit, some smoky pretensions to laugh at – for she attended concerts, visited galleries and would have liked to be liked for her mind – just enough resistance to please and enough repentance to gratify, in a woman saw Markie a long way. In fact, he liked women lowish.

Markie, looking at Emmeline while he brought out the plates, wondered what else there was about Daisy that one could tell her. For they were at a point when talk becomes retrospective: right back at each other's lives they looked with concern or pleasure.

Tonight Emmeline was rather *distraite*. Though she had said she was hungry she did not eat very much; she drank one glass of wine, then sat, cheek on hand, looking sideways into the fire: light blinked on her lashes. Still the room kept for her the ghost of its early strangeness; it would never be quite like other rooms – as though coming in for the first time she had anticipated something upon the threshold. But this touch of strangeness upon her nerves was becoming familiar: an isolation from life she felt here bound her up more closely than life itself. She could not have described the room, told where the clock ticked from, what pictures there were, or whether its colours, shapes, textures, had ever displeased or pleased her. There was the sofa, here – for she put things down here – must be the table; there was darkness over the corner with no lamp and a rug slipped under one's foot by the door. But intense experience interposed like a veil between herself and these objects. When he spoke or approached it was for an instant as though the veil parted: something unknown came through – though he was all the time formlessly near her like heat or light. His being was written all over her; if he was not, she was not: then they both dissipated and hung in the air. But still something restlessly ate up the air, like a flame burning.

XXII

For Markie, her silence was like the reflecting surface of water one would not for worlds disturb – so one drops a stone in. 'Wake up,' said Markie.

She looked his way.

'What are you thinking?'

'I wasn't.' Smiling at the question – that she, for one, was never allowed to ask – she watched him fill up her glass and recork the bottle: when he had done she said, 'But I didn't want any more.'

That, thought Markie, was like her. Had one wished, she would have come with one to the jeweller's; she would have leaned for hours on the glass counter beside one while one had the shop out to choose her a necklace, then said as one left the shop, case in hand: 'But I don't wear pearls.' She was slow, perhaps, in connecting things with herself, and had been happy just now watching the pretty red stream of claret.

He said: 'Well, you'd better drink it.'

Emmeline thought perhaps she was being too silent. Unlike Cecilia, who in the course of just such an evening would have glanced many times at herself in the mirror of one's opinion, Emmeline seldom asked herself if she pleased or how things were going. Just aware of a differing tenor in all their meetings, she accepted as natural his variations of mood. High or low, drifting over the hours, iridescent or darker passing a shadow, she saw their happiness like an immortal bubble, touching a moment objects it seemed to enclose . . . All the same, she did know she was very silent. Cecilia complained that she was inert, Markie said he never knew any woman take less trouble. Could silence bore him?

'*Am* I a bore?' she said.

'Most bores talk too much.'

'I hope I am not,' said Emmeline, sipping her claret. 'Though I still don't see, in a way, how it could be helped.'

'We must face it,' said Markie, solemn.

'I suppose if I did really bore you, you wouldn't say so. Are most of your friends amusing?'

'No,' he said, definite.

'I expect they are. But as you're amusing yourself you might not notice.'

'Only one can be funny at a time, if that's what you mean,' said Markie tartly. To be looked at so dispassionately by Emmeline and told that he was a funny man was a little blighting. Beyond an extraordinary flow of high spirits her nearness and their attraction set up, he did not, in fact, waste much wit on her. Partly because he distinguished acutely between intimacy and society – her presence lay lightly upon one; she was kinder than solitude – partly because his wit, from its very nature, blunted or splintered against a quality that he called her divine humourlessness, and that was in fact a profound irony. He found her – like all naïve and humourless people who did not in any way represent themselves by a manner but had to be taken as they were found – funny: she seemed adorably comic. Her seriousness, her angelic politeness, her cat-like unaccountability all, while exposing themselves to his laughter, remained beyond his derision. If the complete moral calm with which she had stepped in Paris over one line in behaviour surprised, in a sense even shocked him, some elusiveness underlying her generosity, something she still withheld unawares renewed the hunter in him, restoring to love what compliance might have destroyed: its mobility. Something escaped the senses, something broke through the hard intellectual frame of his idea of her: her unconsciousness still had him wholly at its command.

All the same, she had asked if she were a bore. And he asked himself – making her come with him to the fire, before which they stood, his arm round her shoulders, his fingers exploring the arm and shoulder so sensitive to his touch – if she ever could be. The possibility glanced his way like a confederate: he was unwilling ever to love her too much. In his nature some final displacement was still impossible. In Paris he had briefly and even brutally told her they could not marry, that he could not, in the day-to-day sense, ever live with her or try out, as they must in marriage, the balance between nights and days. As their relation took form and the shape of their feeling began to appear in its rhythm, his reasons for that quite instinctive refusal became more apparent. The fact was, she kept him uneasy. While her passivity soothed him, an exaltation at all times latent in her regard and, so great a part of her passion, likely to spring out at any time, alarmed, irked and often fatigued him. He had still the sense, as after that first night in Paris, of having been overshot. Her goodness had an unconscious royalty and was overbearing: under her too high idea of life and himself some part of him groaned, involuntary. Her easiness, her unexactingness, the very absence in her of that prehensile quality he detested in women – that had made at the outset Cecilia's friendliness too like a pretty, firm hand placed on his arm – all argued in her the deep and innocent preassumption that they were each for the other.

In fact, she was not everyone: there were places she could not occupy. He lacked his Daisy who cried, crooned and pitied and called him her dear bad boy. He missed something that, leaving the gift shop, he had been able to brush from his person like Daisy's powder; he missed also that tinkle of falling bric-à-brac, those giggles in the dark.

'The fact is,' he said, 'one can't live on the top of the Alps.'

'Alps?' she said, having travelled further than ever from thought in the warm firelight, under the influence of his touch.

'I can't live at top gear,' he said, rather more lamely, conscious that half his meaning must go astray.

'Oh, no,' said Emmeline, 'that would be tiresome. Why?'

'It occurred to me. One would give out, you know.'

'Oh yes; one would be bored.'

This was all very well – 'All the same,' said Markie, facing her round to him, held by the elbows, so close that staring into each other's pupils they squinted a little, and had to laugh, 'we do disagree, you know.'

'How large your face looks,' she said, drawing away a little to bring it all into focus. Her soft big-pupilled look, indolent and unsearching, passed from feature to feature, caressing the fleshy mask that it loved so well.

Tightening his grip on her elbows, he went on: 'We do disagree.'

'About everything, yes – stop, Markie, you're hurting me rather – I don't think that matters.'

'You *don't* think: that's just the trouble.'

Surprised, she said: 'What is the matter, Markie? Is this your conscience?' Though she had never met Markie's conscience she had heard it sometimes, creeping about the house.

'No,' he said angrily, 'Common sense.'

A shadow of more than incomprehension, of distaste, even of

boredom crossed Emmeline's face which, always transparent to feeling, now seemed, pale and clear in the lamplight, more than half transparent materially. She said: 'You are like an insurance company,' and did not explain why.

'You must know this can't always be this.'

'Nothing goes on,' she said. 'We grow old and don't care, then we die: I don't think it matters.'

'Look at me!' he said sharply.

'I'm looking – what else can I see?'

'God knows: I never dare think what you do see. Nothing at all like things are.'

'Near enough.'

'For you, I daresay.'

'You're unkind,' she exclaimed.

'I'm alarmed.'

'If I'm not – and of course I do see in one way I am ruined – I don't see why you should be.'

'Oh, all right. As you like. But we *are* riding for a fall.'

'I don't care.' Smiling, she drew her finger across his angry uncertain lips in a little line that should conclude the argument.

'I do,' he said, when the finger had gone. 'You know, you've been idiotic.'

'How, a fall?'

'Oh, I don't know . . . But it will be the devil.'

It would be the devil. Her unusual touch on the spirit stirred rare solicitude in him; he was afraid for her. He was, however, a good deal more afraid for himself. He had had a frightening glimpse – as she stood serious, eyeing him, anxious to share the untimely burden of this idea of his but with her most radiant air of being outside calamity – of how very high a structure there was to come down. The tall tower, that rocked by some shock at its base or some flaw in its structure totters and snaps in the air, falls wide; the damage is far-flung: you cannot stand back enough, it is upon you. Markie, in whom something cowered, was much afraid for himself. He was afraid, as she stood there so gently beside him, as much *of* as for Emmeline; it was almost physical.

This irrational fear of her touched him a moment, ice-cold and feathery like any bodily fear, in the mouth and the palms of his hands. She had, as he saw, stepped in Paris clear of the every-day, of conduct with its guarantees and necessities, into the region of the immoderate, where we are more than ourselves. Here are no guarantees. Tragedy is the precedent: Tragedy confounding life with its masterful disproportion. Here figures cast unknown shadows; passion knows no crime, only its own movement; steel and the cord go with the kiss. Innocence walks with violence; violence is innocent, cold as fate; between the mistress's kiss and the blade's is a hairsbreadth only, and no disparity; every door leads to death ... The curtain comes down, the book closes – but who is to say that this is not so?

That Emmeline should have consented to love on his terms was to Markie, now knowing her better, extraordinary. Some idea he had of her reeled every time she appeared in the door of his discreet flat. If such strangeness sweetened possession, it let in an insecurity: he knew less and less where he was with her; reason gave out. As her friend he could only deplore her bad bargain. He had a sound worldly sense of, in her world, impeccability's market, a keen legal mistrust of the disadvantageous. You cannot research in law, bring up fine points for the telling conclusion, cement an uneasy position, in short, make out a strong case, without gaining respect for the right as an asset if not as an absolute. While not discounting the heart, for which you cannot adjudicate (his idea of the heart was hazy) he could not see why she had not shown a better head. The success, in spite of its notable absence of method, of her outrageous Bloomsbury bureau showed a flair for business – if only (as he still believed quite simply) in knowing so well how to exploit her charm. She might have exploited this further: had she held out till he was crazy he would no doubt have married her: that she had not cared to buy marriage appeared incredible ... In view of all this, her wildness appalled Markie. And to this wildness, this flood, this impetus that he could not arrest, there appeared no limit. He dreaded the fall. He could wish he had never disturbed her, never possessed her but left her as he first saw her, smiling at him like a stranger across the room.

Emmeline, feeling suddenly tired, sat down, leaning back on the sofa. She said: 'Are you trying to tell me this ought to be over?'

'Good heavens,' cried Markie, unnerved by her beauty and her directness, 'no!'

'Then don't let us talk,' she said, shutting her eyes as though the bright weight of the room were upon the pupils.

'I was only saying – I'm not dependable.'

'One thing about marriage – one would not have these discussions. Or do married people discuss?'

'You're right,' he said, 'we waste time.'

'They have more time and waste it; but not like *this*. If we were married, you'd have to be with me unless you could think of some reason not to. You'd hate that, wouldn't you? . . . But all the reasons against marriage sound so silly: I suppose it can be a good thing. Cecilia and Henry were happy. The good reason for us not to marry is, we don't want to.'

'It wouldn't suit us.'

'No, it wouldn't suit us at all . . . Besides, you don't get on with Cecilia and I don't think your sister likes me.'

'Family dinners . . .' said Markie.

'Sometimes they're nice.'

'Never – This *does* make you happy?'

'I wish I were everyone.'

'Why?'

'Because then everyone would be happy, and also I'd always be such a change for you.'

He said: 'But I like monotony,' sitting down on the sofa. So the discussion ended, with fatal softness. Shadow drew back, having hesitated on the threshold; draughts died down as though in a heavy curtain . . . The fire fell in; falling rain tapped on the parapet; hardly a sound came up from the street.

'Turn out that lamp,' she said, 'it is in my eyes.'

XXIII

August approached, but Cecilia could still tell no one her summer plans: these not existing she had to envelop herself in an air of mystery, from which soon sprang a rumour that she was engaged. Only Julian did not inquire. Much was possible, nothing seemed to decide itself; everyone warned her against the heat in America. There were enticing alternatives – a tour in France, a cruise, several possible visits – for any single of which a young woman might have been grateful; but some hazy distaste hung over her mind in considering anything. For her part, Emmeline said rather vaguely, she would be staying in Wiltshire in August with Connie Pleach.

'I don't think,' said Cecilia severely, 'that that would be at all a good advertisement for your bureau. You ought to travel.'

Emmeline, whose own decision was really far more acute – for the first time in her life her plans were dependent on someone else's, for the first time she had to move furtively in the dark – said she might go abroad later, suggesting, with unusual lack of feeling, that Cecilia would do well to make up her own mind. And it was, she said almost sharply, an *agency*, not a bureau.

'Don't be snappy, my sweet,' said her sister-in-law, surprised.

There was no doubt that Emmeline's temper was less angelic, or that her candour, while still beyond question, had lost transparency. They felt this at Woburn Place. Lady Waters – in the course of a lengthy call at the agency, in which she scared off at least three diffident clients and removed the last of some circulars for hypothetical friends – had made the same observation: Emmeline lacked equanimity, Emmeline, their relative warned Cecilia, was not herself: it was clear that some strain had arisen between her and Peter Lewis, and that in consequence clients were dropping off. Upon Cecilia's sharply saying that this was nonsense, Lady Waters reported to Gerda that clearly some strain had arisen between Cecilia and Emmeline, for poor Cecilia was not herself at all.

'I only met Mrs Summers once,' Gerda said guardedly. 'And, if you remember, she was not herself that day either. Or so you said.'

'No one can be *more* herself than Cecilia: she is touchingly open-hearted. She seemed so well at Farraways, but of course the place is like home to her, one can see her light up when she arrives . . . I sometimes wonder if there is not something a shade unnatural about Emmeline.'

'How unnatural?' asked Gerda hopefully.

'It would be hard to explain.'

'Frank says he met her once. But she wouldn't, of course, be his type.'

At her own mention of Frank Gerda became very conscious and Lady Waters looked thoughtful. The Daimler, slipping and stopping in the afternoon traffic of Regent Street, took Lady Waters, who had had lunch with Cecilia, with Gerda to see some pictures. The wettest weather was over, the day made a sulky concession to someone's idea of summer. Gerda, who had lunched all alone at Fullers' on salad and ices, then exposed herself (or so she imagined) to much disagreeable attention while waiting at Carrington's corner for Lady Waters, who was unpunctual, anticipated their afternoon of appreciation with some despondency. Lady Waters, however, had met the artist. Gerda's shares with her patroness, just at the moment, seemed rather low: having heard much too much of Cecilia she could not help introducing the subject of Frank.

This was a success: Lady Waters, looking into her deeply, said she must put Frank right out of her mind, at least for the present.

'But he is so sympathetic.'

'I liked Frank,' said Lady Waters. 'But men who are sympathetic are not, alas, always dependable. Julian Tower seems sympathetic but I do not think he is treating Cecilia at all well. I do not expect he means to play fast and loose, but I don't think he can quite realize what he is doing; she cares for him more than she knows. I'm afraid, Gerda, that Julian and Frank are both men who prefer what they have not got.'

'Oh, Frank's really not like that!'

Gerda glanced at a strip of mirror to see herself blushing; her friend's acute silence remained a strong comment upon the blush. She took more interest in Gerda for the rest of the afternoon.

The Blighs' plans for August were still upon the knees of Lady Waters, who had told Gerda, and later had Gilbert to lunch to repeat this to him, that it became imperative for them to get right away together and talk things out. Gilbert agreed, with the reservation that he should also like to play golf and a little bridge;

Gerda, who did not play golf, agreed to go any distance their friend thought suitable provided there should be something to look at when they were not talking things out. Casino, cathedral, she was indifferent; she thought for her nerves' sake she ought to sun-bathe. 'But suppose,' she said, 'we should really *quarrel* out there? It would look so silly to come back separately; besides, I really cannot look after luggage.' Lady Waters said she had understood things could hardly be worse than they were, and Gerda assented meekly. But then what to do with the babies? Gilbert's mother was selfish, her mother was going to Switzerland. It could but occur to the Blighs how nice it would be if the babies were asked to Farraways. But their babies, too far short of adolescence, did not interest their friend.

'You see, we can't talk things out with the babies *there*.'

Lady Waters agreed that this might be difficult. As the Blighs could not hope to enjoy themselves, no one could call them selfish; all the same, she felt bound to remind Gerda that her and Gilbert's relationship was not to each other alone; it was triangular – or, recollecting the number of babies – more strictly, square. 'Oh, I *know*,' Gerda agreed. She was feeling, in spite of Frank, quite the little mother and had bought, while waiting for Lady Waters, two small frilly sun bonnets . . . They arrived at the gallery: Lady Waters, holding her private view tickets, swept upstairs, Gerda bobbing anxiously in her wake. Someone suspiciously like Tim Farquharson, with a young woman in scarlet, slipped out by another door as they came in.

Emmeline, her official morning quite broken up by the length of Georgina's visit, and by Miss Armitage's plain view of the visit, expressed in sniffs and some glaring silences, could not get down to much work in the afternoon. She had been out late with Markie; her head swam, her eyes were heavy; any jar in the office clanged on her nerves. At about four o'clock she left Peter to it and drove home to Oudenarde Road; mortified by this desertion she took a low view of herself and locked up the car despondently. She went round by the garden – hat off, pushing back her hair that felt close and heavy – and wearily mounted the steps to the drawing-room window. Undisturbed shadows, calm outlines of doors and furniture, a bee drumming over a bowl of sweet peas on the indoor silence, all promised solitude.

But Julian, solitary and from his attitude waiting, was in the drawing-room; he stood, back to the window, looking at one of Cecilia's books. More books, aslant on the table, must have been put down restlessly: two cigarettes were ground into the white jade shell. That Julian should smoke in her drawing-room before Cecilia's arrival argued in him (had Emmeline noticed) unusual tension. Surprised that he should not have heard her come up the steps – for by his whole air he was listening, though tuned, perhaps with that exclusiveness of close attention only to pick up sounds from the hall – Emmeline paused in the window. Seeing her shadow, he turned.

'Hullo, Julian, I've come back early.'

'How very nice!'

'Isn't Cecilia here?'

'She wasn't sure of her movements, so I said I'd wait.'

The meeting, though friendly on both sides, even affectionate, was not quite easy: both felt the shock of a presence on taut nerves. Emmeline sat on the end of the sofa and smiled at him, pushing her hair back, but said she could not stay: she was going to have a bath. Her manner, halting and even childish, put Julian in charge: bringing out his cigarette-case mechanically he found himself doing the honours.

'I don't smoke.'

'I remember,' he said, discomfited.

What Emmeline wanted most was to lie full length on the sofa, eyes shut, feet over the end, infinitely relaxing in nerve and muscle. Checked in this, she had hardly energy left to walk upstairs. Fixing on Julian her gentle, unfocused gaze, pulling absently at her hat-ribbon with long fingers, she said no more.

'Look here, Emmeline: you've been doing too much.'

Touched by the note of authority – and what a comfortable relative he might make! – she explained that this was a specially busy season, that their campaign was taking effect and clients were going in dozens to places they'd never heard of. She added that they had a secretary who clicked reproach at them like a waiting taxi.

'Not your Miss Tripp?'

'No . . . we rather wore her out.'

'So she left you?'

'She's having a holiday.'

He could feel her collecting her thoughts at a distance and

speaking to him from a long way off. Something it was an effort for her to see round or over must take up her whole foreground. He would have liked to take momentary but entire command of her life, take away the felt hat on whose brim her fingers kept nervously closing, say: 'Either sit right down or go, my dear,' most of all, to sponge Markie clean off her slate – to undo, in fact, what was not undoable. Small exasperations, defeats, curiosities that kept pricking his love for Cecilia alive could play no part in feeling for Emmeline: he asked himself what in her could have been the first object of Markie's rapacity, and whether even that quickest, most potent and brutal of vanities could realize itself in a single act of destruction.

Emmeline, by coming so softly and suddenly in when all his thoughts were Cecilia's, renewed with him her first appeal, something less disturbing and rarer than charm or beauty. Her presence, so cool to his heated and anxious mood, could have been pure refreshment. But he was haunted – still so clearly seeing her that first night in her silver dress in the alcove, watching ice tip about in her glass – by some quality she had lost: perhaps simply composure. Stumbling upon each other in this empty hour, they both seemed cast up – wrecked in fact, for with each of them something had miscarried – on a bleak little island of intimacy, too small to explore.

Against Markie he felt a profound and disturbing anger. But with Julian anger turned inwards, and while sapping with long roots his nervous being put up few outward shoots. Though her weariness and distraction brought the partisan in him to its most militant, what could he do? Aggression appeared preposterous as the practice of duelling to his fatally mild temper. He had, too, to admit, with the bitterest of inward smiles, that having gained so little ground with Cecilia he had no right on behalf of Emmeline to that transported possessiveness that in more vigorous ages sent the brother out with the whip. In the holy war reason plays no part: in Julian feeling was shredded by cold good sense. Championship has to discount in the woman anything but passivity, to deny that she could not have been undone without some exercise, however fatal, of her discretion and was in fact her own to ruin. Had he every privilege, were he far more than her sister-in-law's so far ineffective suitor, Emmeline would not, he saw clearly, tolerate for a moment his interference. She still believed herself happy; untouchable resolution showed even in her lassitude like a mountain-top on a too clear sky. More, her gentleness masked every shade of will from contrariness to fanaticism. There is one kind of sublime officiousness, anger's or love's, that is overruling: pure anger crystallizes its object, the seducer becomes the abstract of appetite or the thief. But Julian's was impure: horrified reason played too great a part in it; he could not pack Markie – engaging, rational, witty, intensely social – into the box of one idea and run a sword through. He was not disinterested, being aware of sheer man-to-man envy of Markie for cutting so much ice.

Emmeline dropped her hat to the floor. 'No,' she said 'leave it –' and sat looking down. 'I'm sorry I'm sleepy; I so seldom see you. It must be the time of year.'

'I know,' he said sadly, 'we never meet.'

'At that party, you asked why we hadn't, and I said I was out all the time or else having a bath. Though it sounds like what people do say at a party. I think it was true. This house is Cecilia: when I come in I see her, simply, whether she's in or out. Nothing feels part of me, yet I live here too. I feel I leave nothing but steam in the bath. Is your house ever like that?'

'It may well be: I don't know.'

'Who wants to know? – You're quite right. Accounts do balance, or should, but oneself never comes out: it is waste of time. All the same, I should like to live *somewhere*; it would feel more natural. If you were to marry, Julian, your wife would locate you: somewhere would become special, you'd know where you were. But no one could do that for me, and no one seems to expect me to do it for them. When I put cups and saucers away in the office cupboard, it feels as though they had flown there; even boiling our kettle isn't anything like the pleasure it would be to someone else. When I plug the kettle in, then see it boil, I know there is something I'm missing – You know Markie, don't you?'

'A little,' said Julian, leaning against the mantelpiece. A lustre tinkled, the pretty parade of objects, fans, figurines and boxes, continued behind his shoulder.

'If I died,' said Emmeline, 'it wouldn't – though I expect you would all be sorry – be very noticeable. But if Cecilia were dead, every time I looked at those ornaments I should think: "How terrible." – You don't know Markie well?'

'We meet now and then.'

'People seem to think a good deal of him?'

'I know few men of his age with such a sound reputation: he ought to go a long way.'

'He is nice, isn't he?'

'Very,' said Julian, smiling.

'You don't have to agree,' said Emmeline, 'some people don't like him. Cecilia, for one, doesn't like him at all . . . He doesn't live in the Temple, you know; he has a flat in Lower Sloane Street, over his sister's house. His sister is Mrs Dolman, her husband is something to do with gas: those houses are very big. He has a lift for things to come up in, and when he wants to talk to the cook he whistles: when he talks to the sister they telephone. So it is quite independent. Yes, he said he knew you a little. We once saw you having lunch.'

Julian nodded, and named the restaurant.

'He and I don't know many people in common, so I remember. Do you really remember? It was a hot day.'

'You wore a green dress.'

'It seems so long ago.'

'I was with my sister,' said Julian, not knowing what else to say.

'However happy one is,' she went on, with more than her usual air of inconsequence, 'one is glad of a friendly face. Is that why one asks friends to weddings?' She watched the bee glitter above the sweet peas and circle out of the window. 'People seem so pleased when people marry: is that why they go to weddings?'

'Just general good-will.'

'Do you think it really does much? – People's good-will, I mean: does it see one far?'

'I suppose it must be reassuring. And people cement things: "In the presence of friends," and all that: if one must be committed it's better to be committed right up to the hilt.'

She said quickly: 'But what commits one isn't what people know. And why should one want reassurance?'

'Don't you, ever?'

'I don't see why one should . . . Cecilia says when she's happy she feels like sitting alone in a café quite empty but full of looking-glasses, with all the lights on: herself makes a crowd, she says. But hundreds of one's reflection could be so frightening –' She broke off to listen. 'Is that Cecilia now?'

They both listened. 'No.'

'I really must go to my bath – What do you and Cecilia talk

about? – I'm sorry,' she added, colouring, 'all I meant was, what *do* other people talk about, all the time? There must be something to say, but I wonder what? I feel speechless so often, as though I were climbing a mountain.'

'I feel speechless as though I were pulling one foot out after the other across a bog.'

'Oh Julian, but you're not dull! I expect you make people talk; you make me talk now. And yet, if you know what I mean, I have really nothing to say to you. I don't think these are my thoughts. Do you know what people are like?'

'I suppose we all think we do.'

'Cecilia tells me I don't. One couldn't expect, could one, to agree with anyone the whole time?'

'Not the *whole* time, but –'

'Oh surely,' she said, 'disagreements are on the surface? Perhaps between friends the surface was meant to be rough. One has to try to speak: words twist everything; what one agrees about can't be spoken. To talk is always to quarrel a little, or misunderstand. But real peace, no points of view could ever disturb – don't you think so, Julian?'

For a moment he did not answer. Then: 'You do know,' he said, 'that I want to marry Cecilia?'

'Yes – I do hope she will.'

'There seems no reason why she should. But Emmeline, if – in the remotest eventuality – what would become of you?'

'What,' she said rather wildly, 'ever becomes of anyone?'

'I do wish, my dear, you'd have *some* idea . . .'

She looked at him so intently that he was startled and felt a spasm of self-reproach. Then he saw that the face turning his way its narrow angelic oval in fact concealed the entire retreat of thought. She had gone away. With her whole good-will, he no longer had her attention, for which her quick movement of consternation was all penitence. To have wandered, or have been suspended, while he was speaking of what was so near his heart . . . ! Her lips trembled, not daring to ask what he had just said.

'Idea?' she repeated. He cursed himself for a blunder: her mind might have spun itself out on that fine thread of talk that, snapped off by his question, now trailed in the air. It had been fatal to speak of the future: he felt the whole Emmeline in recoil. If she were difficult, even impossible, she was rare and dear enough to be humoured.

To this blank pause, Cecilia came in. They heard the front door click, a pause by the telephone-pad, the drawing-room door whirled open and she was with them.

'Oh Julian, I *am* so sorry – Emmeline darling, home?' She stripped off her white gloves, dropping her handbag into a chair: the room sat up visibly. 'How terrible of me,' she added, animated and happy. 'But why ever not have tea?'

'I forgot,' said Emmeline, stooping to pick up her hat.

'You're tired,' Cecilia said swiftly.

'I'm going to have a bath.'

'I had Georgina to lunch. And oh, just think, Julian, I gave her a pudding I got from her own cook!'

She stopped to watch Emmeline wander out of the room; when the door shut: 'Julian,' she cried, 'what *have* you been saying to Emmeline? She looks all over the place.'

'We just talked,' he said, taken aback.

'I suppose she's just tired. Georgina's convinced that something's wrong at the office.'

'Doesn't Lady Waters exaggerate?'

'Oh yes,' said Cecilia, ringing for tea. 'All the same, you know, there's no smoke . . . Have I wasted much of your afternoon? Georgina gave me a lift to the top of Bond Street, so I did some shopping: a hat . . . She was taking that unfortunate Gerda Bligh to a private view.'

Leaning back in his chair, he assured her she had not wasted his afternoon. He asked her about the hat, and told her about a picture he thought of buying. Whatever had been in his mind before lunch, when he so urgently rang up, had gone now or was adjourned: once or twice while she talked she sent him a flitting glance of inquiry, not knowing if she were glad or sorry.

Julian gone, Cecilia ran up to dress: it was very late, she was dining out. At last, very hurriedly, snapping one bracelet more round her wrist, she tapped at Emmeline's door.

'Come in,' said Emmeline after a moment: she came to the door in her Chinese-blue dressing-gown with the dragons. In there, the bureau gaped open; letters and papers were tumbling out: she did not bring office order into the home. Damp from the bath her hair clung in strands to her neck: her lids drooped; headache was written over her forehead.

'I'm going now,' said Cecilia. 'I'm terribly late – To please me, Emmeline, don't go out again. You –'

'I told Peter I'd go to his party, but I think perhaps I'll ring up.'

'Yes, do. There are *cachets fèvres* in my drawer.'

'I'll find them.'

'Emmeline – there *is* nothing wrong?'

'Nothing, honestly. Have a nice time.'

'Nothing Julian said worried you?'

'No, he was sweet.'

'I do wish you'd give up the office, or take a holiday. I wish you'd at least think it over. Everyone says –'

'I don't want to,' said Emmeline with that impassable note in her voice.

'But you might suddenly want to; you might find it such a bore. You're really too young to get tied up: it is such waste of you, such waste of time –'

It was like Cecilia to rush at essentials with one eye fixed on the clock. Emmeline said: 'Cecilia, you will be most terribly late!'

'Or suppose you got married –'

Emmeline, smiling, re-knotted the cord of her dressing-gown. She said: 'Nobody wants to marry me.'

XXIV

'And another thing,' Mrs Dolman went on, voice twanging over the wire, 'if you can't make your friends go out quietly you'd better keep them all night. Two men in what sounded like ski-ing boots crashed past our door about three o'clock; neither Oswald nor I got another wink. Then your friend with the giggle came down and dropped her evening bag, several keys and a good deal of change, and had quite a hunt for everything, bumping against our door. I may add that she left the lights on. Why didn't you see her out?'

'Who, Daisy? There'd have been far more noise if I had. It was her look-out: she wouldn't go with the others.'

'And please see that your empty bottles go down in the ash-can and don't leave them outside your door. The cat knocked one down today and it was by the mercy of heaven it didn't go through the banisters and splinter on somebody's head. And another thing –'

'You should shut that cat up, it nearly broke my neck for me last night, moping about on your stairs in the dark. Besides, it's dirty – Now shut up, there's a good woman: I'm in a hurry.'

'Cook's taking this week-end off: why, heaven only knows. If I don't let her, it just means she won't come back: I see that in her eye. She's had enough trouble with you. If you want Boulestin sauces at ten minutes' notice you'll have to go somewhere else –'

'– Willingly.'

'So till Monday you'll have to eat out.'

'That leaves me cold,' said Markie. 'I'm going off this week-end too. As it happens. Otherwise ten minutes' notice like this would be damned annoying. If you can't manage servants at your age you'd better shut up shop. Anyhow, what became of that sherry I sent down for sauce? Where's the whisky I didn't lock up? That woman's so tipsy she can't whistle. Now clear off the line for God's sake: I've got some telephoning to do.'

'If you are going off, they'd better turn out the flat. Last time I was in the place smelt like a bar – Shall you want anything forwarded?'

'No, I'll be in on Monday. Yes, they can clean up, but if I find anything missing I walk straight out. And don't let them touch the books, either. That's all, I think.'

'Have a nice week-end,' said his sister agreeably.

'Thanks. I'm going to Wiltshire.'

'And next time your friends come in –'

'Oh, sleep it off!' said Markie. He hung up.

At this time of the morning, the whole flat looked as though it had been slept in. There was a general staleness, rugs rucked up, cushions about the floor, ash everywhere but in the ash-trays. Daisy had left a comb on the mantelpiece; rings from the bottoms of glasses were stamped on the furniture. Markie, shaved but still in his dressing-gown, pulled a suitcase down from the bathroom shelf and began to drop things into it: he was not taking much to Wiltshire. The telephone rang again: 'Damn!' he said wearily. But it was only Emmeline.

'Markie, I'll be ready by one. Do you bring cigarettes, or do I?'

'I will. And the drinks, of course.'

'And her matches are sure to be damp. Do you like ham or tongue?'

'Anything, anything. I'm seeing a man at eleven: don't keep me, there's a good girl.'

'All right – Do you think Connie'll leave soap, or should I –'

'We won't wash. I'll be ready one sharp. Good-bye, angel.'

Emmeline ran the car up some ruts into the lean-to; Markie swung the suitcases out and they went round to unlock the cottage. Connie Pleach had lent Emmeline her cottage out on the downs, not far from Devizes.

They pushed the door open; at the first breath Emmeline, who had not come here before, felt she had been quite right about the matches. The 'woman who came in' had lit a fire; twigs snapped and charred in thin smoke, a kettle hung over them on a hook. Two windows looked at the skyline up the calm grey-green flank of the down, a lovely picture of emptiness whose changing lights flooded at every moment the small grey room. The windows, closed, shut in a faint smell of bleached damp from limp calico curtains: there was a smell of oil lamps. A great gilt harp, one of Connie's heirlooms she could not house in her basement flat, effectively blocked the wall-cupboard beside the grate. A red Recamier couch shed stuffing; there were two string stools, backless, a Windsor chair, broken, and a kitchen table painted cobalt blue.

'Where,' said Markie, looking about, 'does the woman sit down?'

'I don't think she does, much; she generally walks about.' Emmeline, beaming, dropped a whole armful of parcels and added: 'But we'll sit here.' Sitting on the red sofa she held out her arms to him, so very happy to have arrived. He kissed her (for they could always go back to the inn at Devizes); side by side on the sofa they still looked about. A big black-and-white of Prague (one of Emmeline's posters) flapped at them from three drawing-pins; there were some photographs, one rather hackneyed Van Gogh and a framed certificate stating that Connie had joined the Band of Hope. A distinct mustiness drew their attention to bookshelves. 'At least,' she said, 'there are plenty of books.'

'Oh, there are.'

'Now don't,' said Emmeline. But with Markie so cheerfully carping she felt quite un-anxious. Her eyes shone, colour tinged her cheeks; fresh wide air and escape from the pressure of London had restored her equanimity. And she was enjoying, too, the domestic rôle: had she not spent the morning shopping at Fortnum's, determined all should be of the very best? No sardines, no cheese from the village shop should offend Markie. Perhaps her disassociation from cups and saucers, of which she had spoken to Julian, came simply from living with the pervasive Cecilia: here objects had each their full circle of charm and mystery. She patted the red sofa, leaned back to twang the harp; then, getting up, moved the harp and looked into the cupboard. Here she found pewter plates, two Coronation mugs, Breton bowls, a Crown Derby cream jug, a good deal more china from Woolworth's, and several grey dinted spoons. There was a smell of mice. 'Here's Worcestershire sauce,' she said, 'either curry powder or mustard and – oh, poor Connie, she did leave soap!'

'Happy?' said Markie.

'Yes – Shall we keep the harp somewhere else?'

'Have you found the glasses?'

For a moment this worried Emmeline, then she discovered them just at eye-level, ranged in a row. While Markie undid the drinks she went into the scullery; here the oil-cooker was potent: she opened the window. Shadows edgeless and soft in the flooding mild light rolled over the face of the downs; close by the window three hollyhocks bore up their spikes of red frilly flowers. Leaning out over the warm sill, Emmeline touched a hollyhock.

'I say, Markie,' she called in a minute, 'there aren't any stairs.'

Drawing a cork, he shouted: 'Look in a cupboard.'

She looked; there the stairs were, neatly packed in, twisting up to the attic light.

'How clever you are,' she said, muffled, head up the staircase. 'How do you know about cottages?'

'I've heard of them.'

In fact, this Connie's cottage idea of hers had been received by him in the first place with great mistrust. Fancy played little part in his pleasures and he did not lightly let the amenities go. He had anticipated, quite soundly, that she might spend much of their time looking bothered or even stricken and asking where things could be. He had heard enough of week-ends of this kind to be exceedingly funny about them without having had to expose himself to the discomforts of any one cottage. There was a good deal of business with tin-openers, you hauled about buckets and kept running backwards and forwards for milk or beer: what animation arose had a raft-like quality of gratitude for survival. Never feeling that this could be fun, he declined invitations of this kind – so persistently that, just now, he had lugged the suitcases over the bumpy threshold with a dreamlike malicious pleasure, as though he were to hear of this happening to someone else . . . He and she, however, had long been planning to go away. Their brief and irregular meetings – so little fair weather between the last frost of arrival, the earliest shadow of saying good-bye – were unsatisfactory to both of them, wretched for her. Their free time was too short for travel; the risks and banalities of an English hotel she refused to contemplate. It would have been his idea of a joke to have borrowed Farraways, servants, cellar and all (he overlooked Lady Waters). Failing this – which Emmeline did not seem to think funny and would be incapable, anyhow, of bringing off – there had remained Connie's cottage. So Markie let Emmeline have her own way. To play at house with her for two days would not be uncharming; there was also no doubt her first round with a Primus would reduce Emmeline to entire and rare dependence on male capacity. Two days undisturbed possession of her, clear of Paris or London, had a sweetness hard to resist. Markie had measured the map with his thumbnail before starting: Devizes, he always reflected, was quite close by.

'Markie,' she called again, 'there's a pump in here.'

'Do we have to pump it?' he said, suspicious.

'Connie didn't say so.'

He came in, with his drink and hers, to inspect the pump; he waggled the handle but only a gurgle came.

'Never mind,' she said, 'there's water out in that barrel. Or we can ask the woman to find us some in a well: the kettle's full, anyway – Why,' she said, looking askance at her glass, 'have you given me this?'

'To drink.'

'But I'd rather have tea.'

'But it's long past six.'

'Never mind.' They returned to the parlour, where Emmeline, kneeling, began to puff at the twigs with some wheezy bellows. White ash raced round the hearth; up the chimney Emmeline saw a small patch of sky. Though she discouraged the fire, her air was a wordless magnificat. Markie looked at the parcels, there seemed to be a great many. 'What's this?' he said.

'A ham,' said Emmeline proudly, watching him undo the wrappings.

'But, my dear girl, we can't eat a ham in two days!'

'I thought we'd be hungry.'

'We'll have to bury it.'

'In the shop it looked smaller,' she said, discouraged.

'I suppose it's cooked?'

'Yes, they said so.' Rallying she went on: 'When the kettle does boil, let's run everything into one and have high tea.'

Markie hesitated: he foresaw trouble. 'As a matter of fact I thought we might dine in Devizes; I think it might be a good plan. The inn's quite good; I ate there once.'

'Oh *Markie* . . .' She put down the bellows. 'I brought Greek honey and biscuits and everything; I brought special coffee for you to make . . . It was half the point . . . I thought it would be such fun.'

'Yes, angel; lovely tomorrow. But tonight I do feel I should like a good plain dinner: I had no breakfast and half a sandwich for lunch. I'm sorry: all men are beasts. But you know we should take half the evening fussing with plates and things and then be half the night clearing away.'

'I meant to have everything lovely . . .' She had pictured them at the table between the two windows.

'I know. But I feel,' he said firmly, 'dinner might do us good.'

Emmeline said no more; she blinked at the fire; the kettle, now humming, put out a comforting thread of steam. The cottage, the late lovely sense of arrival tugged at her heart. 'Here we are,' she had thought, coming in: but she had been wrong, they were not. For ever coming and going, no peace, no peace. What did Markie always want to avoid? She thought of backing the car out again from the lean-to and bumping over those five miles of by-road to Devizes: she thought of the bald street, and close room, the kind clumsy waiter bumping against her chair. She would not mind, she thought, if this did any *good*: she drooped. 'If you'd told me,' she said, 'I wouldn't have brought the ham. I'm so tired, Markie; I'd hate to drive any more.'

'You're hollow,' said Markie firmly, 'that's what's the matter with you, my girl. You can't stuff with cold tinned food at this hour, it's horribly indigestible. What you want is a good plain –'

'Yes. But the ham isn't out of a tin.'

'Pity *I* can't drive,' he said rather touchily.

Unforgivably, she did not reply. Markie's conviction that this sort of thing had been bound to occur perhaps precipitated the crisis, for a mild crisis it was. He had an irritated conception of Connie's circle – which no doubt Emmeline found sympathetic – as sitting round on these rush mats tearing bully beef with their front teeth and talking art. 'Of course if you put it that way,' he said in reply to her silence, 'we'd better stay here and eat your ham.'

'Oh no . . . when do we start?'

'You'll feel better with dinner inside you,' said Markie, cheered. 'About seven? Then we'll come straight back.'

'I'm afraid we are bound to do that,' said Emmeline icily. 'There's nowhere else we could go.'

Wondering whether to shake her, Markie ignored this; no one is so impossible as a hungry woman who does not know what is the matter. Markie was being more tolerant than one might have expected, for which he got little credit.

'I think,' she said, more or less to herself, 'I'll make tea all the same, as the kettle's boiling: I'd rather like to make tea.' In view of everything else he could not discourage this. So she soon knelt on the hearth-rug, chafing her hands round a mug of tea, looking wisely and sadly into the smoke.

Markie did not drive a car because machinery bored him; also on the principle that it is a mistake to do anything anyone else can do for one: he did nothing at which he could not excel. Secure in the prospect of dinner, he roamed round to look amiably at the bookshelves, took out a yellow volume, blew dust from the top and returned with it to the sofa, where he swung his feet up, opened the book at random and read aloud:

' "Quand on aime, à chaque nouvel objet, qui frappe les yeux ou la mémoire, serré dans une tribune et attentif à écouter une discussion des chambres ou allant au galop relever une grand'garde sous le feu de l'ennemi, toujours l'on ajoute une nouvelle perfection à l'idée qu'on a de sa maîtresse, ou l'on découvre un nouveau moyen, qui d'abord semble excellent, de s'en faire aimer davantage. Chaque pas de l'imagination est payé par un moment de délices. Il n'est pas étonnant qu'une telle manière d'être soit attachante.

' "A l'instant où naît la jalousie, la même habitude de l'âme reste, mais pour produire un effet contraire. Chaque perfection que vous ajoutez à la couronne de l'objet que vous aimez, et qui peut-être en aime un autre, loin de vous procurer une jouissance céleste, vous retourne un poignard dans le coeur. Une voix vous crie: ce plaisir si charmant, c'est ton rival qui en jouira.

' "Et les objets qui vous frappent, sans produire ce premier effet, au lieu de vous montrer comme autrefois un nouveau moyen de vous faire aimer, vous font voir un nouvel avantage du rival.

' "Vous rencontrez une jolie femme galopant dans le parc, et le rival est fameux par ses beaux chevaux, qui lui font faire dix milles en cinquante minutes.

' "Dans cet état la fureur nait facilement; l'on ne se rappelle plus qu'en amour *posséder n'est rien; c'est jouir qui fait tout*; l'on s'exagère le bonheur du rival, l'on s'exagère l'insolence que lui donne ce bonheur, et l'on arrive au comble des tourments, c'est-à-dire à l'extrême malheur, empoisonné encore d'un reste de l'espérance.

' "Le seul remède est peut-être d'observer de très près le bonheur du rival. Souvent vous le verrez s'endormir paisiblement dans le salon où se trouve cette femme, qui, à chaque chapeau qui ressemble au sien et que vous voyez de loin de la rue, arrête les battements de votre coeur –'

'– Rot,' said Markie, putting the book back.

Emmeline, who though already too familiar with *De l'Amour*, from which Cecilia frequently read aloud, had politely stopped stirring her tea to listen, said: 'Why?'

'One's got no time for all that.'

'Stendhal crossed the Alps with an army with a valise strapped on to his horse,' said Emmeline thoughtfully.

'Oh, no doubt,' said Markie, '*he* could have driven a car.'

Before they left for Devizes, Emmeline walked down the grassy garden and picked some cornflowers; she said to herself that they would not be long away. Markie came after her; they stood looking back at the cottage, at those funny surprised dormer windows to which the stairs led up. A few posts pegged the garden away from the endless down; nothing else was in sight. A little smoke from their fire dissolved in the clear evening; the downs in their circle lay colourless under the sky. Some childish idea of kind arms deserting her mind, Emmeline said: 'How alone we shall be tonight.' Like a presence, this cold stillness touched the idea of their love: would they dissolve like the smoke here, having no bounds? The low roof was comforting, but the cottage door, open, showed darkness where they had been.

At a thought, Markie's fingers tightened on hers. But he only observed, looking round the skyline, that this did seem a queer place for Connie to keep a harp.

'Feeling better?' he asked. On the whole, they had not done badly, though he looked doubtfully into his coffee-cup. The waiter hovered, anxious to bring the bill: high up some pale electricity lit the ceiling among the pelmet-shadows, but daylight was in the street. A few other people lingered over the crumbs; someone looked hard at Emmeline, who did not notice, and from Emmeline to Markie. Having by now quite lost the thread of her day she sat looking out of the window, making no movement to go home.

'I'm sorry,' he said, 'I hate your being so tired.'

'I expect dinner was a good plan. You look sleepy, Markie; have you been working late?'

'Some people came in about twelve and stayed all night.'

'Did you have to see them?'

'They never rang up, simply came walking in: like a fool I went to the door.'

'Who?' said Emmeline idly.

'Two men and – oh yes: Daisy.'

'Oh yes,' said Emmeline.

'Of the shop,' said Markie, too easy. 'They said they'd just thought they'd look in: nothing would make them go. I was rude enough. The fact was, Daisy was feeling sociable, but didn't feel quite like coming in on her own.'

'I suppose not. Did they enjoy themselves?'

'I don't think so; I hope not. They drank a good deal and stood round and said nothing particular; Daisy walked on some records and said what a nice flat I'd got.'

'Hadn't she seen it before?'

'I suppose she'd forgotten.'

'What's Daisy like?'

'Oh, very nice. Her uncle's an archdeacon.'

'Oh, don't be tiresome, Markie!'

'There's nothing much else to say. She's kind-hearted and has a nice complexion: she's putting on weight. She's got a hide like an elephant; she's all right when she doesn't talk. I should think she'd bore you: she might not.'

'I don't suppose we shall meet.'

'Her telephone bill's too big: she can't bear to wait till anyone rings her up –'

'– Why must you talk like this?'

'Well, you rattle me, angel; sitting there looking like that.'

'Like what?'

'Death.'

'You overrate yourself, Markie,' she said coldly.

'Sorry,' he said, stung.

'I love you.'

'Then that's all right.'

'Does Daisy know all your friends?'

'She knows them; they don't always know her. I'm sorry, but that's accurate. Oh yes, she has quite a good time; she gets off, if that's what you mean. Those two men she brought in last night she'd picked up at a party.'

'Does she miss you?'

'She never lets old friends go.'

'I'm glad she has a nice time. I expect she's amusing.'

'Oh yes.'

'Do you ever miss her?'

'There's not much to miss: she's a nice creature. She's behaved very well, really.'

'Yes, people do.'

Looking at her oddly and quickly, he said: 'Let's get back to the cottage.'

'Not yet.' Emmeline poured herself out more coffee, clattered her cup about nervously, did not drink. Her look stole his way and retreated under the bronze lashes.

'She was perfectly calm last night,' he said, 'if that's what you want to know. Just a little pathetic, but that was always her way. In her best days she was always rather like the song about the little church at Eastnor. That's Daisy's fun, after all: we all like a bit of sentiment.'

'What did the two men do while she was pathetic?'

'She stayed back while they were starting the car up, to look for her comb.'

'Did she find it?'

'I've no idea – no, it's under my clock.'

'I wish you hadn't told me,' Emmeline said suddenly, raising her eyes to his.

Markie's eyebrows twitched up. 'What,' he said, 'about Daisy stopping?'

Scarlet at the misapprehension, she said quickly: 'About her at all.'

Markie, half-way between chagrin – for Emmeline, most unconscious of critics, did not let blunders pass and he could but be conscious of her vibrations of distaste at much that he said and did – between chagrin and natural gratification, said: 'How could I know you'd mind?'

'I don't mind – How could I possibly?'

'All right, then, you don't, you don't. There's no reason why you should. Do be calmer, angel; you're fussing the waiter – You know you make poor old Daisy sound like a cheap gramophone. And you well know –'

'– You know I don't want to be told things. Markie: I do not need to be pacified. What things you think! I didn't want to be prying – Oh darling, what has become of us?'

'Nothing,' he said shortly.

It was the nearest they came to a scene. She said, looking round for her gloves: 'The other night, what did you mean by the Alps?'

'Mountains. Now get your things and come home. Yes, it's all right, I've got your gloves: they were under the table. Yes, you look lovely' – for Emmeline, turning round rather wildly, had stared at herself in the sideboard mirror. Excited by some new element in her beauty, he sat repeating: 'Lovely,' with rather too pointed calm. 'Perhaps just a bit of powder: you didn't when we came out ... Yes, that's very good. I'd do anything for you, angel: push the car home if you're too sleepy to drive. We'd get back about as quickly, along that road – Emmeline, if you keep on looking at me like that I shall scream. What in hell's the matter?'

'I believe,' said Emmeline, 'we forgot to lock up the cottage.'

Someone had done this for them, no one had stolen the harp. The woman who came in had come in, no doubt to see if they wanted anything more. Also, no doubt, said Markie, to find out what they were like. Emmeline reached up to light the lamp; the hanging lamp swung a little, tilting its shadow about the beams. The last light from the downs went out; in lamplight the windows darkened. The brown paper they had left lying was neatly stacked up, flames flickered under fresh logs – all the same, though, the breath of the cottage was cold – the ham had been put away. What the woman thought of their negligence only Connie would know.

'She's brought eggs,' said Markie, 'twelve, in a plate. She must think we're titans.' He got glasses and put syphons down on the table. Emmeline heard a moth on the window-pane; she caught it and threw it into the dark: it whirled in the light from the window and disappeared. Then she drew the curtains. 'Hullo,' she heard Markie saying, 'she's brought a telegram too, or taken one in. Yours, Emmeline: here –'

She stood still by the window. 'What can it be?'

'Well, look! Perhaps Connie's wishing us luck.'

'Oh no, she –'

Standing under the lamp with his arm round her, Emmeline read the telegram: she read it through twice:

Come back Sunday must talk very urgent indeed –

Cecilia.

Emmeline said: 'She's going to marry Julian.' She stared at the post-office writing, so unlike Cecilia's, while something slid down in her like a dead weight. Timber by timber, Oudenarde Road fell to bits, as small houses are broken up daily to widen the roar of London. She saw the door open on emptiness: blanched walls as though after a fire. Houses shared with women are built on sand. She thought: 'My home, my home.'

'She's going to marry Julian.'

Markie, having quite naturally read the telegram over her shoulder, had put, for a moment, a much more annoying construction upon it. 'You don't think she – '

'No. No, it's Julian.'

This did, after all, seem likely. Relieved, Markie said with sincere good feeling: 'Oh, excellent, splendid: quite the best thing she could do.'

'She wants me home tomorrow.'

'Yes, so I see. But they can't be in such a hurry as all that.'

'She thinks I'm with Connie.'

'While we know you're not.' His arm, tightening, felt Emmeline unaccountably tremble. Two moments, Cecilia's and his, were in conflict: he pulled the telegram not too gently away; those half-shadows behind their talk at Devizes mounting up in him in an impatience ravaging and intense. Damning the bridal Cecilia, he crumpled the paper and threw it into a corner: had they not come here to be alone?

'I know she is right,' said Emmeline, looking round wildly.

'Quite right, quite right.'

'I'm so fond of them both.'

'Well, let's drink to them.'

Shakily, Emmeline took the glass.

The loneliness of the downs, the great weight of darkness over the cottage, these unfamiliar shadows, a sense of being swept strongly apart on a current from all she had held to, made her that night cling closer to Markie, beseeching from the rough and impersonal contact of passion a little comfort and peace. Silence acute and momentary like a wind standing still came in from the dark outside as Markie turned out the lamp and kicked out the fire. The stairs door swung on the bending candles; one more violent and wordless hour disjointed from life was written over the week-end cottage.

XXV

'But how did you know?' said Cecilia, pausing a moment quite breathless from her quick flow of talk. Her mind ran on ahead, she could hardly wait for Emmeline's answer, which did not come.

Emmeline, who could formulate nothing, put up a hand to her cheek that still flamed from the sun and speed of the journey, and that departure. It was Sunday evening, soon after seven o'clock: she was just home.

'I suppose,' Cecilia supplied, a shade grimly, 'it was what everybody expected.'

'It's what I hoped.'

'Darling . . .' Cecilia said, with that odd elation that had not time to be happiness. 'I suppose,' she went on, 'I seemed crazy, sending that wire. But I came in yesterday, after we'd – after it was settled, feeling so strung up. You had to hear first; the idea of not seeing you until Monday night sent me nearly silly. Still, I suppose it was selfish. Did Connie mind?'

'No,' said Emmeline.

'I didn't expect you'd be doing anything special.'

'Oh no, we weren't.'

'Bless you,' exclaimed Cecilia. 'Now this feels like home.'

Reading Markie for Connie, it had been terrible. If this were home, one fled here with battered wings: it would not be home long. Still stunned by the day, Emmeline heard Cecilia's voice from a long way off, and had an impulse to catch at Cecilia's long sleeve floating past, as her sister-in-law paced the drawing-room, shaking ash everywhere and excitedly talking, to assure herself she was once more in kind if oblivious feminine company.

To say that Markie had minded would not be adequate. Any talk of return to Cecilia he blithely discredited overnight, and had taken as done with. This morning Emmeline said she *was* going back; nervousness made her assertive; she could not have put things worse. Upon this, the dead stop of his tenderness, flicked off sharply as electricity, his incomprehension and ice-cold anger had given

209

that hot bright Sunday – downs bald in sunshine, heat quivering in through the cottage doors – the lucidity of a nightmare. He told Emmeline she was mad: that her madness was nothing to him he made plain by a hundred manners of walking away, of releasing himself from her touch, by a cold self-sufficiency that – as he lay, legs crossed, reading on the red sofa, or strolled in the outdoor sunshine – she could never disturb. Yesterday's unborn pleasure, today's might-have-been hung about the cottage, picking out the harp, the hearth and the pictures in lines of agony, afflicting her senses whatever she touched, wherever she turned. If her presence became an irritant, the cottage too small for them both, this was easily cured by strolling out on to the downs when she came in, by turning unconsciously indoors again when she followed. A profound and slighting contempt for her point of view, that must have under-lain at all times his tenderness, was apparent in all that he said and did, most of all in silence. This complete disconnection between them, so disorientating to Emmeline, meant, he made evident, little enough to Markie.

She endured this throughout the morning. Then: 'Markie,' she cried, 'I won't go. We'll stay here tonight. I'm sorry.'

Taking a book from the shelf, Markie turned with raised eye-brows. 'Oh?' he said. 'Stay here? Why?'

'You know I don't want to go!'

'Then we don't see eye to eye: I'm afraid I do.'

'I beg you to stay!'

'We mustn't upset Cecilia.'

Emmeline, meeting his cold eyes, was startled by what she saw. She exclaimed: 'You fight like a woman!'

'You ought to know,' he said, taking his book to the sofa.

Emmeline stood by the fireplace, hands clasped in terrified resolution behind her back. 'You *must* listen,' she said. 'Because you're first now, now you're everyone, was that any reason to hurt Cecilia? Oh, *understand*, Markie: don't just shut up your brain! What reason have I to give her for not coming back? Look at all the lies she's believed about this week-end, about my being here with Connie: she thought I went off rather bored because Connie asked me. She knows Connie couldn't keep me away when she'd said it was urgent. I know this must seem just a small thing, Cecilia's marrying Julian: I know people keep marrying every day. But she, I – she must want me so much, or she'd never have wired. I'm part

210

of Henry; I mean all *that* to Cecilia: I have to be good to her now. Before all this, before you came, I wouldn't have understood: now I know how she feels. She wouldn't have wired if she hadn't thought I'd be longing to come. How *can* she know how things are with me – you and I, here? All this, changing everything for me, how can she understand? If I don't go tonight, there is only one thing I can do: I must tell her why not. I couldn't bear her to think I just failed her for no reason. If I said the car had gone wrong, Cecilia'd think: "Why not a train?"'

'Well, why not?' said Markie, turning over a page.

'If I don't go back I must tell her . . . But I couldn't; I can't, Markie: it would be too cruel. You don't know how she feels. She's . . . not like us, she wouldn't ever see why . . . Just now, when she's so safe and happy – it would be cruel! You see, she'd think I was ruined. She'd blame herself; she'd never be able to understand – Why did that telegram have to come? Interruptions like this, don't you see, are a tax on our sort of love. People in love like Cecilia and Julian, people married, have passports everywhere. They don't get telegrams, nobody sends for them: everyone understands. But you and I – wherever we go there is something to keep us separate. Someone is out to break us. We're not any nearer each other for being tied up in lies!'

Still saying nothing, Markie turned over another page. 'I think you will kill me,' said Emmeline.

Unnerved by her white face he said: 'For God's sake, don't make that fuss in here.'

'But you must understand. You may be bitter, you ought to be fair. *Markie*, put that book down! I ask you to put down that book!'

He put down the book politely, keeping his thumb in the place.

'Listen: I give in, I give up. Cecilia'll just have to bear it. I'll let things be spoilt between her and me. Could you think I wanted to miss our day? Our minutes are all so precious I never know what to do with them. All I ever wanted, all I ask now is to stay. Every time you and I part it tears me to bits. There is no one but you.'

'If we must really go into all this – my dear Emmeline, you put no one first but yourself. Your will, your conscience, your lunatic sensibility. No doubt you are right, but you can't have it both ways, you know.'

'I love you. I beg you stay here with me tonight.'

'Love?' said Markie. 'Love with you's simply a theory. You care for nothing but being right. It's a pity you can't be natural.'

'Oh, Markie. Natural . . .'

'You think you've done something extraordinary.'

'It made you happy.'

'Oh yes.'

'Whatever I am, forgive me. I only ask you to stay.'

'Quite frankly, I don't care to stay in a cottage this size with a cold and hysterical woman.'

'I see,' said Emmeline, dropping her voice suddenly.

Fixing her eyes with his cold eyes, he had that uneasy feeling, that quick touch of physical fear again, as though something were going to spring . . . She turned away, went to the cupboard and began to put out the plates for lunch . . . After lunch she stacked up the plates and wrote a note for the woman, explaining they had been called away, were leaving the ham and some groceries as a present and were sorry they had not had time to eat the eggs. She skewered this note to the ham, left five shillings on the mantelpiece, went upstairs and packed for herself and Markie: the bedroom was too small for two people to pack in at once. She shut the windows and drew the print counterpane over the bed. She forgot to take off the kettle, and left the cornflowers she had picked yesterday in a mug on the window-sill. Markie thanked her for packing for him; he bumped the two suitcases downstairs and into the car. They locked up the cottage and left at about three o'clock.

Neither looked back as the cottage slipped into a fold of the downs: the dazzling white road spun ahead and they made good going. When Emmeline stopped for petrol Markie got out and put through some calls to London: they kept him some time; he apologized pleasantly for the delay. Some plans for the evening: she perfectly understood.

'You must write a nice letter to Connie,' he said as they entered London.

'Yes,' said Emmeline, 'she has been very kind.'

In the drawing-room, looking at Emmeline rather uncertainly, Cecilia said they would have, she supposed, to talk plans. But not plans tonight.

'One thing you haven't told me: when are you and Julian actually getting married?'

'Oh well,' said Cecilia airily, 'that depends.'

'Not on me?' said Emmeline, colouring.

'Oh, darling, no: why?'

'There can't be much to wait for. *There* are your August plans, ready-made.'

'Yes,' Cecilia said, 'things do arrange themselves, don't they. All the same, I naturally feel –'

She broke off. Emmeline said, curious: 'What do you naturally feel?'

'– A poor thing,' said her sister-in-law, with a complete change of tone and surprising bitterness. 'Not very much of a life. I have flopped all ways; I hang on looking pretty about it, like one of those wretched creepers. First Henry, then you, now Julian. I don't think you know how I've leaned on you – and so dishonestly, too. I say to everyone: "Dear vague Emmeline, where would she be without one?" Simply because I find *cachets fèvres* for you, and order your dinner. You were too young to know when it first began, then you grew up into it. How you have suffered my foolishness! Now I go on to Julian, all smooth and easy. But what are you going to do?'

'I'll get a flat: I should like a flat.'

'I wish Julian had married *you*!'

'I do wish he had,' said the smiling Emmeline. She paused, however, and looked at Cecilia, anxious. Now that Cecilia was leaving the Summers, now that Emmeline and what was left of Henry must draw in closer, excluding young Mrs Tower, it must become daily harder to speak without qualifications and growing reserve. Cecilia tonight, with her busy woman's loquacity, appeared already remarried. Catching at a veil that thickened between them, Emmeline said almost sharply: 'Cecilia, you're happy? This *is* all right?'

'Yes,' said Cecilia, 'it is. Though you may well ask. Julian really is good; I've tried all round in my thoughts to slight him, but I'm not able to any more. I don't have to pretend with him; we are easy together. If this went wrong, I'd be done for. It's all far better than I deserve: I cannot feel Julian's fortunate . . . However,' she added, brightening and trying to bite back a smile, 'he's thought it all over, with a thoroughness one can hardly consider flattering: I think he knows what he's doing.'

'And you do love him?' said Emmeline.

Cecilia turned quickly, surprised more by Emmeline's manner

than by the question. It was on the tip of her tongue to say: 'What do *you* know?' An uneasy presence made itself felt: she went small and transparent before this unknown Emmeline. She said at last: 'Yes, I do love him as much as I'm able. I wish there were more of me, but we do know how we stand. I don't think it does to examine things.'

'No, oh *no*.'

'Emmeline –?'

'No, I'm quite sure you're right.'

'I feel that I'm honest – Darling, why can't we adopt you?'

'I'm over age,' said Emmeline thoughtfully.

'I suppose we may have some children. Anyhow, we are finding a house somewhere: one couldn't possibly live in a flat. Poor Julian, moving his pictures – Darling, what fun it will be when this happens to you!'

Emmeline said irrepressibly: 'Don't let's talk about that.' She picked up the cigarette-box, now smoked quite empty, and snapped the lid rather disturbingly to and fro. Cecilia saw with amazement her finger-tips press themselves white on the shagreen box-lid.

'Emmeline, for heaven's sake, tell me –'

In the hall, the telephone rang. Emmeline put down the box: for an instant her heart stood still. Cecilia said: 'Julian,' smiling; everything was forgotten. Emmeline heard her plug the telephone through to her room and go cheerfully up.

Before midnight the house was asleep; Cecilia unstirring lay happy among her pillows. Emmeline, saying her name softly, crept to her door and listened: no answer; one was alone. Down in the hall like a thief she shut the basement door, all the doors, listened. Then she turned on the light in its gay hanging crystals, approached the telephone-table, looked at the clock: Benito appeared from nowhere and ran round her feet.

Very clumsily, slowly, she dialled a number. Looking through the white hall wall as though it were glass she heard the telephone tingle and dot out its double note in the distant flat. No one came. She still listened, seeing distinctly a room she had known too well or been too happy to see, where the repetitive bell made her in some way present, though there must now be nothing but darkness there. He was out. Having wrung from that silence so stamped with his absence no stir or answer, she hung up at last. She looked round the hall, her throat tightening, then fumbling through the directory came on another number and dialled that.

Mrs Dolman was disengaged, even affable. 'Markie?' she said. 'No, I've no idea, I'm afraid: I never do know. Is he not up there? No, he wouldn't be, he was not expected till Monday and they're half way through cleaning the flat ... Yes, he has been in: very cross. But I heard the front door bang, now I come to think. But we live quite apart.'

'Yes,' said Emmeline.

'Is it anything urgent? It *is* rather late, you know.'

'I'm sorry.'

'Oh, all right; I'm not in bed. By the way, who's speaking –'

'I don't think you'd –'

'– Who did you say?'

'Miss Pleach,' said Emmeline.

Mrs Dolman's smile was audible on the wire. 'Well, I'm sorry Miss Pleach, I can't help you –'

'Thank you very much, I –'

'Oh, for nothing. Better luck next time! Here, stop – he's got some friends somewhere in Maida Vale or St John's Wood: Summers: you might try there.'

'I've tried there,' said Emmeline.

'Oh, you have?' remarked Mrs Dolman, smiling again. 'Then I really don't know ...' She ran through some more names, entering with strange gusto into this chase of Markie. 'Or there's a shop,' she concluded, 'Kennett, somewhere near Sydney Place.'

'A shop would be shut,' said Emmeline dully.

'Not *this* shop; it's quite worth trying. K, E, double N –'

'Thank you,' said Emmeline, who had heard. 'I don't think I'd better. It isn't urgent. Only something he left in a car ...'

'*I* see,' said Mrs Dolman. 'Well, good-night.'

'Good-night.'

Emmeline turned the lights off and went upstairs. She stood in the dark in her doorway, she did not know for how long. Then she went down again with cheeks burning, turned the lights on, looked at the clock and found Daisy's number. The receiver felt clammy, her movements were not her own. 'Hullo?' said, almost immediately, Daisy's kind-hearted voice.

'Is Mr Linkwater there?'

Daisy bounded audibly. 'I – I don't know,' she said. 'He may be:

I'll see. Is it urgent?' Emmeline heard her put a hand across the receiver, but small chinks of sound came through. 'I say,' said Daisy, over her shoulder, 'a woman wants you.'

'*Fool*, I'm not here,' said Markie, quite near the telephone. There were indignant whispers; evidently Daisy was quite a fool.

'I'm so sorry,' said Daisy, uncovering the receiver. 'Mr Linkwater's *not* here. Try Sloane 00500.'

'Thank you. Good-night,' said Emmeline.

'*Good*-night.'

XXVI

Dear Uncle Julian,

Your kind letter made me so happy. It is good of you at this time of your great happiness to be so full of thoughts for me. I congratulate you on your engagement and Dorothea wishes to do the same. We both thought Mrs Summers so nice, and when I was at Farraways I found out she had a kind heart, also. It is nice to think she is going to be my aunt. I hope we may have many happy times.

I do not know what else to say except that I hope you will be very happy. Your life must sometimes have been quite lonely, and Mrs Summers will be a great consolation. You will be pleased to hear that Dorothea and I got 'Highly commended' for our garden. If a rabbit had not got in and eaten some of the annuals we might have got the prize, but we are very thankful. The white dress you so kindly gave me to sing in the choir will come in beautifully for your wedding, if it is warm enough. I hope Mrs Summers will like it. Little did we think, did we, for what happy purposes it would be worn.

I think that is all, except to send you my best love and Dorothea's kindest regards.

Your loving niece,
Pauline.

Cecilia read the letter, with several others that Julian had given her, in a taxi, on her way to Rutland Gate. She took taxis all day; she could not get anywhere fast enough. She also re-read, with a smile, a long cable from her mother. She and Julian had now been engaged for some days; it had been announced; the friendly world was upon them. Every day they met to exchange letters; they laughed and talked every night on the telephone.

Lady Waters received Cecilia, whom she had not seen since her engagement, in a glow of maternal importance tempered by slight foreboding. Far more, thought Cecilia, as though one were about to become a mother. She kissed Cecilia on both cheeks. 'This,' she said, releasing her gravely, 'is, I know, what Henry himself would have wished. You must be certain of that.'

'Julian is so very sorry he couldn't come.'

'That is quite all right,' said her aunt, 'he is dining with us tomorrow; I have been telephoning to him. He and I want a long quiet talk.'

'He'll love that,' said Cecilia.

At this point Sir Robert came in hurriedly, wrung Cecilia's hand, seemed to wonder if he should kiss her, and patted her speechlessly on the arm. 'Robert,' his wife explained, 'is delighted. After Emmeline, Cecilia, you come very near his heart.'

Sir Robert looked deprecatingly at Cecilia, murmured that Julian was lucky and disappeared. He was not to be with them for lunch.

'I cannot pretend,' Lady Waters said, 'that this is an entire surprise to me. In fact there have been moments, Cecilia, when I felt tempted to broach the subject, but delicacy prevented me. You are so very much my own niece (when your mother sailed for America she said, you know: "I leave Cecilia with you,") you are so transparent, I could watch Julian winning his way well into your heart. And I admit there were moments when I began to fear things might go astray; one is always alarmed, Cecilia, on behalf of anyone so heart-whole. Well, my dearest child, you are older now than you were, you should bring still more to this marriage. And now, mind, you must not let thoughts of the past stand between you and happiness. You owe this to Julian. *He* comes to you heart-whole (I think I am right in saying?). No, Cecilia, I see no reason why this should not be a success.'

'Neither do I,' said Cecilia, unclasping her fur. Georgina, she felt, was one of the many reasons why she and Julian should not live in London. All the same, one could not imagine living anywhere else. She stripped her gloves off to show her new emerald ring.

'Very nice,' said her aunt. 'You are not superstitious, of course?'

'Oh, no.'

They had quite a nice lunch. Cecilia asked amiably after the Blighs, Tim Farquharson and two or three more of Georgina's unhappy young friends, Georgina said that the Blighs should still win their way through; they had, however, a rather hard fight still ahead.

'Oh, dear, with each other?'

'No, with themselves. They think now of the Pyrenees . . . Frank is rejoining his ship: for the best, I daresay.' She went on to say that

Tim Farquharson had been seen driving round the park with a pale young woman in red, and though recessive when taxed with this was no doubt attracted. 'I daresay,' she added, 'I may hear about it tomorrow, when Tim comes to tea – Oh, and Emmeline will be sorry to hear she has lost a promising client: our vicar is dead.'

'Which vicar?'

'Our vicar at Farraways. I saw he had one of her circulars on his desk.'

'Had he? She never spoke of him.'

Lady Waters impressively cleared her throat. 'Cecilia,' she said, 'I don't want to worry you at such a time' – determination to do so glinting on every feature – 'but have you thought at all about Emmeline?'

Her niece felt inclined to say: '*Naturally* not!' Instead she said: 'Why?'

'There will be, of course, her future to be arranged for, but I am really more anxious about her present. I feel I should tell you. She seems to be taking directions one cannot approve. Without your influence, and with her quiet home life removed, there is no telling, as things are at present, what may become of her. For one thing, as I told you, one gathers on all sides her business is *not* doing well. She is losing her grip on it. I looked in again for a moment the other morning: she was not there: no one seemed to know where she was. That new secretary, who has a pleasant direct manner, was quite clearly anxious, though she would say very little – for which, of course, I respected her. That young Peter Lewis looked really haggard; I've never seen anyone less himself. It is, of course, always possible that his feeling for Emmeline may be changing, in which case their partnership would become difficult. I do not think this likely, from what I know of him, but these things are always possible. Emmeline may be quite unconscious: it might be thoughtful, perhaps, just to drop her a hint.'

'No, for heaven's sake don't do that!'

Lady Waters looked at her sharply. 'Evidently,' she said, 'you do share my anxiety ... Mr Lewis, however, is quite a minor point. Emmeline is attractive; there were moments when I thought Tim – but I daresay that was for the best. She is remarkably innocent for her age, and makes friends quite without discretion. This brings me up to my point ...'

Lady Waters again cleared her throat. 'Yes?' said Cecilia, contracted, nervous and gloomy.

'It is this: I hear on all sides that she's going about with a young man of whom neither Robert nor I can approve: Mark Linkwater. She was seen dining with him at Devizes some nights ago. And Devizes, Cecilia, is some way from London.'

'Oh, yes.'

'Even Robert is worried; I don't know what else he may not have heard. Robert would be quite the last, of course, to blame you, Cecilia. But I must say *I* do feel that – owing, of course, to this recent preoccupation, to your interests and your anxieties lying so much elsewhere – you may have been just a little remiss. One must face facts, you know: she was left in your charge when poor Henry died.'

'Henry never said anything. He wouldn't have dreamed of putting her into anyone's charge. Henry said nothing, Georgina!'

'Then he meant much to be understood. He would have relied on your taking his place: she had nobody else. He would have relied on your common sense –'

'– I had no common sense at that age.'

'A common sense,' her aunt went on, raising her voice, 'that you, rather than Emmeline, seemed liable to develop. Were Henry here now I feel he could only feel –'

This was intolerable. Cecilia put down her fork. Georgina's rounded periods bounced on her nerves. Was this simply the last of Georgina's outrages on good taste or abortions of fancy? Might not the nonsense she talked at all times discredit this? This outbreak of real perspicacity seemed preposterous as a seizure. That Georgina – stately buffoon of so many interludes, source of so many laughs between Emmeline and Cecilia – should sit here putting Cecilia wrong on behalf of Emmeline appeared more than fantastic. That Cecilia's conscience should answer was like a dream. She longed to ask what Sir Robert had heard, if anything; to know if that gentle optimist really were worried or if Georgina had simply harried him into expressing concern. Her heart went leaden; glancing down at her new ring she longed for Julian. 'What do you *mean?*' she said.

'I am telling you,' said her aunt. 'My point is just this: Emmeline is being far worse than simply silly and intellectual: she is doing herself real damage in her own world.'

'Which world?' parried Cecilia.

'There is only one world,' said Lady Waters. 'That young man's reputation is shocking. You may be certain that Robert would never listen to idle gossip, and I, while I have to hear of so much that is painful, am not an alarmist: I realize that up to a point one must live and let live. But how well do you know this young man? Does he come to your house? Have you attempted to put his relations with Emmeline on any regular footing? Myself, I hear nothing good of him.'

Cecilia fell back rather wretchedly on an echo of Julian. 'He's fearfully able; they say he is brilliant. He may be Lord Chancellor, anything . . .'

With dignity, and as it were in inverted commas, Lady Waters sniffed. Cecilia's heart went lower: that sniff was traditional. The fumes subsided, off went the Delphic trappings: here spoke sheer Aunt, empowered by plain good sense. That voice went back through the school-room and to the cradle.

'Lord Chancellor? Not for some time. Meanwhile, he is likely to do, in a quite irresponsible way, a good deal of damage.'

'But what can one do?'

'I'll tell you,' her aunt said, with awful readiness. 'In fact, Cecilia, it is more than time that you knew this and took a strong line. Evidently you know well what I'm talking about, or you would not look so uncomfortable. Your engagement to Julian puts you in a strong position. Till now, I admit, the extremely promiscuous way you made this young man's acquaintance yourself has put you at some disadvantage.'

'But I can't help talking to people in trains.'

'In future I hope you may travel with Julian, or have more ties: no good has come of your running about alone – You are in a position to act: you must act, Cecilia. You owe this to Emmeline; it is the least you can do for Henry. I may say that if you *don't* take this up, I intend to approach Julian. As your connection, Emmeline's good name becomes his affair –'

'No, you mustn't do that: he'd hate it!'

Lady Waters's eyebrows went up, perhaps at this rapid new growth of family selfishness. 'Very well: then listen to me. Either you must have this out with Emmeline, find how she stands with this young man and, with Julian's view to support you, *strongly* discourage the whole affair; or else, invite Mr Linkwater to your house, be as civil to him as you please but make him feel clearly that Emmeline has you and Julian behind her, and that her affairs are your own.'

'But they're not: Emmeline would be furious: we could never say that!'

'And he had better meet Julian,' went on Lady Waters, ignoring the protest.

'They've met,' said Cecilia sulkily.

'Not on these terms. Mr Linkwater's relations with Emmeline must be recognized, or they must stop. If he is up to no good he's not likely, on those terms, to trouble you long.'

'Yes, that's all very well.'

'– It *is* all very well. If you are too idle and selfish to use your influence with Emmeline, who has every confidence in you –'

'But really, I can't ask her *that* –'

'– And if you will not allow me to speak to Julian, I feel I have only,' said Lady Waters, clearing her throat again, 'one course left.' She looked thoughtfully at Cecilia, who, twisting her ring round in agitation, made no reply.

'My relations with Emmeline are more than delicate; she is not my own niece, I do not pretend to be in her confidence and I have no wish to force it. I may say,' added Lady Waters, 'that the idea is repugnant to me. But she is Robert's near relative, virtually his ward: he is devoted to Emmeline and I have seldom seen him so seriously disturbed. I cannot let this go on. If you refuse to do anything, I must approach Emmeline. I shall sift things out and go into the matter thoroughly: this affair of Devizes has really brought things to a head. I am sorry, Cecilia, but you are leaving me no alternative.'

'You mean, catechize Emmeline?'

'If that is what you call it.'

'No, no, no,' said Cecilia: her manner became hysterical. 'No, don't do that, Georgina: I'll have a dinner.'

'A dinner?'

'A dinner.'

'Whom will you ask?'

'Poor dear Markie.'

Lady Waters, noting with grave satisfaction that she had destroyed Cecilia's appetite so that the *soufflé* dwindled cold on her plate, cancelled the cheese course and led her back to the drawing-room, where she applied restoratives, praising her happy new bloom, asking about her trousseau and undertaking to find them a suitable house. Cecilia, talking with nervous rapidity, sipping her coffee, told Georgina much more than she had intended about her engagement to Julian: how when anyone else had proposed it seemed so much out of the question that she had never known how to begin to say no, and so seemed to waver; while to Julian she put up such reasoned and sound opposition that she had paused to consider, and been, considering, lost. Lady Waters, convinced that her niece had loved Julian at sight and had always intended to marry him, listened indulgently. When, at half-past three, Cecilia left to meet Julian her aunt kissed her once more on both cheeks. 'And mind,' she repeated, 'you must not let *anything* worry you.'

When Emmeline asked that night: 'And how was Georgina?' Cecilia said with a sigh: 'Depressingly sane,' and added no more.

Emmeline noted the sign of dismay: she clung to Cecilia's happiness. As in the mortal solitude of an illness someone turns for a moment to smile at a smiling face in the door, she looked forward all day to these evenings spent with Cecilia. Evenings together in the already rather distracted, doomed little house were becoming more frequent, for they had much to discuss and arrange. Julian was generous, friends from the outside world made fewer claims. Emmeline liked to be told little things, to be made to laugh, to enjoy through Cecilia the hundred happy banalities of an engagement. 'What happened today?' she would ask every night, coming home. She was sorry Georgina had not been funny at lunch, or that Cecilia had not had the spirit to find her so.

On evenings when Cecilia went out with Julian, Emmeline walked the roads of St John's Wood or up to Hampstead, quickly, her hands in her pockets. Wet or fine, when rain drew the lamplight out into long reflections, or moths from the sycamores whirled in brown air round the lamps, she walked late; pulling up vaguely at corners or stopping to stare over garden walls. The neighbourhood appeared strange to her. Trees were dull with July; dust and lamplight made the pale houses monotone; she heard voices sharp with late summer fatigue.

She walked, too, by day, the streets of east Bloomsbury: quite often she found herself crowded out of the office. Miss Armitage was no longer funny: the partners, frightened and impotent, did not know where they were. Some contraction in Emmeline, Peter's uneasy withdrawal had left a vacuum that this cold woman rushed in to fill. She held every inch and gained others: she undermined

223

them. Emmeline, upon whom inefficacy was growing, found she had no longer the power to fill her own desk. She sat staring at bottles of coloured ink in the pigeon-holes, or turned over dully the letters put out for her to sign: once she signed something she had not read. This broken spring in her enterprise, this betrayal of everything could no longer appal her. Wrestling for life with something she found she had no hands.

'It's absurd,' she said, meeting the panic in Peter's eye, 'we can sack her any day.'

'Why not?' But they knew that they never would. Everything passed through their secretary's hands; she had tentacles everywhere; without her, these days, they did not know what they were trying to do.

'I'm sorry,' Emmeline said, 'I lost Tripp for you.'

After just a perceptible pause he said: 'Oh well, it couldn't be helped.'

Emmeline thought she would come in one day to find that cold iron woman seated at her own desk. The old gay routine broke up; Miss Armitage made the tea; the partners were never alone. They became more regular, more efficient – but so were Cook's, so were Lunn's. Emmeline saw from the faces of clients how the whole character of the office changed. Coming in to project their holidays they missed that old radiant assurance, that sense of the whole world offered them smiling: holidays became just one thing more to be undertaken, this end of a gruelling summer. Cook's were quicker, Dean and Dawson's more central: just perceptibly, clients were falling away. The Serbs wrote from Paris that Miss Armitage had offended some of their clients. The graphs curled down from the walls and they pinned up time-tables. At five, at a quarter to, daily a little earlier, Emmeline with a murmured apology to Miss Armitage slipped from her desk, put her hat on and went out to walk the streets. Peter never looked up: cracking his finger joints, stooping and staring over the papers, Miss Armitage shoulder to shoulder, Peter worked heavily on.

'You should take a rest,' Miss Armitage said to Emmeline with her gaoler's kindliness. 'You look all to bits.'

'I can't go just now.'

'Oh dear, yes, Miss Summers: we should get on perfectly.'

The pavements off Theobald's Road are hot and narrow; you get jostled into the gutter or bumped on walls. All these years while

Emmeline worked in her quiet office these streets, so noisy and near, had been going on: now she and they were acquainted. One day, scared by a sudden darkness over the sunshine, by an intensification of London's roar in her brain, she turned into an empty tea-shop and sat down, pressing the palms of her hands to a marble table. She bought note-paper from the cashier and wrote, for the first time, to Markie. He did not answer. That week her hair went darker and dull, her face white: if anyone looked at her in the streets it was to wonder from what she was running away. Broken up like a puzzle the glittering summer lay scattered over her mind, cut into shapes of pain that had no other character. Walking the streets blindly she did not know that she thought, till a knuckle grazed on a wall, a shout as she stepped off into the traffic recalled her from depths whose darkness she had not measured. The bleeding knuckle, the angry face of a man shouting down from a lorry were like bright light flashed in her eyes: the nightmare drew back, waiting. One note held her ears through the hollow thunder of traffic: in shells of buildings the whirr of unanswered telephones. These were insistent: she put her hands to her head . . . To please Cecilia, she looked at two or three flats, rubbed grime from the windows to stare out, looked at the sockets for gas-fires, counted the mean little empty rooms.

This evening, seeing Emmeline disappointed, Cecilia was sorry she had nothing more to tell her, and racked her brains. She told her about Tim Farquharson's new young woman in scarlet, and that fearful battle lying before the Blighs. 'And oh,' she said, 'Georgina says you'll be sorry to hear you have lost a client: their vicar's dead.'

'Who's dead?'

'The vicar at Farraways.'

'Oh,' said Emmeline, turning away her face.

'Darling, I didn't know you knew him!'

'He came to tea once, one Sunday . . . He and cousin Robert and I had tea out under the lime. It was very sunny, in May. He liked christenings, he said; he said he enjoyed motoring.'

'I'm so sorry he's dead.'

'Oh well . . .'

XXVII

On Saturday Cecilia, pitching her voice rather high out of over-naturalness, asked if Emmeline would be in on Wednesday night. Emmeline thought for a minute: the emptiness of her evenings was carefully kept from Cecilia. 'Yes,' she said finally, 'why?'

'Markie is coming to dinner; I thought that might be nice.'

Having made this announcement with all the ease in the world, Cecilia became very busy with bright satin patterns spread over her knee – for her trousseau was now well in hand – and did not look up. Shuffling the satins, she was beginning to ask: 'What's happened?' wishing the clock would strike or something go past in the road to disturb the vibrations of what she had just said among the glasses and ornaments, when Emmeline asked quite smoothly, if from a distance: 'Why?'

'You see, Julian ran into him the other day, and Markie was so nice and friendly about our engagement and sent me all sorts of messages. So I felt sorry I'd been such a pig: I rang up and asked him to dinner.'

'What made you do that?' said Emmeline.

'I've been telling you,' said Cecilia, a shade tartly: she held up a strip of scarlet against the light.

'And he said he'd come?'

'Oh yes; he seemed rather touched: we arranged a day.'

Emmeline looked at Cecilia as though they must both be dreaming. Then turning away her eyes dark with fatigue she picked up from the floor a bright inch of satin that slipped from Cecilia's knee. She said: 'Is this your wedding dress?'

'How could I be married in scarlet? Dove grey for widows.'

'Did you say I should be there?'

'I don't remember, I –'

'– Did he ask?'

'I said: "We shall *all* look forward to seeing you" – Julian's coming, you see.'

'Julian . . . Did *Julian* want to?'

'Naturally. We shall be four.'

'Cecilia, why did you ask him?'

'Who, Markie? Because he's a friend of yours.'

'I see. But I don't see him now.'

'What do you mean?'

'We're not great friends now.'

Cecilia thought: 'Then why was he at Devizes?'

Uncertainty and confusion made her shuffle the patterns till she said reasonably: 'You mean to say, you've quarrelled? I'm sorry, darling. But, as he's coming, *he* at least must be wanting to make it up. He seemed anxious to come.'

'You must let me off,' said Emmeline.

'Darling, don't be so foolish; it isn't like you. If *he* can behave – and I've never thought that was Markie's strong point, as you know – surely you can, for an evening across a table? You know you think quarrels are silly: you and I never have them. One's got to behave. You can't creep away, it's all wrong.'

'You must let me off.'

'But I count on you.'

Divided bewilderment, seeing this at once as a trap and a door opening, helplessness, not knowing where to turn, a frightening distrust of Cecilia, who with bright imperious manner seemed ranged with the world against her, all kept Emmeline silent: when at last she said: 'I would so much rather not see him,' it was with such despairing inefficacy and such detachment that the battle seemed already lost, or won. Cecilia, not feeling bound to examine the tone too closely, dismissed a suggestion that this could martyrize Emmeline.

'Put him off?' she said briskly. 'I don't well see how I could. How can I be so uncivil when he's been friendly. We fixed the day: he'd know there was no mistake.'

'Let me be away!' said Emmeline.

Something frightened Cecilia more than she dared admit: it was she who looked young and helpless: with eyes dilating she searched Emmeline's face. 'I don't understand,' she said '– *does* it really matter?' She sat twisting her ring and knitting her hands together; round her, sadly as fallen petals, patterns littered the floor. 'Don't!' she exclaimed involuntarily. 'Darling, you frighten me!'

'I'm sorry: it's nothing.'

'Has something happened?'

'Only things going wrong.'

'Nothing happened in Paris?'

'No. I was very happy.'

'I knew things were all right,' said Cecilia. 'I always trust you.'

'I know,' said Emmeline.

'Then *does* this matter?'

'Not much – Just as you like.'

'Then,' said Cecilia, rallying, 'you really are being foolish. You're making mountains, beloved. Surely poor Markie's not worth all that.'

'Mountains?' repeated Emmeline, struck by the word.

'Yes, I do think mountains. You're certain to have to meet him sometime and somewhere: why not happily here? Parties do seem so often to put things right: there's nothing like looking pretty and being social. We always enjoy our parties – they've always been good parties, haven't they, Emmeline?'

'Always, yes.'

'And this may be one of the last – So you don't mind?' said Cecilia, pressing on her advantage. For a moment she thought she saw in Emmeline's eyes a wandering icy gentleness like insanity's, gentleness with no object. But this was as in a dream. 'You don't really mind?' she said.

'I don't mind,' agreed Emmeline. And before Wednesday this had become nearly true.

Benito lay curled up on Emmeline's dressing-gown. Looking into her wardrobe, crossing her bare arms up which the first chill of evening began to shiver, Emmeline found only two dresses pretty enough for Cecilia's party tonight: the yellow in which she had dined with Markie, the silver in which she had first met Julian. Since Markie's coming she had been out less often: very happy or unhappy one disappears equally. The yellow, unworn for so long, still showed a faint splash of sherry across the front: she had started so violently when the cook whistled. So she put on the silver, slipped her string of crystals over her neck, smoothed her hair and went down: it was early, not eight o'clock.

Julian waited about rather anxiously at the foot of the stairs. He disliked this idea of Cecilia's, suspecting behind it some shadow of Lady Waters, and had opposed it. 'But it is arranged,' she had said with smooth little intonation and raised eyebrows. 'If you don't mind . . .' she added. He did mind. All the same, here he was, pledged to assist at this ghastly farce, trying for all of them, martyr-izing perhaps to one: a farce only Markie's bravado, Emmeline's frozen passivity and his fiancée's rooted distaste for fact in the rough could have ever made possible. Here they all were, the table set, Markie soon to arrive: somehow things had to be carried off. Standing about in the hall, he heard with a start that showed plainly where his anxiety lay – Emmeline's door shut and Emmeline's foot on the stairs. Julian looked up to smile.

Her beauty surprised him. Very tall, silver and shining, her hair tonight at its brightest, face at its most translucent, her unnatural serenity caught at his heart like a cry. Were she dead, she could not have come from farther away. But from this distance, her silver dress sweeping the stairs, all the more Emmeline seemed to arrive at a party, one of those parties from which one is always absent, which heroes and one's friends' friends attend in some kind of heaven; the eternal Party to which Cinderella drove up, upon whose light the doors close. 'Here you are . . .' Julian said, holding out a hand – that, though smiling his way, Emmeline did not see – as her shadow came down the white wall.

A little angry with Julian, who she felt did not wholly support her, Cecilia, afloat on big flame-pink transparent sleeves, was everywhere: touching the flowers, lighting the tall table candles that made a pale ring in daylight, moving the glasses for sherry from place to place. Tonight was the first of her very last parties: no phase of her life had gone out in such festivity. She said to herself, only Markie was coming; but always that charming flutter was at her heart. The drawing-room, heavy and cool in late light with white Chinese peonies, the dining-room, pointed expectant glitter on lakes of polish, reflected her animation. Rooms put off their recent veiled air of being already left and forgotten. Quite pink with endeavour, her two little maids ran about below: claret warmed, salad chilled, the service-lift hummed up and down. Like the fountain-play of all nervous pleasure, tonight had a flexible delicate perpetuity. The doom of the house seemed a rumour and Julian, now going with Emmeline into the drawing-room, as innocent of it as any guest.

Julian thought how much he should miss these evenings at Oudenarde Road. Watching Emmeline watch the fire, he opened some cigarettes and advanced a match-box – already a little the host. Emmeline watched Julian opening the cigarettes: the pretty and smiling occasion was terrible. He unstoppered the sherry, moved a glass vaguely and looked about.

Cecilia swept in; disturbing their grown-up silence, in which she had no part, she stood like an eager child, at a loss, and did not know what to say. The clock-hands crept round: though Markie did not arrive he was still not late.

'Do I look nice?' said Cecilia. They were assuring her she looked lovely when the bell rang.

It was possible that bravado brought Markie to dinner. He unwound his white scarf in the hall and followed the maid in, smiling: delighted to see himself. Shaking hands with Cecilia – from their handshake her fluffy pink sleeve fell away – he agreed that this was very nice. 'I hope I'm not late,' he said; 'I came up from Baldock.'

'From Baldock? What a long way!'

The merit of this long journey flourished about Markie: he did explain, however, that someone had run him up. He glanced down the room: at the end, in late light reflected in from the garden, he saw Emmeline standing with Julian, in a long silver dress that he did not know. She smiled at him like a stranger. Markie advanced, as they did not, the greeting became general.

Chatting over the sherry, Cecilia wondered why she had not asked Markie to dinner like this before. Though still not entirely what she liked, he was competent and had floated, within two minutes of his arrival, what had once looked like being a rather dead weight. Julian warmed up and came forward, leaving Emmeline standing by the white mantelpiece. With his handkerchief, Julian mopped some sherry from the base of Cecilia's glass which was dripping a little: skirting these lovers, so taken up with each other, Markie strolled to the mantelpiece, where he put down his glass.

'Well, Emmeline,' he said quietly, 'how are you?'

'Very well.'

'Very busy?'

'We're sending a good many people to Palestine.'

'Won't that be very hot?'

Possibly Emmeline did not know: she made no reply. Having finished his sherry, Markie looked at her sideways to say something more, but at this point Julian came their way with the decanter.

The maid appeared at the door; they went in to dinner.

Between Cecilia and Emmeline, across the round table from

Julian, Markie, this evening, was at his best. He caught no flies on his tongue; he played gracefully up to Cecilia, gave Julian openings, kept inviting the silent Emmeline into the talk. Such a hum soon hung over the glasses that ten or twelve people might have sat down: his wit, more agreeable, lost its buffeting quality: later, Cecilia remembered nothing particular he had said, just that her spirits went up and she felt gay and successful. Ice encased Emmeline's most vivid smile and her listening attitude, perpetuating her beauty: she was 'behaving' as one would wish.

When just the tip of an angel's wing brushed the table: 'Well,' Markie said to Cecilia, lifting his glass an inch: 'Here's to Switzerland!'

'Why?' said Julian.

'Where Markie met me,' vouchsafed Cecilia, sparkling.

'Though in what part of Switzerland,' Markie said, 'one cannot be certain. In fact, I didn't know it was Switzerland till you told me.'

'Close to a lake.'

'And very nasty it looked – Did you finish that book?'

'Which book?' said Julian.

'A book she was travelling with.'

'No,' said Cecilia. 'Somehow I never took to it. If we could remember what time it was when we met, Emmeline could tell us where, to the very rock. She knows what all trains are doing all over Europe.'

Julian looked at his wrist-watch. 'Eight forty-eight. What is the Simplon-Orient doing now, Emmeline?'

Emmeline told them. Markie asked Julian where he and Cecilia had met: *he* seemed uncertain, she said it had been at Goodwood, the first and last time she had been; it had rained and she fancied no one. 'I talked too much,' she said, 'and sat too long on my foot at lunch; it didn't uncramp for the rest of the afternoon. I never did know anything about horses.'

Markie said he had learnt all about horses he had ever forgotten from men in the bar of the Irish mail: he had asked why one should not have an electric fox: they had been able to give him no reason. Smiling, Cecilia paid tribute to Markie's adaptability: in other company he would have been out with the Quorn . . . Looking across the table Markie reminded Julian that *they* had first met during the Strike: Julian had given Markie a lift to the Courts.

'Those two blondes,' he said, 'that you had in the back flagged another car going west the moment you put them down and drove back up the Strand again. They were having quite a nice morning; I daresay they got their lunch – Whereas you and I,' he added, turning to Emmeline, 'met at this very table. So this is an anniversary.'

'Yes,' she agreed.

Julian said: 'The night I met Emmeline, at a party, we danced till she said, very nicely, should we sit down and talk? When we'd talked a little, she said she wished we were dancing.'

'Emmeline, *is* that true?'

The maid drew the curtains: on the shadows their faces in candle-light sprang out into new life; something contracted a little about the table. Julian said to Cecilia: 'I wish I'd met you in a train.' Dropping her voice she said: 'Why?' – one of those questions between happy lovers that are never answered but float into speculation. Their eyes meeting, each sought in the other's a ghost of that first charming strangeness (a little blurred for these two by the rain at Goodwood) from which they had travelled far. They regretted that odd grace of love in its immaturity. Each tried to picture the other, unknown, balancing down a train corridor; unconscious, each veered round those inches that brought them full-face for a quick rush of words on her part, a wrapt inattention on his. Delicious and intimate confidence, like a match struck between them, was hastily sheltered. So lovers in company step off the spinning disc of talk for their half-moment, to step on again smiling ... Markie, taking the hint – one inch more of Cecilia's gauze-covered shoulder – turned quickly to Emmeline. They were almost but not quite alone: still with the light inflection of someone chatting at dinner he said: 'You are looking lovely: is that dress new?'

'No,' she said, surprised by the question.

His eyebrows went up at her manner; he said quickly: 'Aren't we friends?'

Her wide-apart eyes looked his way with unseeing intentness. 'I didn't think so,' she said.

'Then why am I here?'

She could have said: 'You are not,' for his presence remained unreal. She said at last: 'I don't know.'

'Then why get Cecilia to ask me?'

Emmeline's eyes dilated and darkened suddenly with amazement in her white oval of face. She turned away and sat twisting her glass, looking thoughtfully at her hand, as so often when they had been dining together. Once, by some reflex to his attention, her eyelids fluttered, she opened her lips to speak, as though some strange partner at dinner, dependent on her politeness, were by her side. Markie's quick look, sidelong, examined her fingers' movement about the stem of the wineglass, ran up her bare arm to the shoulder, the throat, then down the long string of crystals hanging over her dress. The look left its track of fire: Emmeline's fingers tightened about the glass.

'Idiot,' he said, still lightly. 'When can we meet?'

She said something inaudible.

'What did you say?'

'Never.'

'– Jane,' Cecilia said suddenly, recollecting herself, looking round. 'Mr Linkwater's glass ... Julian says he has heard of a house,' she went on, to Markie, 'but then we hear of so many. Where would you live? I don't think the house we both want has ever been built.'

'Why not build it?'

'I don't think we know what we want.'

'It would be devastating,' said Markie, 'to have to make up one's mind.'

Cecilia explained that nothing was light enough for her: she wanted something all windows; her distaste for dark walls, she feared sometimes, must be almost morbid. Whereas Julian must have wall-space, to hang his pictures. Chatting to her of Corbusier – still with an eye for Emmeline listening to Julian, cheek on her hand – Markie profoundly regretted coming tonight. Here, tonight, the incalculable had flared out – on his side again, at least – between him and Emmeline, on account of her unforeseen beauty, her distance and her renewed unconsciousness of himself. He was alarmed and unnerved by the violent resurgence of his desire.

So far he had come out lightly: if he had missed her, relief had room to predominate. He had kept a cold sense of her worth: consideration was owed her – was he not here tonight? – with the end in sight always he had the decent obsequies well in hand. It had been high time they parted: a woman who rang up Daisy would stop at nothing; things began to be dangerous, for there is no doubt that angels rush in before fools. He loathed suffering, out of place in the rational scheme: since Devizes, his major feeling had been resentment. The measure of her unhappiness he could have gathered, but did not dare gather fully, from one wild letter. Some idea of disaster, injurious scandal, of her life taken, her brain going, had smoked out at him like a djinn from the cashier's envelope: for a day when alarm and compunction had had their full way with him he avenged himself on her by silence. She had undone herself; she was her own victim; he was unhappy in having touched her; she would not ever be warned. Justice, inscrutable under the bandage, remained Markie's cold ally.

They had parted: no doubt for the best. But, having come just into ear-shot to leave her in better order, he found himself ambushed and did not know how to get free. A confused struggle against this renewed domination, with self-contempt, and a maddening resentment of his desire, sharpened his manner and – though throughout the rest of dinner he did not again look at Emmeline – added a bitter edge to his talk: Cecilia found him less pleasant.

In the drawing-room Cecilia added a log to the fire, while Julian pushed up the chairs. Emmeline thought it must be very late: it was half-past nine. Ten minutes with Julian of rather guarded banality had quite restored Markie's morale: coolly standing by Emmeline's chair he was ready for anything . . . Cecilia unfolded an *Evening Standard* with inch-high headings: the case of the moment was striking and she asked Markie to give them his inside view. This he did, with what seemed the most likeable indiscretion: two of his best friends were briefed for the case, he had met the lady concerned and he did not mind telling them . . . He stood with his back to the fire, very good company. A little wine and the evening had gone to Cecilia's head; she sat encouraging Markie: nothing remained unpalatable. Julian chuckled; Emmeline glanced once again at her wrist-watch: a quarter to ten.

Passing the cigarette-box Emmeline dropped it; the cigarettes scattered: Markie broke off and went down on his knees. In the confusion Cecilia and Julian touched fingers a moment: they smiled and thought: 'Not yet.' Kneeling up beside Emmeline's chair with a handful of cigarettes and reaching over to put them into the box, Markie said quickly! 'There's something I've got to tell you.'

Emmeline stared at him, mute.

'You must listen: when can we –'

'All right, never mind,' called Cecilia, bored by this interruption of stooping and groping 'we'll pick up the rest later.'

Markie stood up: they went on with the case but it dragged rather more. Emmeline leaned back, arms crossed on her knee, fingers curling up idly: she looked at the clock she was too blind to see behind Markie's shoulder. At twenty-past ten he said: 'If you won't think me rude, I must telephone soon for a cab: I've got to get down to King's Cross.'

'Oh dear,' said Cecilia, 'must you?'

'Alas yes; I've got to get back to Baldock. I've got all my things there; not even a toothbrush in town. My sister has shut up the house and taken her family to the sea-side, where one hopes she may drown them. All her servants walked out; she was almost incompetent. So I doubt if I'd ever get into the flat – May I telephone?'

'Couldn't your friends drive you back?'

'No, that wasn't my host; heaven knows where that car is now. We looked up a train; they'll meet me.'

Emmeline stood up and smoothed out her silver dress. She said: 'I'll drive Markie down.'

There was a slight movement about the room; an unmistakable protest. Markie said nothing, looking at Emmeline oddly. Cecilia exclaimed: 'Oh, no, darling, you can't! She mustn't, must she, Markie? You'll easily get a taxi.' 'Easily,' agreed Markie, fixing his eyes on Emmeline. Julian, looking from him to her, thought: 'Tragedy is disparity,' and did not know what this meant. The room felt very close; he opened a window and let in a rush of dark air. Between the uneasy curtains night came in, thinning the lamplight, and made the room darker and less secure. Cecilia, brushing on Julian's elbow her falling pink sleeve, whispered: 'Julian, don't let her go; it's all wrong; I don't want her to.' Julian staring down the dark garden – the plane rustled, in the bowl by the windows peonies stirred – said: what could one do? It remained their affair. 'It isn't right,' wailed Cecilia . . . Meanwhile, Emmeline had left the room to put on her fur coat.

Markie, disarmingly fatalistic, accepted whisky. 'Shall I get the car out?' Julian called up from the hall.

'Yes,' Emmeline called from above.

Benito had moved from Emmeline's dressing-gown on to a scarf of hers that was on the bed. He was still sleeping, one paw out, his little white chin turned up. Bending over Benito to smile, Emmeline touched his chin softly – a shiver of pleasure ran down his flank but he did not stir – and slipped the scarf from beneath him, winding it, warm, round her throat. She took her coat from the cupboard and turned the lights out. As she came downstairs Cecilia ran up to meet her, exclaiming: 'You oughtn't to drive in that dress!'

'Why not? I often have.'

'Then take your gloves – here they are, take them: your hands get so cold.'

Not taking the gauntlets, Emmeline went on down past Cecilia, whom she did not see: Cecilia, helpless, stood back against the wall. They had not parted like this before. In the hall Markie finished his whisky and put the glass down by the telephone. Under the fur coat, the hem of Emmeline's dress glittered past him and out down the steps with their carpet of light. 'Well,' said Markie, looking about for his hat. He said something hearty to Julian and held out his hand to Cecilia, who came down to take his hand in a dream. They said good-night: Markie thanked her, saying how charming it all was: he hoped they might meet again soon. He ran down the steps to where Emmeline sat in the small open car drawn up to the kerb.

'Don't be long,' called Cecilia, coming out after them.

Emmeline, starting the car, did not seem to hear: 'All right,' shouted Markie, 'she won't be long.'

XXVIII

For some minutes they drove in silence. Still on the crest of his impatient resolution to be alone with her, Markie jammed down his hat and leaned back, enjoying the air: the warm lampy evening blew like dust from his brain. He glanced once at Emmeline; but her deliberate profile invited nothing. Turning out of a terrace she bore left, uphill by the Finchley Road.

'Here, I say – this isn't the way to King's Cross!'

'We're going to Baldock.'

'My dear . . .' he said uncertainly, 'that's very nice of you.'

She did not reply. They swung up the winding curves of the Finchley Road, past Swiss Cottage station, past blind shop windows reflecting lamplight and couples halting and sauntering in the cool restless night. Lit parapets, at which he glanced up, uneasy, fretted the darker sky; swept by long spokes of light the wide street was watery. Eyes fixed ahead, never looking his way, she said quietly: 'Well?'

Indecisive, his look stole round, seeing blown-back hair, her white profile, her long bare hands on the wheel: an end of her thin scarf trickled and flew in his face. Slipping ahead through the traffic at even speed, they left down the Finchley Road a long wake of tension.

'Well, Emmeline?'

'You said you had something to say.'

Among street lights crossing like spears his thoughts were at every angle; indecision and stifling urgency held him tongue-tied beside her. Her white fur coat, slipping apart, showed a silver knee and some quenched light running among the folds of her dress: she was so close, his nerves leaped into his finger-tips. Her swerve round the blank black back of a lorry swayed them together.

'– Don't touch me,' she said, contracting.

'Sorry,' he said, with but general reference to the incident. 'But you knew I was always out for what I could get.'

'So that's been all right,' she said, in a tone so gentle and accurate he could detect no bitterness.

'Never,' he said briefly.

Not a line of Emmeline changed: she did not pause to consider this or to wonder, but, slackening speed for a moment took the wide black Hendon way: they bumped over tramlines; a long lit road running brighter with traffic crossed theirs. Left and right, homely windows were now beginning to darken, downstairs then up; large cars racing back to London shot ahead slipping vivid stretches of turf and kerb, sweeping fans of light over ceilings under which people lay half awake. A cold night smell came from the turf. Then: 'I'm sorry,' Emmeline said: at a pressure from her silver slipper the speedometer needle went creeping up.

Turning awkwardly in the small car, he put a hand over hers on the wheel, then felt her fingers harden. 'You're cold,' he said.

'We're going north.'

The cold pole's first magnetism began to tighten upon them as street by street the heat and exasperation of London kept flaking away. The glow slipped from the sky and the North laid its first chilly fingers upon their temples, creeping down into his collar and stirring her hair at the roots. Petrol pumps red and yellow, veins of all speed and dangerous, leapt giant into their lights. As they steadily bore uphill to some funnel-point in the darkness – for though lamps dotted the kerb the road ran and deepened ahead into shades of pitch like a river – this icy rim to the known world began to possess his fancy, till he half expected its pale reflection ahead. Cut apart by cold singing air he and she had no communication, till his waking sense of the live warmth inside her fur coat, of her heart in her breast beating, quickened recollection into desire of her known beauty. While he sat, an image of strangeness, fixedly eyeing the dark, he slipped his touch to her wrist, whose blue veins and every flexible movement were written over his nerves. A sense of that unknown presence within her outline – a presence that slipped behind veils every time they kissed – made his fingers, jumping and burning with fresh excitement, tighten about her tense cold wrist as she drove.

'Mind,' said Emmeline calmly. 'How can I drive?'

'I don't want you to: stop!'

She disengaged her wrist with finality.

He said urgently: 'Listen: turn back. Come back to the flat.'

He waited, thinking his words had been blown past her. Then she looked his way: 'It's shut up, you said.'

'Not really: we could get in.'

'But then why –'

'Why tell them it was shut up? I don't know: it's not their affair.'

With that blink of her lashes, as though something were going to strike her, Emmeline turned away quickly. 'There's no truth left,' she said. 'Or is it I that am mad? There seems to be no truth anywhere. Even our servants lie.'

'I'm left,' he said, 'whether you want me –'

'I only want to be quiet,' said Emmeline.

He insisted: 'Come back to the flat.'

'Was that what you had to say?'

He had little idea. Hendon Circus stood empty, asleep in lamp-light: she crept so slowly over the cross-roads he thought she would surely turn. But she looked up round the façades of pretty suburban elegance and in at dark windows as though someone else had spoken, or someone up there might reply: this halt in her faculties made the car almost stop ... Recollecting herself, she glanced at the clock on the dashboard, they gathered speed and went forward, uphill, then down. He saw 'THE NORTH' written low, like a first whisper, on a yellow A.A. plate with an arrow pointing: they bore steadily north between spaced-out lamps, chilly trees, low rows of houses asleep, to their left a deep lake of darkness: the aerodrome.

'Hendon,' he said. 'I wish we were still flying.'

'So do I,' she said with an irrepressible smile. 'I wish it were still that day.'

That day flooded him, with its tilted plan of two countries, the intoxication of its warm evening, the terrible sweetness of the suc-ceeding night. He said: 'Would you want things different?'

'No, that was our only way.'

'Then can't we go back?'

She glanced at him. 'Back? To where?'

'Then.'

'And tell the same story again and again and again? There's nothing more left ahead of us.'

'I'm sorry, you know,' he said. 'I am most mortally sorry. But I was what I was because I am what I am. You expected too much. What we had always seemed to me good, but you wanted more.'

She cried: 'But nothing ever seemed good to you: nothing was ever enough!'

'Look out: not so fast!' he said, suddenly rigid. Their speed had mounted; they swung in and out from the kerb on the polished black road: grassy breaths from fields rushed at them; like a bubble frozen a little observatory hung on the dark. The car hardly holding the road seemed to him past her control. Recalling his face in the taxi in Paris, she saw he was very frightened. Slowing down, she turned calmly right up the Barnet by-pass.

'I wouldn't kill you,' she said.

'You don't think much of me, do you?'

'How can I judge you? We've both been wrong.'

'All the same, times were good.'

'Yes, they were good,' said Emmeline. 'They are still too close to remember, but that must have been like the sun: it changed everything; you were everywhere. Such little things were happy: the early mornings, Smith's at the corner of Sloane Street, even times we wasted, tables and chairs where we sat. All that can't have been for nothing; it can't just have been a deception. I still think there must have been meant to be something more.'

'Let's look again.'

'No, we've seen.'

'But let's try again. *Could* you marry me?'

'No,' she said. 'I can't marry anyone now.'

'I want you so terribly, Emmeline.'

'No,' she said gently, 'not really. No.'

'You seem right,' he said violently, 'but you're wrong, all the same. I know I did hurt you, I'm sorry: it couldn't be helped. I had had enough, this last week; things were getting too much; I was all for letting things go. I never knew what you were after; I didn't think you knew yourself. I don't think you knew how unfriendly you sometimes were.'

'Poor Markie,' she said. 'I see now.'

'I don't much like anyone, really. I'm not much, I just like a bit of fun. You never let anything be what it was. After Devizes – honestly, yes: I was through. We were up to no good.'

'Yes,' she said, 'yes, I saw.'

'So I thought: that was that.'

'Yes, it was.'

'But it wasn't; it's not!' he cried with a violent movement, unbearably cramped in the car. He watched their lights fly over wires and sheep's stubbed backs. 'I'd forgotten to count all *this* in. I'd forgotten what you were like. As futile as adding up and forgetting

240

a column. When I came in tonight and saw you miles off in that silver dress, saying nothing and tipping your sherry about like you always did, I knew we should never be clear. You wouldn't have smiled like that if you'd thought so, either. My heart sank, I don't mind telling you, Emmeline. I agree it's the devil; it may be a pity we ever met. We may be each other's bad luck, but luck sticks, you know. First you thought too much of me, now you don't trust me an inch, and you're right. But here I still am. And you're something I can't get past. In a sense, I'm done for. This is ten times worse than if I hadn't had you in Paris. If you meant to go back, you should never have loved me then.'

'Then I was wrong,' said Emmeline.

'We reckoned without each other. If you can't stick things out as they were, we'll have to be on a footing: we'll have to marry.'

She repeated: 'I can't marry anyone now.'

'But what *were* you after?'

'It can't have been there.'

'But you love me – or why are we driving to this damned place?'

'You said there was something to say. I thought we'd say good-bye. Our last parting was mean and horrible.'

'But I love you: you're ten times myself!'

'But all our time was a struggle: first trying to understand, then trying not to. I have to be quiet now. You must leave me quiet, Markie.'

'If you take this away, I go right to pieces, Emmeline.'

'That can't be true: you're a man.'

'But it is,' he said, with a frightening drop in his violence.

Appalled, Emmeline said: 'Have I done you harm?'

'That all depends,' said Markie, and looked at her quickly, 'You can't just leave me. No one is dropped, you know, without being damaged.'

'Then forgive me; I ought to have seen.'

'So you can't do that,' he repeated. 'You can't do anyone in. It's a thing you couldn't do.'

'One does oneself in,' said Emmeline.

A drop in her voice, less resolution than deadness, as though this had for years been over, shook him from speech into panic: he fumbled a hand out, gripping her dress. She slowed up the car; he, letting slip the cold silver fabric as though it melted, pushed his hat back, rubbed at his forehead gone clammy and swore in the dark.

She stopped the car, dropping both hands from the wheel in mute acquiescence, as though there were something here they could not get past. Aware of her stillness, of her remoteness that seemed more in time than in space, he said: 'But you must,' and dragged her into his arms. Relaxed in distraction or pity she pressed a cold cheek to his. Night silence surrounded his hurried breathing, her unhappy sigh: he looked in her eyes closely; her senses stirred. But having found only night in her pupils, sensing an absence in her surrender he let her go: 'As you feel,' he said and stared at the two lit dials: the clock, the speedometer.

Still passive on his slackening arm, but as though she were quite alone now, Emmeline looked through the night that like grey water clearing let her distinguish the folded country and hanging darkness of woods. Through this not-quite oblivion – that not a car, while they waited, came by to disturb – their headlights sent unmoving arrows that died ahead. This breathing outline of earth, these little mysterious woods each aloof from the other and moulded like clouds in the air brought to her desolation a healing stillness that had eluded her happy and living, so that she touched for a moment the chilly hand of peace. A sense of standstill, a hush pervaded this half-seen country. Friendly darkness, as over a pillow, and silence in which a clock striking still pinned her to time hung trancelike over this early halt in their journey. But, from beyond, the North – ice and unbreathed air, lights whose reflections since childhood had brightened and chilled her sky, touching to life at all points a sense of unshared beauty – reclaimed her for its clear solitude.

Markie's hand moved under her shoulder. 'Where are you?' he said.

'Still here.'

'No. Come back.'

'I can't.'

'Then why are we stopping?'

'Very well,' she said, leaning forward to the self-starter, 'then we'll go on.'

Fields and woods vanished unknown beyond the headlights. Speed, mounting through her nerves with the consciousness of direction, began to possess Emmeline – who sat fixed, immovable with excitement – and shocked back his numbing faculties into alarm. '*Not so fast,*' he said again.

If she slowed down at all it was imperceptible.

Collecting himself, he found in her furious driving response, were it only an apprehension, to his own pressure: her speed had the startled wildness of flight. He was now quite certain he had not lost her, for she was like someone who plays the piano wildly to drown some crisis they cannot even admit, or question to which there can only be one answer . . . Banks rushed up to take their light each side of the by-pass: afterwards, ghostly young beeches along the kerb. His tension betrayed itself by an unconscious contraction at every car that approached: dawning behind the skyline headlights appeared, widened, dazzled them blind a moment – while he felt their own light car sway under Emmeline's fingers – then sheered past, each time a hairsbreadth nearer, leaving him icy with apprehension about the roof of the mouth. He looked sideways, trying to fix himself by an idea of fixity: three cars, standing empty, nosed into the jaded glare of an all-night café. Lit banks and low dark running skyline plaited their alternation over his brain; beside him she sat in frozen singleness, drinking speed. He thought: 'One must move again; not much time now; we shall be at Baldock.' But this was Hatfield: they slipped round the town like thieves. People still stood in doorways or shadowed blinds. Renewed by this distant flash of town life and warm breath from windows he said, leaning into the cold air close to her cheek as they cleared the last of the town with its sleepy villas: 'Keep driving all night, angel: you won't get away from this!'

Emmeline said nothing.

But, startled by his alternations of panic and triumph, his cold resolution to keep her and bitter enraged desire to throw her off, she turned his way, after a moment of silence, that same dilated and musing look of inquiry that, breaking again and again across their intimacy, had made him feel her no more than delayed on a journey elsewhere, and marked their unchanging distance from one another. This look's familiar strangeness – calling up trees at St Cloud, skylines about Devizes, firelight in his claret on rainy evenings, their closeness in small rooms and smiling encounters in streets – strung and tightened together these memories on a taut cord whose pull at the heart – dull, dragging and sharp like the wrench of a muscle – was far-reaching: this was unforeseen pain. The cold breath and dark depths of his loss appeared suddenly: his thoughts at a standstill seemed to resound agony or started in disarray from this unheard-of finality, breaking down every control. With some desperate idea of assault, but not daring to touch her, not daring to formulate what he could not express till she was in his arms, he moved her way in the car, shouting into the darkness between their faces invective, entreaties, reproaches, stripping the whole past and taxing her with their ruin. He exposed every nerve in their feeling: nothing remained unsaid ... Nervously shaking her hair back, gripping the wheel beside Markie, Emmeline, who said nothing, drove, as though away from the ashy destruction of everything, not looking back. Running dark under their wheels the miles mounted by tens: she felt nothing – Like a shout from the top of a bank, like a loud chord struck on the dark, she saw: 'TO THE NORTH' written black on white, with a long black immovably flying arrow.

Something gave way.

An immense idea of departure – expresses getting steam up and crashing from termini, liners clearing the docks, the shadows of planes rising, caravans winding out into the first dip of the desert – possessed her spirit, now launched like the long arrow. The traveller solitary with his uncertainties, with apprehensions he cannot communicate, seeing the strands of the known snap like paper ribbons, is sustained and more than himself on a great impetus: the faint pain of parting sets free the heart. Blind with new light she was like somebody suddenly not blind, or, after a miracle, somebody moving perplexed by the absence of pain. Like earth shrinking and sinking, irrelevant, under the rising wings of a plane, love with its unseen plan, its constrictions and urgencies, dropped to a depth below Emmeline, who now looked down unmoved at the shadowy map of her pain. For this levitation a total loss of her faculties, of every sense of his presence, the car and herself driving were very little to pay. She was lost to her own identity, a confining husk. Calmly, exaltedly rising and balancing in this ignorance she looked at her hands on the wheel, the silver hem of her dress and asked herself who she was: turning his way, with one unmeasured swerve of the wheel, she tried to recall Markie.

'Look *out* –' he began: and stopped at her glittering look that while so intently fixing him showed in its absence of object a fixed vacancy. She looked into his eyes without consciousness, as though in at the windows of an empty house. His throat tightened, the roof of his mouth went dry: she was not here, he was alone. Little more than his memory ruled her still animate body, so peacefully empty as not to be even haunted.

'Emmeline —'

Her state rushed at him with an appalling perception of physical danger, his sense of her unrelaxed grip on the wheel and unknowing pressure on the accelerator. His old recurring dread of her, latent and long disregarded, must have pointed to this: his dependence, this moment, for life on these long ignorant fingers and silent brain.

'Stop for a moment,' he pleaded, mustering some kind of calm. What he had said meant nothing: speed streamed from her unawares. The road was not empty; swinging almost up the right bank she shot ahead of a lorry: traffic approached them, twice she seemed magnetized into, twice he was stupefied by rushing arcs of light, in which for two moments he felt her suspended by him, fingers just on the wheel. Their survival was barest fortuity: one car pulled up behind them and someone, shouting, looked back . . . 'Emmeline,' he repeated, in desperately wary approach.

Still she heard nothing, or heard some singing silence inside her brain: as the wild swing of their lights scythed the dark ahead his agonized apprehension, a thousand vibrations of impact drew a sharp line, like fog round a lamp, round the circle of mindless serenity where she sat merciless, ignorant of their two lives. Dreading as much as a breath's touch on this taut ungoverned speed, Markie sweating, bit back exclamations, keeping his hand from her hand. He coaxing her gently, he reasoned; as often when they had been alone together. He watched the next lights dawn like doom, make a harsh aurora, bite into the road's hard horizon and, widening, flood the Great North Road from bank to bank. His fingers an inch from the wheel, wondering if he dared stun her, he said hopelessly: '*Emmeline* . . .' with the last calm of impotence. As though hearing her name on his lips for the first time, dazzled, she turned to smile. Head-on, magnetized up the heart of the fan of approaching brightness, the little car, strung on speed, held unswerving way. Someone, shrieking, wrenched at a brake ahead: the great car, bounding, swerved on its impetus. Markie dragged their wheel left: like gnats the two hung in the glare with unmoving faces. Shocked back by the moment, Emmeline saw what was past averting. She said: 'Sorry,' shutting her eyes.

Julian drew the curtains, after the others had left them, over the strip of cold night that disturbed Cecilia. They did not at once settle down: she picked the *Evening Standard* up from the hearthrug and dropped it behind the sofa, shook out some cushions and stood looking into an empty coffee-cup on the mantelpiece. She said: 'You are very good to me, sorry to have been foolish.' She said she thought the evening had gone off quite well, considering; Julian agreed. Her eyes just missed his look but she said no more. The uninterrupted quiet of evenings to come already covered this evening; standing before the fire he tinkled a lustre idly, half sorry this was not to be their home. For her part, her fancy, already leaving these walls, was a little homeless: she thought of their unknown house and the marriage they must achieve there between his serious pictures, her Dresden clock. The tinkling lustre subsided; Cecilia lay on the sofa in front of the fire, her face turned his way, her cheek on a cushion. Still finding her very mysterious he said: 'Your dress *is* lovely,' watching the firelight creep up the thin pink folds.

'It's my trousseau,' she said. 'I shouldn't be wearing it, but one has no control.'

'I'll forget it,' he smiled, 'then see it all over again.'

'No, never forget!' she cried. 'Never forget any moment; they are too few.'

To count this moment utterly free of oblivion she smiled; he came closer; the lemony scent of the Chinese peonies, mounting, enchanted the quietly lamplit room where the fire rustled. She put her arms round his neck and her big chiffon sleeves, warm from her arms and the fire, fell back softly against his face.

Benito was restless tonight: he slipped round the door ajar, a small presence flitting and dark as a thought, a wide wild look over the cushions, something springing and turning and never still. Julian said: 'He's quite a cat now.' 'Yes, he's a dear little bore,' she said. 'Emmeline's fond of him.' She pressed her cheek to the cushion, her dark eyes went from shadow to shadow after the restless kitten. Julian, a little disturbed, said: 'Shall we put him to bed?'

Benito slept in the basement, though morning had often found him in Emmeline's room. Julian cornered the kitten and caught him; after a moment Cecilia followed them into the hall. Here it was chilly; the house seemed still to echo the others' departure. Standing under the light with its hanging crystals Cecilia looked upstairs and saw in the half-dark Emmeline's door ajar. It was later than she expected: she saw by the telephone Markie's white scarf that he had forgotten, Emmeline's gloves that she would not wear.

Suddenly nervous, Cecilia said, turning to Julian: 'Stay with me till she comes home.'

THE END

MORE ABOUT PENGUINS, PELICANS
AND PUFFINS

For further information about books available from Penguins please write to Dept EP, Penguin Books Ltd, Harmondsworth, Middlesex UB7 0DA.

In the U.S.A.: For a complete list of books available from Penguins in the United States write to Dept DG, Penguin Books, 299 Murray Hill Parkway, East Rutherford, New Jersey 07073.

In Canada: For a complete list of books available from Penguins in Canada write to Penguin Books Canada Ltd, 2801 John Street, Markham, Ontario L3R 1B4.

In Australia: For a complete list of books available from Penguins in Australia write to the Marketing Department, Penguin Books Australia Ltd, P.O. Box 257, Ringwood, Victoria 3134.

In New Zealand: For a complete list of books available from Penguins in New Zealand write to the Marketing Department, Penguin Books (N.Z.) Ltd, P.O. Box 4019, Auckland 10.

In India: For a complete list of books available from Penguins in India write to Penguin Overseas Ltd, 706 Eros Apartments, 56 Nehru Place, New Delhi 110019.

THE HEAT OF THE DAY

Wartime London; and Stella's lover, Robert, is suspected of selling information to the enemy. Harrison, shadowing Robert, is none the less prepared to bargain, and the price is Stella.

Elizabeth Bowen writes of three people, estranged from the past and reluctant to trust in the future, with the psychological insight and delicate restraint that have earned her a position among the most distinguished novelists of the century.

'Unerringly, exquisitely, Miss Bowen has caught the very feel of her period. The novel is the most completely detailed and the most beautiful evocation of it that we have yet had or are ever likely to have' – *New Statesman*

'Rarely, to my knowledge, has the late flowering of love in wartime been more poignantly described in fiction; and never, perhaps, more effectively presented as an integral experience, shared equally in all its aspects by a man and a woman' – John Hayward in the *Observer*

THE DEATH OF THE HEART

Sixteen-year-old Portia comes to live with her wealthy older half-brother and his wife, Anna, in London during the thirties. Tormented by the agonies of her first love affair, she is obsessed by the feeling that everyone is laughing at her. And when she discovers that Anna has been reading her diary, she takes a sudden explosive step which pulls everybody up short.

'One of the most sensitive novels written during this troubled century' – John O'London

EVA TROUT

Few writers can match the brilliance of Elizabeth Bowen's prose. And here the formal grace of her style, her flair for mischievous social comedy and the subtlety of her dialogue go into creating one of her most formidable – and moving – heroines.

'Resonant, beautiful and often very funny . . . Eva is triumphantly real, a creation of great imaginative tenderness . . . Elizabeth Bowen is a splendid artist, intelligent, generous and acutely aware, who has been telling her readers for many years that love is a necessity, and that its loss or absence is the greatest tragedy man knows' – Julian Webb in the *Financial Times*.

'Rarely have I come across a novel in which sexual frustration (and sexuality) have been so richly and powerfully conveyed' – Roger Baker in *Books and Bookmen*

THE LITTLE GIRLS

In 1914 they had been eleven years old, three little girls at St Agatha's, a day school on the South Coast. Fifty years later, Dinah, beautiful as ever, advertises in the national newspapers to find the other two – Clare, now established with a successful business, and Sheila, a married woman, glossy, chic and correct.

In this brilliantly orchestrated novel, as subtle and compelling as a mystery story, Elizabeth Bowen asks: can friendship be taken up where it left off? What are the revelations – and the dangers – in summoning up childhood?

'There is that recurring shiver of delight . . . for this story is poetic in its awareness, its stimulus, its beauty of writing; and as full of clues, hints and half-revealed secrets as any thriller' – *Scotsman*

FRIENDS AND RELATIONS

' "Life after all," though Edward, hearing tea approach, the gay dance of china on the silver tray, "is an affair of charm, not an affair of passion." '

But his mother had discovered otherwise. Aristocratic, ageing, still beautiful and still passionately attached to her lover, Lady Elfrida had tasted forbidden fruit, and her affair had become the skeleton in the family cupboard. And for her son Edward, tied to a job in the Civil Service, bound into marriage, sealed by the charming rituals of social intercourse and teatime conversation, his mother's sin, none the less, still has a disturbing potency . . .

In *Friends and Relations*, through nuances of drawing-room comedy, the absurd – potentially explosive – interplay of propriety and passion, Elizabeth Bowen richly earns V. S. Pritchett's tribute: 'Daring by nature and intellect and passionate in imagination, compassionate in heart, she saw to it . . . that her people faced the secrets from which society no longer protected them'.

and

A WORLD OF LOVE
THE HOTEL
THE HOUSE IN PARIS
THE LAST SEPTEMBER
THE COLLECTED STORIES OF ELIZABETH BOWEN

ENGLISH AND AMERICAN LITERATURE

☐ *Helbeck of Bannisdale* **Mrs Humphrey Ward**   £3.50

Edited by Brian Worthington. Written in 1898, a classic to rate with the novels of George Eliot and Charlotte Brontë, this is a subtle and impressive treatment of 'the love between man and woman'.

☐ *The Red Badge of Courage* **Stephen Crane**   £1.50

Introduced by Pascal Covici, Jr. 'A psychological portrayal of fear', and one of the greatest novels ever written about war: the story of a raw Union recruit during the American Civil War.

☐ *Heart of Darkness* **Joseph Conrad**   £0.95

Conrad's most profound exploration of human savagery and despair is contained in this story of Marlowe's search for Mister Kurtz in the jungle of the Belgian Congo: a vision that has haunted readers, novelists and poets throughout the century.

☐ *Selected Writings* **Samuel Johnson**   £3.95

Edited by Patrick Cruttwell. Including generous selections from his Dictionary, his edition of Shakespeare, and his *Lives of the Poets*, plus excerpts from his journalism, letters and private prayers.

☐ *Call It Sleep* **Henry Roth**   £3.50

Published in 1934, this extraordinary novel reveals, through the eyes of David Schearl (the son of immigrant Jews), a profusion of life and family relationships in the teeming jungle of a New York City slum.

☐ *A Journey to the Western Islands of Scotland* **Johnson**
The Journal of a Tour to the Hebrides **Boswell**   £3.50

Edited by Peter Levi. These two journals of their joint tour of Scotland in 1773 are masterpieces of travel-writing, human observation and glorious, sardonic wit.

ENGLISH AND
AMERICAN LITERATURE

☐ *The House in Paris* **Elizabeth Bowen**   £2.50

A novel that crystallizes, with delicacy and wit, the disturbing relationships between children, sex and love. 'All Miss Bowen's most brilliant qualities are here' – Jocelyn Brooke

☐ *Look Homeward, Angel* **Thomas Wolfe**   £4.95

A young boy grows to manhood in small-town America. Here Wolfe displays, said F. Scott Fitzgerald, 'that flair for the extravagant and fantastic which has been an American characteristic from Irving and Poe to Dashiell Hammett'.

☐ *The Aspern Papers* and *The Turn of the Screw*
   Henry James   £1.75

Edited by Anthony Curtis. Containing James's two most dramatic and masterly tales: the first, a story of literary 'spoils and stratagems' set in Venice; the last, a ghost story that still puzzles the critics and terrifies all its readers.

☐ *Martin Eden* **Jack London**   £2.95

Based on the author's own turbulent and legendary life, the story of a young San Franciscan seaman and his struggle to win intellectual and social recognition.

☐ *The Enlarged Devil's Dictionary* **Ambrose Bierce**   £3.95

Edited by Ernest Jerome Hopkins. Containing 1,851 definitions, this spicy, satirical dictionary is for all those 'who prefer dry wines to sweet, sense to sentiment, wit to humour . . .'

☐ *The Unfortunate Traveller and Other Works*
   Thomas Nashe   £2.95

Edited by J. B. Steane. Sketches and writings by one of Shakespeare's most lively contemporaries: the journalist, storyteller, irreverent social critic, jester and entertainer who epitomizes the flavour and bawdy vitality of the Elizabethans.

ENGLISH AND AMERICAN LITERATURE

☐ *News from Nowhere* **William Morris** £2.95

Edited by Asa Briggs. The Utopian novel, plus a selection of designs, letters, verse and writings by this brilliant artist and most unorthodox Victorian.

☐ *Barchester Towers* **Anthony Trollope** £1.95

Edited by Robin Gilmour. Trollope's most popular novel, and a superb comic portrayal of life and society in mid-Victorian England.